I0598357

ALMASI 2

Queen of the Streets
By
Dartanya A. Williams Sr.

Printed in the United States of America
First Printing, 2020
ISBN 13: **9781732612235**
Library of Congress
Ni Jamba La Publishing
Philadelphia, PA 19138
www.dartanyaawilliamssr.com

WELCOME TO THE WORLD OF ALMASI

When you think of Almasi and Dartanya A. Williams Sr. You will think of the words Mastermind of Crime fiction at its finest. Almasi is raw, gritty, and thought provoking. Dartanya has created Almasi from the dark world that many girls from the hood have lived through and survives. The grimy life of survival, gang life, and making hard choices to come into a world to remain safe, to survive and just not struggle for the basic necessities. Almasi is a portrait of a woman we all know and met in our lives. Almasi is an unforgettable character, the queen of the streets, but a well-written portrait of gang life. It is a captivating novel of survival and how easy it is to be betrayed even in the gang life. Are you ready to be hooked into the Almasi series?

Tamyara Brown
www.tamluvstowrite.com
No. 1Best selling Amazon Author, Blogger, Graphic Design & Podcaster

Back into The Shit

It's the beginning of August 2018, I took off for a couple months after I got out of prison.

I thought them devils had me for a minute. My sister Robin went to law school I paid for it all and it was the best money I ever spent. She is now a big-time lawyer, I'm so proud of her now. She's living with this dude name Ismael Blackwell he's a real big square but that's what I like about him I'm so glad she did not hook up with no street Nigga. He's a lawyer too there talking about getting married soon just as long as she's happy makes me overwhelmed with joy for my baby sister.

My son Little Boom is 21 now I got him working at all my laundromats and cleaners ten locations. Five cleaners and five laundromats are all cash businesses. Me and La-Nesa are still business partners with the hair shops. I have my own cellphone stores and my other legitimate businesses that are making me some good loot. Little Boom is responsible for all of them making him know the real meaning of work. He does his job, but that Nigga just love running the streets going after every hot in the ass young whore with a tight outfit on shaking her ass. Now everybody is grown its time I did some living myself. So, I got my mind right after all the bull shit I when through thinking my life was over. That took a big psychological toll on me for real but the way I played it off nobody would know it. Me and Jay Black when to Jamaica and had a blast for real. As you know the drama and the bull shit don't stop until the casket drops nonstop.

After two months of fun & sun plus some hot sex getting my shit off every night with my man loving it. Fuck Stella, I was the one getting my groove back with a vengeance. We came back home I really did not want to come back home because I had to get back to the grindstone putting in mad work, but I have to stay on top of getting this money for the outfit (The Gang BSN).

So, as you know it, I'm back at it again and one day. I had my man Jay Black to look over our books when we got back to doing

BSN business. He showed me that this little nerd ass motherfucker Rocket been skimming off us for a long time. What's really fucked up he's not the only one the girl Natalie we gave a job to after she hooked us up with Tony Bolivar and we gave her top status and protection with BSN. This greedy ass bitch, she been taking big chunks of loot with no shame in her game.

One thing about Jay he's good with numbers he's been in the game for a long time. He came up in the game with Black Inc. The black mafia in Philly when most of them when to Jail and died off he stayed in the game breaking off from them Niggas calling them self's the BCT The Black Cream Team. So, I picked up the phone and called Nails Nathan and Willie Whack-Whack to take care of Rocket's little sneaky ass that way I know it's going to get done right. Then I hit up Rah-Killer to kill Natalie's greedy ass immediately. Then I get the call from Damon Gee, "yo sis, I know you been chillin and enjoying yourself a well deserve vacation and all that. I need to holla at you right away its important Sis."

"Can it wait to later?"

"No, it can't. I'll be at your place in a few minutes I'm talking to you from my whip."

"Okay, I'll have Goliath bring you out to the deck all right."

"Okay, I'm here already I'll be up in a few minutes."

I went out on the deck and made me a drink waiting for him to come up I sit back getting my puff on and sipping my drink. Goliath is walking out on the deck with Damon Gee. Goliath just waves and go back in the front room. Damon bump fist with me

"I can use one of them myself, Sis."

"I'll make you one." I go behind the bar getting his glass putting ice in it than I pour him some rum "so what's up now, Damon?" He picks up his drink sipping on it and replied, "just too much is what's up. The fucking Armenians took off with three containers of our guns and your boy Gill joins up with GTG. They cleaned out one of our warehouses and drop off spots that we have the cocaine in.

"Are you sure it was him?"

"I just got finish looking at the video tapes in the warehouse the dumb motherfuckers did not wear a mask."

"Or he wanted us to know it was him. Did you think of that?"

"But why?"

"Because of Spider that's why."

What the fuck does Spider have to do with it? That Nigga is out of the game now he put you in his spot?"

"I'll tell you why back in the days when my mother and father was killed two of the men from that hit squad was Spider and Crazy Tee. Spider killed Crazy Tee so he would not kill the baby in the house and that baby was me. Crazy Tee is Gill's father."

"Damn, I did not know that shit."

"A lot people don't know so somebody must have told Gill that Spider was the one who killed his father and he's taking it out on us now."

"So, who told him?"

6

"That's easy it only two people in this whole world knows about that shit. That's Spider and that crack head bitch who raise me Dotty. I know Spider did not tell him shit."

"But why?"

"The reason why I took Robin to come live me and cut her ass off from the money she was getting. Plus, I took in Robin paid for her to go to school, now she's successful and that bitch Dotty is a broke down old junkie whore, and you know the old saying misery loves company. She wants to drag up me and Spider's past to get back at both of us."

"But that shit was so long ago nobody is thinking about that shit right now. Almasi your trippin."

"Oh, you don't know these peoples Damon. Black Giovanni is a shot caller in prison he has thousands of soldiers that do shit for him with blind loyalty and they don't give a fuck about how much work you put in. That how the BSN was built he will reach out from prison just to fuck you up to let you know he still run shit on the streets. You're so very wrong my friend that's what these Niggas do to teach you a hard lesson on who they are to show their reach. If the green light is put out on someone it has to be done the way he says it has to be done. Plus, he will look at it like Spider lied to him. That would make Black Giovanni think what else did he lied to him about. See y'all don't know how this shit works and you're in this gang. He can have his people that's getting out to replace us. You never thought about that did you?"

"No, I never looked at it like that it's a lot of fucking politics if you ask me Almasi."

"Your right its all the politics of the shot callers not us. Plus, you don't know what Black Giovanni promise Gill maybe he told him he can take over once he got us out the way you never know. I have to think like that now. What's really fucked up they will send one of y'all close to me to do it did you know that?"

"Damn, that's some real deep shit. So, what are you going to do here?"

"Don't worry about it. I'll take care of it okay just find out where those guns are at for me. We have a lot people who want their shit. We have people waiting on them motherfuckers we might have to smooth things out until we give them another supply of what they need."

"Who are we going to get it from then?"

"I can go holla at the Black Demons they will hook us up to make up all of our orders. Well you go to Tanya and tell her double up to keep shit on track with that missing product."

"I'll get Ty-Kim and Chrome to track down Gill ass and take care of him. He doesn't know where the other warehouse is at.

"Hell no, his peoples that work with him know just as much as him."

"Well, that's good I still say to switch shit up any way as you know Niggas do talk too much."

"Yeah, your right I been doing that it's only a few of us who know where all of them are at." Walking up on the deck is my son Little Boom he bumps fist with Damon "yo, what's up uncle Gee?"

"Nothing much just doing what I do, Nephew. What about you, how you been doing?" "I'm just working hard and doing my thing. Well, I have to roll you take care." He waves at and he play boxing with Damon for a few minutes and he quickly go out the door. "Hey mom, can I borrow the Benz tonight I'm going out."

"What happen to your car, Nigga? You just got that Jawn?"

"Well, it's in the shop Mom. I did not want to wait around for a loner, so I took a cab to get here."

"That just sound like some more of your bullshit to me. Boom but let me get my pocketbook and give you the keys but if you fuck my car up, you're not too big for me to put my foot in your ass!"

Then my man Jay Black came walking in the door coming from work while I'm walk from the deck to get my pocketbook.

"Hey, baby what's up?" He came and kiss me, and I replied, "nothing just getting my keys for Boom." He bumps fist with Jay.

Jay asked, "so when are we going to meet that woman your spending so much time with now of days?"

8

He started laughing as I walked up to Boom,

"yeah, he's right when is this going to happen, son?" "See what you started Mister Jay now I have to hear this all day and night." I quickly go in my bedroom getting the keys for this boy I hold them in front of his face and .

"I should not give you shit what you shame of us or she's butt ugly or something? Little Boom."

"No, I'm not shame of y'all and hell no she's not butt ugly, okay. I'll have y'all meet her later on tonight all right. Now can I have the keys please mom?" I hand them to him.

"You just saying that shit so you can get what you want that's all? No for real I'll bring her by for y'all to meet her okay look I'll keep my word, okay."

"I'll see y'all later on tonight and thank you mom."

"All right Nigga be careful, and he roll out the door with his cocky ass Stroll. Me and Jay walked to the living room sitting on the couch hugged up Jay looks at me and asked, "so what you think he's up to now?"

"I don't know but I don't want him doing what we do."

"I know that shit and I keep his ass busy with the laundromats and cleaners."

"Well baby, I think your too late for that shit with him hanging around Gino Gats, Tanya, Fat Lou-Lou and his crew you know damn well he's getting busy."

"Did he tell you about his own place, yet?"

"No, he did not say shit to me about him having his own place."

"Well I'm telling you now than, but you did not hear it from me, okay."

"Well I knew this day was coming one day he was going to move out I just would have liked if he told me you know what I'm saying?"

"Well don't jump on his ass about it give him time to tell you all right."

"Yeah, your right well I called Willie Whack-Whack and Nails Nathan to find Rocket's little sneaky ass. Good what about Natalie?"

"I got Rah-Killer on that one and check this out were missing three containers of guns. "What? Yeah three of them."

"Plus, Gill hit one of our warehouses taking a shipment of coke but as you know I got more in the stash. I'll have Tanya and her crew to get that to make up what was taking. "You know who took the guns?"

"Yeah, the Armenians it was on their end. So, what are you going to do? I have to call the Black Demons to help us out to fill all those orders.

"So, what did they say?"

"I have to call them."

"Well go call them baby do that shit now so none of that will get backed up on you."

"As you know mommy's work is never done!"

We both started laughing than I lift my head off his chest pulling out my phone calling Top-Cat the president of the black Demon's motorcycle club. He picks up after it rang four times, "hey what's up Ma, I'm glad you're out now hi are you doing?"

"I'm good brother look I need you can I talk on this phone.'

"Yeah, it's cool, my shit is safe. Well, I got hit and I'm going to need a shit load of guns to fill some of these orders."

"I can help you out but some of them might be a little higher than others that's the only thing. I have to be up front with you, Sis."

"Well what every it is I can't lose some of them people, so I'll pay it.

"When are you coming to see me?"

"I'll be there Friday with my list on what I need."

"Sound good, Ma and I have to say I'm happy you beat them devil motherfuckers with your case. You're out here still doing your thing! And if you need some help with anything just let me know from the door."

"Thanks, Tee Cee I will let you know if I need you and I really appreciate your friendship brother.

"I know that and the same here so how is Jay?"

"He's good he's right here. Put him on the horn right quick so I can holla at him." I hand him the phone and asked, "yo, what's up, Nigga?"

"No, what's up with you man you still going to sell me that bike, brother?"

"Oh, hell no for you to go mess that motherfucker up anybody but you."

"You're not right man, but I holla at you later, okay. Tell Jo-Jo he still owes me from that last card game."

"I'll tell him, but you know that Nigga he's a hard payer, but you take it easy and its really good hearing your voice, brother."

"Same here Mister Black cream team. Moja (One)"!

"All right Mister black outlaw biker Moja!" He hands me my phone back "that Nigga is crazy while he's still giggling."

"Where you say you met him at again?"

"In jail. I got locked up for some bull shit parole violation I was up there with him Jo-Jo Outlaw and his right-hand man Doctor Jerry."

Then Poochie walked up to us "he's going to get some smokes do we need anything?"

Jay answered, "yeah, I need some smokes too homey here you go." As Jay reach in his pocket handing him some money and he quickly go out the front door. La'Wadna Aunt-Tee along with Sheree our new housekeeper from El Salvador both coming in the door with the bags of groceries. Goliath is helping them with the bags sitting them on the table busy talking to one another the room is filled with their chatter. Out of nowhere running in the front door is three mask men with guns **Kapacka! Kapacka! Kapacka**! Shooting soon as I seen them. I reached up under my couch getting my AK-47 letting them have it. Jay at the same time whipping out his pistol from the back of his pants firing back at the men who rolled up in my front door. We pen their ass back with our fire power they are ducking low shooting at us, but they can't move forward. I quickly ran towards the kitchen spitting back at the three attackers to get Aunt-Tee out there **Kacpacka! Kacpacktacka!**

I reach where Aunt-Tee is at ducking under the table with bullets flying everywhere. I see she's hit in the arm and leg. Sheree is dead with the blood flowing from her mouth. I tell Aunt-Tee to grab the back of my shirt and move her ass fast! I see Goliath shooting back at them but he's not really too aggressive I notice that from the door.

I yelled at him, "cover me big man!" I stay low running towards the deck and at the same time so did Jay. Soon as I reach the deck with Aunt-Tee holding on the back of me for dear life. I pointed to Jay and he went behind the bar and hit the button that put up the steel gate on the deck. The loud hydraulic sounds of the steel gate **Swoooop!** Going up but I can see two of them running towards the front door.

Soon as the gate when up it locks all the doors and windows. I run up to the video panel behind the bar on my deck to see if they got out the door two of them did get out but one of them did not. The would-be assassin seen the door closed and he could not get it open he panics. He ran towards the window on the left-hand side I can see him than Goliath is running behind him shooting he hits him all in his back. His lifeless body slid down on to the floor with the blood making a trail of blood from the window to the floor. Aunt-Tee and Jay is watching with me looking at the video monitor.

Aunt-Tee asked, "when did you have this put in Almasi that was smart!"

"When me and Jay was on vacation and everyone was gone."

Jay , "one of your so-called bodyguards sold you out. I think it was your boy Poochie soon as he went out to get some smokes this shit happens."

I looked at him and Aunt-Tee and replied, "that was too convenient let me look at some of the DVD tapes of today and yesterday. I can tell you which one of them who did it. "Then we hear some banging on the steel gate its Goliath yelling, "let me in there all gone and I got one of them motherfuckers!"

I yelled back, "hold on big man the shit is on a timer, okay." I lied to him so I can have time to look at my video play back.

I yelled out to him, "just make sure there all gone and see if Poochie is okay?"

"Fuck him he's the one who probably set us up in the first place, Almasi. I'll go look around I be back all right?

"Okay big man! The whole time I was talking to him I was going over every inch of the play back DVD. They both did not know I had video cameras put in all over my house. I had it done at all the places I lay my head at. So, I would know what the fuck is going on in my crib trust no one that's the first thing in a hustler's bible page one chapter one. So, I'm scrolling through it than I hit the jackpot. I see Goliath on the tape early this morning on the phone <u>outside</u>, near the garage than I turn up the sound a little and I can hear him say man the shit is going to be perfect!

"All you have to do when I find out when her aunt La-Wana is coming back from shopping. I'll send Poochie out for some smokes y'all roll in and smoke everybody and roll out its full proof plan it's going to work trust me"

Soon as I hear that I looked at Jay and I ask, "Aunt-Tee did Goliath call you before you got in the spot?"

"He sure did Almasi!"

"Okay, now this stay between the three of us don't say shit about this! Okay and act normal. I'll have Doctor Chow come over and get them hot slug out your arm and leg okay?"

"How you feel?"

"The shit burn like a motherfucker. Well, its better than you being dead, Aunt-Tee I kiss her on the cheek and looked up at Jay." I call doctor Chow and tell him I need him right away.

He will be right there that man is away on the hustle he away come fast because he knows I pay him really good and I give him a big fat ass tip too I hang up.

"What are you going to do about this back-stabbing ass hole we have in are camp?"

"Don't you worry, baby I got something really special for his ass trust me!"

So, What about Sheree's people?"

"She had no family they all got killed by MS-13 in El Salvador that's why I helped her out when she told me the story of her life. It's a shame she made it all the way here in this country ducking bullets to get killed in my fucking kitchen."

"So, we should be good on that end, but I really feel bad about her getting killed with that ass hole setting us up."

Then I called Dun-Dun telling him to come to my crib so I can tell him everything that happen. Plus, I wanted him to tell the others to come over to the house so we can take care of this fucking traitor up in my crib. I hang up and call Puerto Rican Joe, Black Duke, Booby Hill and the new guy Taz Money to come clean up these bodies for me. I let the steel gate up and we all walked back in my place it's a fucking mess.

So, I waited on all of them to come to the crib and doctor Chow to take care of Aunt-Tee who is in a lot of pain.

I'm really happy she's not dead, but Goliath will be real soon and he don't know it yet. I calm down and I had to act normal. I know me I will start going off on a Nigga when I'm mad at them. Instead I chilled out to play this shit right. One the worst things about this game is when someone betrays you it hurts but I'm still alive to get my revenge. It doesn't matter how good you been to them they have their own agenda. I go into my bedroom getting me a big bag of coke and I started getting high ready for whatever. My mind is racing in all kinds of direction to make my next move.

Tracking Down A Nerd and A Greedy Bitch

A half an hour has past, and everybody came all at the same time. Dun-Dun, Mookie, Tony Smokes, Crazy Monk and Poochie. Right behind them is Black Duke, Puerto Rican Joe, Taz Money and Booby Hill. Doctor Chow came and I took him to the back bedroom where Aunt-Tee is at so he can go to work on her wounds. I came back in the living room looking up at Goliath ass and he is doing his best acting job playing it off looking at Poochie sideways. That Nigga should get an Oscar for the performance he put on for real. Before Goliath could lie on Poochie I told them to go outside and stay on post while we talk. I told Booby Hill to stay with both of them and **Hakikisha hakuna kinachchotkea** Poochie *make sure nothing happens to Poochie* I know Goliath don't know any Swahili, so he doesn't know what I so Goliath think I'm going to kill Poochie not him. Then I yelled take both of their guns! Booby Hill nodded his head pointing his gun at them "y'all heard the lady give them up right now!"

While everybody stood there with their guns out on them. Poochie held his head down, he twirled the cigarette in between his fingers while Goliath is had a slick smile thinking his plan to put it on Poochie was going to work. Booby Hill take their guns and yelled, "okay Nigga outside, let's go!"

I to Booby Hill, "don't go far I'll call you when were ready while they clean this shit up for me."

He looks up at me   **"Nimekupa Ma!** I got you Ma."

Soon as they went out the door, I waved my hand for everybody to gather around and I asked, "Jay go get the tablet." He walked up and handed it to me. I turn it on showing all the others what Goliath did. They all glared, and screw faced him. After everybody seen it, I , "we will take him to the scrap yard and deal with his ass after they clean up all the food and the bodies off the floor."

Black Duke took off the mask of the dead would be assassin. He was a white dude. Then Puerto Rican Joe looked at his arms and legs for tattoos seeing the flag on his right arm he's Armenian. He points at it, "that's their national flag right there. Everybody is looked down at the tattoo.

Puerto Rican Joe , "so why is Fat ass working with the Armenian ass holes?"

"It's only one thing Money, Duke!"

I looked at him and agreed, "your right Duke do any of y'all know where his girl Kina live at?"

Jay , "your son knows where she lives at, he's hung out with them a few times or more."

"Okay let me call his ass up the phone." He picks up after it rung three times   "What's up, Mom?"

"Look, I need to ask you something? Do you know where Goliath girl Kina live at?"

"Yeah, Why Mom?"

"Because I just found out that Nigga just tried to have me hit here at the house and I want to go grab his woman too."

"Damn that's fucked up. When did that shit happen?"

"Just an hour ago right after you went out the door. She lives not too far from you at One Brown street at the condo unit three."

"Thanks baby, I see you later come to the city line condo that's where I'll be later on you know where it's at, okay."

"I hear you mom is there anything else you need me to do?"

"No, I'm good I can take it from here all right thanks for your help Boom."

"So, I have to be strapped then?"

"You better Nigga and keep your eyes open to make sure you come see me tonight and be careful."

"I will mom see you later on, okay."

"Okay bye."

I looked up   "yo Dun-Dun you want to go grab this bitch for me?"

"Sure, thing, Sis where she lives at?"

"One Brown street unit three."

"Shit that's right around the corner here."

"Yeah and take her to the strap yard for me and call up Fat Lou-Lou and let him know you're coming."

"Crazy Monk I'll go with you."

"Wait for us there and don't go anywhere okay?"

They both nodding their heads going out of the door. I tapped Jay walking towards the deck with him putting his arm around me while the others clean up all the mess. I go behind the bar and make us some drinks I make his gin on the rocks and my rum with a little bit coke soda but were both snorting some blow.

Meanwhile on the other side of town in South Philly Nails Nathan and Willie Whack-Whack is looking for Rocket. They checked three places and he's nowhere to be found they called me while I'm sipping on my drink and snorting a little blow with Jay. I pick up and asked, "yo, what's up?"

Willie Whack-Whack answered, "hey Almasi, we looked in house, his mother house and his little fuck pad joint as well. Do you know any where he can be at?"

"Yeah, it's this fat hooker name Saquina he's in love with she lives on 2200 block of Oakford street its 2259. She works out her house he should be there.

"Okay thanks were going there right now. I'll let you know how we made out Moja (One)!" Moja! Miles away in the North East Natalie is coming out her two-story house with her new boy toy name Carlos a young good-looking Puerto Rican cock smith for hire. Parked outside of the house is Woo-Woo the new guy down with the psycho body bag crew is behind the wheel of a black GMC truck. Sitting in the back seat with their black mask and machine guns is Rah-Killer and Nugee. Rah-Killer , "she is let's go, Nugee. What about her boy toy Dick slinger?"

"He has to go too, fuck Em! That the last piece of old pussy he will have!" They both laughed jumping out of the truck soon as they both reached her black Benz ready to get in, they started straying them both at the same time **Katpackataka! Kapackactacka!** Hitting Natalie in her face chest and ripping her stomach open with blood and her guts gushing out on her car and on the ground everywhere.

Along with her male prostitute hitting him in the head neck and chest. He falls sideways on the car door with the blood splashing all over it falling to the ground. Woo-Woo came driving up fast as Rah-

Killer and Nugee jumping into the truck as it sped off down the street. Soon as they got on the expressway, I get the call I picked up on the first ring while right after I snort up two fat line of some damn good cocaine.

"Yo Tulipata! (We got them)"

"Kazi Nzur!(Good Job)"

I hang up looking over at Jay and announced, "one down one to go, baby."

"Good, but after they clean this shit up here, I think we should get the fuck out of here."

"Your right soon as there done."

"You know they're going to get the job done we need to get out of here right now, sweetheart."

"First let me get Poochie off the hook, okay."

"Yeah, your right!"

An hour later Puerto Rican Joe came out on the deck "hey Almasi, were all done."

"Thanks' Joe just make sure y'all bring Goliath to the strap yard alive, okay."

"I'll try Almasi."

"Don't try Joe just do that for me."

"Well after you show us that tape everybody wants to kill him."

"Yeah, your right let me call Booby outside he picks up on the first ring."

"Yo, what's up Almasi?"

"Bring them in right now for me please."

"Okay!"

After a few minutes Booby Hill walking in the front door with Poochie and Goliath with a shit eating grin on his grill. I walked up with Jay by my side I to Jay,

"give me your gun baby!"

Goliath yelled out, "I've been waiting on this shit he's pointing at Poochie shoot this Nigga in his fucking head boss lady!"

I take the gun and I put it under his fucking fat black chin. He is looked up at me "what the fuck is you doing" That Nigga set up the hit not me!"

"No Nigga, it was you motherfucker and I was so good to your big black ass and took you under my wing like a brother! And you did this shit to me Nigga you were a fucking nobody working in a shit hole strip club working for peanuts. I took you in!"

Everybody got their guns out on him. Goliath yelled again, "no it was not me it was this Nigga boss lady. I would never do no shit like that to you!"

"Oh, really Goliath"

"Jay, go get the tablet!" He hands it to me, and I hit play letting him see him on the DVD of him setting the hit up on the phone. After it stop, I looked at him   "so what was that Nigga?"

"You didn't not know I have video all over this motherfucker when I was gone!" His whole face it as he lowers his head and started crying like a fucking baby.

"Yo Poochie go with the rest of them to the strap yard with this back-stabbing motherfucker."

I nodded at Booby Hill to give him his gun back soon as he gave him the gun back, he pointed it at Goliath head mashing it on top of it.

I yelled at him   "yo, don't kill him yet wait till y'all get him to the strap yard. Y'all just clean this joint up make sure that Nigga die slow too. Now, get him the fuck out my face y'all!"

All of them started beating on him taking him out the door. I walked to my bedroom with Jay packing me a little bag.I go in my safe taking some money out there toss in a bag to get the hell out of this motherfucker. I got me some things I wanted to take with me, and Jay did the same. I paid Doctor Chow five big stacks. I ask him to take Aunt-Tee home for me while me and Jay got up out of there.

I kissed Aunt-Tee as she hopped out the door with doctor Chow. I walked them to his car, and I went back and me and Jay packed up our shit locked the doors up and rolled out. While we were on our way to my other place at city line avenue condo. We get in Jay's black Benz 500-S than I get a call from Fast Eddie the crooked ass ex-cop Damon Gee have working for him all the time.

"Hey Almasi, we have to meet I have something that you need to hear it's really important."

"Oh yeah, so why you did not go through Damon like you all way do before?"

"This is so hot; I think I should be dealing with you direct. Okay so when did this you have to deal with me direct starts?"

"It's needs to start soon as you can see me because everything, I have to tell you can save your life if you get my meaning."

"Okay give me an hour and I'll call you back so I can set up a place for us to talk, okay?"

"Sure, make sure you call me now it's that good I'm telling you."

"All right I'll hit you back goodbye."

"Yo, that was that crooked ass ex- cop Damon Gee was working with saying what he has, to tell me might save my life Jay."

"Well, have he told y'all any bull shit in the past?"

"No, everything he told us have been spot on."

"Then you need to talk to him. I wish I had some crooked ass insider helping me out I'd be three steps a head of the fucking game."

"Yeah, but now I'm going to need somebody else to watch my back. I can't believe that fucking Goliath Nigga. I pulled his ass up out the fucking gutter and he did that shit to me.

"Baby, I'm going to tell you something and I want you to never forget this okay money make Niggas do strange things. See who ever approach Goliath knew that he would go for it because he's a greedy fuck. But they knew dam well it could have been 20 million dollars. Poochie would have never did that shit to you because he's a real Nigga he makes money it doesn't make him. If Poochie would have knew what he was going to do, he would have told you then smoke that Nigga in front of you to show his loyalty to you. Goliath is just like all these 2018 Niggas is about no loyalty or integrity."

"You're right, Jay so I'm kind of shaky about getting someone else to watch my back now. Jagger was my Nigga for so long now. I need two Jagger's with all this shit going on. Look keep Poochie. You got a lot people to pick from get Puerto Rican Joe, Black Duke, Booby Hill or one of Fat Lou-Lou's guys."

"Like who? Gavin?"

"No Blood Eye that guy he's the one. Trust me. He's your man."

"I'll think about that one."

"I'm telling you Blood Eye is your man get Jagger and his peoples to train him a little more. He would be your pit bull from the door."

Soon as we reach my city line avenue condo Jay carry all our bags up into the crib. We both got settle in snorting blow and drinking martinis. Back in South Philly its midnight Willie Whack-Whack is at the back of the house of the hooker name Saquina Nails Nathan is in the front of the crib. They simultaneously kicked the doors in they were up stair getting busy. They were so loud the two of them never heard them coming into the house. They both checked the basement and the first floor making sure no one was in the house Willie Whack-Whack creeped up the stairs first with Nails Nathan right behind his partner.

They both walked up to the door hearing all these loud sex noises with the loud sounds of the bed squeaking up and down. Nails Nathan looks at his boy Willie Whack-Whack putting up three fingers up to let him know when they were going to rush in the door. One two three they both bust the door down with their gun pointing at them. The big fat woman Saquina is in shock she's putting up her hands. She was sitting on his face jumping up and down she stops with her eyes became wide. He can't see them, yet she is yelling out please don't Poooofff! Nails shoots her in the middle of her chest with his pistol with the silencer on the end of it. She falls over on the side of the bed and Rocket jumps up Pooofff! Pooofff! Willie Whack-Whack shoot him in the head twice and his lifeless body falls back on top of the bed backwards with the blood splashed all over it. Nails Nathan walks over towards where Saquina body fell at on the right-hand side of the bed Pooofff! Pooofff! He shoots her two more time to make sure she's dead. Nails Nathan say man could you let a big bitch like that sit on your face like that man wouldn't that kill your ass? Willie Whack-Whack, yeah it just did! Nails Nathan giggles good point let's get the fuck out of here! Willie Whack-Whack , "man, I love a big sexy woman, but I won't let them sit on my face. I have to get on my knees to eat the pussy out that Nigga must had have a strong ass neck."

Nails Nathan , "well that Nigga had his last big good meal at least." They both laughing and when out the house in the darkness.

They're Going to Take Over Your Shit

Me and Jay get settled in at the condo I go in the bedroom unpacking some of our things chatting about our plans were going to do most of the week. When I get the call, I look at my caller ID and it say Manny Williams its Willie Whack-Whack's fake name. I pick it up **"Habari njema haki** *Good news, right?"*

"**Dada nzuri sana habari** *Very good news sister!*"

"**Oh really? Tulipata** *We got him.*"

"**Familia nzuri ya kazi** *Good work family!* "

"**Okay dada kuzungumza nawe baadaye** *Okay sister talk to you later.*"

I looked up at Jay laying on the bed "well they got Rocket little greedy ass too." "Good now don't for get to call that dirty ex-cop back than you and me can have some alone time." As his eyes get wide and licking his lips like he's fucking L L or something. I got something to put on his lips for real it's hot and very wet.

I smiled, "Yeah, you right about that baby but where am I going to meet him at?"

Tell him you meet him at the parking lot of the Saks Fifth avenue parking lot not too far from here."

"I'll go with you sweetheart to watch your back."

"Okay, that sounds good thanks, honey."

This is something I love about our relationship having someone who really loves me plus he knows the game. He helps me out, but he also let me run my business plus he doesn't be trippin with a big male monster ego. So, I call Fast Eddie the ex-dirty cop back he picks up on the first ring.

"Hey what's up you ready to meet?"

"Yeah meet me at the parking lot of Saks Fifth avenue in a half an hour come alone."

"Okay I will you make sure you do the same I see you there."

He hangs up I just want to hear what this motherfucker has to say. Most the time he be going through Damon Gee, but his information be right on the money doe.

24

"Well look at it like this whatever he has to tell you must be some real shit just for you to hear you know what I'm saying."

"Yeah, I guess your right I won't know until I get there."

Then we can hear someone coming in the front door I pull out my pistol just in case it's not my son he's the only one with a key to my place. We both quickly walk towards the front door soon as I looked up, I see it's my son Little Boom with his Girlfriend their both smiling. I quickly put my gun in the back of my jeans and say so we finally get to meet the mystery woman in your life this is so nice to see here. We all started laughing as I got closer to her, I can see she have a little pot belly and a big smile on her face. My son announced, "Mom, this is Laquitta. Laquitta this is my mother, Miss Almasi."

"Just call me Almasi, please." I walked up, and I give her a hug "I'm so very glad to meet you honey come in here and have a seat." I point at Jay "this is my soon to be husband Jay."

He smiles at her and greeted her, "hi are you doing dear nice to meet you as well."

I asked, "would you like something cold to drink?"

"Yes, I would please its, still hot outside even when the sun goes down."

"Yeah, I know girl."

"but it feels good in here, Almasi."

"I'll be right back with something cold to drink." I look over at Jay and asked, "you need something a beer will be fine for me honey."

Okay I'm thinking to myself this girl looks pregnant. Do I say something or just let them tell me about it? I'm going to see what they're going to do then rather me jump the gun. I get some cold spring waters and a beer for Jay I walked back handing them their water and Jay his beer.

"Sit down, Mom I have something important to tell you." He had a big ass smile on his face. I sit down sipping on my water as he continues, "mom, I have some good news for you. Your about to become a grandmother. Laquitta is about to have a baby. We have to tell you this as well me and her have our own place not too far from here in Bala Cynwyd."

"Wow, that some really good news." I jump up and I walked over to her hugging and kissing her. I then kiss my son too. I to her, "so how many months are you?"

"I'm five months now."

"Okay, do you know what it's going to be."

"Yes, it's a boy Miss Almasi."

"What I just tell you call me Almasi or Mom, okay."

"Yes, mom." A wide smile appeared, and I hugged her again.

"Now that's what I want to hear. I'm really happy for y'all."

I'm thinking to myself I never would have thought I live long enough to become a mother yet alone a grandmother.

Then Little Boom , "well, I told you I would bring her by for you to meet her. We're getting ready to go back home we both are tired running around shopping for things for the house and the baby too. So, we are going get up out of here all right, mom. We will make a longer visit next time."

"Okay, just let me know and I'll cook for all of us. Let me walk y'all to the front door and it was nice meeting you Laquitta. Y'all take care and don't be a fucking stranger stop by and see me some time you hear."

"I'm going to hold both of y'all to our little dinner together all right."

"that sounds nice we will be back for that mom don't you worry."

"I know you will the way I throw down girl Little Boom love my cooking too."

"Yes, I do mom you're a really good cook."

"See how you think he got so big."

They both started laughing walking out the door waving goodbye. As they went out the door Jay came walking up and, "we have to go to meet your cop friend."

"Oh yeah." I locked the door up and we quickly go to my whip I toss Jay the keys so he can drive. We drive a little way from the condo, and we see a car sitting by itself he pulls up beside the dark blue sedan. I looked inside and see it was him, so I get out looking around seeing that he's bye himself. I open the door and I sit next to him in the front seat checking him out. I , "what's up Eddie?"

"Look I just got some news about your organization."

"What news you got about my organization?"

"Well tell me do this sound about right the shot caller of the BSN name Black Giovanni wants to take over your drug operation now that Philly, Nokey Blaze and Spider is out of the game. He has a gang who is selling a lot of drugs from prison now a lot of them are coming to take over the streets."

I heard there all getting out soon and you don't have any real heavy hitters watching your back they can take you out and put their people in your place.

"Do you know the name of this gang that's supposed to take over my shit? "

"That's why I'm here honey so you can pay me for the name of the gang and their leaders, so you know who you're gunning for."

"You're going to have to pay me 250,000 dollars for the name of the gang and it's leaders."

"Why should I pay you a half a million dollars for this information?"

"Because I'm also going to help you that's why, sweetheart because they done killed some good people of mine. I know you don't like me, but I will help you kill their ass."

"So, if you're going to help me why are your black mailing me for some more information than?"

"How about if I give you a job working with me and I'll pay you way more than the 250,000 dollars you're asking me for what about that?"

"Well I'm listening what kind of money your talking about Almasi?"

"Look as you know we have more than a few cops on the payroll you pay them out for us, and you get paid every week 90,000 a week."

"That's 540,000 dollars in one months' time. That's way more than what you asking for right?

"Yeah that some good money. I'll pay for your first month tonight. Now I have to say is you bull shitting me?"

"No, I don't bull shit when it comes to money, but you are going have to work for its doe Eddie."

"Oh, I'll work for it so you going to give it to me tonight?"

"Yeah wait here let me make a call so somebody bring you the money okay." I get out the car and I jump back in my whip pulling out my phone. Jay asked, "so what did he say?"

"I will tell you in a minute let me make this call baby."

I call Tanya she picks up after it ringing two times say hey what's up boss lady?

"Look I need you to take out 600,000 dollars and bring it to me at Saks Fifth Avenue parking lot right now."

"Okay girlfriend and come by yourself too."

"Sure, thing I'm on my way."

I hang up and jump back in the car to talk to Jay he to me, "what are you doing?"

"I'm giving this motherfucker a job that's what I'm doing."

"Why the fuck is you doing that for just kill that cracker ass motherfucker and that will be that!"

"No baby I know what I'm doing I can get more out this white man by giving him a job than to just kill him I need him right now."

"I really want to hear this shit on why you need him. I know I was right Black Giovanni is making a move on us and he's using the excuse of something that happen over 30 years ago to clear us out and move in his own peoples."

"Is that what he told you?"

"No, he doesn't know the whole story. He was just coming to me so he can cash in and get a job that's all he wanted from the door. But he did tell me there coming after us because we don't have any heavy hitters backing us up. This will be a good time to take us out because of their drug thing is growing fast and they have to give out more jobs for people."

"Yeah I can see what you're talking about now by Black Giovanni being a shot caller. He's running to a bunch of drug dealers coming in and out of the system. If he gets some of them working for him. Not only is he expanding he's taken over the majority of the market that's what you call a power move like a motherfucker."

"Yeah it is, and he want us to be the ones crushed under the wheels of his progress. A half an hour blaze past fast as me and Jay is talking then we both see some head lights come inside of the parking lot pulling up in a white Benz is Tanya by herself, she pulls right beside me.

I wave for her to rolled down her window and I point for her to give Fast Eddie the money sitting in his car. Tanya jumps out with this big gym bag walking up to his window tapping on it he rolls the window down and she hands him the bag. Soon as she hands it to him, I get out and walked over bumping fist with her.

I thanked Tanya, she just smiles I wave my hand and she gets back into her whip and she take off from the parking lot. I get back in the car sitting next to Eddie , "count it."

He looks up at me unzipping the bag counting it , "well it looks good to me I thinking you was bull shitting me at first."

"Oh no Mister Fast Eddie I don't fuck around when it comes to money okay."

"Now this how it works the girl who just gave you the bag she's going to tell you where to go to pick up the loot every week."

"Okay, I hear you."

"Then you're going to drop off to each one the people on the list she texts you on who to give it to you got it?"

"Yeah, I got it Almasi."

"Now Eddie if the money doesn't reach them people, we ask you to give it too you know you're dead."

"Oh, I know that I'm not a fucking dummy over here I will not double cross you, Almasi."

"I'm just letting you know I have to tell you that and your family too just know that.", "Look this is what I really wanted in the first place was a job I really appreciate this Almasi, I'm going to really show you with all this bull shit that about to go down soon.

"So, what's going down Eddie?" And I looked him right in his face.

"They call themselves the Chain Gang Clique. They are the ones who going to move on you Black Giovanni's peoples from prison the shot caller from that click his name is John Knotty."

"Oh yeah, can your people in prison tell us all the people that's not down with them or have some kind of grudge against them?"

"Yeah, I love the way you think that's really smart. I'll talk to my peoples and get that information for you okay."

"Good, just let me know. I'll pay them out of my cut not yours I want you to enjoy your money you earned it tonight."

"Look, I'm going to go she's going to text you with the locations and the list okay."

"Look, you're going to have to talk to Damon Gee. I know he's going to be pissed off I came right to you."

"Don't worry about Damon I run shit as you know. I'll tell him and the others you work for us full time now your cool and thank you.

"No, thank you, Almasi, I won't let you down."

"I know you won't. I talk to you later, okay." He bumps fist with me smiling his ass off. I jump out the car and hopped into my whip and I tell Jay to take off please

As were driving away Jay asked again, "so what he tell you?"

"He told me that the Chain Gang Click is going to move in on us do you know anything about these Niggas."

"No, not too much I heard of them before, but I know who do?"

"Who then?"

"My cousin Mikey Zulu he knows all them Niggas from what I know so far is that the Zulu's are at war with the Chain gang Niggas in the joint. "As you know inside goes with the outside, so shit is really hot on the streets between the two gangs."

"Is he up about this time of night?"

"Yeah, he is you want to go see him now?"

"Yes, baby I have to because I want to get a jump on these Niggas shit there going to move in on me so I can be a head of the fucking game."

"Okay than after that can we have some alone time with the two of us sweetheart. Know what baby I'll give you a nice sloppy ass blow job like it's your birthday okay."

His eyes got wide as fucking broad street, "oh yeah that sounds like a winner, I'm looking forward to that shit!" I reach over rubbing his Dick   "I'm make your toes curl and rock your fine ass black ass world!" We both started laughing while were driving to North Philly.

MEETING THE ZULU HOARD

It doesn't take us long to get to North Philly Jay pulls up at this brown stone house at 17th & Diamond street. Jay parks pulling out his phone and the phone is ringing. Jay is looking over at me smiling "you're about to meet this crazy ass motherfucker."

"Yo! What's up Cuz!"

"I need to holla at you, brother about some real shit that's about to jump off."

"Well just let me know, Cuz and I'll take care of their ass for you!"

"I know Cuz that why I love you. Look, I'm downstairs in front of your crib right now, Bro."

"Okay, I'll send my peoples to come get you stay there they be right down one."

After a few minutes I looked up and it about five big Niggas looking inside of the car. Jay announced, "it's cool baby, come on. We both get out the car I make sure I got my gun close to get busy. One of the big men walked up to Jay and asked, "yo, what's up? I'm Reggie Zulu come with me." He looks over at me, "oh, your girl can wait in the car Bro."

"No, she comes with me, plus you don't know who you talking to over there that's Almasi."

"Oh snap!"

"You mean Glock Mommy is here in the house!"

"Yes, that's me, brother. I'm so sorry my *Udadewabo* (**Sister**)."

Jay scratched his head and asked, "what he just say baby?"

"He sister in Zulu but I'm an *Indlovukazi* (**Queen**)."

Reggie Zulu cleared throat and corrected himself,

"my bad your right, *indlovukazi* (**Queen**)" Follow me. Well you know I don't know none of that mumbo-jumbo shit, I barely speak English. All of us started laughing rolling with all these big thug Niggas inside of the house. I'm looking around and they have armed

32

guards on every floor we all walked up to the second floor and this guy walked up to us stopping us.

Reggie Zulu assured us, "their cool Tommy Mikey sent me to come get them, okay."

He puts up his hand to hold us back pulls out his phone calling Mikey. He picks up on the first ring and yelled, "it's cool, Tommy, let them up!"

We walked up another flight of steps and when we got to the top of the stairs. Its two more men with machine guns dressed in all black. They both just stepped to the side with Reggie Zulu pushing the large wooden door open. Soon as we stepped inside this place is huge on the right its people sitting on the black leather couches eye balling us the whole place smell like weed. The smoke is thick in the air. Then on the left its some more people sitting around at tables eating drinking and getting their puff on and their thick too. No wonder they call them the Zulu hoard it's a lot of them motherfuckers. Reggie waves at them walking towards the back and sitting up on a big Leopard skin throne is this very tall dark skin dude with this voluptuous woman with a black cat suit on sitting on his lap. He looks down with a big smile on his face "let me up, baby so I can talk to my peoples here." She gets up smiling. He smacks her on the ass as she walks away.

He steps down and yelled, "Cuz!" They hugged.

"I want you to meet my queen."

"Well, your queen needs no introductions here Almasi Glock Mommy!"

"Welcome, Ma!"

"I'm Mikey Zulu. I'm glad you're here and for you looking out for our peoples down with El Barero from the 3rd street Mob. He shakes my hand with both his hands bowing,

"he you're the one who put him on, and he put us on what is it that you need from us?"

"Is there any where we can talk?"

"Sure, thing I got you look at this shit my Cuz hooked up with Glock mommy queen of the fucking streets over here come this way

33

please." Then he points at Reggie for him to follow us as Mikey Zulu put his arm around his Cousins shoulders walking towards there large doors on the left-hand side of this huge room. Mikey Zulu push the door open into this room with red lights on and this not to long table.

He sits at the head of the table and Reggie turn on the lights and the room get bright. Jay gets my chair for me to sit down and he sit down next to his cousin on the left.

Reggie sits on the right-hand side of the table. Mikey Zulu asked, "so, what is it you need Almasi?"

"Well, do you know about the Chain Gang Clique?

"Yeah, I know them motherfuckers we had to take care of a few of them in the joint they can't fuck with us we run shit inside and out."

"Why are they fucking with you?"

"Something like that they supposed to be making a move on me that what I heard from this crooked ass cop." I have on my payroll he got it from a prison guard friend of his.

Mikey Zulu, "oh yeah, yo Reggie get Fats on the horn and check this shit out for us, please." Reggie stands up pulling out his phone and he walks towards the right as the phone rings.

"So, where you meet my fucking Cuz at Almasi?"

" Jay is smiling saying dam your nosey, Nigga."

"I just want to know how this Nigga got so lucky that's all."

"Well,I met him at his car dealership when I ask for a bullet proof Benz wagon." Mikey Zulu began laughing.

"I would have step to you too, Ma."

"I don't know so you were buying a new whip and you met this crazy ass, Nigga". "Yo, that's like the pot calling the kettle black!"

We all started snickering when Reggie came back standing near us hanging up "your information is right on the money, Almasi!"

Black Giovanni's nephew name John Knotty is about to get out and they want him and his people to take over the upper management of the BSN.

"Man, that's fucked up! How long you been down with BSN Almasi?"

"21 years Mikey I was doing hits when I was 17 years old working my way up in the game."

"Well, I'm so glad you came here to see me about this shit. I got your back for real."

"Those Niggas aren't shit doing that to you when you put in a lifetime of fucking service!"

"Look I'll call EL Barero and let him know what's going on."

"No, I'll do that Dawg, okay. I just want you to get all your people ready for this shit that going to go down."

"Okay, Glock Mommy. I'll put the word out but you going to need some more peoples down with you too. Just in case some of them Niggas who say there, down with you and they're not."

"Yeah, your right about that shit."

"Who else can we get to be down with us BSN got a lot of Niggas shook and my queen here is part of the reason why."

"Mikey Zulu, I got some of my peoples but you going have to hook them up big time because most of them is just getting out of prison their ready to fight but they need a lot of fucking incentive, Ma."

"You know what I'm saying. As you already know I got keys on speed dial" "Can you hook up a sit down with these Niggas and who are they Mikey is they any good I don't want to get some Niggas."

"They can't take all the heat that flowing their way. Mikey Zulu I would not bring them up if they can't do the job, Ma. Everybody know my word is gold on the streets."

Jay asked, "so who are these Niggas spit it out?"

Mikey Zulu laughed, "S.O.S these Niggas are no joke my Nigga."

"damn, why I didn't think of that shit your right they ran the jails and still do if you ask me."

"What the fuck is S.O.S.?"

"yo, Smash on Site is a bunch of fucking brutal killers but like he they don't come cheap doe but there worth every fucking dime the shit is perfect."

"It doesn't matter can you hook up a sit down for me' I'll make sure I hook you up as well Mikey."

"Okay Ma, I'll make some calls and see if I can hook it up this weekend is that cool?"

"Yeah, but I need it sooner than that I don't know when these Niggas are getting out?"

"Yeah, your right about that hold on he pulls out his phone and he make his call while he was making his call. I hit up Jagger to let him know what the hell is going on. He picks up on the second ring

"Hey, what's up, boss lady hi you doing? Not to good I'm going to need you to come to my spot tomorrow. Jagger yeah what happen boss lady? Look I holla at that crooked ass cop Fast Eddie and he told me that Black Giovanni is going to make a move on me and put his nephew John Knotty and his crew in my spot.

"Oh, really, well you know I got your back where you at now?"

"I'm at Mikey Zulu's crib he's going to hook up a sit down with some of the S.O.S. Niggas to see if they're going to be down with me on this thing."

Jagger laughed, "oh yeah."

"Why are you laughing?"

Jagger continued, "yo John Spartacus that's the head of the gang Smash on site is my brother.:

"Get the fuck out of here you for real?"

Have I ever lied to you, sis?"

"No, Jagger I told you he was running the prison but he's out now. I been putting him on so they can get on their feet."

"Good, can you bring him to the crib with you tomorrow?"

"Yeah, I can do that what time?"

"About two in the afternoon is good for me."

"We will be there Moja **(One)"**

"Moja!"

Mikey Zulu replied, "I'll try again tomorrow he not picking up Almasi, but I'll stay on it for you, okay."

I didn't tell him I got the hook up already, so he doesn't feel bad. "Okay, Mikey you do that I'm going to get up out of here. Thank you so much for your help, Bro."

I hug him and Jay joked, "all right now that's enough motherfucker!" And he pulls Mikey back playing. We all started laughing, "yo, I just gave her a fucking hug over here, Nigga."

Jay busted his chops   "but she doesn't know you like I do; Nigga let's get the fuck out of here baby." I know he just playing with his cousin. Mikey Zulu , "yo, Reggie make sure they get to their whip safely okay, brother."

"you know it, Reggie."

We came out of the room walking out when Reggie pointing at a couple guys and they started walking with him as we all head towards the steps. We get down the long stairs going out the front door with Reggie Zulu and his two men in front of us. Right before we were about to jump in the car. A car came speeding up Straying bullets at us I can see the muzzle flash in the dark. **Kapackataka! Kapackatacka! Kapackatackata!** Jay jumped on top of me taking me to the ground when I get my gun out. While Reggie and his men are firing back at the drive bye shooters. Pat! Pat! Pat! Pat! Pat! I can feel something wet dripping down on my face when I looked up, I see its blood. I push up to check Jay out I'm scared out of my fucking mine. I hear the car taking off down the dark street. Jay yelled, "I'm hit, but I'm all right." I looked up and he's hit all in his arm and legs.

Reggie came running up, "are you two all right?" I screamed, "he's hit."

"I got you, man." He helps him over to the steps "we have to get you to a doctor!" Reggie ran up the street as I sit next to him with my gun still in my hand looking both ways ready to blast anything coming my way. Reggie came with his whip riding up on the sidewalk right up to us as he jumps out helping me get Jay inside the car. Reggie jumps back in getting behind the wheel taking off down the street. He drives about four blocks pulling up at this place that looks like a fucking funeral home.

Reggie , "help me get him inside." He gets up to the door I hear this loud buzzing sound on the door. Reggie pushed the door open and this heavy-set older woman with mix gray hair came running up taking him to the back room. Soon as me Reggie and this older woman help him sit on this long white Gurnee. Then a few minutes later I see Reggie and this older woman bring in another man who was also shot laying him on the other Gurnee across from us. Right than when I looked at the other man it was one of the men Reggie picked out to walk with us outside to our car.

Then the older woman walked up to me and Jay and introduced herself, "my name is Octavia everyone calls me doctor O. I'm going to get the bullets out of you, okay. Missy, I'm need you to sit over there while I work, okay?" I just nodded my head yes and move out the way fast keeping my eyes open checking out this place that looks like an operating room in a hospital. Soon as I sat in that chair out of her way she really when to work she took her scissors cutting his jeans leg all the way off then she when over to the other dude saying hey Ronny, I'm going to get that slug out of you okay. She points to Reggie,

" help me move him on his side, baby."While he's helping her move him, she's going to work with her scissors cutting his shirt off of him at the same time.

Then she tosses it inside of the trash can near the Gurnee she quickly puts on her rubber gloves on than pulls her steel cart in between the two Gurnee's in the middle of the room.

With all her equipment she gets a needle ready then she sticks Jay in his leg saying to me after this he won't feel shit trust me honey not really looking at me still working. She tosses the needle in the trash and she picks up another needle and she stick the dude Ronny in his side. She tosses that needle and grab the long tool and she came up to Jay and asked, "how you feel?"

He's mumbled gibberish, "oh, you're ready, Nigga." She takes one of her tools digging in his leg pulling out the first slug dropping in the pan filled with liquid. Then the second one dropping it in the pan than the third one super swift and I can see the clear liquid turn red in the small round pan on top of her steel cart. Then she turns around getting another tool working on the dude Ronny digging dropping the hot led into another pan on top of her steel cart. She reaches up under the cart pulling out a bottle of gin taking large swigs.

While that was going on Reggie came to me asking me for our car keys, I quickly reached in Jay pocket giving him the keys to the car not taking my eyes off of this woman doing her thing she have mad skills to pay the bills. She is reaching for her tool and she started cutting his shirt arm off tossing it in the trash putting the scissors on her cart getting her long tool pulling out the slugs one by one dropping them in the pan. She turns around doing the same thing to the guy Ronny just watching this woman work was amazing. She was all done wrapping up both their wounds super-fast and professional. she reaches up under the cart and she finish off that bottle of gin winking her eye at me fixing her wig wiping the sweat from her round brown head. Reggie came up handing her three stacks she sticks it into her white house coat reaching under her cart getting a large bottle of pills handing me a hand full saying give this to him for pain okay with her eyes getting wide with a smirk on her face. Reggie , "we have to get the hell out of here before the cops come checking shit out, I got y'all car in the back now. I moved it back there while your man was getting worked on. You ready Almasi help me with him." We lift Jay walking to the back door. When we pushed the door open were both holding up Jay on each side of his arms. Soon as we stepped out of the doorway just a little out of nowhere stepping out the darkness it was two men holding a pistol to my head and one on Reggie Zulu.

The mask man holding a gun to my head is not saying a word, but I can see in his eyes from that mask if I move, I know I'm dead. But the mask man holding the gun to Reggie Zulu dome yelled, "give me your gun motherfucker!"

Reggie Zulu yelling back at him, "it's in the front of my jeans take it, Nigga." Soon as the gun men reach to get Reggie's gun from his belt line. Miss Octavia steps up fast with a shotgun. **Boom!** At the same time, I pushed the other dude he stumbles back as I whipped out my gun getting low and shot him in the head **Kapacka!** I had to let Jay go he fell to the floor. Then I hear Boom! Octavia shot the other man we did not see popping up from out of the dark on the right. The last man that popped up fell to the ground.

Octavia , "you two both owe me big time and make sure you give me something before the week is out or don't bring any of your fucking people here anymore. Matter of fact if you don't have my money. I'll come and get it and both you young bucks don't want me to come get my money because I'm not coming to fucking talk to your young dumb ass."

I looked her right in the face   "don't you worry, Miss Octavia. I'll have my people drop it off to you the very next day."

She looked me up and down   "don't be bullshitting me, child! Reggie Zulu , "no she not bull shitting you, Miss Octavia. This is Almasi her word is real."

"I heard that name before and they say your one bad bitch when it comes to a gun, I tell you what fuck what you owe me!"

"Reggie, just make sure you bring her young ass back here next week and me and her can have a contest on who is the best that's all."

"Okay,than I'll do that but first we have to find out who set us up."

Miss Octavia shouted, "oh shit, that's easy they were Tommy Zulu boys."

Then she points at each one of them dead on the ground and continued, "that's Jimmy, Moose and Crazy ass Eric look for yourself? Reggie quickly go over looking at the men really fast he lift the black mask on each one of the men and came back to help me with Jay, "Doctor O, you were right how did you know they had mask on?"

Octavia joked, "all the fucking tattoos you Niggas have on your body I know every last one you motherfuckers even in the dark!"

We both looked at each other nodding our head yes. Then Reggie Zulu .

"Ms. Octavia, we have to go now I'll set that contest up next week, okay." I just looked at her and smiled as we help Jay to the car, we put him in the back seat, and I sat up front. Soon as Reggie pulled off driving towards the street, I asked him, "so who you got your money on?"

"Look, I never seen you shoot so I have to have my money on Miss Octavia she's one old crazy bitch, but she can shoot."

"Well, you're going to lose your money, brother."

"Oh yeah, we will see about that!"

"So, what are you going to do about one you men setting us up?"

"No disrespect to you Almasi but Zulu take care of Zulu no out siders. I'll take care of Tommy myself okay."

I did not say any more on that I just told him where to go to take us home. He made sure we go in the crib safely and Reggie help me take Jay to the bedroom and he called one of his peoples to come pick him up and after an hour or so he rolled out with one of his men taking him back home. After walking Reggie Zulu to the door, I came and laid next to Jay knocked out sleep and soon after I fell asleep too with the night we had.

The next day when I got up, I kept checking on Jay he was sleeping well than he got up looking up at me and asked,

"So, what happen to my sloppy blow job, Ma?" We just laughed as I gave him two more of them pills that Miss Octavia gave me. He just looked at me saying what the fuck is this. Just take them Nigga you're going to be hurting you need to take them! He rolled his eyes, but he took them I changed his dressing of his wounds gave him something to eat and he laid back down and when to sleep quickly.

41

Almasi 2
Queen of The Streets
By Dartanya A. Williams Sr.

While I when and worked the horn getting ready for this hell that about to come down on me but a bitch like my self is going to be ready for sure.

Have A Sit Down with The People I Trust

Later, the next day early that afternoon the first person at my door is Jagger. He came with Poochie soon as I seen him, I came up and I hugged him.

"You cool?"

"Yeah, I'm good, but you did have me worry for a minute there with that ass hole Goliath Ma."

"Well, I'm sorry about that we had to make him think he was getting away with it you were safe the whole time. I told Booby Hill what was up right in Goliath face."

"Oh, when you were speaking Swahili?"

"You better know it." We both started laughing as Jagger came up and hugged me.

"I heard what happen are you and Jay all right?"

"Well Jay jumped in front of the bullets taking me to the ground but he's all right now."

"Wow, you make me think that I should have never step off, Almasi?"

"No, don't say that shit, Bro. I gave you my blessing for you to go do your thing baby boy. It's your time now!"

"Well, I'm here now. I got your back, Ma!"

"I sure, hope so now my Nigga because all of this bull shit is about to come down on me. For real your bull shittin me, right?"

"No sit down and I'll tell you all the fuck about it."

Poochie and Jagger sat down, and I sat in my big chair looking up at them. "Check this shit out Black Giovanni is making a move on us after we done build all this up."

Jagger , "so, he's getting his peoples to run shit."

"That just what he's doing he got his prison gang people getting out called the Chain gang to take all the top spots."

Poochie chimed in, "yeah, I know them, but they don't have your kind of plug to hook them up to keep shit a float. I always you were a smart motherfucker I told Jagger that from the door." We all started laughing. Jagger chimed, "yeah, so what are we going to do here?"

"First off, I'm going to sit down with Tony Bolivar and make sure we keep our shit locked down. Next, I'm going to link up with EL Barero and his peoples so they can know what's up. I already talked to the Zulu's that's when Jay got shot last night and I think Black Giovanni got into one of their ears to take us out to get that money. But I really don't know but I don't fucking believe in coincidences neither."

Poochie , "your right about that shit, Ma! They paid them Niggas to try to take y'all out that's how they move I know all there moves Almasi. I was locked up with them foul ass Niggas."

"So, what you are telling me about your brother's crew?"

Jagger yelled, "yeah S.O.S these Niggas are no joke."

"So, do you think he will be down?"

Jagger , "yeah, but you have to put them on with something a lot bigger than what I hooked them up with first and they will be down. As you know money talks and bull shit walks all day down the street you know what I'm saying."

"Call him right now you not saying nothing but a fucking word it's on right now fuck that." Jagger is on the horn when the doorbell is ringing. I looked over at Poochie and asked, "can you get that for me, homey?"

He quickly gets up to get the door after a few minutes he came back with Damon Gee walked up and bumped fist with me, "what's up Almasi?"

"Have a seat I have to talk to you about something, Bro."

"Yeah, I'm here to tell you a few things as well, Sis."

"Yeah, did you find my canisters of guns."

"No, but I did find out where the head of the Armenian mob stay at."

"That sounds good.;

"Yeah and I also got word from Jane Doe she wants to holla at you?"

"Oh, hell no sound like a set up to me Damon when she reached out to you?"

"Just the other day."

Jagger cut in, sorry I don't mean to interrupt you two off while you're talking but my brother he have a truck at Girard & Frankford avenue than we can sit down and talk."

"Okay." I put my finger up at everyone while I pull out my phone and called up Quan Khuu.

"Hey, what up sweetheart what can I do for you today?"

"Look, I need about 200 bricks delivered at Girard & Frankford it will be a truck down the street from the food market, okay."

"I got you, no problem it will be here in a half an hour make sure your people are there. They will be there. All right I holla at you later one!"

"Now that's done Jagger don't let me regret this shit later."

Jagger chimed in, "trust me it's going to be the best money you ever spend Almasi."

"Yeah, if you say so Nigga if they cross me, I'll smoke all of them myself and you know that."

I point back at Damon   "yo brother look I put Fast Eddie on the payroll, okay?"

"Sure, thing Almasi can I ask you why though?"

"Yeah, he going to help save my ass that's why."

Damon , "okay so what about Jane Doe? What you want me to tell her she just wants you to hear her out that's all what you don't trust me sis?"

"Yeah, I trust you I don't trust her, but I'll sit down with her to hear her out okay. You set it up."

I asked them to hold on for a minute I take and call Fat Lou-Lou he picks up after it rings three times.

"Hey, what's up boss lady what can I do for you today sweetheart."

"Look, that dude you got working their name Blood Eye Bob."

"Yeah what about him he's a hell of a worker. Well I'll send somebody to come pick him up I need him."

"Okay, Almasi. I don't know if I'll get somebody as good as him, doe?"

"Don't worry I got somebody I'll send to you."

"Who then?"

"Don't worry I'll send you someone good all right." I hang up screaming

that fat motherfucker!

"Now, where was I?"

Oh, let me call Arturo! Arturo is the right-hand man of Tony Bolivar here in the states. This dude picks up on the first ring.

"Yo what's up pretty lady how are you doing today."

Not to good I need to talk to you about something important.

Arturo replied in his thick accent, "okay is it one hour important or next day important? It's one hour important."

"Well I'll see you in one hour at the Ritz Carlton okay goodbye."

I get up out my seat and to Jagger and Poochie, "I need you two to roll with me to this meeting. Poochie call my Aunt-Tee so she can stay here with Jay until I get back all right, I'm going to get dressed."

Damon Gee asked, "what are we going to do about the Armenian's?"

"We'll talk about that when I get back, I got something for their ass!"

"Your rolling?"

"Yeah, I'm going to get out of here I have a lot of shit to do. All right I see you later!" We bump fist as he goes out the door. I went to my bedroom to get ready for my meeting. I put on something nice because I'm going to the Ritz Carlton, so I have to blend in just a little. I check on Jay laying in the bed he's still doped up from them pills I gave him. I still tell him I'm rolling out and I'll be back. He's just mumbling because he's really out of it. So, I'm done getting myself together I walked back in the living room and ask Poochie,

"Did you call her?"

"Yeah, she should be here any minute she is taking an Uber."

Soon as he that the doorbell is ringing. Poochie saying that's her right there. He quickly goes to the door and he was right it was her she came in hugging me.

"Aunt-Tee just keep an eye on him and fix him something to eat when he gets up. He has not eaten anything after I gave him them pills for pain Aunt-Tee thanks so much coming here the last minute for me."

"Oh, don't worry about that, baby I'm here for you any time you need me so go do what you have to do honey."

"How is your leg Aunt-Tee?"

"I'm good baby you know me I'm one tough bitch from North Philly!"

We all laughed, and I say you better know it! We hugged again and I wave at Jagger and Poochie to roll out with me right before we when out the door Jagger gives Aunt-Tee a hug, "I have not seen you in a while."

"I know baby you better go okay."

"I miss your coffee Aunt-Tee you'll be seeing more of me for now on okay I'll talk to you later." We all quickly when out the door with Aunt-Tee standing in the doorway waving us goodbye and a cigarette hanging from her thick lips.

My Sit Down at The Ritz

Poochie drove my black Benz wagon it took us about a half hour to get there in downtown center city. We pulled up and Poochie let the valet take the whip as we quickly when inside this big luxury palace. This white dude came up to us and asked, "may I help you."

"Yes, I'm here to see Mister Arturo."

"Oh yes, right this way he's at the table over here."

He walked us over to his table he stood up saying thank you so much! He pulled out a 50-dollar bill handing to the tall well-dressed white dude he smiled and bow and walked away. We sat down with Arturo waving for us to sit down smiling I introduce him to Poochie. He knew Jagger shaking his hand. He greeted him, "nice to see you again, brother. Now would you guys like a drink or something?"

"Yes, I'll take one my brothers here are on duty okay."

Both not saying a word just nodded their heads yes with a smile. Arturo is waving his hand at the waiter to come over, "yes Sir."

"I'll have rum on the rocks."

He looked over at me and the lady, "Anything she wants."

I looked up at him and asked, "I want a Martini, please."

"Yes, coming right up Miss."

Arturo looks at me, "okay, what is it you wanted to tell me?"

"Well, it looks like I'm going to have some big trouble from some shot callers from my gang."

"Oh yeah like what?"

"Like they want to push me out and put in their own peoples."

"That's not going to happen things are going to fucking smooth plus me and Tony will not hook these guys up in the first place."

"I know that they just might have their own plug you know what I'm saying. I don't care what these guys want to do there not messing with our business!"

"No disrespect to you but we are not just some little old street gang or something. Were an international organization you know what I mean Almasi. Well I came here to tell you what was going on that's all."

"That's good I'm glad we had this talk and I don't want you to worry one little hair on your very pretty head sweetheart." The waiter came back with our drinks setting them in front of us. Arturo lifts his drink up and tilted his glass, "I will never let anything stand in the way of our business. I'll take care of this so-called troubles your having okay and I'm going to show all of them the real meaning of a shot caller."

I lift my glass with my martini, and I tapped his glass lightly and similed, **"Wao wate waliokufa** Their all dead."

Arturo looks at me and asked, "what did you just say?"

"I just their all dead!"

"Yeah, you got that one right, honey!" We all started laughing while we were drinking. I was thinking to myself right then and there fuck the BSN.

I'm going to have my own thing.

Arturo stood, "look, I'm going to get up out of here. You need to do your own thing and cut your gang loose and do business for yourself. Your just too smart and talented to be fooling with these scum bags from the gutter."

I just looked at him not saying anything as he stood up. I stood up and I hugged him, "thanks for meeting with me today."

"Hey, you don't have to thank me just keep doing what you do."

He quickly started walking towards the front door while I waved at Poochie and Jagger with big smiles on their faces. We all walked outside with Poochie calling the valet so he can get our whip. He quickly came back with the car but without saying a word. They both was feeling like me empowered. Poochie gave the valet 20 dollars and we all jump in taking off down the street with Poochie behind the wheel smirking. I looked over at him and asked, " what is you smirking about, Nigga?"

"Well it looks like the BSN is a done deal if you ask me. If they're going to be fucking with you after all the work, you put in for them."

I don't say anything, but my wheels are turning like a motherfucker. I turn up the radio when I hear a song from the nineties when I was loving the life.

"Now, I know all this shit is not what it's all cracked up to be but right now. I'm feeling good even doe I know it's going to be one hell of a hard road. I'm going to make this shit happen for me. He's right I been sharing the profit with everyone like a good little soldier just to get pushed out."

It took us about an hour and a half to get home the traffic was jammed the fuck up. Jagger Phone rings and it's his brother John Spartacus he talks for a few minutes and he hangs up.

Jagger responded, "my brother everything is good in the hood."

I turned and looked at Jagger, "good just make sure they come and see me so I can tell them what's what all right?"

"I got you Almasi. I'll make sure they come holla at you for sure. A half an hour later when we came up in the crib and Jay was sitting up on the couch watching sport center. I sat next to him and gave him a kiss,

"How do you feel baby? I'm feeling a little better now it still stings but I need more of those pills you had."

"Okay, you have to eat something then I'll give it to you."

Aunt-Tee jumped up and answered, "I'll fix you something baby."

"Well if you can fix me a big old steak, Aunt-Tee. That would be more than fine with me."

"You got a big old T-bone coming your way Jay!"

We all started laughing and I pulled out my phone.

I called Tanya up she picked right up.

"Hey what's up, Almasi?"

"Yo, I need for you to do two things for me, okay."

"Sure, what you need for me to do?"

"I need for you go pick up Blood Eye Bob and bring him to my crib. Then I'm need for you to sit with me a little so I can tell you what's next okay."

"I'm on it right now. I see you when I get there one!"

I lean back on Jay and he asked, "so where did you go?"

"I went to have a sit down with Arturo."

"So, what happen?"

"He told me not to worry about nothing and he also told me I need to start my own thing. He is right, too."

"He is right those motherfuckers want to bump you out after you held shit, down for them for years you need to do your own thing!"

"Yeah, I know that, but I know I'm not going to get a lot of these guys to follow me with my own thing. All they know is BSN."

"Don't worry about the ones that not going to follow you. You have to just weed out the fucking fakes that all when you're going on your own."

"Do you think I have to get any more muscle to watch my back?"

"Yes, but get new guys because you want loyalty from the root of the tree you know what I'm saying?"

"Yeah, I understand." Then I hear the doorbell and Poochie get the door and he is walking in is Tanya with Blood Eye Bob. Jay just looked at me, "I see you listen to what I told ya, honey."

"Yeah, I did!" I winked my eye at Jay. He is smiling his ass off than I spoke to Blood Eye Bob standing in front of me with his big muscular body with all his scar's and tattoos. He asked, what's up?" Tanya stood next to me on the couch bumping fist with me not saying a word. Then I ask him how is your Swahili brother?

Blood Eye Bob replied, "**Kweli nzuri Really good!**"

"Okay I want you to work with me watching my back. Are you down with that?"

"Well it's not just about the money but I do want some more money so I can take care of my family."

"Okay that's done what else?"

51

Almasi 2
Queen of The Streets
By Dartanya A. Williams Sr.

"I want a new whip and a lot of access to lot of tools so I can get busy?"

"Okay, I can do that for you. Anything else?"

"So, can I get some of that loot at the end of the day so I can give some to my wifey Mary so we can get a new place to live."

"Sure, I'll do that, but would you like for me to get La-Nesa to hook you up something really nice?"

"Yeah, I would like that but I'm still going to need that loot so she can get off my back." "Okay at the end of the day I'll give you eight bands to get started. I want you to work with Jagger and Poochie, so you know my routine and shit like that?"

"Sure, I'm with that thanks." I stood up shaking his hand saying welcome to this side of the family brother.

"Thanks, Almasi I won't let you down."

"I know that brother I waved Jagger over so he can show him the ropes." I knew right then and there he was the right man for the job Jay was right. He just looked at me and smiled. I pulled out my phone and called La-Nesa she picked up all happy to hear from me. I ask her if she could hook up Blood Eye Bob a really nice place to live, she give her a couple days and she can get something really fly for him.

"Okay sounds good do that for me please."

"How is little Boom?"

"Girl that Nigga is fine he got this girl he's living with and there about to have a baby."

She started laughing, "girl, you're on the late train mine have kids all over the fucking place." We laughed and talked for a while than Damon Gee came back to the crib and asked, "you ready to talk?"

"Yeah, let's go out on the deck." Tanya is ready to get up and go I told her no you're in on this one too. She just smiled and walked with us walking out towards my deck area Jay stay on the couch laying back watching TV. Soon as we sat down at the bar Damon looked at me and announced, "I hooked up that sit down with you and Jane Doe."

"When did you set it up for?"

"Is tomorrow afternoon good for you?"

"Yeah, I can do that but where at? "

"At our warehouse is that cool?"

"Sure, she not scared to come there?"

"No, she's good with it she on the up and up Almasi."

"Well how you do you know I won't kill her soon as I see her."

"Well it will be no skin off my fucking back I just wanted you to hear her out that's all. We can use some more peoples good with a gun after all the shit I been hearing."

"So, what you been hearing Damon?"

"Well, I heard that it going to be a shakeup in upper management and these new guys called the chain gang is going to move in on us."

"Yeah and who is going to be their plug?"

"Well I heard it supposed to be your old friend Emillano."

"Oh, really okay I tape Tanya.

"Yo, call your boy Gino right now tell him get ready to ride okay." She just nodding her head yes. I call up Ty-Kim he picks up after the phone rings three times.

"Yo, what's up sis?"

"Yo, I need you and your boy Chrome to **Hoja juu ya mtu move** *on somebody right now*.**"

"Uko Wapi *Where you at?* "

"Condo two. Okay Mimi nipo hapo *I be right there*.**"

**"Damon Gee, so what are we going to do about the Armenians now?"

**"I'm give that to Rah-Killer tomorrow that way I know it's going to get done right. But I'm going to put her up on that right now that your reminding me about them motherfuckers. Now that you know where their top man lay his head at."

**"Yeah here is his address."

He hands me a piece of paper with the address on it I look at it and smile while I call up Rah-Killer. She picks up after the phone rings four times.

"Yeah, what's up Almasi? Is everything all right?"

"Yeah everything is good **Nina kazi fulani kwa ajili yenu!**"

"*I got some work for you!* Una jua mimi niko chini."

"*You Know I'm down!*"

"Nzuri *Good* come past the crib around two so I can give you all the details. All right?" "Okay **Moja**(One)!"

I told Tanya, "hey baby why don't you make us some drinks while were waiting on Ty-Kim and Chrome to get here, all right?"

"Sure, thing Almasi and Gino is on his way too."

"Good, I want this shit done tonight."

A half an hour blaze past and Chrome Ty-Kim and Gino Gats all show up at the same time. Soon as they came up walking on the deck I stood up and bump fist with all of them and asked, "y'all ready to punch in?"

Chrome answered, "you know me I was born ready, sis." We all started laughing and he looked me in my face, "yo Almasi, I'm hearing some crazy ass shit in the streets about you and the BSN. What the fuck is going on?"

I looked him right back in his face with the others waiting for me to say something.

"Look, I'm not going to lie to you and I'm glad you're right up front with it as well. Some of the Niggas rolling with the shot callers want me out."

Ty-Kim replied, "I don't understand why they want you out when you were the one holding shit down all this time that's fucked up."

"Well that the way it goes Ty man. I just want to know is y'all rolling with me or your rolling with them?

"It's just the way it is that's all?"

Gino cut in, "well, I started out with you and that's who I'm rolling with you. I got your back!"

I looked at Chrome "I don't have to say it you know fucking well I'm down with you. I don't know these Niggas. I'm with you!"

Ty-Kim chimed in, "I'm with you fuck all that! But are you not calling a big meeting to let everybody know what's up?"

54

I looked at all of them and answered, "not yet, I want to see who is really down with me first."

I Had to Kill an Old Foe

All of them are not saying anything just nodding their heads and then I say to all of them. "now that bull shit is out of the way are y'all ready to go to work or what?

They all started snickering,

"Look I ask you two Ty-Kim and Chrome to do this because y'all know where Emillano live at I want his ass dead tonight!

"Can you do that for me?

Ty-Kim announce, "say no more were on it and it will be done tonight, sis.

"See, that's the shit I want to hear!"

"I bump fist with him giggling. Tanya also stood up bumping fist with me and chimed in, were not going to let you down Almasi!

"I know y'all won't just **Nitaomba kwawgu** *(Holler at me)* **when it's all done."**

All four of them walked from the deck Ty-Kim, Chrome, Gino Gats and Tanya right behind them strolling.

Damon Gee asked, "well, I could use another drink before I go. I looked at him so now it just you and me here. So, what do you think I'll make it past this bull shit with the Chain Gang?"

"Sure, we will with me helping you know fucking well we will out smart all these motherfuckers, but it won't be easy doe."

"Know what I'll join you with that drink but were drinking some cold Cristal I have back there in the little refrigerator."

He goes to the back of the bar going in the refrigerator pulling it out

"So, what are we celebrating?"

"We are celebrating our freedom from the BSN!"

We laughed while he popped the bottle while we were getting our drink on the crew, I send to take care of Emillano get to his spot two hours later in Glendale. It's a little suburb outside Philadelphia with big high price homes and lot of the houses have a nice piece of land on it as well. They took two cars Chrome and Ty-Kim in one whip there in the back of the big house. Gino Gats and Tanya in the other whip in the front of the house. Ty-Kim he called Gino Gats saying its only two bodyguards up front take them out its nobody in the back Moja (One).

Gino Gats turns to Tanya and whispered, "Ty-Kim we have to take the motherfucker out in the front its nobody in the back. So, are you ready? Tanya didn't say word she's screwing on the silencer on the tip of her gun nodding her head yes with a cigarette hanging from her thick sexy lips. Gino Gats looked at her gun and asked, "where the fuck you get that from?"

His mouth dropped open and he thinking to himself why he doesn't have one. Tanya blurted out, "Almasi gave it to me about two weeks ago."

Gino Gnats snapped, "Well you go up front and kill them I'll back you up. After that I will text Ty-Kim and Chrome.

Tanya blurted out, "I can do this by myself soon as you see me smoke their ass. You text Ty-Kim and Chrome okay you good with that?"

"All right do you!" With a funny look on his face twisted up Tanya doesn't pay him any mine she pulls her black mask over her face and gets out the car walking really slowly towards the house staying low. Then she laid all the way on the ground creeping up on the two bodyguards standing in the front of the large house she's crawling on the grass on the long lawn.

Tanya took her times creeping up on the two men in the dark soon as she got about 20 feet from them Tanya took aim and started shooting Pooofff! Pooofff! Pooofff! Pooofff! Hitting the two men twice in the chest. Gino Gats sitting in the car watching talking under his breath dam this bitch is good! Gino Gats quickly text Ty-Kim a skull and cross bone Emoji.

Ty-Kim looked at his phone soon as it when **Bing!** Ty-Kim saying **Walikuwa juu (**Were up!**)** They both put on their black mask and leather gloves. They both jump out of the car walking up to the house with their machine guns the closer they got to the house the faster they started walking. Chrome kicks in the back-door Boom! Ty-Kim and Chrome check the first floor real fast then they both head up the long stair well creeping up in the dark. A man at the top of the steps with a gun Ty-Kim and Chrome open up on him **Kapacka! Kapackatacka! Kapackacka!** The man fell backwards on his ass they both step over the bloody dead man's body. They see the shadow of a person running into the room on the right-hand side of the house. Ty-Kim quickly got low and started shooting hitting the man in the back-running inside of the room.

The man fell forward falling to the floor yelling in pain Chrome when to go running up to shoot the man in the doorway Ty-Kim pulls him back for him to get low on the ground. Soon as Chrome got down on the ground gun shots started coming from out of the doorway hitting the walls just missing them.
Ty-Kim yelled, **"Sasa (Now)!"**
They both stood up at the same time shooting walking forward towards the bedroom door on the right. The closer they got the more they were hitting the man with the gun the man fell to the floor bleeding yelling in deep pain they walked up on the man stepping over the dead corpse in the doorway. When they looked down and seen it was Emillano they both stood over him all shot up riddled with bullets he was breathing hard looking up at the two mask men. Ty-Kim pulling out his pistol from the back of his black pants **Kapacka! Kapacka! Kacpacka!** Shooting him in the head three times. Chrome pulls out his phone taking pictures and sends the pictures to me at the crib real, quickly to show me that Emillano is dead. They both looked over towards the left and they see a woman peeking her head up from behind the bed shaking. Ty-Kim pointing his gun at the woman saying come up from behind the bed right now! The woman stands up with her hands up in the air it's a beautiful dark skin Latino woman with a pink sexy nightgown on. Ty-Kim lower his gun looking at the sexy woman. They both stared at one another thinking if they should kill her. She pointed toward a large painting of

a bull fighter on the wall, "it's over a million dollars in there if you let me live you can have it."

Ty-Kim yelled, "all right open it up!"

The woman screamed, "how do I know you won't kill me soon as I open up the safe."

Ty-Kim asked, "what's your name?"

"My name is Cambria."

"Okay, Cambria we came here to kill your boyfriend over there we did not come take any money. We don't give a fuck about the money okay, but I will not kill you if you open it up and we will give you some of it okay."

Cambria walks over to the painting on the wall on the left she slides it to the side and she quickly hit the buttons on the safe and it pops open. Ty-Kim walks over along with Chrome they both look inside.

Chrome jumped in, "shit it more than a million dollars in here honey your better try more like eight if you ask me hand, me two of them pillowcases over there."

Cambria quickly get both the pillowcases from off the bed handing them to Ty- Kim and Chrome. They both started taking the money out in stacks when they were almost done Chrome pulled out his gun from the back of his pants pointing at Cambria's head she jumps back. Ty-Kim puts up his hand, "**Usifanye hivyo** *Don't do that!*"

She never seen our faces and she have nothing to do with that no-good motherfucker just chill. Ty-Kim takes the rest of the money out of the safe and he walks over and place it on the bed.

Ty-Kim looks up at Cambria and responded, "that more then, enuff loot for you to get the fuck out of town and not say a fucking word about what happen here."

Cambria went and sat on the end of the bed right near the large pile of money, "thank you so much."

Ty-Kim turns to Chrome and shouted, **"Inachukua tu pesa na kwenda** Lets just take the money and go."

Chrome puts the pillowcase filled with loot over his shoulder, "lets, get the fuck out of here."

He looked at Cambria walking out of the door as they both step over the bloody bodies on the floor and quickly walking out of the large house to the car. Soon as Chrome got behind the wheel to take off Ty-Kim text Gino Gats and Tanya a basketball. They take off along with Chrome and Ty-Kim in the back of the house. An hour later I'm really twisted with Damon I'm ready to go to bed Ty-Kim interrupted my sleep, "I just wanted to tell you not only did we killed that motherfucker we got about seven million dollars out of the deal as well."

"Get the fuck out of here Dawg?"

"Yeah, it was this sexy kitten in there with him she if we don't kill her its over million dollars in the safe, so she opens, it and we took the money and I kept my word I did not kill her."

"Well if y'all had on mask your good to go."

"I just wanted to tell you that so I can give you some of it."

"No, you just split that up with Chrome thank for being honest my Nigga most people would not say a word."

"Look I seen the pictures good job I holla at you later Moja(One)"

"Moja!" I told Damon I was going to bed now that I'm all fucked up messing around with his ass, he started laughing saying no me fucking around with you Almasi!

We both were giggling are ass off then I told him to get somebody to take him home, so he called up Woo-Woo to come pick him up this Nigga is six" six 350 pounds of tattoo ghetto bad ass who is no fucking joke. He did time with Booby Hill and Lurch who is down with the BSN Gang. He came and picked him up in about a half hour and to me could not got a better guy to watch his back while he's twisted. I walked them to the door, and I waved watching them drive off from my window and I when to bed flopping down on the bed next to Jay already knocked out sleep. But in the middle of the night this Nigga rolled over rubbing his Dick on my ass while I

60

was half sleep, so I turn over and started jerking his fat black love muscle making it harder. Then I just started sucking on the top of the head of his soldier standing at attention the more I started working my head and tongue on his meat the wetter it got. When it started making a lot of spit flowing it started rolling down to his balls with me jacking his shalf at the same time. Then shit started getting really sloppy sticky and nasty and to tell you the truth I was enjoying this shit just as much as he was. I was in a zone sucking on his sweet black meat.

I thought back to the days I would never be doing any kind of shit like this but the older I got the freakier. I became. He already knows I don't do fucking anal fuck that shit! Plus, If I don't suck him off, he will find some ho in the street to do that shit. I really love this man so what's a sloppy ass blow job to knock this Nigga socks off. It helps to keep the spark in our relationship popping off the chain. To make his ass pop a vain in his Goddam brain.

I'll do just about anything for Jay within reason to make his ass cum and be happy. I had that Nigga singing and moaning a like a motherfucker pumping and gyrating his hips up groaning loud. I knew he was ready to cum by the way he was grunting. Panting jolting and making loud sexual noises. **Ooooooh** here it cum!

Oh, shit this Nigga looks like he had been backed up for about six months or something with all that shit gushing out of his one-eyed black snake. I pull my head back really swift not to get it in my mouth and let it shoot out with all his dripping Dick juice running down on me. With a good hand full of his man hood pointing it under my chin and rubbed all of his super-hot love juices all over my titties. All warm and sticky on my nipples feel so good and freaky. I don't care what other bitches say I hate the taste of cum I want to do some freaky ass shit but I'm just not there yet with that.

This Nigga was jumping up and down in the bed like he was having convulsions or something. Jay is breathing hard looking up at me with them sexy brown eyes of his. I can't front when I see him like that damn that shit turns me on like a lightning bolt hitting me straight in my dome for real. I wipe my mouth off real fast and he kiss me on my cheek I get up going in the bathroom in our room and rinse my mouth out with some Listerine. Then I get a tub of hot water, some dove soap, and a wash rag. I set it on the nightstand and start soaping him up a little and wash him off with the warm rag. I wiped him off that Nigga. He loves that shit. He starts to moan so sexy to me in so much pleasure when I do that for him.

He stared into my eyes lovingly and touched my face.

He then replied "it's like floating up to the clouds and no other woman ever did that for him before."

After I've done that, I light up a cigarette I puff on it and I hand it to him.

"Yes, I treat my man like a fucking King for sure because I'm a fucking queen from the door."

I go in the bathroom and jump in the shower right quick and I come back smelling all good and shit and boom this Nigga is ready to fuck after I lay next to his ass. I know what buttons to hit on this Nigga. But I go to sleep and he cannot say I didn't take care of him really good so he can't get mad about me going to sleep. When I got up that morning, we get a quickie in to start off our day because I had a lot of shit to do. That same afternoon I sat down with Jagger's brother John Spartacus along with his number two-man Donzilla we all sat on the deck with drinks just the four of us me Jagger, Jay, Donzilla and John Spartacus. He told me he was going to need some help bagging up all that dope he never had that much dope to bag up in his life. We all laughed, and I told him he's going to have to get use to that because that's the level was on. I would help them get up to speed by bring in my peoples to help him bag that shit. But he's going have to do something else for me first while I help him, I got him by the short ones he can't say no or come half ass on what I need him to do.

I away do that shit to Niggas who always say they want a lot of dope until it's time to bag that shit up when I drop it on their ass. What they don't know is that within our organization were a big network of people who work for us doing that shit they just think of the money their going to get but you can't make the loot until you bring the fucking piggy to market so they will need me to be in the mix with what every these motherfuckers are doing I'm three and four steps ahead of Niggas every time laughing to myself.

I laid out the plan what I wanted him to do to them Chain Gang Niggas he loved it He told me something that I wanted to hear as well. he told me that he can get close to Black Giovanni inside of the prison because he has his top soldier on the inside name **Bookey**.

As soon we start, pumping him and his team some work that will get the job done. he told me that Tommy Zulu was dead after that shit when down that night because he's really cool, with Reggie Zulu, and he had to clean house with about six more Niggas.

Black Giovanni promise Tommy Zulu a large cut of the dope money coming inside of the prison because it like double the price on the streets and gave them some front money to take y'all out.

His boy Moose broker the deal," Y'all killed him that night along with Crazy ass Eric Jimmy and Nugee was the one who was following y'all."

To tell them where you were at after, some cat name Mick Molly did the drive bye on y'all with this guy name Gill.

I asked, "are you sure?"

"Yeah, some dude name Fat Hector do that name ring a bell."

"Yeah, I know that Nigga he supposed to be down with me."

"Well they before they killed Tommy Zulu that Fat Hector was real pissed off about one your peoples name Chrome got Philly spot instead of him and he was not going to drop his BSN flag along with some other old head Nigga helping them. Do you know the name of the old head who is helping them?"

"No, I don't I'm sorry Almasi they did not tell me his name they just he was one of the old heads down with Nokey Blaze that's all."

"Wow you done told me a lot brother." As I looked over at my man Jay nodding his head.

looked up at me saying, "looks like were going have to do some house cleaning are motherfucking self as well."

"You ain't lying my brother."

63

I looked up and said toJohn Spartacus, "you don't have any problem taking care of these Niggas for us, do you?"

"Oh, hell no Ma after you been so good to us and you been holding my brother down all these years, I feel like I been part of the family for all this time."

We all started laughing I announce to everybody as y'all know this stay within all of us here I don't want none of them to know what fucking hit them.

Then John Spartacus asked, "Who the hell is Zelda?"

"That's Nokey Blaze wife why?"

Well she been going up to the prison meeting up with Black Giovanni putting all these Niggas in motion that what I heard.

"Do Nokey Blaze know about this Shit?"

"I don't know Ma. That's what I heard so far."

Jay and Jagger just looked up at me not saying a word. When John Spartacus and his boy Donzilla rolled out from my place He promised he was going to take care of that shit and he was glad to meet me. I bump fist with him saying look we always was family we just did not know it yet.

He laughed, "that's true I walked them to the door along with his brother Jagger and Jagger walked both of them to their truck in the large driveway."

As I waved to them goodbye. Me and Jay when in the bedroom so we can talk alone. Soon as I close the door behind me, I to Jay sitting on the bed,

"How in the fuck are were going to find out if Nokey Blaze is backing his wife up to do this shit? I know she wants me dead for smoking her sister Neeie."

Jay looked up at me, "well, get your boy Damon Gee to look in on it and see if he can find out shit as you know he's really good at things like that."

"it really doesn't matter were going have to smoke Nokey Blaze after we take out his wife. This is something we will not be able to fucking avoid in this situation."

"your right but as you already know in this game it's so many things you have to do that's fucked up that you don't want to do."

After we came out of our bedroom, Jagger came back getting on post with Blood Eye and Poochie to watch are backs. We spend the rest of the afternoon plotting and puffing going inside of my movie theater room I had built in my spot. It seats about 25 people and we never get time to enjoy it to watch movies. So, we both sit up in the front of our new theater. I call it the Queen dome with two ounces of weed. Jay bought it from this crazy ass white boy name Frankie Bong. This strain of weed is called mellow yellow. We twisted up about eight blunts, pop some popcorn, and had two big gulp size cups of iced tea.

Sitting back in the large leather chairs checking out some good gangster movies like this Japanese joint called Outrage, Sugar Hill, Hoodlum, and both of our favorite Shottas.

A Shooting Contest with Miss Octavia

A week blew past I went and talked to my Nigga Tee Cee from the Black Demons at his spot in Pots town. He is helping me replace my big gun order. Plus, he told me he had my back with the Chain Gang situation bull shit. I just have to keep my eye on Niggas that supposed be down with my crew. Then Reggie Zulu set up that shooting contest with Miss Octavia on Friday night and I had to go through with it no matter how crazy it was. But before all that go down, we had to get back at the Armenians who took my big shipment of guns. The last time we were fighting these, motherfuckers they put up a hell of a fight. This time around I plan to cut their fucking heart out of their chest while it's still beating. Damon got these motherfuckers clocked. The big man name of the Armenian mob here in the United States, is Eamon Krikjian and his right-hand man Hai Dorian is engaged to Eamon's daughter name Kaia.

So, I came up with a plan and I'll drop it on my peoples when I meet them at my warehouse. I got up early so I can have a sit down with Jane Doe to feel this bitch out. In the back of my mind I don't trust her. I promised Damon I'll hear her out before I kill her ass. I got myself together everybody was ready to roll out at 10:30 on the dot. I had Poochie and Jagger training Blood Eye he sat in the front seat with Poochie driving. and Jagger turned on some funky ass hip hop sounds the whole way to ride to South Philly. It took us about hour and a half to get there with all the traffic all fucked up. Soon as we got there Tanya, Gino Gats, Black Duke and Puerto Rican Joe is there already. I bump fist with all of them speaking as I go to my office. My phone rings I check it and looked at my caller ID its Damon Gee.

"Yo what's up, sis?"

"I'm good when are you getting here? I need you so I can drop this game plan on these Niggas on how I want this thing done."

I'm on my way.Look, I have to tell you this before you want to smoke Jane Doe when she gets there."

"How you know I was going to kill her?"

"Look I've been around you from the beginning."

"I don't trust that bitch, Damon man."

"Look she's going to help us with this Chain Gang thing were going to face."

"Yeah how?

"She's really closes to John Knotty's sister. Her name is Bryah and she can tell us where they hang at. So, I need for you to be cool so we can wipe these motherfuckers off the map."

"Okay, I'll back up and see how this horse shit on a platter plays out if she cross, us I'll kill her and anybody who looks like her."

"And you would have every right too, trust me on this one I'm the one who got you out that bull shit with the D.A. Just trust me on this, Sis. Okay, I'll fall back on killing her this better not be some more sucker ass shit now. I can't make any fucking mistakes at this point and you know this."

"Don't worry I got this I'll be right there Moja(One)!"

Soon as I hang up with Damon Gee Rah-Killer came tapping on my office door I wave her in, and I point at the chair smiling. Rah-Killer sits down lighting up a cigarette blowing out some smoke saying I'm ready to go. That's just what I want to hear Rah-Rah I called in Willie Whack-Whack and Nails Nathan to put in this work.

You know I can do this shit with my crew. I know but what I'm doing here is hitting them all at the same time, so I need more manpower to get this shit done. Just let me quarter back this shit it's going to be off the chain when it's done right trust me!"

A few minutes later Nails Nathan and Willie Whack-Whack came to my office door knocking with them wicked grins on their grills. I tell them to come in and have a seat I bump fist with both of them. They all say family at the same time. Rah-Killer had a sinister smile and they sit down in front of my desk.

Almasi 2
Queen of The Streets
By Dartanya A. Williams Sr.

I tell them were waiting on Damon Gee so were all making small talk until Damon came in with Jane Doe, Fly Ty and Ayden soon as I looked up at her I had fire in my eyes, but I knew I had to chill the fuck out. I speak and bump fist with all the others but when she came up to me last, I felt funny.

I asked, hi you are doing?

I'm good. I really need to holla at you Almasi. Okay but I need to holla at my peoples about something and you and me can get down to what we need to do to clear the air. Sounds good to me. I waved towards Booby Hill sitting with the others outside of the office he quickly came up to me and I get Jane a drink while I holla at everybody right quick.

" I'll call y'all in when I'm done okay?

I look at Jane Doe and sad nothing is going to happen to you Damon told me some really good news you have for us and I need you to come closer with the family cool?"

"Yeah, I'm cool." Booby Hill smile and walk her out of the office while Damon Gee pat her on the back saying see everything is everything baby. She smiles walking outside of the office closing the door behind herself. Everybody sat down and gather around me while I give them the run down how I want this shit done. After I gave them the game plan, they all rolled out the door Damon Gee stayed, and I waved Booby Hill sitting with Jane Doe sitting with the others in the gangster lounge. Booby Hill just walked her to the door I just winked my eye at him, and he just put his fist up I say to him close that door for me please brother. I tell Jane Doe to sit next to me Damon is on the other side of me and it's just the three of us.

I looked Jane Doe right in her face and asked, "so what was you thinking about when you tried to Jack one of our pill mills?"

"Look I got tricked into that shit. I did not know it was the gangs pill mill or I wouldn't done that shit with him but after that I did not fuck wit Jasper anymore."

"No, I got the fuck out of town after that shit once I knew he was a fucking clown."

68

"So why you did not come to our meeting at the scrap yard that's when I heard you was down with Jasper?"

Jasper told me that y'all was going to kill me along with Knock Daddy and Bulls Eyes. My name was mixed up with them setting up Petey Q."

I looked over at Damon Gee and he nodded his head.

He replies, "that's true I heard the same thing from Jasper that why I told Almasi to hear you out. I knew Jasper had everybody all fucked up in the game. Now it's time for you to make amends with us here and now."

"So that means I'm back down with BSN than?"

"Look, I don't know if you heard but it's some Niggas who been running BSN from prison. They want to push us out and run things." Jane Doe asked,

"Who?"

"The Chain gang Clique."

Her mouth drops open and she shouts, "I know all them Niggas! I used to fuck with Crazy Paulie and plus I'm really close to Bryah." She looks at Joe Doe and raises my eyebrow

So, this is your test. You help us take them out and you can bring in a crew and run shit with us. do you think you can do this?"

"Yeah, I can do that but if were not BSN anymore. What's the name of the family now?"

Look, we have to think big now were no longer little ass ghetto dope dealing operation. were a Giant money-making conglomerate."

"That's it, **GMMC?"**

"Yep, that's it!! I came up with that the other day when I had my sit down with Arturo."

Damon Gee responded, "that sounds good to me.so what the fuck are we do going to do with these fucking tattoos we have now?"

We all started laughing.

"Now we got all that bull shit out of the way do you want a drink?"

"Sure, and something to smoke too!"

Almasi 2
Queen of The Streets
By Dartanya A. Williams Sr.

We all started giggling I pulled out my bottle of Belvedere from my bottom desk draw along with some big red cups and set them on top of my desk.

Damon Gee yelling, "oh it's fucking on now!"

Jane Doe pulls out her pocketbook a big plastic bag filled with weed.

Jane Doe replied, "I miss this shit getting it in with some real Gee's."

I pulled Damon Gee to the side telling him about the shit with Zelda. *I asked him* to snoop around and see if he can find out anything about Nokey Blaze. I told him to try to find out who's the traitor in our family.

Damon suggested, "look why don't you get Jane Doe to take some of them out before she sets that other thing up."

"that's would be a good idea." So, I sat back down and to Jane Doe I got something for you to do right away. She responded, "name it and it's done!"

I announced, "I want Nugee dead before the week is out."

She asked, "do Rah- Killer know about this?"

I answered, "She will after it is none."

Jane Doe smile, well it done then right."

I thought to myself only thing I must do is break the bad news to Rah- Killer about her boy.

The Armenian Mob Hit

While we were kicking the Willie boo-boo in my office my hit team is just arriving at the Chestnut hill mansion. The two vans filled with five men are what I call the slaughterhouse five. No one comes out alive. Nugee is behind the wheel of the first work van with Rah-Killer beside him riding shot gun. He pulls up at the front of the big house on the hill with the big black gate. In the cargo area is Woo-Woo Lurch and Mick Molly. Dressed in all black rocked cocked and ready to rock with their machine guns. In the back of the house is Billy Blunt behind the wheel and Bullet Head Joney riding shot gun puffing on a short cigar. In the cargo area is Willie Whack-Whack, Nails Nathan and Crowbar Carl. All of them have on earpieces so they all can be in communication with one another.

Rah-Killer commanded, "okay, **Kuua kilakitu kinachchoendelea** *Kill everything moving!"*

Rah- Killer jumps out the work van along with Woo-Woo, Lurch and Mick Molly.

Nugee stay with the van for the getaway. They all head towards the front gate of the house. At the same time in the back of the house is ***Timu mbili*** *team two*. Billy Blunts behind the wheel, machine gun in his lap, and two pistols on his hips. He bumps fist with each one of them stepping out of the van super smooth like the old pros of the death machine. That never leave you soul when you a real gangster from the gutter. **Timu mbili** *Team two* rolling towards the back of the house like hungry savages with blood in their eyes. Soon as they started up the hill towards the pool area, they can hear the dogs barking and snarling. All eight of them running up on them ugly sharp teeth beast is ready to chew somebody ass out. Bullet Head Joney waving his hands up in the air Willie Whack-Whack and Nails Nathan both got down on their knees real slow taking aim. With Each one of them holding RPG-7 Flames ripping out the barrows like hell lava sparks on top of a volcano. **Kadoom!** Then you hear a loud hollering sound all at the same time. Dogs are crying and they smell that smoky funky stench of burning animal flesh. They are screaming in deep pain. All of **Timu mbili** *Team two* **are** getting low so none of the dog's parts that are flying get on them. It's like a thousand pieces of shit coming at you. Blood and dog guts splatter all over the nice green lawn. Globs of sticky burning dog flesh smoking like a barbeque from hell.

Mick Molly popped up first ready to kick some ass. He started popping off the heads of the six men coming towards them. Along with Crowbar Carl Nails Nathan, Willie Whack-Whack. With a glow of the muzzle flash spitting hot shit. All you see is men falling to their death they are worm food in a blink of an eye. Mist of blood and death screams fill the air as each one of the men coming towards them never seen it coming. Laying low in the grass Bullet Head Joney mopping up the rest of the men with smoke flames and flying flesh ripping from their bodies. They all haul ass towards the white brick back entrance. Crowbar Carl set the putty on the large door and ducked off to the side. **Boom!**

Meanwhile in the front of the house Lurch blew the gate off the Hinges and the Moja Team. He is at the front door they smoke about eight men on their way running through them like a hot knife to fucking butter. Rah-Killer on the right waving for the rest of them to move up fast ready to kick some more ass. Lurch kicked the door in **Kadoom!** Woo-Woo on her left firing at the first five-gun men coming hot heavy bringing hell fire. But Rah-Killer, Woo-Woo and Lurch is laying down flat on the ground shooting upwards. Letting the front door goon squad to run right into awaiting instant death. After they all hit the floor hard yelling and crying from the on slot of bullets. Smoke coming off their bodies like a Sunday afternoon cook out. Rah-Killer, Lurch and Woo-Woo pops up all at the same time running inside the house like a bolt of fucking lighting.
Shooting and looking both ways back and forth mowing down anything moving their way. Woo-Woo and Lurch quickly run up the

large steps on the right-hand side of this large modern-day palace. Crowbar Carl and Bullet Head Joney post up outside the door. Willie Whack-Whack and Nails Nathan staying on post on the first floor inside of the house both teams meet up to fight all together. Toting their machine guns like the season vets they are. Mick Molly and Rah-Killer right behind them staying low but moving swiftly. Lurch and Woo-Woo rushing towards killing the few men who were left. Mick Molly and Rah-Killer ran towards the three rooms checking for whose left in the mansion. Woo-Woo rush up on the left shooting and killing the Goons in the rooms. **Barrrrrraaattttt!** Mick Molly kicks down the big white door on the left. **Boom!**

Lurch enters in the room and there is Eamon Krikjian laying on the bed with four women with nothing on. He raised his hands and they know who he is. Lurch yelled, "get down on your knees. Do it now!"

Woo-Woo came up with them pointing his machine gun towards the four sexy young women who begins to scream. Eamon Krikjian is down on his knees doing as he told looking up as Woo-Woo mashes his machine gun to his head. Then he looks over at Lurch just nodding his head yes. **Kapacka! Ra tat tat tat kacpack!**

Shooting all four of the young women who falls back to the bed in a big bloody mess. Eamon Krikjian looked on his horror and pees on himself not moving cold steel to his head not moving. With Woo-Woo staying there waiting to kill him last. At the same time Mick Molly and Rah-Killer burst in the back room on the right killing four more men falling to the floor screaming in deep pain.

As Hai Dorian Eamon's right-hand man is the last man standing. He is holding a hand grenade looking at the two black mask killers pointing their machine guns at him.

Hai yells, "stand back or we all go motherfuckers!"

Rah-Killer swings her machine gun and takes aim at Hai who's to the side right before Hai is ready to pull the pen on the hand grenade. Rah-Killer shoots him right in the middle of his head. **Kapacka!** His lifeless body hit the hardwood floor making a loud thumping sound.

Almasi 2
Queen of The Streets
By Dartanya A. Williams Sr.

When she looks over smiling Mick Molly is on the floor because he hit the deck. Rah-Killer looked down and was him on the floor. She screamed, "get the fuck up off the floor!"

Rah-Killer walks over and pick up the hand grenade rolling on the floor. She is showing it to him, "I smoked his ass before he could pull the pin.

Mickc Molly yelled, "How the fuck you knew it would not go off shit?"

"Beause I'm good that's why motherfucker let's get the fuck out of here!"

Soon as they came out the back-room Lurch steps out in the large hallway waving his hand at the both of them. Mick Molly and Rah-Killer quickly walked into the large room soon as they walked inside while Woo-Woo had Eamon Krikian on his knees waiting for them to come back in the room. Rah-Killer smiles bumping fist with Woo-Woo pulling out her Rambo knife placing it under his chin.

Rah-Killer looking him deep in his eyes what made you think you could fuck us, and you would not die motherfucker? Eamon yelled, "just kill me and get it over with I don't need to hear you talking shit!"

Rah-Killer yelled, "you ain't nothing but a word ass hole!" Rah-Killer pushed the big knife upwards under his chin Eamon screaming in pain as she pushed it all the way up into his head with blood shooting up out of his mouth and eyes. Rah-Killer pulls the knife out of his head watching him fall over to the floor with the blood gushing out of his head. Rah-Killer looking up at Lurch and Mick Molly "didn't I promise all you no good motherfuckers a good time?"

They both started giggling really loud.

Rah-Killer yelled, **"Ondoke Nje** *Roll out!* "And just like the crack troops they are every one of them started running out side by side in two's in and out of the house towards the vans. Rah-Killer was the last one out and she shouted to Nugee in the earpiece to get in position. **Team Timu mbili** got to their work van first with Billy Blunt smiling as each one of them running inside. Crowbar Carl, Bullet Head Joney, Nails Nathan and Willie Whack-Whack. Then at the front door Lurch,

Woo-Woo, Mick Molly and Rah-Killer soon as she sat down next to Nugee she bumps fist with him yelling, **"Ondoke nje** *Move Out!"*

Both of the work vans blazed out of there off the set as fast as they roll in there. Later on, that night I called Rah-Killer over to my spot. She came about an hour later and I took her to my deck alone telling her what was going on with Zelda. Nokey Blaze's wife and then I dropped it on her telling her I know about her boy Nugee, Mick Molly is working with Fat Hector and the Chain Gang to take us out. She did not believe me at first, but I called up John Spartacus to tell her the same story he told me. She knows John Spartacus is straight up and would not just be lying. I knew she was hurt but she announced, "let me take care of Nugee."

"No, I got Jane Doe to take care of it for me."

To see if she's on the up and up to come back into the fold.

Without me telling her she knows if she says something to any of them, she knew she was dead as well with that look in her eyes. When I look at her, I could tell from the glossy look in her eyes that she was hurt. "you know me, sis I will keep that shit to myself you have my word on that."

I pulled out some coke and we made some lines. We rolled up 100-dollar bill and she snorted up two fat lines. I did two lines and made her a drink from behind the bar. She no gin this time give me some whiskey please. I took the bottle of Jack Daniels and slide it over to her. Then she grabbed it from the top of the bar she opens the top and holds the bottle up in the air., "to you sis you save my life and I'll never forget it as long as I live!'

She started drinking right out of the bottle. We both got fucked up together and I got Jagger to take her back home safe. I went to bed with Jay knowing that my sister was hurt. She knows I was giving her a heads up. We both found out about the game its really fucked up when you have to kill someone close to you for real.

It's Show Time

Two days blaze past its Friday night 10:30 P.M. And it's almost fucking show time with this shooting contest with Miss Octavia. I'm kind of hype about this because this is my time to shine and show these motherfuckers a bitch like me got skills. Reggie Zulu set this up I don't want them to get mad after I beat this old bitch. She might can do her thing, but I know damn well she won't beat me when it comes to shooting. Jay was still messed up, so he stayed home but he wished me luck and went back to sleep still all drugged up off of them pills.

We all ride to North Philly three car's deep me Damon Gee behind the wheel, Poochie and Blood Eye in the back seat. Following behind us in his Benz truck is Jagger, his homeboy's Steve Swiga and Gun Ho Moe. Then Rah-Killer with her girl Kimberly We ride to this big abandon factory near 22nd & Lehigh avenue Damon Gee parked in front of the church Jagger parked right behind us. Rah-Killer parked up the street and walked back. We all got out at the same time, but we waited on Rah-Killer and her girlfriend Kimberly to come up to us. Jagger walking over to me and the others , "hey Almasi, I want you to meet two of the best **Askari** *soldiers* in Philly."

As he pointing to each one of them, "this is my man Steve Swiga and this is the one and only Gun Ho Moe." They both bump fist with me smiling.

Gun Ho Moe asked, "I heard you're really good with a gun."

"I'm one of the best you'll see tonight brother you better put your money on me, Nigga." "That just what I'm going to do to **Da Da's** *sister.*"

Damon shouted, "shit, I got six bands on you for sure easy fucking money!"

Jagger replied, "yeah, I got eight bands on you Almasi."

Rah- Killer also chimed in, "shit, I got 10 bands on you sister and if they don't want to pay me after you kick this bitch ass."

Almasi 2
Queen of The Streets
By Dartanya A. Williams Sr.

"I'll smoke everything moving out this motherfucker!" All of us started laughing we all started walking across the street and two of the Zulu's came walking up, "hey, what's up?" I'm Eric Zulu and this is Tony Zulu." I bump fist with the two men I seen the two of them the first time I went to their spot. There about four men on post in front of the door on the side in the dark. Two of the men quickly pointed at the large door for us to go inside we walk in there. And I see Mikey Zulu with about eight of his men all around him and his women giggling and laughing loud. Standing with them is Reggie Zulu soon as he seen me, he quickly walked over to me bumping fist and asked, "you ready for this, Ma?"

"Oh yeah, where she at?"

"She's coming don't worry she will be here."

"So, you got you money on her?"

"I sure do she done put a lot of money in my pocket, so I have to stick with that I'm sorry."

"Oh, you will be after I'm done with her you will see for yourself."

As soon as I told them that coming in the door is Ms. Octavia with about four of her peoples.

Her two son Nick, Dashawn, and her daughter in law Viera married to Nick plus Miss Octavia man Mister Melvin. I can see it in all of their eyes they just know she's going to win. Miss Octavia smirk at me standing with all of her peoples. She walked over to me and shook my hand, "good luck."

I just nodded my head as I see Reggie Zulu putting up the targets. The place is well lit, and I'm ready. Reggie Zulu call both of us to where he has all the targets at. The first one he put 8 bottles on the wooden table about 70 feet away.

Reggie looks at both of us , "I'm going to flip this coin and I want you to call it before I toss it up?"

Miss Octavia shouted, "heads!"

Reggie Zulu lets us look at the coin before he flips it. He tossed it up in the air and he let it hit the ground. We all look at the coin its heads. Miss Octavia smiles at me as her son Nick came over handing her the gun. Reggie Zulu pointed at the red painted line for her to stand behind.

He asked, "did everybody putting in their bets?"

I see Mikey Zulu and Damon Gee making bets with one another and all the others putting in their bets all you hear is loud chatter filling the large space along with smoke and loud hip hop music. Reggie Zulu looks at Mikey and he gives him the high sign to get started. He turns to Miss Octavia and asked, "are you ready?"

Ms. Octavia yelled, "hell yeah!"

She stood behind the line taking aim **Pat! Pat! Pat! Pat! Pat!** She hit seven out of the eight of the bottles. Sean Zulu moves the bottles and set up the new ones quickly looks at Reggie let him know that its ready.

Reggie Zulu looks at me and asked, "are you ready?"

I just nodded my head and I stay focus and took aim **Pat! Pat! Pat! Pat! Pat!** I hit all eight of them all of my peoples are cheering and clapping.

Next set up I see they had these plates on a wire swinging back and forth like a pendulum six of them swigging not hitting one another. Miss Octavia steps up, taking aim, and she hit all six of the plates. All of her peoples go off screaming.

I know I have to top this shit, so I wink my eye at Damon Gee and the others. I take aim, I shoot all six of the plates and then I shoot the wires that the plates were hanging from. I hit everyone. All of my people go **Wooooo!** I watch Miss Octavia reloading her pistol as Sean Zulu put up the watermelons on a pole. This time he puts them back a little further eight of them. Ms. Octavia's son hands her a shot gun. She steps up taking aim shooting she hit six out of the eight. All of her people are applauding. Damon Gee reached in the back of his black jeans walking up to me handing me desert eagle while Sean Zulu is putting the next set up. He points at Reggie Zulu he looks at me saying you good to go. I just nodded my head, but I twirl the pistol on my finger then I started shooting hitting all eight of them then I hit every one of the poles splitting them in half with the wood flying in the air.

I looked over at Miss Octavia winking my eye as she's fixing her wig with a cigarette hanging from her lips. All of my peoples went off yelling, "I looked over at the Zulu's and all of them they all had that look of worry on all of their grills."

Now I see her sons walking over with the apples now were doing the William Tell. Nick and Dashawn put the apples on top of their heads she takes aim shooting she hit both of the apples from off their heads and all of her peoples are clapping. I called Damon Gee over I whisper in his ear to get six apples and get Jagger to stand with him. So, Damon Gee and Jagger putting an apple on top of their heads and holding an apple in each hand. I stepped up shooting each of the apples off their heads and out of their hands. All of my people started yelling I can see that the Zulu's is getting upset.

Now Miss Octavia gets a blind fold as her son Nick puts a pineapple on top of his head. Mister Melvin ties the blind fold on her head, and he walks her up to the red line she takes aim everybody is holding their breath the whole place gets quiet. Miss Octavia shoot the pineapple off his head and they all are cheering loud. I wave Damon Gee over to me telling him to get four pineapples and he knows what to do. Jagger puts the blindfold on me, but Miss Octavia's people's Mr. Melvin and Deshawn came over to check the blindfold on me. Jagger looks at all of them and asked, "are y'all satisfied?"

They answered, "yes."

Damon Gee shouted, "get ready!"

Jagger walks me over to the red line. I took aim and yelled to, Damon Gee, "you ready?" "Yeah!"

I shot the pineapples off his head and his hands and the one that he was holding in between his legs. He tossed it up in the air and I shot and hit that one as well. Blash! Once I heard all of my peoples yelling, I knew I won this shit. Jagger took off my blindfold all them Niggas was mad. But Miss Octavia had some class about her she came over to me and began with, "look you got this one for real your good."

"Thanks, you gave me a run for my money doe."

She hugged me all of her people was mad as shit. Damon Gee quickly when over to Mikey Zulu trying to slip out the door talking shit with his crew. Blood Eye is standing in front of them and asked, "where y'all going?"

Right beside him is Rah-Killer, "hey Mikey you know what's up?"

He just smiled and he hands the stacks over to Damon Gee and Rah-Killer knowing he made a bet with her as well along with Jagger. Reggie Zulu came up and made sure everybody who place a bet got paid so it won't be no shit. Then her son Dashawn came up to me while were all about to roll out the door and made a snide remark, "next time you be taking me on."

I just look at him and nodded my head, "yeah when you get your weight up, I'll take you on."

"So how much then?"

"Get up 50 large and I'll take you on young N!"

He just looked at me as we all started walking out the door giggling now all these Niggas are going to be coming out the wood works to take me on. I jump in the whip with my team and they were going off because they all won a lot of money and everyone, of them wanted to celebrate. I called up Mookie and let him know we were stopping by his club I know he's going to roll out the red carpet for us. He told me he was at his other strip club, but he was going to be there and make sure we all have a good time. I hang up with him and it took us about a half an hour to get to club Elite. We park in the large parking lot across the street from the club we get out I made sure we were together. Then Big Frank Mookie's manager he came running up and told us to all of us to hang back. It's a car they keep going around the parking lot my people just called me letting me know.

I looked at him saying oh yeah all of us is pulling out our guns getting ready for some shit to go down. Then Gun Ho Moe pulls out two great big pistols stepping up in front of everybody. A dark sedan came speeding up on our left-hand side banging on us **Packa! Packa! Packa! Packa!** Everybody shooting back all you hear is the loud thunderous sounds of all of our guns going off all at the same time. All of us hitting the deck Damon Gee jump on top of me to cover me. But not Gun Ho Moe he just squatted just a little shooting his two big pistols hitting the two-gun men and the driver. He just looked over at me winking his eye at me. I tapped Poochie and Blood Eye for all of us to get the fuck up out of there. Damon Gee hops behind the wheel with all of us inside of my truck taking off right behind us is Jagger Steve Swiga and Gun Ho Moe. Rah-Killer and Kimberly drove off in another direction all we see people running and red and blue flashing lights. We all split up and all of us made it back home I called everybody to make sure everybody was cool.

I found out the next day the men Gun Ho Moe killed was Dashawn Miss Octavia's son and his crew. I knew that Nigga was mad that I won the shooting contest, but I did not think he would come to get us, but he paid with his fucking life. Now I heard that Miss Octavia and her peoples are out to get us after that shit. The Zulu's told me they would chill that shit out. I still knew not only did we have to watch our backs from the Chain Gang Niggas wanting to take our shit over. Now this small group of Niggas want us dead as well as the cops being up our ass. They came to me asking me all kinds of crazy shit talking really greasy. The same two *Dick Head detectives. Detective Thomas Miles and his partner Jason Kovalski they suppose, to be the ones who was going to bring me and my team down for good with a fucking task force just for us.*

They already know what happen to those other two ass holes who was fucking with us detective **James Schultz** *and his sell out Nigga partner detective* **Kenny Williamson.** *The pussy ass Detective Schultz got it first he was out on his deck playing with his kids when Jagger Gill and Fly Ty rolled up on him with black mask smoking his ass right in front of his wife and kids shooting him up multiple times all over his body. His wife Debra passed out from* *the shock but the three of them did not touch the kids like I ask them to. Jagger was pissed off at both of them the way they talked to us at the hospital talking shit when Blue got shot up. Yeah, it was a lot heat on us, and his partner detective Williamson vailed to bring us down a long with the FBI. The shit was a joke there just as dirty as the fucking cops with their fucking hand out.*

Plus, they could not prove shit and the uncle Tom ass Nigga detective Williamson was creeping around, but he could not do shit when they found out detective Schultz and his partner detective Williamson was taking money off of drug dealers in East falls projects working with a big ass network of rogue police officers. My man Damon Gee did it again expose them two ass holes. Then what made if even better one the cops took immunity and gave all them dirty ass cops up. All of the cops and the FBI all felt like fools, so that open the door for detective Williamson to get his next. A few months later While Williamson was on trial for corruption, he was driving home one night with his girlfriend name Keisha when a car crashed in the back of him. He pulled over jumping up and down yelling at the young man who crashed into him walking up out the dark behind him was me I with a silencer on my pistol.I shot him three times in his dome and walked away nice and smooth the girl in the car never seen what the fuck what happen. I had one of my young boys name Yokey one of Black Dukes peoples from North Philly to crash into his ass he got paid really well too plus he knew if he open up his mouth he was dead but everything when super smooth like I planned. He got ghost from the scene after I step out of the darkness the car was stolen four months ago. So, the cops had nothing to go on prints nothing but the three slugs I put in his fucking disrespectful black ass.

After that, a lot of them cops back the fuck up off us with all of their bull shit investigations. They acted like they were turning up the heat on us but most of them did not want to wind up dead. Each one of them that came with the bull shit we put them in the ground for real and they stop fucking with us. Then we had a whole shit load of them on our payroll after a while.

So, these two asshole cops don't know what going to happen to their ass after they called me all kinds of low life Nigga bitches and all the other shit they can think.

Queen of The Streets
By Dartanya A. Williams Sr.

I came to my spot and hit up Damon Gee to give me everything he can get to take care of these two motherfuckers as well they will never know what fucking hit them. I didn't have to wait long for something unfortunate shit to happen to them two ass holes cops.

One-week later detective Thomas Miles was shopping with his wife Belinda at BJ's warehouse. In the parking lot when a mysterious black truck came up and ran his ass over killing him on the spot while he was putting groceries in the back of his SUV. They could not come and ask me anything about it because of the description his wife gave saying it was a large white male who was driving. I had Top-Cat from the Demon MC's hook it up for me he gets one his brother bikers from out of the Milwaukee chapter name Big Trucker. He is a half black and half white criminal who looks like a white man. He did it and he got paid really good and he was glad to do it for me he hate cops.

An hour after detective Miles got ran over detective Jason Kovalski packed up all his shit and left town with his wife Blanche, he thinks I don't know where he's hiding at. He's in New Mexico with his sister Shelly and her husband Rick and their three kids. I let him get relaxed and fucking laid back comfortable.

Then I'll send somebody to smoke his fat white ass as well for fucking with me. The One thing.

I like about being in this position I'm in you fuck with me your fucking dead no matter who you are judge, district attorney cop whatever I I'm not the bitch to be fucked wit.

Three days later Jane Doe went to work she had Nugee's address and was ready to do what I ask her to do. Nugee was sleep in his house in West Oak lane he lived on Williams street a lovely two-story town house with a nice lawn and a two-car garage. It's 3 in the morning Jane Doe parked about two blocks from the house she was dressed in all black with rubber gloves and she had the black mask up on her head like a hat. Soon as she came to the back of the house, she pulled the black mask over her face. She gets to the back door "kick the door real swift and came inside of the house she gently closing the door. She came up through the basement up to the first floor then up to the second floor creeping up towards the bedroom. The bedroom door is open she peeks in seeing the two of them sleep

Almasi 2
Queen of The Streets
By Dartanya A. Williams Sr.

Nugee and his wifey Kala Jane Doe slowly came up on the two of them knocked out sleep **Puuuooofff! Puuuooofff! Puuuooofff! Puuuooofff!** It's a thick mist of blood flying up in the air she put two slugs in each one of their heads. Jane Doe quickly when downstairs going out the front door locking the door and closing it behind herself, she quickly put the mask up on her head again. Just like it was a hat walking nice and slow with nobody outside. All nice and easy to her car two blocks away going the other way jumps in her whip and pulls off real smooth. When I got up the next morning around 11, drinking coffee in my kitchen I got the text saying in bold letters **Imefanywa** *It's done.*

After about two hours later the whole gang knew that Nugee was dead. Kala's mother came over to the house and she could not get in. then she broke in the house from the glass deck door after she kept calling. She came in the house an found them upstairs in a bloody mess all hysterical she called the cops. After that, the cops went around talking to most of us in the gang and I acted shocked that he was dead. After a shit load of questions from the cops and then some detectives all up our ass like a fucking small thong on a fat bitch. But as you know I'm an old pro at this shit but this time both of these homicide detectives was acting like they were going lock all of us up all cocky and shit, so it made me start to think. So, when they were done talking shit, I called up Fast Eddie to find out what's going on.

He told me that Blue's wife Taye went to the FBI talking shit about all of us and they have her under wraps and none of us suppose, to know about. I already know they can't prove anything. Fast Eddie also told me she was the one who told the cops that I was the one running the gang when they first locked me up to go to PFDC The Philadelphia Federal Detention Center. I started writing my book about my life thinking I was done I'm glad I burned that motherfucker up. The whole fucking time I'm thinking it was detective Williamson and detective Schultz doing their investigation on us that brought me in. It was that bitch Taye and Tamika giving up the tapes on us to the cops and the feds. I didn't know all this fucking time wow. Well, one of them will never talk to the cracker ass cops never again.

Family Problems

It's one month later and the beginning of September. I got everyone that's down with me to have our BSN tattoos removed with Doctor Chow. He is also a tattoo remover it costed us a nice grip, but I had to do it. It's was like the motherfucker was never there in the first place. I loved it. As soon as we did that shit the Chain Gang came at us really hard and fast from the gate. Its Wednesday 3 P.M. Mookie is closing his strip club called Chocolate Dreams at front & Allegheny he's with his manager at that location.

Sugar man and two of his top workers Sammy and Johnny O made sure all the girls got to all of their vehicles safely. Once all the customers were all gone. A big black truck rides up on them jumping out is four men with guns none of them wearing mask Crazy Pauly, Nicky Ice, Byron Glock, and Marko Nash. Crazy Pauly yelled, "yo Mookie, come with us so we won't kill all of your workers here. It's up to you motherfucker if you want them to live or not!

Mookie pulled out his gun pointing it at all four of the men nice and calm saying so let them go then and I'll come with you, Nigga. Crazy Pauly waves his hand with the gun in, "go man you don't have shit to do with this get the fuck up out of here go!"
Sugar Man, Sammy and Johnny O ran off in the large parking lot and fade out in the darkness. Mookie turned to the four men and asked, "what you four faggot's want?
Crazy Pauly yells back, "oh, you're one brave motherfucker!"

What they didn't know is Mookie pulls a hand grenade from his pocket holding it by his side and his gun in the other.

"Crazy Pauly, come on and get in the truck Nigga or were going to smoke your ass right here and now!

Mookie just laughed tossing the hand grenade at them in that split-second Nicky Ice stepped up to take aim at Mookie **Kaboom!** Blowing his ass up all of his body parts and blood slashed all over the three men making a big mess and Mookie was in the wind gone. At the same time on the other side of town Tony Smokes is in the back of his smoke shop at the Cedarbrook mall with his woman Nashawn and her sister Kasamira. When Fat Hector came tapping on the back door. Kasamira knowing who he is letting him inside of the store. Fat Hector is always flirting with her when he comes by the store. He asks, "so when are you going to let me take you out with your fine ass self? I know what to do with that juicy fat ass of your girl."

Kasamira giggles, "soon as your wife Ronna is not fucking wit you no more that's when Nigga."

"Oh, you got jokes for days they both laughing as he walks in. Fat Hector left the back door open while he walks up in the office talking shit with Tony Smokes and Nashawn there both glad to see him as they both speak to him. Nashawn she's sitting in her man's lap in the office chair giggling and laughing while there counting the money, they made that day.

Fat Hector snicker, "see, as soon as someone is not around you two are right at it doing the nasty! Byron Glock, Queisha Loot and Nasir Murder they creep inside the store quickly. Nasir Murder grabs Kasamira mashing his gun to her head pulling her into to the back room. The three goons came up in the office guns blazing. Fat Hector was all a part of the plot to kill them. Fat Hector played along for a minute putting his hands up in the air. As soon as Tony Smokes went to pull his gun out of his desk Fat Hector pull his gun out on him.

"Don't do that shit, Nigga. Youu already know I will shoot your ass dead!"

Tony Smokes shook his head in shame, "damn Hector man I never would think you would sell us the fuck out man!

Byron Glock quickly reach over and grabs Nashawn. Tony Smoke leaped for the gun in his desk Queisha started shooting **Pat! Pat! Pat! Pat!** Hitting him in the neck,chest and head. Killing Tony Smokes before he could get the gun. Nashawn went off trying to fight back with Byron tussling with him. Queisha yelled to Byron, "shoot that bitch so we can get the fuck out of here!" **Kapow!** Byron Glock shot her in the head she falls to the floor not too far from Tony Smokes body in a pool of blood.

Nasir took Kasamira to one of the storerooms and began to rape her while holding the gun to her bend over. Fat Hector look around for the surveillance tape machine seeing Nasir Murder raping the young girl. Fat Hector walked up and shot her in the head **Plow!** Her lifeless body fell forward headfirst hitting the floor **Doom!** Nasir yelled, "what the fuck you do that shit for. I was not done man!

Fat Hector screamed back in his face, "well your done now, motherfucker!"

You just fucked up big time you don't know about DNA, Dickhead?"

Nasir Murder, "so, what we're going to do?"

Pulling up his jeans he asked Fat Hector, "No, Nigga! What the fuck are you going to do is the question? You're going to have to take the body with us and burn it!"

Queisha and Byron Glock came in the storeroom and yell, "come on y'all we have to get the fuck out of here come on!"

"Fat Hector, "yo, we have to give your dumb ass boy a hand with this body on the floor." Queisha walk up, "For what? The bitch is dead. Let's go!"

Fat Hector smirked, "yeah, but your boy here done fuck the bitch and his DNA is up in her dead pussy."

Queisha yelled at him, "your one dumb ass Nigga. I tell you!"

She points to Byron, "yo, help your boy get this dead bitch off the floor so we can go. Shit! Get a trash bag so this don't be a bigger mess then it already is! Byron Glock looking over at Nasir saying well hurry up Nigga this is your fucking mess where we have to take, a body with us after we done killed everybody in here! Nasir looking in the storage room finding some big trash bags in the back on top of the shelf. Queisha told Fat Hector,"find that surveillance tape while there doing this shit."

Fat Hector replied, "that's what I was doing when I ran across this your boy acting like he has not had no pussy in years!"

Queisha chimed in, "well, he's been locked up for the last ten years, doe. He didn't have to do that shit. I could have hooked him up with one of them stupid ass hoes from around the way for real." Fat Hector laughed walking in the other room looking for the surveillance tape DVD machine. Nasir and Byron by this time wrapped Nashawn body in the large trash bags and duct tape. Queisha walked a head of them with the car keys as Byron and Nasir started carrying out of the room to the car outside. Queisha looking both ways then not seeing anyone outside waving them to the car opening the car trunk and they tossed her inside.

Queisha told them to get in the car. She went back to see what Fat Hector was doing and he was coming out the back door soon as she walked up.
"You ready?"
"Yeah let's go!"
They both ran back to the car jumping in taking off from the dark parking lot. Now I'm home late night getting my groove back now that Jay was feeling better were right in the middle of fucking. My phone was ringing off the hook. As you know I did not get it until we got our shit off. Soon as we both came, I sit on the side of my bed, I a little out of breath, I light up a Newport and checked my messages. It was Mookie telling me that the Chain Gang just tried to kill him at his strip club and for me to call him back. By the time I got the second message from Dun-Dun telling me that Tony Smokes and Nashawn was dead. Soon as I heard that shit, I went the fuck off! I just about fell off the bed Jay laying in the bed jumping up, "what's the matter, baby?"
The tears begin falling from my eyes like somebody turned on a fucking water faucet. It was like somebody hit me in my chest with a sludge hammer too. Jay came to me consoling me as I just let it go with my man. After I got a good cry, I got myself together I jumped in the shower got dressed and I texted everybody to meet me at the America street warehouse.

Almasi 2
Queen of The Streets
By Dartanya A. Williams Sr.

Two hours later in the wee hours in the morning what I didn't know was that Fat Hector went to the scrap yard with Crazy Paulie, Rowdy Sean, Queisha Loot, Byron Glock, and Nasir Murder. Fat Hector banged on the big gray steel door soon as the new guy Ro-Boo peeked out seeing it Fat Hector knowing who he was he opened the door **Boom!** Shooting Ro-Boo in the face he fell to the floor. As all of them bum rushing their way inside Gavin, Fat Lou-Lou, Poppy Low, and Mister Fat Back, Seen Fat Hector on the camera in the back room where they were at. They all call it the count room where they kept the money. The five of them were back there counting loot from all of the rounds, they did that day. Soon as they seen them came in slaughtering everyone inside. Big Josh, Little Bee-bee his girl Muffin were all killed on the first floor. Gavin, Fat Lou-Lou Poppy Low, and Mister Fat Back. They took all the large bags of loot with them escaped through the back door that leads to a tunnel.

On the other side of the street this group of killers don't know anything about. I'm at the warehouse waiting for everybody to show up. Most of them are coming in one by one. Jane Doe shows up with her peoples her brother Bucky Guns Tia Slim and Neckbone. Ty-Kim, Woo-Woo, Lurch, Nails Nathan Willie Whack-Whack, Mick Molly, Booby Hill, Crazy Monk, Dun-Dun and Rah-Killer. I tell everybody to go to the back room we all called the conference room in this large warehouse area. I had it hooked up but not too nice because you never know when the cops would run up in there. So were all sitting at the table when my phone rings. I pick it up and I hear Chrome say, "Yo, it's me, sis. "Hey, what's up my Nigga where you at?"

Look I'm on my way there and I got some foul shit to tell you, Almasi."

"Okay, I'll have the boys let you in."

"I'll be there in a few. Moja One!" I hang up thinking what the fuck is going on now. Chrome came in speaking to everybody in the room and he came up, and I just looked at Blood Eye letting him know it's cool for him to sit next to me.

So, he got up standing up near me Damon Gee came in the room sitting on the other side of the table winking his eye at me.

"Hey Blood Eye man could you get me a cold beer, please?" He just nodded his head quickly getting me a beer handing it to me. I looked at Chrome "so what's up?" He hesitated for a minute looking up at everybody in the room. I looked at him nodding my head letting him know he could speak freely. I did not want any of my people to think I'm holding anything that's going on behind their backs specially with what's going on with these Chain Gang Niggas.

I don't want anybody to have an excuse to turn on me for some dumb shit I have to be thinking on my toes and I can't make any fucking mistake from here on out. Chrome blurted out, "Look Philly's man, Fat Hector is wildin out for real."

"Like what?"

"Well, I found out he's fucking La-Rinda Philly's wife now that you gave me Philly's territory to run. He's been sneaking around with Brenton's brother Diesel and his crew since he came back."

"Yeah, I did not know he came back to town he sure did not let me know about that shit after his brother got killed. I been looking out for him and his whole crew. I knew he did not check in with you. He told me he did those Niggas is up to some for real, Almasi. "Yeah well, we going to have to check them Niggas real fast then."

"Yeah and Fat Hector been talking a whole lot of shit too, Ma."

"Yeah like what he been saying. He told me that he should have got the spot when Philly when on the limb. He's not removing his BSN tattoo he worked too hard to get the motherfucker. And been going on that he tried to kill Ayden too. Everybody sitting at the table is grumbling loud."

"Where is he's at now?"

"He's in a fucking coma in Jefferson hospital." Then my phone rings, "excuse me for a minute I have to take this."

I sip on my drink and I answer the phone, "yo, what's up?"

"Yo Almasi, this is Lou-Lou."

"Yo, what's up big man what's shaking?"

Almasi 2
Queen of The Streets
By Dartanya A. Williams Sr.

" Hey, your boy, Fat Hector is a fucking low life traitor he just came to the strap yard with a bunch of Niggas I never seen before and they killed Ro-Boo, Big Josh, Little Bee-Bee and his girl Muffin!"

"Get the fuck out of here Dawg you seen his face."

"Yeah, we seen him on the cameras on the walls. They got most of the product that was there, but they did not get none of the money we were in the count room when it when down. So, we got the cash out of there and hauled ass."

"Okay, where y'all at now?"

"Were here with your girl Tanya at the Nice Town warehouse."

"Stay there I'm going to send y'all some help up there just in case Fat Hector and them chain gang Niggas roll up there."

"How you know their Chain gang motherfucker's, doe?"

"I just know look if you see Diesel and his crew come there don't let them in its a fucking set up all right."

"I got you, boss lady!"

"I'm sending Jagger and his peoples there, so you let them in but not Diesel and them Niggas. You heard me?"

"Yeah, I heard you Moja!"

"Moja!" I quickly hang up and started calling Jagger he picks up after two rings.

"Yo, what's up sis?"

"Hey Jagger, I need you and your peoples to get to the Nice town warehouse right now. I just found out Fat Hector is a fucking traitor!"

"He just went to the strap yard and killed four of are peoples how fast can you get there?" "I can be there in a half, yo!"

"Okay, call me when you get there and stay there. I'm on my way Moja!" I looked at Chrome "see soon as you tell me about that fat motherfucker, he just was at the strap yard and killed four of are people jacking the product."

Chrome asked, "who did they killed?"

The new guy Ro-Boo, Big Josh, Little Bee-Bee and his girl Muffin. Rah-Killer yelled, "from the end of the table why don't you send some of us there to take care of them motherfuckers!"

91

"Because I need y'all here that's why! Plus, I need for Jagger and his peoples to earn some of that loot they been making." Everyone at the table is laughed,

"do not worry I have something really special for y'all to do so just chill out all right, Rah."

Meanwhile, back at the Nice Town warehouse Jagger and his crew get there in a half an hour just like he promised. Steve Swiga, Gun Ho Moe, Little Bay-Bay, Flip Diddy, John Rocka and Frank Iilly. Tanya Gino Gats, Puerto Rican Joe Black Leon, Fat Lou-Lou, Gavin, Mister Fat Back and Poppy Low is already there. And just like I told them to send that no-good ass Nigga Diesel to come knock, on the door so he can get inside with all the others with Fat Hector to bum rush the place. Crazy Paulie, Rowdy Sean, Quisha Loot, Marko Nash and Nasir Murder hiding in the background soon as they see the door open, they come rushing up. But Tanya was holding down the spot came up with the plan huddling up with Jagger Fat Lou-Lou and Gavin. After Fat Lou-Lou told her and all the others what was up with Diesel ass. Diesel his boy Shaka and Tee-Bop came knocking on the doors in the dock area.

While they were coming up to the door thinking there going bum rush all of them at the Nice Town warehouse. Tanya had Steve Swiga, Gun Ho Moe, Little Bay- Bay, Frank Iilly and Flip Diddy around the back way to get behind the so- called ambushers. Tanya told Gino Gats to open the door but to close it fast once Puerto Rican Joe and Fat Lou- Lou pull his ass in the door. Puerto Rican Joe and Fat Lou- Lou yanked Diesel ass in the door tossing him to the floor soon as he hit the ground. Gino Gats and Mister Fat Back they slam the door back. Boom!

Jagger, John Rocka, Fat Back, Fat Lou- Lou and Gavin was all over Diesel ass beating the shit out of him taking his gun. Shocka and Tee- Bop ran up banging on the door yelling. Tanya open up one of the slots on the big thick metal door letting them have it with some hot shit. **Kapacka! Kapacka! Kacpacka!** She hit Shaka in his stomach he fell backwards hitting the ground doom! Tee- Bop ran off not getting hit running towards the others hiding all around the warehouse soon as Tee- Bop ducked behind one of their cars hiding Quisha , "yo, we have to get the fuck out of here they know what's up!"

Marko nodded his head, "your right let's get the fuck out of here before they get more men out here on our ass. Come on!"

All of them started to jump in their cars, and trucks ready to jet. Nasir , "yo, what about Shaka man we got go get him fucked that!"

Quisha yelled at him, "well, you go get him then! Can't you see it's a fucking trap so they can kill all of us Nigga!"

Shocka is laying on the ground screaming, "yo, somebody help me!"

Holding his stomach with the blood gushing out Tee- Bop just could not want to leave Shaka laying there bleeding to death on the ground. Shaka is about 20 feet away from him screaming in deep pain on the ground. Popping up out of the darkness behind all of them is Steve Swiga, Gun Ho Moe, Little Bay- Bay, Frank Iilly and Flip Diddy spitting bullets towards all of them ducking down near their cars and trucks. **Baaaarrrrrtttttt! Kackackpackaa! Katackpackataca!**

Quisha Loot shouted out, "I fucking told y'all it was a Gawd dam trap! Not even shooting back Crazy Paulie, Quisha Loot jumped in their truck and took off. **Eeeeeerrrrrrrr!** Rowdy Sean is hit in his leg and back, but he was still running up to the truck. Crazy Paulie jumped in and fell to his death reaching for the truck door. **Kadoom!** Marko and Nasir Murder in a wild panic started shooting back running towards their car but Gun Ho Moe, and Little Bay-Bay both toting theirAK-47 machine guns. They ran up on the two of them straying them hitting them in the face, neck, and chest with chunks of their flesh ripped from their bodies flying in the air. Tee- Bop never reach Shocka laying down on the ground. He ran off right into Steve Swinga and Frank Iilly. Tee- Bop dove to get into his car but was cut down with a barrage of hot led in his ass. **Katttackapakca Katactatackapacka! Katatckkaypackata!** Tee-Bop's lifeless bullet riddled body lying in a large pool of blood near his kitted up black Benz. All chrome out with the dull yellow streetlights shining down on his body with smoke floating off his corpse. The five machine gun

93

assassins disappeared just like the smoke floating up from the dead bodies on the ground. Meanwhile back at the warehouse at America street I have most of my people around the table in the back room. I get the call from Tanya she tells me about what went down. She told me she got Puerto Rican Joe and the others to clean up the bodies from around the warehouse. I tell her good job as I see Big Chrome, Dun- Dun, Mookie, Woo- Woo Black Duke, Ty-Kim, Lurch, Taz Money and Booby Hill roll in the door taking their seats. The room is filled with chatter and smoke I hang up with her.

I whispered to Damon Gee, "I'm waiting on John Spartacus."

I called Jagger on the phone right quick he picks up after just two rings and

"Yo, what's up?"

"Where is your brother at?"

"He is on his way there, Ma."

Soon as I that he came rolling in the door. "Jagger, here he comes I holla at you later. Moja! (One)."

I smiled at him as him and his right-hand man Donzilla sit down but his other three peoples with them stood up behind them Ron Gucci, Killer Cody, and Patty Racks. *I looked over at Jane Doe on the left she knows what I want her to do.*

I bang on the table and called our meeting to order, "all right my Niggas I will not keep y'all here long because it's all kinds of shit going on with the whole **Kikundi** *gang*. I know you see some new faces around the **Meza** *Table* I'm going to have a real cipher after I weed out all the fucking **Panya** *Rats* all around us. As everybody started giggling Jane Doe, Tia Slim, Bucky Guns and Neckbone is standing behind Mick Molly. Jane Doe sticks her pistol to his neck as Tia Slim take his gun. Bucky Guns called out, "get the fuck up and do it slow too, Nigga or I'll smoke you here and fucking now!

Mick Molly stood up with shock expression on his face with everybody looking over towards him. I stand up and announce, "well if most of y'all did not know is Fat Hector is a fucking traitor and he was working in behalf of the fucking Chain Gang Niggas! And Mick over here tried to kill me and my man Jay in a drive by when I had a sit down with the Zulu's. The whole room started groaning loud. Mick Molly looked up at everybody and screech, "I was not the only one where the fuck is Crowbar Carl. He was in that shit too!"

Rah- Killer stood up and chimed in, "your fucking lying. Carl had nothing to do with y'all backstabbing bull shit he is not here now because he's taking care of his sick little girl, she has cancer. I looked him right in his face saying it is your fault my friend Tony Smokes is dead! I just nodded my head Tia Slim pulled him away from the table as Bucky Guns and Jane Doe take aim **Tackacka! Boom!** Bucky Guns shooting him in his chest making a large hole and you can see a big chuck flying from his body and Jane Doe shooting him in the head as the blood gushing out of his dome laying on the ground. I looked over at everybody in the room saying all traitors will be dealt with on the fucking spot! I lift up my sleeve showing everyone in the room I had my BSN tattoo removed after a lifetime of fucking service if your rolling with me or them Niggas it is up to you! All eyes were on me everybody started standing up clapping their hands. *I know with this war with the chain gang is going to be long and really bloody.*

And I already know I just might lose some of my peoples, but I know right now they will follow me into hell with a bucket of water. Arturo really opened up my eyes to things to think and move on another level and that's just what I'm going to do from here on out. A week later we had a private service for Tony Sanders aka Tony Smokes our brother and friend with his woman Nashawn Davis. We had it at a secret location, so we don't have any bullshit going down. It was sad and even with all the blood were going spill in the streets it won't bring him back to us.

They Kidnaped Robin

Two months went by and now it's getting cold outside around this time of year. I had to change up everything I was doing and decided I want to stop selling guns and start selling Molly pills. Arturo hook me up with this Germen dude Fritz Burger in the beginning of November of 2018. We had a sit down at the Warwick Hotel at Rittenhouse square. I go up to the penthouse with Poochie and Blood Eye, Arturo is up there with his goons Zack and Jewy. Soon as we get up there, we all shake hands, but Arturo say for them to wait in the other room while we talk. I agree and just nodded my head at my men while they chilled with Arturo's men shooting the shit. I went in the other room with these large white doors with glass allow Arturo to lead the way. Arturo is a tan handsome man, with a wicked smile. He pushed the door open and sitting at this large round table is this short bald head man as we walked up. He stood up sticking his hand out as Arturo introduce me to him, "Fritz this is Almasi. Almasi this is Fritz the chemical engineer genius in the flesh."

He smiles, "you are oh to kind my friend it's nice to meet you, young lady. I hear so many good things about you."

Arturo points at our seats we sit down as he kept talking as I was told you have the knowhow and the people to move this product along the whole east coast and even the Midwest.

"I do and I'll have a good foot hole on the left coast as well if the numbers are right."

"Oh, the numbers are there young lady let me run them by you while we drink some wine." He takes the bottle of wine and started opening it.

Meanwhile while I'm negotiating a new deal at the same time my sister Robin is on her way to court. She's working on a big murder case. While coming out of her apartment to go jump in her whip in the parking lot of the Dorchester apartment building in center city. They jumped out from behind the park cars is four thug Niggas who overpower her. She puts up a good fight, but these men are

just too strong for her to deal with. A black van come speeding up and they toss
her inside with the men jumping in their self's and take off out of the parking lot.

Its 3:30 in the afternoon I'm done working everything out with
Arturo and my new partner Fritz. I shake hand with both of them
walking out to the other room waving my hand for my men to come
over to me so we can all roll. I get the call from Damon Gee. I pull
my phone out and put it to my ear while I'm walking with Blood Eye
and Poochie to the elevator.

"Yo, what's up Damon?"

"Hey, I got some really bad news to give you."

"Yeah, and what's that after I done cut a very sweet ass deal
today."

"Well, I just got the call from some Nigga saying that they have
your sister Robin. They they want ten million dollars in cash or she's
dead."

"Is it real?"

"I'm almost at her apartment right now I'll be there in a few
minutes to see. I'm calling her phone its going straight to voice mail."

"Okay, stay there I'm on my way Moja*(One)!*"

I to Poochie and Blood Eye, "come on y'all we have to ride like
the wind to my sister spot to see if this shit is real!"

Poochie , "what happen, Almasi?"

"Damon Gee just hit me and that somebody grabbed Robin."

"What? That's fucked up!"

"Well, they might be fucking with us were going to go find out is
it real or not."

Bye this time we were talking we reach the ground floor and was
in front of the hotel Blood Eye quickly tips the valet as he ran and got
the car.

Blood Eye , "if this shit is real, we need to tell everybody to
watch their backs."

"Your right Blood Eye but first we have to make sure it's true."

The tall white boy came up with my black Benz wagon jumping
out handing Poochie the keys. We all hopped in and took off quicker

than a motherfucker can blink their eyes. She doesn't live to far from where we are at, she lives at 15th & Locust street just about two blocks away. I'm really nervous but I'm playing it real cool doe. Its only took us five minutes to get there we park in the parking lot across the street from her building we quickly run over there. As soon as we get to the lobby area Damon Gee is standing there "he's not home and I called her boss Janet."

She did not show up for court today and that's not like her. I thought to myself the shit is real. She never doesn't show up for fucking court. I look at Damon Gee,

"what are we going to do?"

"We can get our people looking but that's going to waste a lot of fucking time only thing we can do is wait until they call me again."

"Who do you think it is?"

"You don't have to ask that shit you know it's the Chain Gang Niggas. After we done kicked their ass with that shoot out at the nice town warehouse a couple months ago."

"Yeah, your right I wish we would have killed all of them."

Me too Blood Eye, "yo, what you were saying early tell all of your peoples to watch their backs."

Damon text everybody and let them know to be locked down and watch their ass while there on the move with everything their doing.

"Okay, where are we going to now?"

"For right now we're all going to are home base and wait for a call or something. I don't know it yet but the Niggas who snatch her was Crazy Paulie, Sammy Steel, Byron Glock and Frank Homicide. They took my sister up at this farmhouse in Pottstown They have her tied up in the back room.

Back in South Philly at my warehouse on Washington avenue six hours done pass and no call its 9:30 P.M. I'm in my office on the phone with my man Jay. I told him what happen he's talking to me to keep me calm down.

I have Lurch, Woo-Woo Taz- Money and Booby Hill on post. Damon Gee is in the office with me along with Dun-Dun and Fly Ty.

98

He told me a few months ago he was going to give up the life. Chillin in the gangster lounge is Jane Doe and her crew Buckey Guns Neckbone and Tia Slim sitting with Puerto Rican Joe Black Duke, Mookie and Crazy Monk.

I had Tanya holding down our new warehouse in North Philly that the Chain Gang Niggas don't know about at Sedgley avenue and I also moved Fat Lou- Lou and his crew to our new scrap yard in South West Philly and the Chain Gang Niggas don't know where that's at either.

I have four more my girl La-Nesa hook me up with. I'm going to move Puerto Rican Joe and them up when I get the pills flowing in, but they don't know it yet. My phone started ringing I get it really quick and it's the hospital asking for Miss Miller.

I answer, "this is Miss Miller who may I say is calling?"

"This is Miss Stein at Jefferson hospital."

"Yes, Miss Stein how is Ayden doing?"

I'm sorry to tell you this but he passed this afternoon. Does he have any other family other than yourself?"

"No just me. Thank you, Miss Stein. I'll have my people to pick up the body to plan arrangements. Are you also going to take care of the bill as well? I'm assuming Miss Miller."

"Yes, I'll have that to you in the morning thank you Miss Stein."

I hang up and I look up at Dun- Dun and, "that was the hospital they Ayden pass this afternoon."

"Wow, he hung in there for a long time too and he really don't have any family at all, Almasi?"

"He has a brother but he's doing life so you might as well say nobody but us because he can't do nothing for him in there." Then Damon Gee gets the call he jumps up pointing saying its them I say put it on speaker. This deep heavy ass voice yelled, "I want to talk to Almasi!"

I answer, "this is Almasi, motherfucker. What is it you want?"

"Yo, what I want is for you to follow our instruction and we won't have to kill your sister okay!"

"I hear you. What is you want me to do hear?"

"I want you to give us ten million dollars put five million dollars in two bags. You have 48 hours to get the money together. I'll call you back and tell you where to drop them off at.

And I know you have it so don't even try bullshitting me the clock is ticking."

I looked at Damon "I need you and Tanya to get that money together really quick too."

"You know I can get it done. You better call your girl so she can get to work." So, I start working the horn I call Tanya telling her to get the money from the stash and put that money together and bring it here. Now while I have them running around putting this money together.

In Pottstown at the farmhouse my sister Robin is working this Nigga. My sister Robin is a gorgeous ass woman she is what Niggas in the street call a brick house. They leave Frank Homicide on post by himself watching her while there figuring out all the spots to tell us where to drop the money off at. Frank snorting coke looking her up and down with lust in his eyes. He's thinking he can get some before they have to turn her loose when they get the money.

Robin asked him, "can I have some?"

He looks at her, "shit why not your tied up."

He walked over to her scooping out the cocaine from the bag and hold it up to her nose for her to snort the white powder. He gives her a hit in each one of her nostrils right after she take the hit, and now she's shaking her legs. She has on a blue dress on and he's looking down at her really nice thick sexy legs. He's laughed, "damn girl was it that good?"

She smirked,"oh hell yes! When I snort coke, it makes me horny."

His stretched his eyes wide looking down under her dress. He can see her pink panties Robin see that he's peeking up under her dress. She continues to shake her legs just a little more cocking her legs open so he can get a better look

Robin asked, "how about giving me some more of that raw Dawg shit, my Nigga."

Frank grinned and announced, "what with you talking like that you're not from the hood girl."

"What you don't know Nigga I'm from right on 24th street. I lived on the 1600 block of Ringgold street Nigga all my life."

"Yeah, I have peoples from down there."

"Oh yeah like who?"

"Do you know La' Wanda Black and them?"

"Yeah who don't know big butt La' Wanda and them and her girl road Dawg Tyshell." "Yeah, I use to fuck with her some time back you do know them Niggas."

"Sure, I do come on and give me some more of that." As she's looking up at him with her bedroom eye's he's eating it all up from the door.

He looks at the bag, "I'm almost out, but I be right back." He quickly goes to his stash and Robin is trying to wiggle out of the duct tape they have on her hands, but she can't get lose.

Frank Homicide comes back with a big bag of coke and announced, "all right baby girl now if I give you some more what are you going to do for me?"

Licking his lips with lust glowing in his eyes looking at her sexy body.

"Well what can I do with my fucking hands tied like this we can have a little fun before any of your people come back. What they don't know won't hurt them."

"Yeah, your right about that but you're going to try to run out of here if I untie your ass."

"Look, I don't want you to kill me. I'll be good I know they don't call you homicide for nothing now."

"Yeah, you're right about that baby." He came up putting his hand up her dress rubbing her pussy and Robin started moaning, "I like that shit, baby can't you feel my panties getting wet?"

She looked him deep in his eyes and she can see that she got his ass now. He puts his hand back up under her dress rubbing even harder as Robin shaking her legs back and forth faster and it's turning him on then he sticks his finger in her coochie his finger started

101

getting sticky and wet. Robin started making these loud sexual noises opening and closing her legs. Frank Homicide is all excited he takes his knife from his back pocket and he cuts the duct tape from the back of her hands in all the excitement of getting some hot nookie. He set the knife down somewhere and he pulls his pants down holding on to his rock-hard tool. He points it towards his sweet wet target with her dress pulled up. Now he gets on top of her and he get what he wants. He is enjoying himself and after he bust that nut, super-fast. He was no better after that. He is laying up with her snorting more cocaine. He even went and fixed her something to eat.

When he went to fix the food for her, she found his knife laying on the floor up under some of the blankets on the floor right near where they had sex at. Near the wet spot on the blanket she puts the knife down her bra. Robin also was looking around the room for her pocketbook then she saw it up on the dresser. She removed the rest of the duct tape off her wrist. Frank came back with that happy he just got some good pussy look on his dark grill. He came in with a plate of beef sausage and eggs. He makes up a makeshift table with some boxes and some wood in the room.

Robin is all smiles he gives her a plastic fork Robin blessed the food as she holds his hand smiling his ass off. They started eating they have a real nice conversation after their done he gets up to get her plate soon as he reached over to get the plate. Robin took the knife and stabbed him right in his neck. **Woom!**

He fell over with the blood gushing out of his neck he fell to the floor face first making a loud thumping sound **Tooopp!** She quickly ran over to the dresser getting her pocketbook pulling out her phone. She had me on speed dial I'm chillin in the office soon as I seen her caller ID pop up on my phone, I almost shit on myself.

I screamed, "Robin are you, all right?"

"Yes, I'm okay. You're going to have to come and get me before one of them Niggas come back!"

"Where are you at?"

"I don't know it some kind of farmhouse or something."

"Okay, then turn on your GPS and I'll send out my people to find you no matter where you at."

"That's a good ideal but I'm going to get the hell out of here too because I had to kill one of them to get my pocketbook. That's how I called you."

"Be careful I'm coming to get you and I'll find out. How's the charge on your phone?"

"Its good right now but it won't be for long."

"Just keep you phone on even if it goes dead just keep it on, I'm on my way!"

"Yo Dun, Damon and Ty come on that was Robin said she killed one of them to get lose!"

Damon asked, "What? Thank Gawd let's go get her ass right now!"

"Hold up I'm going to need you to watch that money and hold down the fort for me."

"You still want me to put this shit together when she just got lose from these Niggas."

"No just stay with the loot, okay."

I looked Damon right in his eyes, "**Ikiwa kitu kinitokea kwangn unachukua** *If something happens to me you take over.*"

And he knows just what I'm talking about too. I can see it in his face he doesn't like it but as you know we all deal with reality in this dangerous ass lifestyle were living.

I yelled out for Ty and Dun-Dun come with me. I quickly walk out to the gangster lounge putting on my black leather jacket and I , "yo, Jane you and your peoples, Joe, Duke, Mookie and Monk suit up were going to go get my sister."

Poochie Blood Eye go get my whip **Ondoka nje** *Move out!*

We all started going towards the door fast and Booby Hill on post asked, "is everything all right, Almasi?"

"Were going to go get my sister right now Booby you stay here and hold shit down."

"No, I'm going with you! Woo-Woo and the others got this Ma."

"Okay, come on." He ran to get his coat and we all went outside with the cold wind blowing as Poochie and Blood Eye went to go get my truck.

Puerto Rican Joe, Black Duke got in there black GMC truck at the same time Jane Doe and her crew is in their vehicle ready to ride. Mookie and Crazy Monk got in Mookie's dark blue truck. Then Booby Hill jumped in his truck last. Poochie took off down the street with Blood Eye riding shotgun. I sat in the back seat holding on to my phone praying to Gawd nothing happens to my sister. So, we all hit the expressway flying up the blacktop blazing I'm playing it cool, but my heart is beating fast like a car going 1000 miles an hour. I want to kill everything moving for real right about now. After an hour and a half on the highway I check my phone to see how close. We are to her with four trucks deep right about now I wish I had more but I'm picking up her signal on her phone at where she's at. We are not too far were close. I call her the phone rings three times she picks up I put the phone on speaker, "hey sis, I'm in TGI Fridays."

"Yeah, I see where you're at it's on Schuylkill Road. How the hell did you get there?" "Somebody gave me a lift could you please get here. I'll feel more safer when you do get here, sis."

"I'll be there in a minute or so."

I hang up I call everybody starting with Puerto Rican Joe then Jane Doe and her peoples. Crazy Monk with Mookie then Booby Hill riding bye him self I let all of them know that she's at TGI Fridays at the Coventry Mall at West Schuylkill road. We all converge at TGI Fridays swiftly I pull my pistol out putting it in my lap getting ready for whatever. Soon as we pull up, I see her running out into the parking lot.

Poochie yelled, "I see her!"

I yelled out, "Stop! Stop!"

I jump out with my gun by my side looking both ways hugging her.

I look her over   "damn girl, you had me worry about your ass!"

Almasi 2
Queen of The Streets
By Dartanya A. Williams Sr.

I see all my peoples in their trucks inside of the parking lot I put up my fist up in the air everybody knows the signal.

"Come on!"

I pulled her inside of my truck and I quickly shut the door and asked, "how the fuck did they get you in the first-place, baby?"

"Well, I was going to court my fiancé Ismael is out of town in Boston because his mother is sick. So, when he goes to see her, he usually walks with me to my car if he has to work or not. I'm walking by myself and these four Niggas came out of nowhere and grabbed me up."

"Well you are going have to move out of there, baby girl."

"Yeah, your right I told you what I did to get out of there."

"Well we can talk about that later you did what you had to do baby. I'm not going to tell you how many Niggas I had to kill to get where I'm at now. So, don't worry about it they would have killed you if I gave them the money or not."

They Tried That Shit Again

We came back to the city with Robin and I told her that she had to stay with me until she finds a place. All of us were happy she was not hurt, but as you know I have to get some get back on them motherfuckers from the door for sure. It's about 12:45 A.M. my son Little Boom was finishing his rounds of all the stores picking up money and dropping it off at the bank deposit boxes. Little Boom took the rest of the money to the safe were we have at the storage locker at Columbus boulevard what he did not know was he was being followed by some more Chain Gang Niggas. Jarrett White, Sleam Shells, Tony Prince, Big Kacky Shank and Yaky. Three men in each car sit back watching him walking up in the large row of storage lockers. They made their move on him in the dark.

Jarret White, the leader of this thug ass group sends. Big Nacky, Shank, and Yaky in their first they run up to the long pathway of the lockers. They all started walking slowly until they ran across one of the storage lockers seeing the large steel door up. On the right-hand side, but the lights are off they all have their guns out ready to move in on Little Boom. Big Nacky walked up inside of it slowly and he turned the lights on and it's nobody in there. They all are looking around they don't see him Big Nacky pulled his phone out calling Jarret. He picked up fast, "yo Jay he's not in here."

"What Nigga? He kept looking but he did not come our way. So, he got to be in there somewhere."

"Alright man!"

Soon as he puts is phone in his pocket. Little Boom creeps up on his left without him seeing him until it was too late. **Kapacka!** Shooting Big Nacky in his face his large frame hits the ground **Doom!** Yaky and Shank turned around really fast shooting wildly and Little Boom is gone ducking inside one of the locker rooms. On the left with the secret door in the back of it these Niggas no nothing about. They go after him not knowing which way he when in the darkness. Yaky started walking quickly seeing another locker door up with the lights off again. He stopped holding Shank back and he turned the lights on. Click popping up on their right this time. **Kapacka!** Shooting Yaky in the back of his head his lifeless body hits the floor inside of the locker room. **Plang!** Shank is shooting everywhere like he lost his mind. **Plow! Plow! Plow! Plow! Plow! Plow!**

Little Boom stepped out holding his gun on him he points his gun back at him and Little Boom , "your out of fucking bullets ass hole." Shank went to pull the trigger *Click! Click! Click! Click! Click!* Little Boom walked over pulling the large locker room door down smiled at him, "don't move motherfucker or your dead."
 Shank threw the gun at him Little Boom ducks and shoots **Kapacka! Kapacka!** Shooting him in each one of his knees. He fell to the ground and screamed in deep pain with the blood shooting out.
 Little Boom walked up to him putting his gun to his head and asked, "who sent you?"
 He's still yelling in pain wiggling on the floor not saying anything crying and yelling. His phone started ringing. Little Boom quickly reached up in his pocket getting his phone   "oh your master is calling you now."
 Little Boom puts the phone to his ear   "your boy is a little preoccupied at the time."
 "Why don't you come in here and get him?"
 "He's real fucked up now he could use your help!"
 Jarett on the other end of the phone yelled, "your dead motherfucker!"
 Little Boom , "okay, listen up really good, Nigga." He pointed his gun to Shank's head. **Kapacka!**
 "Can you hear me now!"
 Slean and Tony Prince was creeping up the pathway of lockers they heard where the shot came from. Tony Prince on the right side of the door and Sleam on the left-hand side of the steel door. They look at one another not saying anything. They lift the door up at the same time. **Woom!**

They both rushed inside of the locker and he's gone. They only see Shank on the ground in a big pool of blood. There both looking around they don't look up. He's hanging up on the ceiling with his legs wrapped around the poles going across. Little Boom with two guns in each one of his hands makes a noise. **Pisssss!** They both look up **Kapacka! Kapacka!** Little Boom shot each one of them in the head. They hit the ground. **Doom! Doom!** Their bloody bodies stretched out on the floor Jarrett calls Tony Prince phone it rings and rings. Then he calls Sleam phone it just rings while he's calling the two dead men just at, that moment. Little Boom crept up on Jarrett soon as he gets up on him, he's about forty feet away from him Jarrett pulls off super- fast like a bolt of fucking lighting. Once the men do not pick up Jarret drives and jumps on Columbus Boulevard and he takes off up the dull yellow lit road getting the fuck out of there Little Boom is shooting at him but he's too far to hit anything while he's moving too quickly. Little Boom calls me telling me what happen, and I send a crew up there to clean up the bodies. It took them about five hours to clean everything up.

My New Deals Keep us Moving Forward

We already have them two homicide detectives Detective Miles and detective Kovalski up on our ass like a tight pear of fucking drawers. I made sure everything was cleaned up and done right. I sent Booby Hill and Chrome to supervise everything with the manpower Jane Doe's crew Tia Slim, Buckey Guns, Neckbone. Along with Black Duke, Taz- Money and Puerto Rican Joe so I know it was done right. I holla at Fast Eddie he told me they had a task force just for us as well. I got Fast Eddie on a mission as well and I want him to tell me who is the lead detective of the task force.

That's checking up on us and he he don't know who it is yet. If he doesn't come up with a name after a week or so I'll dust his coat. I have another dirty ass cop to take his place. I have on my pay roll name detective Don Wilson Nails Nathan is putting me down with him after he called me.

He called me asking me about everything that happen with my son and all that bullshit with my baby sister getting kidnaped. I had a sit down with him after I holla at my son about getting more protection. Now I have to assigned someone to be my son's bodyguard me and Jay talked about it and we both agree on Booby Hill. He gave me a hard way to go on this shit, but he has a baby on the way, and I want him to still be around to see his child come into this world.

A week later on a cold ass Saturday night I had a sit down with my son Little Boom, me, Jay, and Booby Hill at the new warehouse at Sedgley avenue. Soon as we went to the back room to talk, I get the call from Rah- Killer and she needs to talk to me.

I , "come on up to the new joint so we can talk. She she was on her way. I called Tanya while she was on post and told her that Rah-Killer was on her way up to holla at me."

She that she doesn't trust her anymore after we had Nugee hit she's been acting funny. I told her just keep an eye on her but still let her in so we can talk. So, we all sit down, and I have my son sitting next to me on my left and Jay sitting on my right next to Booby Hill.

My son Little Boom , "look mom, I don't need nobody watching my back. You see how I took care of all of them Niggas and lit their ass up too."

"I know that baby, but they underestimated you. They did not know I trained you and been around some of the best killers in the world. The next time they will send someone who will not take you lightly because you did kill all them Niggas."

Jay , "she's right the next time they will come with some real pros. Them thug Niggas from off the street you know. We love you it not that we think you're soft."

He looked up at the both of us saying, "okay, it nothing against you Booby. I know your shit is tight and I really respect you man."

Booby Hill , "I know that brother just let me, and my team keep you safe.So, you don't have to worry about any of the dumb shit, okay."

"Sure!" They both stood up and hugged one another. Right at that time Rah- Killer came and Tanya is looking at her sideways along with Gino Gats and some of the new Niggas she brought in. Big De Shawn, Akbar, Mojo, Tone, Jaleam, and Fat Jacks I don't know none of these Niggas. Her and Gino knew these Niggas from the streets. *She already knows if anything goes sideway it's both their ass is on the line.* Tanya walks Rah- Killer to the back room where we were at.

Tanya knocks on the door I answer, "come on in."

Tanya walked her inside not saying a word, but her face told it all. She waved at me and turning around. Soon as she went and close the door behind herself

Rah- Killer , "to me what the fuck is up with her?"

"I don't know Rah- Rah. So, what's up with you my sister?"

"First of all, hi all of y'all doing? What's up Boom, Booby, Jay?" They all wave back at her as she sits down not too far from me. She had a blunt hanging from her thick lips and look while I was chillin. Your boy came to holla at me.

"Who is that?"

110

"Gill."

"What?" *I just sat back checking her out.*

"Yeah, at the club."

"I was shocked to see him there because it's a gay club and I know most the people who go there."

"So, what he had to tell you Rah?"

"He told me that Spider killed his father Crazy Tee to save you when you were a baby and you are a no good, fucking snake just like Spider is. He heard about my boy Nugee and I need to join his team."

"Oh yeah, *I look over at Jay Booby and Little Boom* But check this out I'm playing him so we can draw this Nigga in so we can take care of his ass."

"So, he thinks you're going be down with him then?"

"Yes, he wants me to set one of y'all up."

"Who?"

"You! Almasi he wants me to set you up."

"Okay keep making him think that shit. Has he told you how he wants to set me up?"

"No not yet we only talked once. I guess he's feeling me out to see if I'm going along with the plan."

"Well if you're going to do some of this spy work for us try to find out who is the old head that's helping them other then, Zelda's Nokey Blaze wife, okay."

"Sure, I can do that for you Almasi."

"Alright then now I'm going to be looking for you to come throw on this here for me and all your thug brothers."

We both started laughing and we roll out there together to go to my crib to get our drink and smoke on for a few hours. *I kept in the back of my mind if she doesn't make this happen. I'm going have give her to the dirt nap. I think she knows that as well. I would hate to do it, but I'll do what I have to do.* My son went home to his crib along with Booby Hill, me, my crew, and Rah-Killer went to my house sitting at my large bar getting fucked up.

Poochie and Blood Eye is on post while we talk shit, we got high talking about old times and where we'd been and where we are going to go in the future for vacation. Then I had Poochie to take her home to make sure she was all right. The next day, I slept in a little late, but got up. Jay just stayed in the bed but what woke me up is the smell of this good food jumping off flowing through the whole house. I knew dam well my sister Robin was not throwing down she barely fucking cooks sometimes, so I got washed and dressed. I came into to see its Aunt-Tee La-Wanda doing some switching in the kitchen. Shit, I lit up like a big Christmas tree in Rockefeller center during the holidays when I saw her. She turned around with that round brown face of hers and big grin, "hey did you miss me?" "Oh, hell yes, I miss you girl!"

I ran over giving her a big hug "I knew dam well that was not Robin in there throwing down like that when I smelled that food in the air. So how you been? I heard a lot shit while I was away healing up this old leg of mine."

"You know me I been rolling with the fucking punches that's all, Aunt-Tee. Soon as I that I hear Robin running up all excited to Aunt La- Wanda yelling, "Aunt-Teeeeeee!" *Jumping up and down like a schoolgirl at recess* running up hugging her,

"Damn, it's been a long-time since I saw you!"

"I know baby now what it is. I want to know is you, all right?"

"Yeah, I'm good Aunt-Tee. Are you sure girl they didn't-…"?

"Oh no, none of that went down Aunt-Tee for real doe." *Waving her hands in the air* "Okay"

"Okay you look good you done grew up on me girl."

"Good morning, Robin!"

She replied, "hey sis, good morning to you as well with a big smile on her face."

Aunt-Tee "y'all go head and sit down. So, we all can eat okay."

Robin , "let me help you Aunt-Tee dam it so good to see you."

La- Wanda , "you can take those boys on post their plates for me okay."

"Sure, thing Aunt-Tee."

La-Wanda winks her eye at me smiling. We sit down and started eating then Jay got up speaking to everyone and he to Aunt-Tee, "welcome back Aunt-Tee you, all right?" "Yeah, I'm good baby."

"What about yourself?"

"Well I'm getting there I be going back to work real soon to go check up on things." Then he came over kissing me "what's up honey?"

"Hey baby, I didn't get you up because I knew you stayed up late last night." He started giggling. La-Wanda pointed at him , "sit down, baby. I got you something to eat."

As Robin is taking the two plates to Blood Eye and Poochie.

Meeting My Long-Lost Brother

We just got finish eating some good down-home grub when I get the call from Damon Gee. I look at the caller ID and I to myself it must be something hot with him calling me so early. I pick it up "hey, what's up Gee?"

"Look, I need to holla at you about something really important."

"Okay, what is it spit it out Nigga."

"No, not on the phone, Almasi. I'll be there in a half hour or so. Okay."

"Okay! **Moja** *(One)"*

"Moja!"

I went to go help to clean up the dishes, Aunt-Tee no waving her hands smiling.

"You go do what you have to do, baby."

"I got this." Jay gets up he is waving me towards the bedroom I get up to follow him. I looked over and I see Robin talking with Poochie. I go in the bedroom with Jay closing the door.

"Yeah baby what is it?"

He sat on the bed. "Look, I'm feeling a lot better and I have to get back to my dealership to find out what the fuck is going on with my own two eyes. You know what I mean?" "Okay baby! Do what you have to do."

"I just wanted you to be on top of your game before you went back."

"Thanks, I'm going back tomorrow but I love helping you out every day."

"You want to know what I appreciate it baby and I'm going to miss you being around the house every day." I walk up on him and I jump on top of him kissing Jay. We hear a knock at the door. We both stop fooling around playing rolling around on the bed. Yelling on the other side of the door is Aunt-Tee joked , "yo, you two in their messing around Damon is here to see you Almasi!"

114

I slide off Jay were both giggling as he smacked me on my ass were both laughing knowing we both want to fuck. I turn to him and smirk, "don't start nothing you can't finish Nigga."

"Yeah whatever." He just smiled as I went out the door to holla at Damon. He's sitting at the kitchen table drinking coffee with a cigarette hanging from his thick lips with Aunt-Tee talking shit, "good morning, Almasi."

"What's so fucking important you could not say over the Gawd dam phone." Damon Gee looks up and asked, "could you excuse us please Aunt-Tee."

"Oh yes y'all go head and talk baby. I'll go in here and watch some of my stories that's on right about now. She puffed on her cigarette cocked to side of her large lips with lipstick on it.

"Thank you, Aunt-Tee I love your coffee lifting up his cup smiling. She smiles back waving at him and walked into the next room. Damon looked me in my face and announced, "were having a sit down tonight with your long-lost brother Mustafa."

"What the fuck is you talking about?"

"Look, I know the whole story okay with you, Black Giovanni Spider and the whole nine. He knows too."

"What?"

"Yeah, he hired Lane West to check you out and he paid him to tell him everything." Mustafa wants to sit down with you because he needs your help as well.

"Yeah why?"

"Well three of his top guys got hit in a double cross Shyheam, Rasul, and his father figure of his Jimmy Muhammad an old-time gangster. Who broker mostly all the drug deals on the east coast now there dry as a fucking bone with product?"

"So, he needs us for muscle and product too."

"Yes, he does it's up to you to say yes or no?"

"So, how is it that? The Colombians and the Mexican's are not in the mix here. I don't understand?"

He did the same shit we did but he hooked up with some heavy ass motherfuckers from Ecuador the big man their name is Tito Quito. I don't think that's his real name but that's what they call him."

"Okay what time you set this shit up for?"

"9 at his spot."

"Where is that at?"

"Camden over the bridge and half an hour drive everything will be cool you can trust me on that."

"Okay I'll hear him out and see what's up on this shit. Do they know who killed their peoples?"

"Yeah, the Chain Gang Niggas the same people were at war with we can use all the allies we can get right about now."

"Yeah, your right but were also in the middle of a real dog fight too Damon."

"Well you think about what you want to do. I have to go I be back to roll with you to the meeting. He drinks the rest of his coffee and he started walking towards the front door r quickly. He bumps fist with Poochie and Blood Eye and kissed Robin on the cheek, "you take care of your self-sweetheart" He roll out the door with his super cool stroll to his whip outside. Way on the other side of town Fat Hector is supervising two hit teams on El Braero with Gill, and Crazy Paulie Queisha Loot with three more thugs that just got out of jail Shake, Poke and Yo- Yo. There are two cars outsides of El Braero's house in the North East in the front and back.

One of El Braero's men sold him out name Choo-Choo letting them know he has no bodyguards around him in the daytime because of his wife Maria. I want them to appear to be normal with the kids and to their neighbors, so they don't think their drug dealers. *I don't know why they did that because people were going to think that about them anyway because their Puerto Rican.* Fat Hector is parked a block away talking to them on the phone. Sammy Steel behind the wheel Crazy Paulie riding shotgun with Shake and Poke in the car in the front of the house. In the back of the house is Little Bo behind the wheel Gill riding shotgun with Yo-yo and Queisha Loot.

Fat Hector calls Crazy Paulie,, "yo, I want y'all to make your move first Gill and the others will be in the back just in case somebody roll out the back of the house okay. Y'all smoke their ass soon as you see them."

Crazy Paulie yelled, "I got you one!" Soon as he hangs up, "let's roll out and do this shit y'all."

Crazy Paulie gets out the car along with Shake and Poke all of them putting on their black mask on and gloves toting their machine guns running up to the front door.

El Barero is in the kitchen with his little girl Rose he named after his aunt who is teaching him how to speak Spanish. His wife is upstairs with their son Malik he named after his homeboy who helped save his life in prison. He's playing with his daughter Rose having a good time and he looked up and seen us on his surveillance cameras. He has outside in the front of his crib. He can see on his TV monitors on the wall on the right-hand side of the kitchen three mask men running up to the spot with machine guns in shock. He quickly scoops up his daughter running towards the steps with her little legs dangling.

He's yelled to his wife, "get to the safe room, yo Maria!" She runs to the top of the steps, "what's going on baby."

"Get to the safe room right now!"

"Here take Rose!"

He run up the rest of the way up to the top of the steps. She quickly grabbing her out of his big tattoo arms saying what about you baby.

"Don't worry about me just go hurry up! You know where the trap door is at inside of the safe room just get you and the kids out of here and go to your mother's house and I'll come and meet y'all there!"

She quickly kissed El Barero and ran to the middle room with the safe room with Malik and Rose closing and locking the large steel doors behind herself. El Barero ran to the back room getting his machine gun and his pistols in his steel case loading up the clips and he hits his speed dial on his phone.

Almasi 2
Queen of The Streets
By Dartanya A. Williams Sr.

To Mister Pete his right-hand man in his organization of the 3rd street Mob. Mister Pete picks up on the first ring El Barero just,"it's going down! **Boom!"**

Crazy Paulie Shake and Poke is in the front door looking around on the first floor of the house. El Barero sling his AK-47 machine gun in front of his self-getting ready for anybody to come through the door. His plan is to kill as many of them as he can and then duck into his trap door inside of the closet that leads to a tunnel across the street. The safe room has a trap door as well to the tunnel his wife knows they can't get into the thick steel doors that are bullet proof, but Maria is halfway through the tunnel with the kids taking them to safety. By this time, the three machine gun mask killers checked the basement and there running up the steps looking inside of the bedroom on the left-hand side seeing it nobody in there.

Then the three of them running in the middle room Crazy Paulie see the big metal doors yelling, "fuck, it's a safe room!"

"what the fuck is a safe room?"

Poke yelled, "let's blast the doors off with are machine guns Paulie!"

Crazy Paulie screamed, "its bullet proof ass hole!"

Poke yelled again, "let's see it could be a fucking fake out!" He aims and start shooting **Kattacatacata**! All three of them are ducking from the bullets bouncing off it. **Aaaaaaaaaa!** The bullets bounce off the thick bullet proof steel doors hitting Poke in his legs and there bleeding. Crazy Paulie yelled at him falling to the floor. "I told you ass hole it was bullet proof!"

"How long you been in jail, motherfucker? I told your dumb ass!"

"Yo, Shake, go check that back room right quick to make sure all of them are in here I have an ideal were going to burn them out."

Shake quickly runs in the back room he looks both ways not seeing El Barero heard him coming up the hallway. He ducked inside of the closet inside. He hits the button on the top of the closet and the wall slid to the side and he jumps in. The wall closed behind him. El Barero is inside of the trap door waiting on Mister Pete and his crew to roll up. Shake is looking around in the back room not seeing anyone in there. He even goes to the closet door opening it seeing nothing, but a solid wall and the closet looks empty. Shake runs back in the middle room and to, "Crazy Paulie nobody is in their Dawg."

Soon as he said that Mister Pete along with Butter, Maro and Vegas came in the front door armed and ready to blast everything in fucking sight. Upstairs Crazy Paulie hear loud footsteps downstairs he yelled, "let's get the fuck out of here!"

"Help me get this Nigga off the floor can you walk?"

Poke in deep pain, "I can hop, shit."

"Well hop your ass on, Nigga. Somebody just rolled in here on us. Come on let's go out the back. Soon as the three of them started running in the hallway towards the back room. They all hear all this loud machine gun fire coming from where there about to run towards out the window.

It sounded like world war three out there.

Crazy Paulie yelled, "come on!"

They run towards the back room just as they about to go out the window. El Barero pops out of the closet on the left. **Kapackatatac!** Hitting Poke in his back ripping his shit to shreds with blood and his flesh splatter all over the walls. Crazy Paulie and Shake jump out the window **Tisssssssssss!**

They both fall to the ground in the middle of a war zone with bullets flying everywhere. They all can hear the sirens from the police coming towards them all. El Barero's men Big Wokey, Raul, Raymundo Gregrio and El Ray is shooting it out with Gill, Queisha Loot and Yo- yo in the back of the house. By this time Mister Pete and the others is running in the back room they noticed El Barero he yelled, "it's me! It's me don't shoot!" They all rush looking down from out the window. They watched all of them running for their life shooting. In all the chaos and confusion Crazy Paulie and Shake got ghost from off the set. With all the shooting going on Queisha Loot Gill and Yo-yo made it out of by the skin of their fucking teeth. And that coward Fat Hector took off soon as the shooting started, they know they botched the hit doing it in the daytime.

Later, that same day El Barero called me telling me what happen. Now he's on the run because the cops want to know what happen with one dead body upstairs in the back room. I told him to lay low and were going to kill all the people who came to his home to kill him. He told me his wife Maria is pissed off with him and she took his kids with her to Miami to stay with her sister Tiffany. I apologized about what happen to him. I also told him to come holla at me tomorrow at the new warehouse on Sedgley avenue. He said he will be there. I hung up feeling bad that shit happen to him. It's dark out and it's time to go do this sit down with **Hadid Ajundi**. It means iron soldiers in Arabic.

I'm nervous to meet my long-lost brother face to face. We drive over the bridge Poochie is driving. Blood Eye is by his side and Damon Gee sitting in the back seat with me telling me to make a deal with them because were, going to need them. With this war were in with the Chain Gang. We pulled up to this not to big warehouse with these stone face men with beards and that killer glow in their eye standing outside. One of the men dressed in all black comes up to the truck as Damon Gee got out and shook hands with him. Damon waved to us to get out the truck. Blood Eye and Poochie right by my side walking up in the place the whole warehouse smelled like burned coffee beans.

Soon as we walked in this well-lit joint in the middle of the warehouse is a long steel table with two men sitting and about six men standing around with machine guns on post. Soon as we came up to the table this tall dark skin brother dressed in all black with a not to long beard stood up. He looked me in my face sticking his hand out for me to shake his hand. *But what was weird was the way he was looking at me like he seen me before or something it was so fucking strange.* I shook his hand and introduce himself, "my name is Mustafa I'm so glad to finally meet you."

"The same here brother. I'm Almasi. I'm really glad to meet you as well."

"Wow, it's like seeing a ghost you look just like my mother."

He goes in his pocket pulling out his wallet then he quickly pulls out this picture showing it to me. When I looked at it and sat down fast. All my emotions hit me at the same time when I looked at it. He's right I looked just like her it was like looking in a mirror. *People just don't know when you never seen a picture of your real mother in your entire life. It fucks you up and messes with your mind.* Damon Gee walked over to Poochie and Blood Eye telling them to step outside. Mustafa waved his hand for his men to leave the room as well they all walked out swiftly.

It's just the three of us in the room me, Damon Gee and Mustafa. He looked at me, "it's all right you can let it all out if you want to." When I looked up at him, he had tears in his eyes and asked, "are you all right?"

"Yes, what about you?"

"No, I'm not all right. You look just like her." He stood up and came over to me hugging me. He continued, "I don't care what happens. You're my family and we should try to make up for all of this pain, hurt and lost time for real."

"Your right, brother. I just did not know what to do once I found out about you and my sister I never met before."

"It's all right all that bull shit was not our fault. We can thank Allah (God) for the time we have now." I hugged him again, "can I have this picture please?"

"Sure, I have some better ones then that one I must give to you, but you can have that one for right now. I have some pictures of our mother and father together too."

"Thanks brother. I want to see them too."

"Don't worry when we hook up again, I'll have them for you for you alright."

We both sit down across from one another, "when I found out you was running shit I knew right then and there you were really my sister it's in the blood."

We both started to chuckle.

He looked up at me and his face became serious, "I can't lie I really need your help with this situation, and I can understand if you can't do it. I'm not trying to pull on our now family ties, but I have a lot of people depending on me right now. We can both help one another in all of this bull shit."

"Okay I can do this for you but the people I deal with is not putting up with any type of shorts or fuck ups on your end and you will have to make that shit up fast."

"I hear you my people are 100 percent and I know we would have to prove that to you." "Yes, you do, and you have to bring something to the table as well."

"I have something nobody have."

"Yeah and what is that?"

"I have most of the prisons on the east coast and a couple in the Midwest."

"Now that what the fuck I'm talking about brother of mine."

"So, we have a deal, then right?"

"Yes, we do but you're going to have to find out who is the Rat in your camp. You're going have to do it fast."

"Yeah, your right I'm working on that as we speak. Okay, just get that done weed all of them out because that's fucking things up for you, brother."

"I got this believe me little sister."

"I like that when you call me little sister, I was dreaming of this day would come and now it's here."

"I know I had to pay someone to find you and it was worth every dime too little sister." "Check this out1 I'm going to let you meet the man I was named after. Him and Black Giovanni came up in the game together in the gang. He can help you as well with this war with the Chain Gang Niggas."

"Yeah what's his name, bro?"

"His name is Mustafa Gats. Your father Leon told our mother Teja to name me after him I'm going to take you to him."

"Yeah, for real when?"

"I'll try to do it next week. I'll hook it up, okay."

"Little sister put your number in my phone." he hands me his phone as I put my number in it.

"Now make sure you call me not just for business now."

"Oh, I will call to holla at you as well little sister. I got you."

"How about if you come over to the house for dinner how about that then?"

"Yeah, I would love that I heard you was a good cook too. Yeah, I'll be there just say when."

"Wow you really did have me checked out. How about this Sunday bring your wife, okay? "Sure, I'll do just that little sister." As we both stood up and hugged one another.

I started crying again now I really met my real family is something I thought would never happen in my lifetime after all these years. *I went home with my crew and I just kept looking at that picture smiling. It made me feel normal for some reason. A week blaze past and Fast Eddie got me the name of the dude who is the head of the task force. His name is Ted Schultz he's the brother of James Schultz the cop we took care of that was fucking with us. So, I know he's going to be a die-hard motherfucker. But I have plans for his ass I'm going to get that dirty ass cop Don Wilson to take him out. He already took care of Blue's wife Taye that was talking to the FBI detective Don Wilson had some peoples inside of the FBI safe house that was watching her ass. He had her food poisoned and she's dead now. It cost me a fat grip to get it done but it was worth every fucking dime. He showed me the proof and Damon Gee checked it out and found out it was true.*

Mustafa came over to my house for dinner with his wife Tammy and we had a really good time getting to know one another. I also introduce the two of them to my son Little Boom and his girlfriend Laquitta who came over to eat with us. I already knew what real family was with my peoples with no blood running through our veins. Now that I have blood family. I felt stronger somehow. But I know now I want to groom Damon Gee to take over all this shit for real. He doesn't want it, but I know he would be my best choice. Next would be Jagger or Dun-Dun. I know Dun-Dun want to do. He's been wanting it for a long time. Now he's been down longer then Jagger so it going to be really hard to pick one of them out of the two of them. My whole week went good. I got the big shipment of Molly pills from my new Germen partner Fritz Burger, I moved Puerto Rican Joe up and had him take over that operation. I let him pick his crew he was really happy about that shit. I called up Tee Cee from the Black Demons MC's that he can have all the gun sales I was letting him take all of my customers.

A Truce is Good for Business

Tee Cee was happy to get all that new business I passed over to him real smooth. Two weeks later I had that sit down with my brother's Mustafa's name sake Mustafa Gats in the beginning of December. We had the meeting at my new strap yard in South West Philly. When I walked into the meeting, I had Fat Lou- Lou holding down the spot. I also had SOS Smash On Sight crew, John Spartacus and his right-hand man Donzilla there to hook up with El Barero's 3rd street Mob boys. So, they can put something together so he can get his get back on them Niggas who try to take him out. *That's me killing two, birds with one stone that's what I do best.* My brother told me that Mustafa Gats was bringing Fat Wally the leader of GTG *The Germen Town Gangsters.* For a truce I was down for that because I heard that the Chain Gang Niggas killed ten of thcir pcoples in a bloody war and shut down all their drug hook up's, from the docks and trucking routes. Now they needed me to put them on right then and there. You know that old saying, "the enemy of my enemy is my friend rings true right about now."

Now all my peoples are on the right-hand side of the room and all of them came in with this tall older man. He had a short white beard, black hat, long black Kashmir coat on and black leather gloves. He walked over by himself he hugs my brother Mustafa then he shook my hand, "I'm so glad you hooked this up for us thank you, young lady."

"Oh, it's my pleasure brother please have a seat where we have a long steel tool table in the middle of the warehouse. He walks over to the left-hand side of the table. I point to Blood Eye to walk Fat Wally and his crew over to us. Smoky, Kay Dawg, Lonnie Lit, Rick Ruger, And Fat Wally's brother Mango.

They all came over strolling with the big man Fat Wally all of them sat down mean mugging. All of them are super tough with tight hard grills and their macho man horse shit. *But I knew nothing was going to jump off because I had the upper hand these Niggas need a plug and I'm the big Dawg in town now and they all want to eat.* I step up and lean over towards Fat Wally to shake his hand. We shake hands and sat down. With Poochie on my right and Blood Eye on my left. *I know this truce is good business plus I know I can take care of Gill's lousy ass. Yet, make a hell of a lot of money in the process with more transporters and foot soldiers to move a shit load of fucking product I got.* All of my peoples behind me is standing up I looked him in his face. "okay, what is it going to take for us to stop from keeping this shit going on?"

Fat Wally looks over to his brother, "well, we need more room to operate for one. Cool I'll move some of my spots near you back five blocks are that enough?"

Fat Wally looks over to his brother, the others and Mango, they began politicking and whispering, "no, it has to be 10."

"Okay, I'm with that. So, what else?"

Fat Wally added, "and were going to need that hook up y'all have with the cops."

I replied, "I can do that, but your going have to kick into the pot on that shit.

"You know damn well those cops are fucking greedy fuck that."

Fat Wally replied, "okay, we can do that we need some of those dirty motherfuckers so we can operate. We don't have none of them on our side like y'all do."

I answered, "they only fuck with you if you have a lot of loot other than that they will not risk their career for nickels and dimes."

We both started laughing I stood up to shake his hand. He looks up at me,

"look, I know you heard what happen, right?"

"Yeah, I heard a little something. I didn't hear the whole story but yeah, I heard so what's up?"

I quickly lied to him, so he doesn't feel so bad and that way I can make the deal with them. I will have them working for me for more than two years with all the shit I got flowing.

"Well we need a new plug and if you can front us something, we can past it back to you really quick."

"Yeah, I can do that, but you have to give me something in return."

"Yeah and what is that?"

"I heard Gill is down with y'all. Now you give me him with his head on a fucking platter and we have a deal."

Fat Wally looked over at his peoples his brother Mango stood up and came over whisper in his ear. He then went and sat back down smirking.

"Okay, then give us the first three months of work on consignment and we will help you do it any way you want to do it."

"Okay, I'll do you one better I'll give you four months of girl and boy if you take some of this Molly product to sell but you have to turn all that in doe. After the four months you flip 40-60 after that with the girl and boy."

"Make it 50 50 with everything and we got a deal."

"Okay." I stood up and we shook hands again. Me and Fat Wally and our 10-year war was gone.

Fat Wally asked, "so when do we get our drop?"

I looked at him and answered, "are you ready for this drop, doe?"

All of them started laughing with his brother Mango saying, "Oh hell! Yes, were ready!"

"How many people you got to bag this shit up?"

"Oh about 20 Niggas."

All of us started laughing and I replied, "you're going need, more Niggas then that for what I'm going to drop on you."

I turned to El Barero and kicked it like this, "come here for a minute."

He came over giggling he stood by my side. I schooled him, "would you tell my new partners over their how many people he's going to need to bag up the first drop. 87 in one spot and another 80 in another."

They all looked at one another in shock and I cut in, and that's not counting the Molly you going to need about 30 more people to handle that. Fat Wally replied, "are you just fucking with us?"

El Barero chimed in, "don't worry I'll help you out. I'm a fucking expert at that shit now." *Then he turns to me winking his eye letting me know when I gave him his first big drop now. He has one of the best drug factory workers in the city now thanks to me.* Fat Wally asked, "so when are we going to get it?"

I replied, "well, you're going to get 500 keys of heroin wherever you want it to be drop off at.

Fat Wally question, "you can't move that much shit in one day. All of us started laughing I pointed at Fat Lou- Lou and asked, "get that for me."

He walked towards the back and came back with eight fat stacks of money sitting it on the table in front of me. With a smirk on my face, "this is all yours if I don't deliver what I promise."

"If I don't get it this is all yours, okay."

All of them looked at each other with Fat Wally he responded with a nod, "all right I believe you." He pulled out his card writing down the address then walking around the table handing it to me and grinned, "okay, drop it off here tomorrow." It was the address to the huge abandon church on Germantown avenue and I know just what he was talking about. He looks up at me and continue to speak, "oh yeah, your boy here is going to help us bag this shit up right."

I spit it to him. "yeah, that is what he said, brother that's what he's going to do and that's 500 keys a month of coke and dope."

Fat Wally replied, "damn, I didn't know y'all was rolling like that shit! 500 keys a month? "Yeah, you're going to have to step up your game, big man. You wanted to get on another level than here it is for you to do your thing and you're still your own boss. So, don't fuck it up, now."

Fat Wally assured Almasi with a smile on his face, "oh no none of that. Wow, that's a lot of shit to move."

We all had a drink or two I thanked my brother and Mustafa Gats for putting us together. I hooked him up with a real nice fat finder fee too. Mustafa Gats pull me on the side and replied, "thank you for the gift."

"Oh, you don't have to thank me that's just the way we do things. We take care of our business for sure."

"I see that. Look, I have someone else I need to introduce you to."

I replied, "oh yeah, is it as good as this deal here?"

"Yeah, even better his name is Charlie Cham-plane on the west coast he got shit on lock. I can hook up a sit down with him, me and you. I did time together in Leavenworth."

"Okay, set it up. You got my number, right."

"Yeah, I got it from my nephew. I'll call you in about a month or two and let you know where we can have the meeting at, okay."

"Sure thing, Mister Mustafa. Just call me uncle because were all family now, baby girl."

He gave me a hug and he walked away with my brother holding a big stack of cash. I told Fat Lou- Lou to get the rest of our money from off the table. He put it back in the two gym bags of money were brought with us to smooth things over for Niggas. We all rolled out the door together jumping in our trucks and drove off. We sat back to my hold up spot and talked about our new deal. I reminded everybody not to fuck this up for us it's a lot of money to be made.

The next day I'm chillin in the crib with Aunt-Tee it around 11 A.M. We are sitting at the kitchen table drinking coffee talking shit puffing on our Newports. Its only been a few weeks and I miss Jay being with me every day now. He went back to work at his dealership where they make bullet proof cars and the best traps for cars in the world. I get the call from my son all excited screaming, "Laquitta is about to have the baby! I'm rushing her to the hospital."

"Oh, shit I jumped up and yelled, "Aunt-Tee Little Boom girlfriend is about to have the baby!"

"Oh, my Gawd Almasi we have to go right now Jesus!" We both ran getting our coats with the quickness. I ran up to Poochie and Blood Eye on post at the front door.

"Yo, we have to go Little Boom's girlfriend is about to have the baby!"

So, we all quickly ran out the door together Blood Eye made sure to lock up the doors as the four of us jumps in my black Benz wagon. Blood Eye rode shotgun with Poochie behind the wheel me and Aunt-Tee in the back seat jumping up and down like a roach on a fucking hot plate. Poochie takes off like a stock car racer in Daytona. I told Poochie to take me to Lankenau hospital it took us about 20 minutes to get there. Me and Aunt-Tee jumped out running up to the emergency ward soon as we ran inside up to the information desk. The fat white lady that look just like Melissa McCarthy said they just went back there with the father that we have to wait out. In the waiting room were both going off. Aunt-Tee is supposed to be calming me down. Now she is about to punch the fat white lady in the mouth for getting smart with her. I chilled everything out with the fat white lady telling her were all just excited about the baby coming please could you accept our apologies. Because we knew dam well when she had the phone up to her head, she was going to call security on are black ass from the door. I made Aunt-Tee apologize to the fat white bitch and she accepted it with a big smirk on her fat ass grill. *You know how them crackers get when they have a little power over a Nigga.* Now me and Aunt-Tee is pacing the floor wearing a fucking hole in it as Poochie and Blood Eye come inside with us. I can't keep still like a junkie who is dope sick and needs a fix.

One hour seems like three hours I see Little Boom coming from the back with some light blue scrubs on and a surgeons mask hanging from his neck and a big bright smile on his grill hugging me saying it's a boy and he weights 10 pounds 11 ounces.

"Wow, he's a fucking whopper me and Aunt-Tee started hugging and kissing one another jumping up and down celebrating.

"What did y'all name the baby?"

Little Boom look at me,"I damn sure did not name him Byron. His name is Baheam, mom."

"Don't look at me like that that's his name."

I was thinking he did not want to name him after himself because of his father Big Boom aka Byron Wilson. That Nigga is doing three life sentences. I know he would get pissed off if I let him know that his son done had a little Boy. I know some Nigga is going to tell him even on death row Niggas get more news on the streets then people walking around free. "Okay, I love it and I kissed him. So how is Laquitta doing?"

'She's fine mom I'm going to talk to the doctors because their taking her up to her room and I'll let y'all know when you can come see the baby."

"Okay, sweetheart come back and let us know when."

I sat down and Aunt-Tee, "so, how do it feels to be a grandmother over here?"

"Shit, I'm not a grandmother. I'm a Glam-mother, baby don't get that shit twisted, girl. I still look good fuck that shit."

We both laughed and talked shit for an hour or so waiting we even went outside and smoked a joint to celebrate. Aunt-Tee love smoking white boys (Rolled up joints) with Top paper she hates blunts. When Little Boom came down and told us that she was in room 608. I told Poochie to come with us and I told Blood Eye to wait for us in the car and keep an eye on things we can't be slipping right about now. The three of us went upstairs and I could not wait to see my grandson. Wow I was thinking to myself how I thought I would not live to see 30. I'm a grandmother this shit blew my fucking mind. We ride up and soon as we get up their Poochie wait outside the door me and Aunt-Tee walk in the room all excited. Laquitta was sitting up I came over to her and kissed her on the cheek and asked, "how do you feel, baby?"

"I'm still in a lot of pain to tell you the truth, Miss Almasi."

"See, what I told you before girl to call me Mom, okay. Tell the nurse to give you something for the pain fuck that after dropping that big load."

She started snickering and replied, "your right, mom!"

Aunt-Tee chimed in and introduced herself, "you don't know me, but I'm Little Boom's aunt La-Wanda."

"Hi, Little Boom talks about you all the time. He said you help raise him along with his mother its like I know you already."

We all started laughing then Laquitta told the nurse is going to bring the baby up, "okay, I can't wait to meet my grandson."

131

Soon as I said that the big heavyset light brown skin nurse came in the room with the baby in her arms smiling. The nurse hands Laquitta the baby my heart is beating fast. As she holds the baby in her arms I stood there and looked in his beautiful face. I felt so proud and so happy. She turns the baby towards me, "say hi to your grandmother, Baheam. She asked do you want to hold him, Mom?"

"Yes, I do."

She hands me the baby and when I held him in my arms, I wanted to cry this was a beautiful moment in my life I was overwhelmed with joy. I was looking down at this handsome little child. He looks just like his father as I rocked him back and forth in my arms. It gave me a flash back when I had Little Boom. This had to be one of the happiest days of my life.

When we came home that day, I was feeling good then I get the call from Fat Wally saying for me to meet him at this abandon church on Germantown avenue that they had Gill their overseeing some of the girl's bagging up heroin. They have the back room ready for us to take him out and he said we had to do him a favor after we kill him. Fat Wally told me to come to the side door on the right, so I told Poochie and Blood Eye to suit up. Then I called up Jagger and his crew to meet me there just in case if it's a set up and I told Rah- Killer to be there as well she sounded shook up on the phone, but she she would be there. Its 2P.M. I made Poochie park up the street and we walk up everybody showed up. I told Jagger and his crew to come up after I go inside. I knock on the large side door and Big Smoky came to the door letting me in. Me, Poochie and Blood Eye walked quickly to the back office where Fat Wally is at. Soon as we walked in the small cluttered office that smell like weed and it was still smoky in their too. He got up fast to shake my hand and asked, "you ready?"

I responded, "I have to call Rah- Killer in here with me and then I'll be ready."

He replied, "cool, I'll wait."

I pull my phone out and call Rah- Killer to come on in. It takes her a few minutes to come up she knocks on the door and Big Smoky goes to get her while we wait. She came in while Big Smoky brings her inside of the office and I bump fist with her, and I announced, "okay, were ready."

Fat Wally pointed to the back, "take them back there and take Lonnie and Kay Dawg with you."

Big Smoky pulled out his phone and called Kay Dawg and Lonnie. They came up fast and we all are walking with them as they led the way to this huge room in the back on the left. Big Smoky open the large wooden doors and it four tables of women with nothing on bagging up heroin. Gill had his back to us while he was talking to one of the bodyguards named Shine. Soon as he seen us walking up, he took his saw off shotgun sticking it to Gill's head taking his gun from the front of his jeans. Gill screamed, "what the fuck is you doing man?"

When he turned around and seen me, Poochie, Blood Eye and Rah- Killer he knew what was up.

He yelled, "all you no good motherfuckers sold me out for this snake bitch!"

I walked up closer to him and begin spitting my reason why, "at one time you were my brother and I had nothing to do with your father getting killed. I was a baby when that shit went down."

Kay Dawg and Lonnie Lit stick their guns in his back pulling him downstairs. With all of us following them down to this other back room on the left pushing him inside this huge brick room but all along the floor is plastic. Big Smoky closed the door behind himself I whipped out my gun and Poochie Blood Eye and Rah-Killer pulls their guns out as well I looked at him and sneered, "so you were going to set me up, right?"

"I was just fucking with Rah talking shit!"

Rah-Killer chimed in and snapped, "no, you wanted me to set Almasi up, Nigga."

"Oh, hell no that was your idea." Me, Poochie and Blood Eye looked over at Rah- Killer not saying a word.

I took aim at Gill yelling, "you're a lying ass motherfucker!"
Kapacka! I shot him in his stomach he curled over holding his
stomach with all this blood on his hands yelling in pain. I looked over
to Rah- Killer, "I know you was thinking we were going to kill you
that was not going down, my sister."

"I knew you would not cross me we go way back. I want you to
remember that okay. I hear you, sis. Now I want you to shoot this
Nigga for making people looking at you all funny in the gang!"

Patacka! Rah- Killer shot Gill in his chest he falls down to the
ground really hard **Doom!** He's laying down bleeding but he's
breathing really hard. I just look at Poochie and Blood Eye they just
started shooting **Patackac! Patkca! Kaboom! Kapow! Packatcaka!**
Shooting him in the head neck and his eyes. His bloody body is
ripped apart from the bullets. Soon as were ready to roll the door
opened up really fast and its two more of Fat Wally's bodyguards
pushing in another dude none of us knew.

Big Smoky screeched, "this is the man who sold us out to the
chain gang. His name is Romey. He's Fat Wally's brother in law he
told his sister Shelly that he would not kill him or any of his men.
that's where you Niggas come in at."

I asked, "oh so this is the little favor he told me about. Well, I
see what he's doing that way. He did not lie to his sister that's fucked
up!"

We all laughed. Poochie joked, "well he did not lie to her if we
smoke his ass."

Big Smoky jumped in , "now you get it."

I looked at him and he's crying like a little bitch he yelled, "if
y'all shoot me every last one of y'all going to die!"

I took aim, "whatever motherfucker!"

All three of us started shooting **Kapacka! Plow! Kapackow!
Pacakac! Kadoom!** His bloody body falls next to Gill laid out. Fat
Wally's crew started working fast wrapping the bodies up quickly in
the plastic on the floor. As we all rolled out the door and went home
blasting loud hip hop, music all along the way to the crib.

Almasi 2
Queen of The Streets
By Dartanya A. Williams Sr.

Coyote Comes to Town

Things is running smooth the Molly pills it started a little slow but by the end of the month shit was picking up. I felt good that I put Puerto Rican Joe in charge of that operation he knew what he was doing. A week later my grandson came home, and I damn near brought the whole store getting things for him. While I'm in the baby section in Target feeling all happy about my grandson thinking what will be really cute on him and walking up on me is Philly. I looked up , "oh snap when you get back in town Nigga. Yo Poochie let him past." *I can see in his eyes he was really upset about this shit pissed off.*

Blood Eye and Poochie is standing in front of Philly blocking his way towards me I gave them the signal nodding my head to let him past. He walked past my two goons looking them up and down specially at Poochie. He came up and gave me a hug, "oh, it's really good to see you, Almasi."

"The same here how is your father doing?"

"He's alright! I heard a lot of good things about you, Ma. I told you that you were the right person for the job. "

"Yeah, you did say it but if I knew all the bullshit that came with it, I would have not taken it Gee."

We both started chuckling, "I need to talk to you about your boy, Fat Hector. Well as you know he's a dead man walking for real. It's just a matter of time, man."

"Yeah well, I'm here to make sure that shit get done a little faster."

"Oh, really, well I could use your help brother always. You know that we can go talk at my spot when I'm done here."

"Don't tell me you had another baby over here on me, Almasi."

"Oh, hell no, I'm buying some shit for my new grandson."

"Word, what Little Boom had a shorty yo?"

"Yeah last week he had a little boy name Baheam."

135

"Wow, I knew that Nigga when he was a little fat kid wow."

"Yeah, he's a man now."

"Is he in the life?"

"Well, I tried to keep him out the shit but yeah, he's in the life. I didn't want him in that shit but he's doing his thing too I can't lie."

"Okay, Okay I have to meet him now."

"I'll tell him to stop by the spot when we get there, okay."

"Yeah, do that I want to see him and what's up with your boys here?"

"What? My men, shit, I have to have them here with me you know what time it is Philly."

"Yeah, I know you're the fucking Don Diva for real doe, now."

We both started laughing.

"Meet me at the spot in about an hour you know where it's at."

"No, where is it? It's at 23rd and Washington Avenue. It's 2301 the big building on the right gray steel door you can park over on the left, okay."

"Sure, thing **Indlovukazi** *(Queen)*. I'll see you then **Moja** *(One)* Moja!"

An hour later, I drop off the baby clothes to Laquitta and I got to chance to meet her mother La Vonne and her stepfather Jody. I rapped to them for a little bit and rolled out. *That Nigga Jody was trying to holla at me about business. I was not paying this small-time Nigga any mine, but I was cool about it, doe. This Nigga just wanted to get put on, but I don't know him, so I kept it moving. On my way to the spot I called up Dun-Dun telling him that Philly popped up on me. I need him to get somebody to follow him and see what he's doing. I told him I don't want him dead. I just want to know what he's up to while he's back in town.*

Dun-Dun said, "that he got me, and he got somebody that's really good to keep a tail on him." I told him thank you and to keep me in the loop on everything and I hung up. So, I drive back to my hold up spot. I have Black Duke holding the spot down now that I moved him up. So now Black Duke have his crazy ass family all around him, his brother

Bango, his cousin Stomp, his brother Yokey and his brother in law Jimmy Goon married to his sister Dorsey. They were tight I saw that over time being around them over the years. And Crazy Jamel his stepbrother Black Duke came up with when his mother Miss May Ann married Mister Earl when Duke was only 8 years old. And I trust them all because Black Duke been down from day one.

He kept all of them in line and he trained them well. *I call them the KBC the killer black crew.* Soon as I came in the door, I waved for Poochie and Blood Eye to keep walking so I can talk to Jamel alone. I bump fist with Crazy Jamel on post *he's a real true to life thug Nigga. He's tall, good-looking, tattoo muscular ghetto hunk, but he's not afraid of a living soul on two fucking legs. This Nigga is a real fucking character I love to hear him talk shit because he's hilarious.*

Jamel chimed in and let me know, "**Baadhi ya dude alikuja kukutana nawe** *(Some dude came to holla at you)*"

"Oh Yeah **Jina lake lilikuwa nani mbwa***I (What was his name dawg)*"

"His name is Coyote. He's one of Arturo's men. What kind of Nigga call himself Coyote?"

We both giggled.

"Oh, okay thanks are you working with Jimmy on his Swahili?"

"Yeah, I'm on his ass, Almasi everyday Ma."

We both started laughing. I started to walk, and then I stopped. He , "why are you by yourself on the door?"

Black Duke got Yokey cleaning the bathrooms because he fucked up missing a pickup. "Okay, did he make him go back and get it?"

"Oh, hell yes and he's on shit house duty as well too. You know Black Duke don't play that shit. He was going to shoot his monkey ass."

"Okay **Nzuri** *(Good)*! **Majadiliano yote mazuri** *(Alright good talk).*"

I giggled to myself and walked towards the gangster lounge. I spoke to everybody and walked to my office. I close the door behind myself soon as I sat down. Black Duke came and knocked on the glass door.

I waved my hand telling him, "come in brother he came in and sat next to me and kicked some hard facts, "yo, some dude came here saying he was Arturo's man. I told him to come back when you get in. "

"Okay **Nzuri** (*good*) I don't want nobody waiting for me unless I say so."

Then Bango came and tapped on the door I waved him in he opens the door and announced, "some dude name Philly is here to see you."

"Yeah let him in."

"You want us to check him?"

"No, he's cool. Can you walk him back here for me please?"

They walked him back to my office he sat down, looked at each of the big gangster dudes, "wow your security is tight up in this bitch, Almasi."

"It has to be, Gee were at war with the Chain Gang motherfuckers."

"Who the fuck are they, Almasi?"

"Their Black Giovanni people from out of prison wants to take over are drug operations."

"Ain't Black Giovanni BSN what the fuck is going on here?"

"Yeah, he is but he wants his people to move me out and put their people in."

"Damn, I didn't know that shit. I put in all these years of work in for the gang and now they want me out."

I was thinking to myself I could not talk to him about the crazy shit his mom is doing. I think he here to feel me out with that shit, so I don't say shit about that with him. I think he just might be the old head that's helping the chain gang Niggas. Even doe he wants Fat Hector dead for fucking his wife Le-Rinda. She ran off with him too and I don't trust his ass for real. I'm just playing along with him for now then I'm going to kill him.

"Okay, you said you was here to help get this Nigga you you're here to make it happen faster. What's the plan?"

"Well my no good, ass fucking wife Le-Rinda don't know her father is sick. I'm going to put him into a nursing home when she shows up and grab her funky ass."

"Yeah well that will get her. So, what about him?"

"We grab is son Ray. He's 18 years old he loves the ground he walks on. Soon as he come out in the open, we take his fucking ass out. I need your help to do it, Almasi. I have no soldiers anymore."

"Okay, I can do."

Bango taps on my door and announce in a deep voice, "yo, Almasi it that dude again name Coyote.

I asked, "is he by himself?"

"No, he got about four dudes with him."

"Okay, tell them you have to check them no weapons and seat them into the conference room. I'll come and talk to them." Philly has not mention anything. He's just sitting back then Bango came back, he's coming in by himself."

"Okay than take him to the conference room and make sure he's clean too."

"Look Philly I get with you on that thing just let me know when you're ready to make your move as you know I got the manpower."

It's Too Much Drama Going on All around Me

Philly stood up and had a phony ass smile on his face.

"For sure, I'm going to let you take care of your business alright." I hugged him and I walked him to the door I waved Poochie, Blood Eye, Stomp and Jimmy Goon with me to the conference room. Soon as I walked inside of the room, Coyote stood up, nod and a grin, "hey, what's up. I'm Coyote."

I walked up and shook his hand. We both sat down. *He's a tall dark skin man with tattoos all over his body and even on his face. His eyes tell you everything about him. I can tell he's one dangerous ass motherfucker. You could not be a scary person being around someone like this because he looks like he done killed more people that you could fill this whole room up with bodies. But I never took my eyes off of this Nigga for one second. One wrong move from this motherfucker I'll cap his ass in the fucking head and have my boys toss his body in the dirty ass Schuylkill river.* He pulled out his phone hitting the speed dial and Arturo picked up on the first ring. Coyote put it on speaker, and he set it on the table.

"Hey pretty lady how is you doing, today? I'm doing fine what's going on with you?" "Well I just sent you Coyote to take care of things for you."

"I got my peoples to take care of things for me, my friend. I'm cool."

"No, you don't understand Coyote is an expert at taking care of anything your having problems with."

"I'm talking about cops, FBI, gang members whatever trust me, honey."

"Okay Arturo, I'll test him out with this shit you're talking about. *I'm looking over at this guy and I don't trust his ass from the door.*"

"Yes, I want you to do that to see that I'm for real. I heard about your thing with the task force put him on that and see what I'm talking about."

140

"Alright I'm going to do that too. You're going to need him. Trust me my pretty lady friend I'll talk to you later my dear."

"Alright Arturo you take care goodbye."

At the time   I didn't know what he was talking about but Gawd dam I found out really fucking fast doe.

Coyote picked up his phone and put it in his pocket, "now were all set right, Almasi?"

"Yeah Coyote, I'll call you with what I want to do. I have to take care of a few things at the end of the week. You and me, will sit down and I'll give you a list of things I need done, are you cool with that?"

"Yeah sweetheart." He pulls a phone from his inside pocket. "this is a phone its untraceable."

He hands it to me and continued, "And you're going to have to get a satellite phone too. I'll have one for you when I see you again." He gets up and nods his head, "it was nice meeting with you. I see you soon." I get up I waved to Black Duke to stay where he is. I walked him to the door Bango sitting in the gangster lounge walks with me along with Stomp, Yokey and Crazy Jamel is at the door. They open the door and let him out. I just waved as he went to his truck with his henchman waiting for him. They open the door for him. He hops in and I point for Yokey to close the door I quickly walked back to my office where Black Duke is sitting next to my desk. I close the door quickly and sit down. Black Duke looked up at me and asked, "what the fuck was that all about? What we got fucking babysitters now?"

"Well it looks that way, but you don't see what I see brother **Angalia Zaidi** *(Look deeper)."*

"Yeah and what's that they want to take over our shit too like the chain gang?"

"No something is going on that's what's up and there, not telling us Duke. I'm going have to find out before the shit hit the fan and splatter all the fuck over all of us."

"Well get your boy Damon Gee he's always finding shit out faster then anybody else." "That's just what I'm going to do too."

Almasi 2
Queen of The Streets
By Dartanya A. Williams Sr.

"I don't want to be out of order asking you this but why he's always on the move?"

'No, you're not out of order asking me. That's what he does so he can tell us what the fuck is going on out there."

I pick up the phone and call Damon Gee he picks up after the phone rings three times. "Yo, what's up boss lady?"

"Look I need for you to check out this dude name Coyote Arturo send down here to give us a hand with the operation."

"Oh yeah well it sounds like something real fishy with that shit, Almasi. I'll check him out for you for sure."

"Look, I'm glad you called I got something hot for you too as well."

"What's that Gee?"

"You know good and fucking well I'm not telling you over the phone. I'll meet you at the crib later on. You're going what to hear this bullshit it has to do with your long-lost brother's peoples too."

"Yeah and guess who popped up on me today?"

"Who?"

"Philly!"

"Oh yeah, well, I'm going have to see what that Nigga is up to as well Almasi. I don't trust his ass popping up right about now. "

"Yeah, I know I'm shopping for the baby and this Nigga pops up on me in Target."

"Did you ever think who told that motherfucker where you were at?"

"No, I didn't think about that I was really surprised to see his ass."

"So how did he act when you started talking to him?"

"He acted like he never rolled out on us and he ask me to help him get Fat Hector and his wife La-Rinda."

"Well he could be on the up and up, but I don't trust his ass. it smells like a set up to me to get close to you to take you out Almasi."

"If I see him, I'll kill him on the spot I'm telling you so don't have me around him."

"You just might be right, Gee. I got Dun-Dun and his people tailing his every move while he's back in town."

"Well I told you how I feel I would not let him stay in town to fucking long. He's up to something I have to go I talk to you later on tonight **Moja** *(One)*!"

"Moja!"

Soon as I hang up, I get a call from my sister Robin.

"Hey sis what's up with you?"

"Well I'm really pissed off right about now to tell you the truth."

"Why what happen Robin?"

"I just got some real fucked up news about Ismael fucking ass! Yeah what did he do honey?"

"This Nigga been playing me all this time. He's telling me he's going to see his mother that was sick and all this shit when I just found out he got a whole family in Boston with this bitch!"

"What get the fuck out of here, girl?"

"Yeah, this Nigga got two kids with this bitch too. A boy and a girl."

"Damn, so how did you find out all this shit, Robin?"

"Well, you're going to be mad, so I really don't want to tell you sis."

"Look, I'm not going to get upset you can tell me."

"Well, I talked to Poochie and told him I think Ismael is creeping out on me. So, he told me that he knows a dude that can look into it but he's really super high but he's good. I hired him to follow is ass around."

"Was the guy name Lane West you hired?"

"Yes, that's him and he told me some other shit I can't tell you over the phone too."

"Oh yeah well what time you get off today?"

"I'll be home around five were done with that murder case we won that one. I got the dude off he knows you."

"Oh, really what's his name?"

"His name is Rico Salazar he's from North Philly do you know him?"

"No baby I don't know that name."

"Okay, he knows you sis; well I be home soon. I talk to you then sis goodbye." *That name Rico Salazar kept ringing in my head I can't place that name for the life of me.*

The rest of the day I just worked the horn to make sure everybody is doing their job and at 4 O' clock I went home with Poochie and Blood Eye. Soon as I got in the door my phone rings, I looked at the caller ID and I see the name Billy Bell Fat Lou- Lou's phony name on his phone. I pick it up really quick,

"hey what's up Lou, what's going on?"

"I got some bad news to give you, Almasi. The trucking company's we were moving shit out with got blown up, so I had to rent some vans to get the rest of the shit out. I had to use extra planes too they also hit the landing strips too. Good thing I have other routes thanks to your son Little Boom he's a real smart kid."

"Well that was good thinking. Did we lose any of the loads?"

"No, they blown them up before we got the shit out, I called up your son and Booby Hill and his crew for some muscle to make sure the shit got out."

"Was it the chain gang crew?"

"No, they were all Hispanic motherfuckers."

"Okay thanks Lou. I don't know what I do without you brother."

"You away looked out for me so I'm looking out for you sweetheart. Look, I have to get back to work I'll come past and tell you how everything went, okay **Moja** *(One)!*"

"Moja!"

By this time, I sat on the couch watching TV my sister came in the door looking sad. I patted the seat for her to sit next to me.

She came and flopped down next to me like a little kid that just got their toys taken away from them.

I asked, "are you all right, baby girl?"

She replied, "no, I feel used up, sis."

"Look it's going to hurt for a while, but you will find someone who will love you for you baby."

144

"He just got with me to infiltrate inside of your legitimate organizations with lawyers and vendors putting money inside of his pocket for him to take care of that bitch and little rug rats in Boston and I helped him."

"Who told you all this Lane West?"

"Yes, and I feel shame now."

"You didn't know what he was up to baby girl. Tell me the names of the peoples he got close within my organizations and stores. I'll weed them out okay. Don't beat yourself up Robin. I'll take care of this shit. There just leeches and easy to get rid of. Look I'm going to fix us something to eat. you just might feel a little better after you had something to eat sis."

"I'm not really hungry sis. I'm going to my room and lay down."

"Well when you get up, I'm going to need those names after you take a little nap."

"Okay I will give them to you don't you worry sis."

She quickly walked to her room I went and got busy in the kitchen. I made a bake chicken with green beans and sweet corn. Soon as I was done cooking Jay came home with that, he worked too many hours in the day look on his handsome face. His face brightens up when he seen me. He came up behind me kissing me on the cheek , "I have something to tell you, Almasi and it's not good."

"What's that baby?"

"We got hit with eight trucks going to Atlanta." *this is where we send product in the trap cars and trucks at Jay's car dealer ship.*

"Who told you?"

"One of my peoples, name Day-Day that work for my dealership in Atlanta. Some Spics knocked us off and they never got the, shipment."

"Well it been happening all day today those motherfuckers blew up two of the trucking companies and the landing strip of the airplanes too. He told me they were some Hispanic cats."

"Did y'all set off a war with the Colombians or something?"

"Not that I know of, Jay. It's fucking news to me."

145

"So, what about your peoples that dude Arturo. Where is he from?"

"He's from Venezuela why?"

"Looks like it's a fucking war and you're in the middle of it with you getting hit all over the fucking place"

"Well I'm going to call that fucking Coyote who showed up at my place. He did not tell me shit that there at war with these motherfuckers."

"Yeah you better do that right away, honey."

"I will after I eat." This have been one fucked up day despite all the bullshit that went on me and Jay had a good conversation about my son and the new baby. He also discussed getting back on track with the product flowing. we both been there before so we don't let it get us down. *When you're a real hustler crazy shit happens all the time, but you can't let it stop you from keeping your paper rolling in no matter what.*

Soon as we got done eating Damon Gee came in the door and walked up to us in the kitchen. He greeted us, "how y'all doing? Damn, it really smells good."

Would you like some, Gee?"

"I sure would."

I got up to make him a plate, "I really need to talk to you, Almasi. he looks over at Jay and gives that this is a private conversation look. Nothing personal it is just business."

Jay got up a, "I get the hint he stood up kissing me. I'll go in the bedroom and watch sport center."

"Thanks honey, I'll come and holla at you about your thing when I'm done."

He walked to the bedroom and went inside and closed the door.

"First of all you're in the middle of a fucking war with the Colombians and the Venezuela crews. The Venezuela's hit this Colombian boat for over 300 tons of cocaine. when they supposed to be working together shit went bad and there hitting back on us."

"That's why that motherfucker came up here saying he's here to help us. They knew what was going the fuck on from the door."

146

Almasi 2
Queen of The Streets
By Dartanya A. Williams Sr.

"Now on that thing with your brother Mustafa. This dude name Kaleam is the fucking rat in their crew because this girl name Shashawa. One of his women is fucking pissed with him because Kaleam is fucking her best friend and she's pregnant now. Her name is Kala."

So how you find all this shit out?" She came to me knowing I'm down with you when I'm up in Mookie's club. She heard that the **Hadid Ajundi** came to us to get product and she's letting me know that Kaleam is a fucking snake cutting side deals with Tito Quito right hand man from Ecuador name Eloy Rodas."

"Wow she knew all of that."

"When she mention that I knew she was telling me the truth."

"Yes, she is if she knew all that shit, she really wanted some pay back on that Nigga's ass for real!"

"And you know this. So, I hooked her up with some loot and she told me where he lay his head at too. I have to give her some more loot I need for you to give it to me for her okay."

"How much is she talking about?"

"10 large that's all. I didn't have that much on me you know I don't carry around a lot of loot on me with these jack ass Niggas everywhere."

"Okay, I'll hook you up in the morning come past the office and get it alright."

"Sure thing, Almasi. I will come about 11 to get it."

"Gee, you know there's no hell's fury like a woman scorn."

 We both started laughing.

Damon Gee replied, "you got that shit right!"

So, you're going to call him and let him know about this shit?"

"Yeah, like right now."

"I'm going to tell him to come over here so I can put him down with this shit and then I'm going to call that fucking Coyote character too."

"Yeah one other thing too."

"And what's that it can't get any better than what you just told me."

Almasi 2
Queen of The Streets
By Dartanya A. Williams Sr.

"Guess who else is in town, Almasi?"

"Who?"

"Your boy Xavier and his wife Tachell that was the other thing I could not tell you over the phone too."

"Yeah where is he staying at? "

"He told he has nowhere to stay. He told me to holla at you and clear it so he just don't come popping up on you. Plus, he doesn't know where you live at. I told him I have to talk to you about it and I got his number."

"So where is he right now?"

"He's in Mookie's apartment's over top the barber shop we took over after we smoked Blue. "

"When did all this happen?"

"Last night after I talked to that crazy chick about your brother and that Mustafa thing." "Why you didn't call me last night about that shit, Nigga?"

"You were dealing with that thing with Fat Wally and his crew."

"So, you heard about that then?"

"Yeah and about the favor too." We both started snickering.

Man call that Nigga up. How does he look, Gee?"

"To tell you the truth he looks broke. I don't know what happen in Miami, but he looks good. I can tell he's not rolling like he was when he rolled out of here with that hoop-dee he came here with. I know that."

"Call him right now fuck that!"

Damon Gee makes the call giggling his ass off and X picked up after the phone rang three times.

"Yo, what's up?"

"I'm sitting with her right now here." Damon hands me the phone.

"Hey what's up Nigga what's up with you, X!"

"I'm just hanging in there; Shorty I need to holla at you for real, yo."

"Well where you at now?"

"I'm at Blue's old spot right now."

"Look, I'm going to send a car to come and get you, okay?"

"Yeah, I'll like that Almasi. It's so good to hear your voice girl!"

"The same here just hang tight I'm going to send my man Poochie to come get you. Don't go anywhere alright."

"I won't I'll be right here Shorty."

I got up walking towards the front door, "yo, Poochie I need for you to go to South West Philly 56 street at the apartment over top of the barbershop and pick up X for me, okay."

"Sure thing, boss lady."

"Oh, and when you come back, I need to talk to you about something okay take the Benz."

"Okay Almasi."

He started walking and he stopped and asked, "is it something bad you want to talk to me about."

"Yeah but go do that for me and I'll holla at you then." Then he quickly went out the door. I walk back to the kitchen where Damon is sitting at the table puffing up a storm on his Newport and drinking coffee. I announced, "I have a feeling that Philly is up to something like you but what's fucked up is Poochie is his stepson."

"I know so talk to him about it and see where he's at with it. Plus, from what I know Philly was just married to his mother and there not together anymore. He married another fucking woman, Almasi."

"Yeah, but I still have to holla at him about it regardless."

"Yeah, your right about that shit."

I picked up my phone and called Mustafa. He answered after the second ring.

"Hey, little sister, how are you this evening?"

"I'm good, but I need for you to come over here so we can talk."

"I got something for your ears only brother."

"Okay, that sounds important over here."

"Yes, it is what time can you get here?"

"I can be there about an hour or so."

"Okay, good make sure your alone nobody else need to hear this okay."

"Alright see you then."

I looked over at Damon Gee and asked, "how do you think he's going to take it that one his top men is cutting side deals?"

"Shit he better take it like a man. fuck that." I got up to make some more coffee and after a half an hour blaze past walking in the door is X and his wife Tachell.

They both walked up into the kitchen I hugged X first then Tachell , "oh shit it good to see y'all."

X looked around, "wow Almasi, you're really doing the dam thing now you got a really nice crib here."

"Well y'all help me get here have a fucking seat, Nigga. Y'all want something to drink?"

"Yeah, I'll have some rum if you have it?"

'Tachell chimed in, "I'll have the same, baby." Then they both came over and hugged Damon Gee. It felt good we all can get together again for real the BBC *Body Bag Crew* back together again. We all fell out laughing I waved Blood Eye over and introduced him to the old crew, "Blood Eye, this is X and his wife Tachell." He nodded his head not saying a word.

"Could you get them some rum on the rocks for us please, Blood Eye?"

"Sure thing, Almasi." She walks over towards the left where my big bar is at and I asked, "have y'all seen Spider?"

"Hell no, I have not seen that Nigga in years. Now after we went to Miami that was it, I seen him the last time you seen that motherfucker." We all started laughing then I asked him, "what brings you back in town **Ndugu** *(brother)?*"

"Look, I'm going to keep it real with you, Almasi. I'm broke, and I need a job for real."

"Okay, you got it but what happen in Miami doe?"

"Shit, I was rolling with the coke then I get the fucking bright idea once I got a little money that I was going to go straight. Then I tried to gamble to get some of that kind of loot I was used to back and lost more money. I had to started selling all my prize whips and boats to just a survive. Now I'm back here to make a long story short."

"Alright, you know I got you Nigga!" I pulled out my phone and called Tanya she picks up after the phone rings twice.

"Hey, what's up, boss lady?"

"Hey baby, I need for you to bring me 30 large over here to the spot okay?"

"Sure thing, Almasi. Also, do me a favor and go past La-Nesa office and tell her to give me those keys to the Condo. I need them for my peoples who just came in town please." "You got it, Almasi. I'm on that right now." I hang up the phone and look up at X and Tachell, "y'all don't have to worry about shit I got you."

"I don't know how to repay you for this Almasi. Thank you so much." He stood up and hugged me.

"X, what was it you told me a long time ago? Don't fuck up this good day by crying Nigga."

We all started chuckling. Tachell came over to me crying and hugging me.

"Almasi, you just don't know what this means to us right now."

Poochie walk in and announced, "Almasi, your brother is here to see you."

"Okay thank you Poochie."

I waved him over towards the kitchen and I introduce Mustafa to X and his wife Tachell and he already knew Damon.

"Excuse me for a minute,y'all while me and Damon go holla at my brother in the back for a minute.". X waved his hand "go ahead and do what you do baby. We'll be right here." Me and X walked Mustafa to my back room on the right soon as we went back there. My brother admired the room, "wow, this room is bigger than my whole house little sister. This is off the chain." I just smiled and I point to the brown leather lounge chair on the left. Me and Damon Gee sat in the two leather chairs on the right.

Mustafa looked up at the two of us and asked, "okay, what is it?"

I replied, "I found out the rat in your organization."

"Yeah, who is it?"

"Damon said, "his name is Kaleam and he's been cutting side deals with a dude name Eloy Rodas." He just looked up at both of us not saying a word putting his head back. I looked up at him, "so you knew, brother?"

"Well I had my suspicions, but I could not prove it with the other brothers. Once I seen them two always hanging out with one another. Who told you?"

Damon announced, "some chick name Shashawa."

"Wow that woman been holding him down the whole time while he was in prison when his family turned their back on him. He must have done something really bad for her to tell on him."

"Yeah, he got her best friend pregnant that's what he did Mustafa."

"Yeah that will do it for sure."

"Well I hate to have gave you that bad news brother, but I had to do it."

"Oh no that had to be done and Tito Quito been up my ass to find out what was going on. That's why he did not want to hook us up anymore that why I came to you for some product."

"Well now you know what's up."

"I really appreciate this little sister. Everyone told me y'all really got y'all shit together." "This proves it." He stood up and hugged me, "thank you so much for this I have to go." Damon stood up and shakes his hand. We both walked him out of my backroom down the long hallway to my kitchen area and then to the front door. He waved goodbye in a hurry. I can see that Nigga was hot. We waved back as he quickly went to his car in the driveway and took off.

I closed the door and walked back into the front room where Tanya is sitting on the couch with a big black and red Nike gym bag super smooth. She stood up bumping fist with me , "Poochie, told me to wait for you here handing me the keys to the Condo." I hand them back to her.

"Okay!"

I want you to hand that to X over there in the kitchen while I go holla at Poochie right quick. We started to walk towards the back room so we can talk.

Damon Gee announced, "I'm going to roll, sis."

He hugs me, "I'll be past in the morning for that loot."

He waves at X and Tachell look I got to go. I see y'all later okay. They wave back and he went out the door. I tap Poochie on the arm, "let's go talk, brother."

We walked down the hallway to my back room, and he sat next to me in the big brown leather chairs sitting back real cool and calm.

I looked him right in his eyes, "look, I think your stepfather is up to something while he's back in town did, he say anything to you."

"Hell no, and as you know I don't fuck wit him after he fucked my mother over and hooked up with that no good, bitch La-Rinda. You see what happen to his ass!"

I started giggling and he even louder, "she ran off and started fucking Fat Hector."

"I just wanted to know where your head was at on that, brother. If he's doing what I think he's doing. He's one dead ass motherfucker."

Poochie assured me, "he will get what's coming to his ass, Almasi. I wanted to fuck his ass up when I saw him in Target when he popped up on your ass, but I chilled out knowing not to make moves. Without you giving me the green light on that shit."

We both started chuckling loud.

I stood up and announce, "okay, you can go back on post. Good talk." I went back in the kitchen with X and Tachell getting their drink on talking to one another. *Damon Gee must have known they were broke, even with them still dressed fly as shit after he seen that hoop-dee. They were driving he knew then because X use to have every kind of fly whip that was out all the time.* When I came out from the back room, I told Tanya she can roll out. I thanked her and bump fist with her and told her to come to the office tomorrow as she when out the door. I came out waving at X and Tachell to come in the living room they both walked from the kitchen and sat down on the couch leaning back smiling.

I asked, "are you two all right now?"

"Oh hell, yes were good you just have to tell me where the fuck is this place at?"

"It's about five blocks from here on the right. You can't miss it X it's a luxury Condon called Luxury Gold towers. I own it and ten others like it and the place is already furnished all y'all have to do is buy some new gear and your all set. Oh, hold up for a minute you're going to need a whip too." I stood up went over to my key bowl near the front door on top my wooden dressers pulling out the key to my dark blue 2017 Cadillac Escalade. I walked back over to him handing him the keys saying hold that until we get you a new one.

"Thank you Almasi. I really appreciate all this." I sat back down, "oh, don't you worry you going to work your ass off for real for real for this shit!"

The three of us started giggling then he just stops, chuckling "whatever happen to the BSN?"

"Well like you told me earlier about making a long story short. They wanted to fuck me over after all these years it's still a BSN but I'm not part of it. I got my own shit jumping off from here on out!"

I rolled up my sleeve showing both of them that I had my tattoo removed they were both in fucking shock with their mouth open wide. He asked, "what the fuck I'm going to do with this shit on my arm?"

"I was thinking it was for life. Well if you're going to roll with me you going to have to black it out or have it removed off your arm or go join them chain gang Niggas!"

"I'm going to kill every one of them motherfuckers if it's the last thing I do for real. They killed Tony Smokes and his wife."

"What Tony is dead?"

"Yes, he's dead. They tried to kill my son Little Boom plus they kidnaped my sister too. She got lucky and got away from them or they would have killed her as well."

"Wow, I did not know that Almasi. A lot of shit done change when I was gone. Yeah it did and you know GTG?"

"Yeah about them Niggas we still at war with them?"

"No there down with us now."

"What the fuck is Fat Wally still the head of the gang?"

"Yeah, he's working with us now and so is the 3rd street mob boys."

"Gawd damn, how you pull that shit off?"

"You know me I know I worked my magic on their ass!"

We began snickering because they know how I be working Niggas with my deals.

X asked, "so what about Fly Ty he's still down right?"

"Yeah, he wants to get out of the life and so do Crazy Monk. Now that your back I get you to work with him on something I got cooked up. I'll tell you about it tomorrow okay."

"Well you know me I can't wait to get to work and get this money."

"I hope you can get use to me being in charge. I'm not trying to be smart, but shit is different now."

"Don't worry Shorty I know how to take orders not just give them out. I'll be fine with you running shit. I rolled out so I lost my rank plus like you said BSN is done."

"It's a whole new thing now who you got to remove your tattoo? Doctor Chow did it for all of us everybody that's down with me had theirs's removed."

X looked me right in my eyes , "well, you call that doctor and make an appointment for me too."

Tachell chimed in, "me too!"

"Sound good to me. Now I don't want y'all to bitch up when I call him now."

X folded his arm and puffed out his chest, "you know I never bitched up a day in my life shorty."

We all started snickering. I asked, "y'all want another drink or something?"

"Oh, fuck yeah but you're going to have to hit us off with some of that nose candy up in this motherfucker, mommy."

"Yeah, I got you. I'll be right back I walked into my bedroom I called up Damon Gee he picked up fast and answered, "what's up, Almasi? I need for you to check X out for me too, okay. I know he's cool, but I want to make sure as well."

"I'm way head of you I started doing that last night. I'll let you know if anything comes up, I'll talk to you later. **Moja** *(One)*"

"Moja!"

I went up in my stash in my dresser draw with Jay laying on the bed, "what you are you doing having a party without me, baby?"

"Oh, hell no, you can come join us. I want you to meet some of my people I started out in the gang with from back in the days."

He got up from the bed and walked out with me while I was carrying a large zip lock bag of cocaine. Jay and I both walked up to them and I introduced my man, "this is Jay and Jay this is X and Tachell." X stood up shaking Jay hand, "nice to meet you, brother. I knew shorty from back in the days."

Jay chuckled, "Shorty?" *He looked me over and started snickering.* I just flag him and join in laughing,

"yeah, that's what we used to call her back in the days when she was slinging crack on the block."

Me and Jay sat down giggling, "yeah with my little crew then they were all super tough too."

X asked "whatever happen to some of them. Almasi?"

"Well Big Kim got killed with her brother Jo-Boo in that Gorilla Boulevard war. Little Row-Row he overdoses a few years ago. Queisha she got out the game and got married and had six little rug rats." *Everybody started giggling loud.* La-Nesa and me are still partner's in our hair shops and she runs her own real estate company. Shamika got killed in the war with Emillano Vagus.

Tachell shook his head, "wow, that's fucked up. Did y'all get him back?"

"Oh yeah that motherfucker got the dirt nap for sure. I can't tell you who did it, but he got his from the door." I poured out a big pile of coke on top of my coffee table making lines with my business card. X asked, "yo, Jay, so what do you do homes?"

I run five car dealerships here in Philly, three in New Jersey, and five of them down South."

"Wow, so I can get something really nice from you then?"

"Oh yeah when you and Tachell get rolling I can hook you up with the flyiest shit you ever seen in your life."

"Well, I'll be seeing you next month Nigga for real!"

We all started snickering loud I rolled up a 100-dollar bill and I hand it to Jay and Jay past it down to Tachell, "lady's first."

"Why, thank you." She bends over and started snorting some of the lines off the coffee table. I got up getting everybody a beer and we party until the sun came up the next day having a fucking blast.

X and Tachell went to their new crib after we party all fucking night. When I got up later on, I got those names from my sister Robin before she when to work at 10 O' clock. I went back to bed still high flopping down on the bed. I never got to call that motherfucker Coyote. When I did get up from sleeping late, I did call him, and he's on top of everything. He upgraded our trucks and planes. I had a sit down with a biker gang in Canada who wants to do business with us because they need better product. Along with the Haitians I been wanting to hook up with that thing for a while now. I thanked him, and I hung up.

I know what he did by him hooking up new business for us. I won't be upset about him not telling me about the war with the Colombians. I called up Fly Ty and told him to meet me at my office so we can talk about him getting out of the life.

He told me he'll be there. Jay got up late too, but he jumped up and went to work before I put my feet on the floor to get ready. He kissed me and went out the door washed dressed and ready to go. I get washed and dressed and got out the door around 1:30 with Poochie and Blood Eye who were on post at 6 in the morning. Even after staying late while we partied our ass off. By the time I got to my office everybody was there Tanya, Fly Ty and Black Duke. Soon as I came in the door, I bumped fist with Black Duke, and I told him I need to talk to Fly Ty alone.

He replied, Sure Ma, but I need to holla at you after your done with Damon Gee. He was here to get that money for that girl that's what he told me."

"Did you give it to him?"

"Yeah, I did give it to him."

"Good I'm glad you took care of it, thanks Duke I'm talk to you after I talk to my man here." I tap Fly Ty on his arm, "let's talk my friend." We quickly walked to my office and he closed the door behind himself. I sat at my desk and he sat in front of me.

"I'm going to get right to it, okay. I need you to do something for me before you go do what you want to do."

"Sure, what is it you want me to do?"

"Well as you know Philly is back in town and if he's doing what I think he's doing I want you to fix his wagon for him. After we kill Fat Hector. I want you to rig his car or where he stays at. I'll let you know you don't have a problem with that do you?"

"Hell, no I would not trust him right about now myself. I think he's trying to set you up for Nokey Blaze and the Chain Gang crew."

"I know. You sound just like Damon Gee he was going to kill him on the spot."

Fly Ty chimed in, "I feel the same fucking way Almasi. Why don't you give me the green light on that shit?"

"I would but we have to get Fat Hector first. We need to draw his ass out to kill him and that way we kill two birds with one stone. You know that's my thing."

"I heard X is back in town too do you trust him?

"Hell, yes more than Philly don't worry I'm checking him out too as we speak."

"I already know he'll pass with flying colors and if he doesn't, I'll have Dun-Dun to punch his fucking ticket to meet Jesus."

We both started laughing, "look we are done for now, but I'll let you know what the game plan is, and I'll talk to you later."

"Alright let me know now. He stood up and hugged me and went out the door." Soon as he went out Black Duke came in and announced, "Fat Lou-Lou was here for you too."

"I'll call him right now thanks."

The phone rang four times and I answered, "yo thanks for the new planes and trucks."

"I to him you know me I'm on top of shit big man." *I just took credit for it fuck it.* "Well thank Ma- Ma but I'm still going to need more muscle now that shit is flowing to make sure we don't get hit again."

"I got you let me makes some calls for you, brother."

"Okay Ma and thanks again." Crazy Jamel came knocking on the door, "Almasi, it's this guy name X here to see you?"

"Yeah walk him back here he's going to be working with us. He's cool."

I still checked him. He's clean."

"Okay then bring him in for me please."

A few minutes later here come X and he came in hugging Black Duke.

"Wow, it's good to see you man."

"The same here look I have to go."

I told X, "close that door for me please he closes the door."

"X, I need you to go help Fat Lou- Lou out I'm going to call Rah- Killer that who you going to be working with." He stood up and waved at Bango to come over fast. I told him to come in this is X they both shook hands.

"Look, go get my man here are two machine guns, two Glock pistols and some clips for me, okay."

"Coming right up Almasi." He looked up at X walking out of my office to go to the gun stash in the back of the warehouse.

I called Rah- Killer she picked up quickly, "what's up, sister?"

"Look I need you to go give Fat Lou-Lou a hand and watch his back."

"I'm on my way I'll be there in an hour **Moja** *(One)!*" Bango came back with a green duffle bag handing it to X , "here check it out."

159

He set it on top of my desk checking his guns and loading the clips. I hand him the address, "this where you're going ask for Lou-Lou. he'll tell you what you have to do."

"I got it. Can I ask you to do you have anything for Tachell to do? She told me to ask you."

"Yeah, I do but I'm really busy right now. I'll call her and let her know later on, okay. Tell her I got her don't worry about it. I need for you to roll right now." He went out the door and I called Tanya in my office. I share with her my game plan with Philly if he's not right. I was super busy that whole day getting a lot done I came late, and I stayed late. When I came, I was home burned out? But I did not care because this is the job I work hard and play hard like a motherfucker. *My plan is to groom Dun-Dun to my spot and it will be my turn to kick back and enjoy my life with my new grandson. I also want to try to talk to my son about pulling back from all this shit as well. I know that's going to be a really hard job to do but I still have to try to talk some sense into his ass. I'm going to set up a sit down with Arturo and let him know that Dun-Dun is going to take over all operations. I will make Jagger number two I know this shit will work. Shit, Spider just rolled out on me and told me to hold shit down until he came back, but he never did come back. And if Arturo don't want me to get out that's when I know I'm going to have a real problem. I know I can talk him into it, and I know they will kill me and my whole family without even thinking about it. I never wanted this life for myself I really had no choice in the matter for real. So far, I had a good run its time for me to get out. I've been really lucky so far but its only but so much luck you can have in this fucking life. And I don't want to be around when the shit runs out on me.*

Kidnaping Fat Hector's son Ray-Ray

Three days later I sat down with Coyote crazy ass. He gave me a new banging ass satellite phone and apologized sincerely to me for not telling me about the war with the Colombians. He they were set up and his peoples had nothing to do with that bullshit. He he had the sit down with the Bikers and the Haitians in Canada is all going down next month. I came to the office soon as I sat down Dun-Dun called me announcing his peoples seen Philly meeting up with his mother Zelda and the old head Jasquez and John Knotty the leader of the Chain gang. And on another day with Big Cyrus Crazy Paulie and Jasquez.

"Yeah, now we know who the old head who is helping them now."

"Yeah, what do you want to do?"

"I need you to be helping Philly with the kidnapping of Fat Hector's son Ray-Ray after we put him up somewhere. I'll have Fly Ty to put a bomb under his car when he drives off." "So, what about the kid Ray-Ray?"

"Kill him too."

"What about La-Rinda?"

"What about that bitch she doesn't get a pass. Do she?"

"Oh, Hell, no I'll have Willie Whack-Whack and Nails Nathan to take care of her ass. They can track down a flea on a shaggy dog's ass."

We both started giggling.

"Look, I'm going to talk to Fly Ty and tell him it's a go after that he want to get out of the life."

"Really, he wants to get out."

"Yeah, that's what he said, brother. He wants out."

"Yeah, everybody told me that shit then they be right back after they been broke like a motherfucker. Then there right back at it again once you get this shit under your skin you never want to stop."

"Well, I been thinking about it myself, Dun."

"Get the fuck out of here and who's going to take your spot?"

"You, Nigga you're going to take my spot that's who."

"So, when are you thinking about rolling?"

"Right after we kill the chain gang leader John Knotty and you can take it from there."

"What about Nokey Blaze he have to go too."

"I know that, but we have to get somebody we can trust to do that shit."

"I'll do it just give me the green light and I won't miss I'm telling you Almasi."

"I would love to let you do that for me **Ndugu** *(brother)* but Nokey Blaze is not like the rest of these regular thug Niggas out here. He's a wiley ass fucking horse he's been around for a really long time, Dawg."

"You kill me with these old school terms Almasi. What does that mean Doe **Malkia** *(Queen)?* "

"That means he's unpredictable and too smart for us to take care of his ass it's that simple were going to need a specialist to do this shit."

"How about that crazy ass dude your peoples hooked you up with from Venezuela?"

"Oh no, I don't trust that guy I'll talk to Damon Gee and some of the others and figure this shit out."

"I'll let you know what I just need for you the do the dam thing with Fat Hector son, okay."

"Okay, let me know Moja (One)!"

"Moja!"

Later, that week me and Philly met up here at my office to put this shit together. I still had Dun-Dun's young boy working for me name *Little Luke. He was Low- Low's son who overdose a couple years ago who use to be down with my little crack slinging crew. I was a young girl wet behind the ears in South Philly on the block back then. Dun-Dun gave him a job knowing his mother Miss Mandy from the old hood in South Philly he's the one watching*

Philly every fucking move. He's good too. He also told Dun-Dun that they had a man on me for a fucking month now a two-man team. Rondell and Lavan two suburban sneaky ass Niggas for hire they been in the game for about a minute too long when I'm done with them. We have the plan set up for Friday night to snatch Raymond goofy ass or Ray-Ray Hernandez is what everybody calls him. He's a real party animal ass hole Nigga whose father spoiled the shit out of him with a lot of money.He blows every fuckin dime showing off for his peoples. Most of them just use him up to get high and have a good time with this little dumb ass rich kid. My crew had everything set up right with Dun-Dun overseeing everything.

He's parked across the street on the left not too far from the club call Melita's 4535 North 5th street that sets on the right-hand side of the street. Philly is parked in a car not too far from Dun- Dun on the same side of the street. He can't wait for everything to go down to get even with the man who is fucking his wife by getting his son. Mookie the wheel man and Crazy Monk Taz- Money in one truck parked on West Raymond street near the corner of the club where they can see the front door. Parked right behind them is Flip Diddy from Jagger's crew behind the wheel. Tanya and Gino Gats in the other black truck. Parked a block away on 5th street is Little Bay- Bay another one of Jagger men behind the wheel with Woo-Woo and Lurch sitting up in an, kitted up dark blue SUV. Frank Iilly the wheel man with Gun Ho Moe and Steve Swiga Dun-Dun made sure everybody had ear pieces that way all of them are all on the same page on with the communication to pull this shit off right.

It's12:45 and Ray- Ray came riding up 5th street with his two boys. They are two Dick riding Puerto Rican motherfuckers Mateo and Sebastian two shit bag coke head young guys from North Philly. The two girls with them Candice and Dominique two coke head young Puerto Rican nasty ass whores down for whatever. These bitches done sucked more Dick then eight porn stars combined. Now in that truck they only had two bodyguard goons with them is Santiago and His road dawg Thiago. The white town car behind them is Alonso and Esteban two of Fat Hector's men from his old hood he grew up with their both not any real soldiers they just playing the part for some money. Soon as the first truck came up a block near the club Dun- Dun with his night vision binoculars checking everything out announced in his earpiece to everyone, "**Twende sasa** *(Here we go!)*"

Just as he said that Fly Ty sneaks up on Philly car a new dark green Impala placing a bomb under it. Soon as he did that the two men that was watching his back Rondell and Lavan pull off in their whip to warn him. Soon as they started up their car to pull off Pooouuufff! Pooouuufff! Pooouuufff! Pooouuufff! They were hit twice in the face and twice in the chest each with the blood all over the car windows. The killers reached inside of the car and got both of their phones off their dead bodies and took off into the darkness. The two specialist I hired to take care of their ass Jagger told me about them name Dime Piece and Bop-Diglo two crazy ass young black psycho killers from North Philly.

I told them if they do good on this, I had some bigger shit for them to do but they were not cheap neither. The truck with Ray- Ray and the asshole party crew pulls up in front of the club. The SUV with Frank Illy came up first behind the white town car. Mookie turned the corner along with Flip Diddy right behind him as Crazy Monk and Taz- Money jumps out. At the same time Tanya and Gino Gats guns blazing shooting killing Mateo and Sebastian on the spot. The two women ran off not getting hit by all the gun fire by some miracle. They ran across the street not hurt ducking out of the way. Simultaneously, Little Bay- Bay pulled up Woo-Woo and Lurch open fire on the white town car before they could get out to help Santiago and Thiago. Hearing the shots from right then the left and it was raining bullets out there at the time. Gun Ho Moe and Steve Swiga is shooting at Santiago and Thiago as well it was too much for them to handle. They were both in shock getting hit all at the same time Thiago was hit in his head in the wild shoot out falling on the club wall bleeding from his head dead. Santiago tried to pull Ray- Ray to protect him but Tanya and Gino Gats came up spitting hot led in their ass killing Santiago. Shooting him in every part of his body he fell backwards on the ground and Tanya came up and shot him **Kapacka!** right in his Dick blowing it off.

Almasi 2
Queen of The Streets
By Dartanya A. Williams Sr.

Gino Gats and Tanya quickly grabbed Ray-Ray along with Crazy Monk and Taz- Money covering them to the truck to toss Ray-Ray inside the vehicle with Mookie behind the wheel. Crazy Monk and Taz- Money hops in and takes off down the dull yellow lit street. Blazing right behind them is Flip Diddy with Tanya and Gino Gats jumps in and they sped off.

At the same time did Little Bay-Bay, Woo-Woo and Lurch Frank Illy with Gun Ho Moe and Steve Swiga got ghost in the blink of an eye for real. Philly was happy pulling off to go meet up with the others at the warehouse on Sedgley Avenue. They had him tied up with duct tape in an iron chair in this dusty ass room in the back on the right in the dark. Dun-Dun called me and told me it was done. I was home chillin with my man Jay watching Power season five over again. Jay missed most of it running the streets and working his ass off doing his thing for both of us moving those things. We never seen more than episode three before we started fucking on the couch. I'm spread eagle and I have my left leg up on the top of the couch and my right leg wrapped around Jay's strong ass sweaty back. Jay is digging in pushing back with his feet for traction pumping on me. He's really putting his back into it too. Were both moaning and groaning even with the TV up loud we both can hear that sound of my pussy popping smacking and cracking like when you fry bacon in an old black skillet.

Then from out of nowhere he took and put both of his big muscular tattoo arms under both my legs and he picked me up standing up fucking me like I was a rubber fuck doll right by the couch. *Wow I'm loving this shit I didn't get fucked like this when I was a teenager. Better late than never.* Now he's standing up fucking me all I see is starlight's and moon rockets blasting off. If he keeps this shit up, he fucked me into a super-hot cum coma. I took both my thick legs and wrapped them around him. He's grunting loud it fills the whole room like hard-core hip-hop music knocking off the walls with him stroking the shit out of me like a crazed sex maniac. We have sparks rocking in this hot ass deep nasty groove we got going on like were both possessed out of are mines. Pumping right back on his wild nasty black ass getting it good hitting my Gee spot. I'm dripping wet like Niagara Falls. I have both my arms around his neck kissing him and I can hear our meat slapping together with every stroke and boom squirting like a water fountain. I started coming and he started moaning even louder with all of my super-hot orgasm gushing all over his thick black erection dripping down his legs on to the floor. Jay started backing up making sure he feels the couch with the back of his legs, and he sits down. Now I'm on top of his fine black ass jumping up and down like a wild woman riding his Dick like I was Sally star on a strong ass black stallion.

I take both my hands and push him back like I'm hold him there just gyrating my hips working his ass over. He's mumbling talking in fucking tongues soon as I seen his face started getting twisted up. Wam! He let it go yelling, "Oh shit baby here it cum!"

I can feel all of his hot jizz shooting up inside of me it made me feel like I was about to cum again. He's shaking and holding me tighter while I'm digging my nails deep down inside of his chest screaming in deep pleasurable sexual bliss. I just lean over and kissed Jay then I just collapsed on top his sexy sweaty dark body. I laid there for a little while before I got up and sat up slowly sitting by his legs reaching on the end table on my left getting my cigarettes.

I'm covered in sweat breathing hard trying to get myself together. I'm floating on a fucking cloud with tingles and goosebumps running up and down my back and legs. I'm lightheaded. I light up two cigarettes at the same time puffing hard *still thinking of that good fucking Jay just put on me.* I reached over handing him the one I lit up for him with Jay looking up at me with that look in his eyes I just love the way he looks at me like that.

I asked him, "what the fuck was that with you picking me up in the fucking air Nigga?" We both started giggling soon as I got up to go to my bedroom Jay smacked me on my ass, I walked to my bedroom getting a large zip up *(Bag of coke). While me and Jay was getting busy what we didn't know was Robin and Poochie was getting it on as well in the back room. In the back of my mind I knew that was going to happen.*

Almasi 2
Queen of The Streets
By Dartanya A. Williams Sr.

Robin is bend over with her hands on the end of the bed and Poochie is hitting it from the back rocking the shit out of her doggy style. They are blasting old school love song so nobody can hear them fucking like minks in heat. Soon as I got washed up after having knock down drag out sex with Jay, I get the call from Dun- Dun telling me to get there before Philly kill Ray- Ray Hernandez at the warehouse because he's been working him over for hours. I told him I was on my way there after I got dressed Jay ask me where I was going in the middle of the night. I told him I had to take care of something I'll be back. I kissed Jay and quickly walked out of my bedroom. I called up Blood Eye and Poochie so I can roll out to the warehouse at Sedgley avenue. I hung up and called Damon Gee he picked up on the first ring and responded, "I'm on my way, Ma! Moja (One)!"

I didn't know Poochie was in the backroom with my sister Robin until I seen him walk past my bedroom while I was getting myself together. I didn't say anything about it she's grown. He waited for me at the front door he didn't know I seen him. Blood Eye came driving up in front of the crib calling me, "he's ready to go he's outside." Poochie is thinking I was going to say something, but I did not say a word about it long as he's ready for duty I'm cool with it. I check my two guns I lit up a cigarette, fixed my coat and go out the door. As the cold wind hit my face Poochie right by my side he opens the door for me, and Blood Eye. We took off down the cold dark street. It took us about a half an hour to get there soon as I walked in the door Tanya walks up to me bumping fist with me.

"Hey what's up, Almasi? We have him back here. Dun- Dun called you so this Nigga doesn't kill this boy."

"How bad is he?"

"Real bad you'll see." I'm looking around to make sure all these Niggas are on point and on post because I know Fat Hector is going off right about now and he just might know where we're at. So, you have to think about shit like that if not somebody will come up on you and smoke your ass,so you have to be ready for whatever in this game.

I have not heard from Willie Whack- Whack and Nails Nathan yet. I asked, "Tanya **Nihawa watu wa karibu** *Is these guys tight?*" As we are walking towards the backroom Tanya replied, "they better be, or I'll take care of them myself Almasi."

"**Nzuri** *(Good)!* **Umekuja kwa muda mrefu mimi ninajivunia wewe** *You came a long way I'm proud of you.*"

"**Asante Almasi** *Thank you Almasi.*" *I like Tanya she's a very pretty light skin woman, but I could see all the change with her to with all the tattoos. When I look into her eyes now their cold and distant like most killers I know so well in this life. I see that she's evolved from a dumb ass college kid into a real fucking gangster now.* I walked in the back room they have this boy nude tied to a metal chair and he's a bloody mess. Philly is still beating on him.

I yelled, "that's enough Phil I know you hate his father, but he has to be alive for all of this shit to work **Ndugu** *(Brother)!* "

Philly is all sweaty and he turns around looking at me with his face all twisted up. He sneered, "**Nataka mwanawe amekufa pia** *I want his son dead too!* "

I walked up to him and yelled, "**Bado** *(Not yet)!*" Philly went to hit him again I ran up pushing him back and screamed, "**Kuacha** *(Stop)!*"

He went to push me back Tanya, Poochie and Blood Eye whip out their gun pointing them at him making him stop right in his tracks as his eyes get wide. He looked up at me and laughed," you ready to make this call or what Glock Mommy?"

"I'm waiting on Damon Gee soon as he gets here, he'll make the call."

"So, where the fuck he's at?"

"Look Philly chill the fuck out all right! He's on his way!"

Soon as Damon Gee walked up, he just looked him up and down not saying anything to him. He bumps fist with me and announced, "let me do this right quick because I can't stand to be around this motherfucker."

He yelled, "what you say, Nigga?"

I step up and screamed, "chill the fuck out before I put three hot slugs in your fucking dome, and I mean it! I'm the one who run shit around here Philly. So, slow your roll alright." He looked me up and down then he looks over at Damon Gee, "I'll come holla at you when all this shit is over with. Partner make the call!" Damon Gee pulls out his phone dialing the number.

The phone rings five times and someone picks up and yelled, "who the fuck is this?"

"This is the Nigga that have your son that's who the fuck I am, Nigga!"

"Well whoever you are your one dead ass motherfucker for grabbing my son in the first place!"

"Check this out, fat motherfucker if you don't come up with any of the money were asking for, he's dead. So, fuck all the big bad wolf shit your talking about Nigga!"

"Okay how much is you talking about then?"

"Eight million dollars you got two hours to get it together and I know you got it so don't bull shit me motherfucker. The clock is ticking bitch!" Damon Gee hangs up the phone. Philly said, "I didn't like your ass at first, but I just love that shit." He bumps fist with Damon. He gives a wicked ass smile because he knows *it's a bomb under his car. Fly Ty is out there ready to blow his dumb ass up, so he is playing along. He winks his eye at me.* My phone rings I get it and its Willie Whack- Whack announcing, "**Tulipata bitch** *(We got the bitch)!*"

"**Nzuri** *(Good)* bring her here for me right quick."

"You got it we will be right there!"

"Yo, check it out y'all, Willie Whack-Whack and Nails Nathan just got that bitch La-Rinda. They are bringing her here as we speak."

Philly smiled rubbing his hands together, "see that why I love working with you, Almasi you always get shit done!" We all sit down in the folding chairs along the wall not too far from Ray- Ray all fucked up nodding with blood dripping from his mouth. I announce, "Tanya go to the door so you can let Willie and Nails in the door for me."

She just nods her head walking quickly towards the front door. Ten minutes later Nails Nathan and Willie Whack- Whack is pushing La- Rinda inside of the room with her going off screaming, "kill me right here you don't have to push me into some dark ass room!"

Soon as she gets in the room, she looks up at me and began pleading her case, "You know I didn't have anything to do with Fat Hector crazy ass, Almasi? He did all that bull shit on his own. I had nothing to do with him killing Tony Smokes and Nashawn." I swear to God!"

Then she looks over at Ray- Ray and cried, "oh shit Ray- Ray poor baby.' She walks over to him Philly and he screams, "don't touch him bitch!"

"I knew you would have something to do with this shit!" He smacks her hard. **Plow!** She falls, to the floor hard crying loud.

"You no good fucking, Ho. I wasted my time and money on your ass, and you run off with some fat ass motherfucker. I should kill your ass right here and now!" I stood up and pushed him back, "Phil that's enough, okay. 'Dun- Dun came in the room whispered in my ear, "Little Luke that Fat Hector just got all the money. His boy Jarrett went and picked it all up."

"Okay thanks let me call Jagger right quick."

I looked at my watch I called Jagger he picks up after three rings, "hey what's up?"

"Are your peoples in place?"

"Yeah both of them is there right now waiting on y'all there the real pros. Almasi don't you worry they get the job done that's why they're so fucking high price."

"Okay thanks. I holla at you later." I look at Damon Gee okay make the call. Damon Gee pulls out his phone with a smirk on his face. He makes the call to Fat Hector who he picks up right away yelling, "it's not a full two hours motherfucker!"

"Look asshole meet us at the scrap yard at 4th and Sedgley avenue with the money. I already know you went and had it picked up. Oh yeah, I wanted to tell you tough guy we also got your bitch La-Rinda!"

Almasi 2
Queen of The Streets
By Dartanya A. Williams Sr.

"Bullshit Nigga"! Damon Gee points up at Tanya, she quickly pulls out her gun walking up to her mashing it up to La- Rinda's head walking her over to where Damon Gee was standing at. Tanya mashing the gun a little harder, "say something bitch!"

"Oh, baby, they're going to kill me-**Kook!**' Tanya hits her in the head with her gun making her yell holding her head falling back Tanya yelled, "shut up bitch! "

Damon Gee asked, "can you hear me now, fat ass motherfucker? Be there don't have me waiting or I'll kill both of them if you don't show up!" Damon Gee hangs up looking at me smiling.

"Okay Tanya get Gino Woo-Woo and Lurch with you! Nails, Willie, y'all go get Taz- Money, Crazy Monk and Dun- Dun you go with them with Ray- Ray. Untie his ass and take him with yall don't kill him until Fat Hector is dead."

La-Rinda looking up at me and asked, "what about me, Almasi? I didn't do shit to none of y'all!" She *looked up at me with them puppy dog eyes looking all sad and shit.* I looked her right in her face, smirked and pointed to Philly, "that's not up to me. That's on Philly over here." Philly looks at her making a trigger finger at her head like he's shooting her she began crying as Tanya started dragging her out the door. I announced, "Philly you can follow them when they go to the strap yard, okay."

"Sure thing, Almasi. Thanks for everything. Just make sure you come back here to celebrate with me after Fat Hector is dead alright." He bumps fist with me. He smiles and he walks behind everybody heading towards the front door. I walked with Poochie and Blood Eye near the front door as I watched all of them roll out and the dude Mojo and Fat Jacks is on the front door closing it behind them.

Me, Poochie and Blood Eye sat down at the table near the water cooler on the right-hand side of the large space. Tanya hooked this joint up nice too. The girl knows what's she's doing I'm looking around when Big De Shawn came over to us chillin and greeted, "hello my name is De Shawn. Is there anything I can get you, Almasi?"

"If you guys have any coffee, I would love some right about now, brother."

"Yes, believe it or not we have a really nice coffee machine in here. I'll get you some right away. Hold on y'all want some coffee?"

Poochie and Blood Eye both replied yes make that three and some cream and sugar too big guy. He walked to go get it after a few minutes he came back with the coffee setting them on the table in front of me and announced, "this is better than Starbucks shit for real."

"Thank you, brother. I like to ask you something do you speak Swahili.'

"Well Tanya is teaching me a little now."

"Yeah like what?"

"Moja means one, **Nenda** means Go, **Nzuri** means Good, **Tulipata** means We got them, **Bunduki** means Guns."

"Good, you've been studying keep that shit up and you can move up in the world if you play your cards right."

Meanwhile, everyone has arrived at the strap yard and Fat Hector is already there. They are looking around to see if we had someone there already. Taz-Money is driving the black GMC truck with Ray- Ray Hernandez in the back seat. pull up in the wide opening pulling up on the left-hand side of the yard. Right beside them is Tanya and them with Woo-Woo behind the wheel of a dark blue Explorer. Tanya is riding shotgun Gino Gats and Lurch is in the back with their guns on La- Rinda. Philly is still in his whip before getting out he text Rondell asking you still got my back. What he doesn't know is that Rondell and Lavan is dead. Dime Piece and Bop- Diglo took Rondell and Lavan's phones after killing them. Dime Piece text him back saying you know it.

He texts back saying kill everything that move out there. They text back we got you. Philly seen that and smirked. He jumps out of the car and he is standing behind them. Tanya and Gino Gats are waiting for Fat Hector to come out in the open so he can shoot him. Fat Hector has Crazy Paulie with him. Fat Hector in one car a black Benz in in the black Pathfinder is Jarrett Blade behind the wheel Queisha Loot riding shotgun with Jimmy Yams, Big Cyus's little Brother Billy Bands, Ziggy Ock, and Joe Knuckles. Crazy Paul gets out of the car with a suitcase moving with him at the same time is Ziggy Ock, Joe Knuckles and Billy

Almasi 2
Queen of The Streets
By Dartanya A. Williams Sr.

Bands is with him every step he makes towards the center of the dirt wide space surrounded by tall stack of cars on the strap pile. Queisha Loot steps out the black Pathfinder truck holding her gun looking around. Philly get out his car walking up front, but he can't see Fat Hector, Dun- Dun, Crazy Monk and Willie Whack-Whack is walking up with them. Nails Nathan is with Ray- Ray Taz- Money have his gun out holding the wheel ready knowing it about to go down. Dun-Dun yells out, "that's far enough give us the money and we will give you Ray-Ray!"

Crazy Paulie , "okay. I'll drop the money over here because I don't trust none of you motherfuckers from the door for real." Soon as he went to drop the large black bag it was so heavy.

He had looked up at everyone with their guns out not taking his eyes off of none of them backing up slowly with his gun pointed forward on them. **Sssssuuuupppp! Sssssuuuupppp!** *The shots were low sounding hitting Fat Hector in his head twice with his head leaning back in the car seat with blood running down in face to his fat chest. Crazy Paulie dropped the bag and it hit the ground with dust flying up in the air pointing his gun up shooting wildly. The second everybody heard the soft shot, everybody started shooting and all hell broke loose bullets flying everywhere under the Dall yellow streetlights above the strap yard. All you see is sparks from everybody pistols trying to kill one another. Nails Nathan pushed Ray- Ray out of the back of the truck and he dragged him behind one the tall stack of cars* **Kapacka! Kapacka! Kapacka!** *Shooting him in the head three times like he was told to do by me once Fat Hector was dead.*

The he came from behind the large pile of cars and joined in the gun battle. Philly creeping up ducking looks up and see that Fat Hector is dead. He's pissed off he didn't do it, but he was happy he was dead. When Lurched jump out to help out in the fight Philly ran over in all the confusion to the dark blue Explorer opening the back door **Kapacka! Kapacka!** *Shooting La-Rinda two times in the head her body slumped over falling out of the backseat bleeding falling face first into the dirt. Woo- Woo looked up but he did not shoot at Philly running away laughing. He jumped in his whip backing up from the strap yard getting the fuck out of there. Dun- Dun shoots Jimmy Yams in his neck and mouth he's dead laid out in the dirt. But Dun- Dun ran over picking up the big black bag of money with dirt all over it. He runs back to the truck still turning around blasting his gun after picking it up. Crazy Monk shot Billy Bands up but he ran back to the*

173

Almasi 2
Queen of The Streets
By Dartanya A. Williams Sr.

black Pathfinder long with Ziggy Ock and Joe Knuckles jumping in as Queisha Loot helping Ziggy Ock and Joe Knuckles into the black Pathfinder as Jarrett turning around getting the fuck out of dodge driving towards the other end of the strap yard the way they came inside of there in the large opening. Crazy Paulie his hit in the top of his shoulder and his left arm but he made to the black Benz. Soon as he sat in the car, breathing hard with his heart feeling like it was going to pop out his fucking chest he looked over seeing Fat Hector dead with his eyes wide open.

His dead body lean back with blood running out of the top of his head and mouth. He quickly slides over opening the door pushing Fat Hector's dead body out of the car. He had a hard time doing it, but he done it fast knowing his ass will be dead if he stays any longer. He
drives off faster than a motherfuckin Hill Billy red neck Nascar stock car racer. Everybody got ghost from the scene Philly is on his phone calling Rondell while he's driving but he's not getting no answer. What he doesn't know is Fly Ty is not too far behind him. Soon as Philly went to drive up the ramp to get on the expressway. Fly Ty hits his remote to the bomb under Philly's whip **Kaboom!** Debris, metal and glass flying in the air with black smoke and flames shooting up to the clouds. I'm chillin drinking coffee when I got the call. its Fly Ty announced, **"Imefanywa** *It's done."*

"Okay, brother **Asante** *Thank you!!*

"You're welcome, Almasi, but now I'm out I'm going to Las Vegas to do my own thing."

"Okay, cool if you need anything or you get in a tight spot you call me okay."

" I will and thank you **Moja** *(One)*"

"Moja!" I stand up and I waved over De Shawn. He came over I , "you get a little more work under your belt and keep working on your Swahili it will be more opportunities for yourself and your crew okay." I bump fist with him, and I rolled out with Poochie and Blood Eye. When I got home Dun- Dun called me to let me know the money that was in the large black bag was fake. I already knew their plan was to kill everybody out there and to get his son back. He was not worry about La-Rinda nasty ass, but we already killed their hit men who supposed to call in more men.

Once they got to where we were doing the drop off at then they would kill me as well. There hit team never got the call because Rondell and Lavan were dead. They knew if they would have rolled up to the spot, they be dead to, so they never follow through not hearing from Rolldell Lavan or Philly neither.

When Sunday came, I made a big dinner and I had all of the boys over to eat. Black Duke and his wife Tya, Ty- Kim and his wife Lashawna, Booby Hill and his wife Nakida, Puerto Rican Joe and his wife Stephanie, Jagger and his girlfriend Ta-Lisa, Dun-Dun and his wife Twanda, Poochie and Robin Blood Eye and his wife Mary. I cooked a two big Turkeys and I stuffed them with wild rice, and I cooked two rump roasts along with macaroni and cheese and some down-home collard greens. I had Tawni, Tya and Nakida help me serve everybody at the table. We all throw down and had a good time talking and eating as a family. This is my family for better or worse and I refuse to let anyone of these sucker's ass holes and haters to take us down or out.

One of the Snakes is Dead

It's the end of December we had a beautiful Christmas and I went crazy buying all kinds of shit for the baby. The war we were in the middle of with the Colombians all slowed down as well. I have to omit that crazy ass Nigga Coyote did take care of business. He helped us get more trucks and planes to move the product out super smooth. And all the blood suckers that were all inside of my legitimate companies that ass hole Ismael had planned inside of my businesses I got rid of all of them one by one. Me and my son Little Boom got replacements as quick as we got them out the door. I put Dime Piece and Bop-Diglo to take care of the task force lead investigator Ted Schultz with the help from detective Don Wilson and Fast Eddie two dirty cops I have on my payroll. I told them I wanted him dead soon as the new year comes in. It's December 28th Friday afternoon Christmas came on a Tuesday the holidays came and when really fast, so I had a sit down with Jagger's brother John Spartacus to see where he's at with the plan on taking out Black Giovanni. I'm sitting in my office talking to Black Duke about keeping shit on track with everything and I ask him about how is X working out? **Nzuri kweli** *Real good* but his **Mjinga Punda Mke** *Sneaky ass wife* I don't trust her at all Ma.

Yeah like what you know you can tell me Duke. She showed up at Mookie's club without X and she was all in Bango's face acting like she was going to give him some pussy.

But my man Jimmy Goon shut that shit down and told her to get the fuck up out of the club. He got Mookie's peoples to toss her ass out. "I didn't know she was like that."

"Well I think she's up to something if you want to know."

"Well thanks I'll keep my eye on her ass from here on out if you think she's up to something and keep this shit with us."

"Oh, I already talk to Bango and Jimmy Goon about this shit not to say shit to X about what happen."

"**Nzuri** *Good!* "

Then my phone rings I looked at my caller ID it's Damon Gee I picked it up real fast and asked, "what's up Nigga? Did you have a nice holiday you never came over for dinner?"

"Yeah, I'm sorry about that Almasi but Dominique had me go meet her folks on that same night on Christmas."

"I could not just roll out on them."

"Okay, I feel you on that one, so you had to meet the folks. It must be getting serious than."

"Yeah it is I gave her a ring, so I had to follow through with meeting her parents."

"Awww shit you put a ring on it she has to be the one Dawg."

"Yes, she is look I call to tell you that your boy Black Giovanni is dead. I just got word from S.O.S. I got it from the number two man in the prison Joey Diamonds." I hung up with him and I called my peoples to make sure it was real and its confirmed from my man Zippy it's true. "So, who did it?"

He answered, "S.O.S. Did it. A Nigga name Willie Locks from order from Crusher the head of the S.O.S. in prison."

"**Nzuri** *Good* News! That's what I want to here. Thanks Gee."

"No problem Ma."

"I'm going to get off this horn with you I have a million things to do. If I hear anything else, I'll hit you back but so far that Nigga is dead. I'll holla at you later Man **Moja** *One!*"

I turned to Black Duke, "Black Giovanni is dead!"

Black Duke pump his fist up in the air and yelled, "It's about fucking time!" Soon as I hung up with Damon Gee, I see Crazy Jamel knocking on the glass on my office door. I looked up and I see John Spartacus standing beside him. I wave my hand for him to come in. I wave at Crazy Jamel, "thanks Mel." *He waves and close the door back going back on post.* I asked John Spartacus, "please have a seat."

He leans over and bump fist with me than Black Duke. He sat down and looked me in my face and told me, "well, I came to tell you that we got the shit done, Almasi and I really appreciate everything you've done for me and my team."

"Well your brother told me that you knew what y'all was doing I'm really happy your down with us to tell you the truth brother."

"But what we need now is that new shit to mix the heroin with."

"What new shit are you talking about?"

"You know Fentanyl everybody is going fucking crazy over it. I know you can get us some of it that would wipe out the motherfucking competition for sure Almasi."

"Well I'll get right on that for you brother and thanks for coming by to holla at me today. let me walk you to the door."

I stood up and he gave me a hug smiling as we started walking towards the front door, he bumps fist with Crazy Jamel and Bango then me before he went outside. I felt like fucking jumping and skipping all fucking day knowing that Black Giovanni is dead. We just pulled out their fucking heart it's just a matter of time that I can crush the whole group of them Chain gang Niggas. I went back to my office and told Black Duke I need to make some calls. He replied, "cool if you need me, I'll be in the back." He got up and close the door behind himself. I quickly pulled out my phone and called Jane Doe the phone rings three times after she picked up.

"Hey what's up Almasi?"

"Yo, what's up girl look I need for you to come in and holla at me I have a job for you to do for me."

"Sure, when you want me to come?"

"Meet me at Mookie's club tonight in his office, okay."

"Cool, I'll be there around 12:30 okay."

"Sounds good to me I see you there. Moja One!" Soon as I hung up with Jane Doe, I quickly call my boo Jay to give him the good news. He picks up on the first ring and asked, "hey baby is everything good?"

"Yeah everything is lovely."

He chimed in Swahili, "**Nadhani mstari huu umepigwa angalia kile unachosema upendo** *I think this line is tapped watch what you say love.*"

178

I replied, "**Sawa Nakusikia** *Okay I hear you!* "

"But, it still really good to hear your voice, baby."

"I just call to tell you that Boom is dropping the baby past the house while they go out for a little while." That's all *a real quick lie for anybody that's listening in on the fucking call.* "Okay, that will be cool he's a real good baby. Look I have to go. I have to take care of something." I talk to you later on at the house. Love you, good-bye."

"Love you too bye."

I hit the button hanging up thinking to myself one of them guys that Jay is working with is a fucking snitch. Black Duke came knocking on my door I waved for him to come in. "I just looked up on the cameras in the back EL Barero and three of his men is coming up to the front door."

I announced, "he's cool but he usually calls me before he come go tell Bango and Jamel to walk them back here to my office." I sit back and wait a few minutes past and they walked them to the door.

I get up and hug EL Barero, "what's up, big man?"

I bump fist with Mister Pete his right-hand man, Butter and some dark skin curly head dude I never seen before. EL Barero introduced him, "this is Montaga." I bump fist with him last.

"What's up? Good to see y'all. Please have a seat. How can I help y'all today?"

EL Barero spoke quickly, "look, I wanted to call you before I came, but I think somebody is listening to us on the phones."

"I just was talking about that with my man Jay. He told me not to talk on the phone because I was going to tell him that Black Giovanni is dead.*" What I notice is that the dude Montaga is real fucking nervous after I said that. and I don't know why.*

EL Barero commented, "word that's some good news for us but I came to tell you is that the Zulu's are not really down with us."

"Yeah, when y'all found out about this shit?"

EL Barero raised his voice, "show her the video Pete"

Mister Pete stands up handed me his phone and announced, "Mikey Zulu was acting funny for the last few months, so I put Marco on his ass, and he got this last night."

I'm looking at it and Its John Knotty Big Cyus, Mikey Zulu and Derick Zulu all smiles drinking, laughing and talking to one another in the club. I'm looking at it and my reaction was, "wow them Niggas was playing me this whole time." I cut it off and I hand the phone back to Mister Pete.

EL Barero raised, "I'm thinking they were cool too we were the ones that put them Niggas on. Now they stop taking our shipments too. Do you know who's their new plug?"

"I think it might be the Mexicans. Soon as they stop taking the shipments y'all should have let me know."

"How long ago they did not take it?"

"Only last month *but he cuts his eyes over at Montaga.*"

Now I know what is going on now this motherfucker is the one who fucked up and he's bringing him here to show me the one who did it. These Niggas know all of our shit we have to switch all that shit up today.

"I already did it Almasi. I'm just finding out about this myself I been so busy as you know we have a really big operation now thanks to you. So, I'm here to tell you soon as I found out baby girl."

"Well, thank you my friend but now I have to make a move on them like right now. "

EL Barero replied, "and so do I Ma!"

When I looked up Mister Pete stood up behind the dude Montaga with a gun with a silencer on it **Pooouuufff! Pooouuufff! Pooouuufff!** His lifeless body falls to the floor then a pool of blood started gushing out of his head on the floor. Wow that's how you take care of fucking business.

EL Barero stood up and soften his tone, "I'm so sorry about this, Almasi. I grew up with this guy and he's been down with me for years I treated him like my real brother. I never knew he was the one who was going to cross me cutting a deal with the fucking Zulus!"

Mister Pete chimed in, "Vegas is the one who told us about him so we had him followed every day at the end of the video you will see him meeting with them too."

"I'll clean this up sorry for the mess, but we had to do this like this to show you we still down with you."

"No, I got this." I stand up I get my satellite phone and I walk out the office waving my hand for my people to come. I tell Crazy Jamel Blood Eye and Poochie sitting on the couch. They jump up, "I need for y'all stay here with him to stay on post and don't let nobody in here!"

I pointed at Bango, Stomp, Yokey, Jimmy Goon waving my hand for them to follow me. They all walked in looking down at the body on the floor face down in a pool of blood. I point my hand and announce, "clean this up for me please fellas and get rid of the body too. Fucking piece of shit."

I looked up at EL Barero with a smirk he smiles back at me. I told EL Barero, Butter and Mister Pete we can finish talking in my conference room.

"Come on" I waved my hand for them to follow me. Black Duke came walking up in front of me and asked, "what happen?"

I answered, "EL Barero was just showing me that one of these foul ass motherfuckers who tried to cross me that's al.l They took care of it brother just make sure they clean that shit up in my office and get rid of the body the right way for me Duke okay."

"Yeah, you know me I'm on it, Almasi."

The four of us walked to my conference room they all were looking around and impress with the setup of my conference room.

"Please have a seat gentleman." They all sat down still looking around. I looked at all of them and asked, "what y'all know about Fentanyl?"

EL Barero replied, "that's the shit a lot of these, motherfuckers are mixing the heroin with to make them come back. But the only thing about that is when you put the Fentanyl with the heroin is that's all they want after you mix that shit with it."

"Okay!"

I get the satellite phone Coyote gave me and I called up Jagger the phone rings about four times before he picks up and answered, "what's up **Malkia** *Queen?* "

"You **Kaka** *Brother!*"

181

"Look, I need for y'all to hit the Zulu's with everything y'all got tonight. Yeah, we can do that you want any souvenirs."

"Yeah, I want Mikey Zulu's fucking head in a hat box. "

"Done! Say no more Moja *One!*"

I looked at EL Barero, "you can join in on the fun if you want to its up to you, brother."

He started laughing, "I think they got it. I know for sure them Niggas is good as dead."

He gives me a high five chuckling, and I ask, "y'all want a drink?" He looked up still laughing replying, "sure, do you have any Tequila around here, Ma."

"Sure, I do Nigga. I pick up the satellite phone and call Black Duke. He picks up on the first ring I asked, "yo Duke, bring me a bottle of Tequila from the back for me, please." "You got it, Almasi!"

Just a few minutes later Black Duke came with a bottle of Tequila with a big smile on his face. He came in the conference room handing it to me and he's ready to walk back out.

I asked, "where the fuck you are going at Nigga? This is a celebration with my family over here fuck that! You can go check in on them Niggas after we do this toast."

I reach down in the desk by the water cooler getting a whole sleeve of red cups handing each one them one Mister Pete, Butter, EL Barero, Black Duke and myself. I open the bottle up and I started pouring everybody some a real nice size shot. After I was done, I put my cup up in the air cheering, "this is to the birth of the GMMC!"

EL Barero asked, "what does that stand for Ma?"

"It stands for the Giant money-making conglomerate!"

He , "shit, I like that Almasi!"

I replied, "this is a toast to the GMMC. BSN is dead!"

We all tap our cups together and drank down the big shot of Tequila fast. Everybody making that face after drinking it down.

I announced, "who ever got the worm I want it!"

Mister Pete , "well, here you go Ma- Ma have fun with it!" As he pours it in my cup, and I drink it down fast looking up at everybody laughing and all of them started cheering.

EL Barero asked, "do you know where you going to get the Fentanyl from?"

"I have a couple people I can holla at."

I put up my finger and I called Tanya she picks up "hey what's up, Almasi?" "Look, I need for you and Gino to go get all new phones. Get my son Little Boom and Booby Hill and his peoples to help you, okay. I need this done today my son know where all the new phones are at. In the warehouse at my phone store in center city."

"Okay, Almasi. I'm on that right now."

"Good, call me back after your done so I can have all the new numbers."

"**Moja** *One!* "

"**Moja!** "

EL Barero looked up at me and stood up, "well, I hate to drink and run but were going to get the hell out of here and let you get back to work Ma."

"Okay, brother how is your Spanish going?"

"**Estoy muy bien con eso ahora senorita mealgera que preguntes.** *I'm really good with it now young lady. I'm glad you ask.*"

"Oh yeah, you are getting really good with your Spanish. I know your aunt Rose is proud of you brother."

"Yes, she is, and I love it."

I hug him as we both giggled while I play punch him with his large belly jiggling up and down. We both have big bright smiles on our faces then I bump fist with Butter, and Mister Pete.

Showing them to the door, "let me walk y'all to the door." I watch them jump in their truck and waved as they drove off. I went back inside closing the front door fast with the cold wind blowing hard outside. I quickly walked back to the conference room until they finish cleaning up my office up from them smoking that no-good motherfucker who tried to cross me scraping his brains from off my floor. I'm sitting at the long table I lit up a cigarette I didn't even get to puff on it really good when I get this text message. **Bing!** I looked up at it quickly holding the phone up and I see this black bitch with

183

her head chopped off with this big white hairy hand holding her from her hair. I'm sitting their tripping because I don't recognize who it is. At the bottom of the picture it says you're going to be just like this bitch really soon. I called up Black Duke he picks up on the first ring, "what's up, Almasi?"

"Look come back here right quick. I have something to show you."

He quickly came inside the conference room announcing, "your office is all clean up now you can go in there if you want it's all good now."

"Good walk with me to my office so I can show you this bull shit!"

We walk to my office I looked around, "damn those Niggas work fast."

"I know we trained their ass really good, Ma."

We both laughed as I walked inside, I told Black Duke, "close that door behind you please."

Black Duke sat down next to me as I hold up the phone so he can see it.

He stares at it hard, "looks like somebody is threating you, Ma. We're going have to get to the bottom of this shit ASAP. But I have one question doe Almasi."

"What's that?"

"Who is this bitch?"

"The fuck if I know she looks a little familiar, but I just can't put my finger on the shit. I'm sitting here tripping my ass off for real."

"What is this motherfucker threating you?"

"Oh, hell no, you have to bring ass to kick ass. You don't know me by now Nigga!"

"On who the bitch is with her head chopped the fuck off and what the fuck it has to do with me that's why."

"Yeah but were going have to still lock shit down like you always say don't underestimate no body in this fucked up game. There are your own words, Almasi."

"Your right Nigga, I'll make some calls."

"Yeah like right now, I'll wait."

"What Nigga who you talking to?"

"I'm talking to you I'm here to make sure you walk out of here alive every fucking day. So, you can call up Ty- Kim, Willie Whack-Whack and Nails Nathan right about now."

I looked up at him I was pissed off at him, but I picked up the phone and called Willie Whack-Whack on my satellite phone. I roll my eyes at Black Duke but he didn't pay me any mine he was cool looking up at me with his arms folded like he was my father or something. I told Willie Whack- Whack to holla at Nails for me too I need to talk to him about what's going on right now. Then I called Ty-Kim and Chrome and told them what was going on too. After I hang the phone up, I looked up at Black Duke not saying a word he asked, "now was that hard Nigga?

I just started giggling bumping fist with him , have a drink with me motherfucker until they get here."

So, I pulled out my bottle of gin from my bottom desk draw and two red cups pour us a big shot with no ice.

"Okay, one drink after that we have to lock this joint down. Look, don't let this bull shit fuck your day up, Ma."

"Yeah, your right but I have to meet up with Jane Doe at Mookie's club tonight."

"No!"

He's waving his hands up in the air at me, "call her back and tell her to meet you at the penthouse that way you have plenty of security around you. I'll set it all up that way you'll be safe."

"You are right." I quickly called Jane Doe and I told her things changed up.

"I need for you to meet me at the penthouse." She was cool with that and I hung up.

I point to his drink, alright Duke now drink up, Nigga!"

"Man, you pour a lot of fucking gin in here shit!" He gups it down and he stood up and slam the glass on the table, "alright, it's time to get back to work I'll make sure to let you know when everybody gets here, Ma."

I replied, "okay." I really wanted him to sit with me so we can bull shit some more and snort a little coke as well. He was right it was time to get back on my fucking game. I can't lie I was a little high, but I know I can still get all of my shit done just long as I don't get fucked up, I'm good. Soon as he went out the door, I called up Damon Gee so he can help me figure who the hell was this on this fucking crazy ass text somebody sent me. The phone rings about five times before this Nigga picked it up, I answered, "yo, what's up Gee!"

"Hey, what's up boss lady?"

"Look some crazy motherfucker sent me a text with this black bitch head chopped off saying I'm going to be like this bitch real soon."

"Oh yeah, I'm on my way right now **Moja** *One!*" The minute I hung up Black Duke came walking in the door with Willie Whack-Whack asking, "what's up sis? What the fuck is going on?"

I can see in his dark grill he was really concern about this shit and knowing this Nigga *he will kill everything in his path if someone is fucking with me.* As Black Duke close the door and sat down next to me. Willie Whack- Whack quickly pulls up a chair and pointed to the phone, "let me see this fucking text!"

I sat up in my chair and I hands it to him he looked at it and yelled, "I know this bitch!" "Yeah, who the fuck is she Willie?"

"Man, that's the bitch we did the Russian hit with at that fancy ass hotel in New Jersey. Her name is Tajae'. Damn, that ho bitch could suck a Dick!" He hands me back my phone.

"Okay, now we know it's the fucking Russians and were going have to dig right back in their ass again."

Willie Whack- Whack replied , "well, we still got something for their ass and were stronger now."

"You're right." We bump fist giggling I asked, "where the fuck is Nail's at Willie?"

He replied, "he's on his way I'll call him to find out where he's at."

I , "hold up use this right here. I think someone is listening to our calls."

"Oh yeah, so what you're doing about that shit?"

"I'm on it right now. I got my son and Tanya on that as we speak."

"Okay, good." He called and the phone rings about six times than his wife Catrina picks the phone up crying,

Willie asked, "what's the matter, Catrina?" She is crying, then she started crying some more saying in a broken voice, "Nathan is dead!"

"What?"

"Yeah, he was getting in his car to meet you and this tall white dude with long hair came up and started shooting him. I had to take cover getting on the floor with the kids. Look, I have to call you back Willie it's the police."

Willie hands the phone back to me with tears in his eyes and announced, "Nails is dead!" "What?"

"Yeah, his wife Catrina told me some tall white dude with long hair came up on him in his whip and shot him up." He stood up and quickly grabbed the half of bottle of gin from off my desk. He started drinking right out of the bottle.

Black Duke replied, "looks like the fucking Russians is making their move on us."

Willie Whack- Whack past the bottle to Black Duke he didn't want to drink but he did it for his friend taking a swig hugging him. Bango came tapping on the office door and announced, "Ty- Kim and Chrome is here. They both walked in the office Bango close the door back as they both walked in with Ty-Kim looking over at Willie crying asking,

"what the fuck happened?"

I looked up at him and softly announced, "Nails Nathan is dead."

"Wow, y'all know who did it?" *I can see he's really pissed off about this shit.* I told him, "the Russians did it after I called you. Willie came in here and ID the bitch in the picture text. I got on my phone he told me it was that bitch Tajae we used to pull the shit off to do the hit on the Russians. Ty- Kim so their hitting us for some pay back then."

187

Chrome chimed in, "well that guy we killed was not just some ordinary Russian gangster he was the top man in their outfit here on the east coast so it going to be some pay back." Willie Whack-Whack jumped in and commented, "yeah but were going have to find out who this fucking hit man is and kill him, "Where is Damon Gee at? He can find out more shit with all the peoples he knows out there in the streets so we can take care of this motherfucker with the quickness!"

"He's on his way I called him after I talked to y'all."

Then Tanya came knocking on the door walking in with a large black Nike gym bag she bumps fist with me. She speaks to everybody in the room asking, "what happen?"

She put the bag on my desk. I look at her and announce, "Nails Nathan just got killed."

"Oh, shit that's fucked up he was a good man. I loved all of his stories about back in the days when y'all was coming up. I'm going to miss his ass."

"Is my son with you?"

"Yeah him and Booby Hill and his brother Ticky is in the truck."

"Where is Gino at?" I made him stay at the warehouse with the young boys to keep an eye on them. We have too much shit up in there to leave them alone you know what I'm saying."

"How many phones you got here?"

"60 in the bag. I gave everybody else their phones and here is the list of numbers with their names next to the numbers."

"Okay, good go tell them to meet me in the conference room in five minutes for me please."

Tanya walks out of the office and I began to talk to everyone in the room.

"I need for all of you to talk to your peoples and let them know what's going on. I'm going to talk to my son Booby Hill and his brother Ticky so they be in the loop on these fucking Red fellas okay."

I reached in my pocketbook getting my zip up bag of blow I set it on the desk. I pulled out a small round mirror and another bottle of gin I got back up from out the drawer. I looked at Willie who look sad about his friend and crime partner. I dump out a large pile of the coke on top of the mirror. Ty- Kim pulls out a twenty dollar bill out his pocket rolling it up handing it to Willie. He took it from his hands slowly and started snorting the coke from off the mirror along with Ty- Kim and me. I get a nice buzz,

"I'll be right back let me go holla at these Niggas okay." They all just nodded their heads as I walked to the conference room. It's my son Little Boom, Ticky, Booby Hill and Gee Dawg Booby Hill's top hatchet man.

There all sitting down I speak to all of them. I come and hug my son, "look, I need for y'all to keep your eyes open because were under attack again with these Russian assholes' looking for some get back on us. And I wanted to tell each one of you I love the way y'all stepped up with the Columbian thing jump off. I'm going to give y'all a bonus. I'm going into another business and I'm going to need your crew to work with Puerto Rican Joe and his peoples."

Little Boom asked, "so what is this new business your talking about mom?"

"Fentanyl."

"Yeah, your right that's what taking over the streets right now I have a contact for that. Who is it and who do you have mind?"

"This Chinese cat name Tiger Mi he's in the Triads he's away buying a lot of phones off of me."

"The Chinese mob okay set it up Boom. I trust you baby I just want to hear some good numbers on that shit."

All of them started giggling *I can see Gee Dawg talking low than elbowing my son. I'm just playing it off like I don't see it.*

"So, when are we going to get that bonus you were talking about mom?"

" I'll have Tanya bring it to you today after everybody make all their drops let me call Carlo Cash and see what's up." I make the call Carlo picks up really fast and he greeted me, "well hello Boss lady! How can I help you today?"

"Everybody just got done you need something."

"Yeah, get your boy Bubbles to drop off ten bands at my office."

"Sure, thing boss lady it will be there in one hour."

"Thanks Carlo **Moja** *One!*"

"Moja!"

I looked up at my son and announced, "one hour make sure y'all wait for it right here." Bango came knocking on the door than he came in and asked, "Rah- Killer is here to see you."

"Okay I'm coming." I wave my hand at all of them and winking my eye at them before I rolled out the door. I'm walking with Bango to my office Rah- Killer is in the office hugging and talking with Willie, Ty- Kim and Black Duke consoling one another. I came in the door asking, "what's up with you, sis?"

She came over hugging me replying, "man, I heard what happen and I came right here that's fucked up."

"Who told you?"

"Dun- D anounced, "he's on his way look I need to holla at you alone, please Almasi." "You and me, can step into the lady's room so we can talk."

We both walked out my office into the lady's bathroom not too far from my office.

"Look, I came to ask you if I can go to Las Vegas with Fly Ty."

"Well right now I need you to be working with Black Duke, Lou-Lou and X if I can bring up some more people as good as you than I'll give you my blessing."

"So how long you think that will take?"

I don't know I'm still getting hit from all sides from the Columbians, the fucking Zulu's done cross me and now this Russian ass hole is running around here killing our peoples too."

"How about if I do something big for you."

"Yeah that will work for me."

"Who is it and who do you have in mind?

"John Knotty if you knock him off for me then you can go to Las Vegas with Fly Ty and be his number two with some loot in your pocket as well."

"Okay I can do that you know me, girl."

"Well, get that done for me and you can roll out. Listen, if you cross me you know what happens, right."

"Yes, I do I'll never do that, Almasi."

"Okay, I'm just letting you know Rah."

"You should know by now that's not in my fucking make up!" I just looked at her not saying a word.

"Let me get in there with the boys and finish bull shittin with them you don't have to worry. I'm going to get that done for you."

I hugged her and we both walked out the bathroom were both puffing on are New ports like a train going down a fucking track. We both go in my office talking shit with the crew when Dun- Dun and Damon Gee came and we all had good wild ass Nails Nathan stories laughing are ass off. Carlo man Bubbles came dropping off the bonus I told them they would get they were all happy. At five on the dot I got the fuck out of there I had Blood Eye and Poochie take me to the penthouse. I called Jay to let him know I was coming home late. I also told him about what happen to Nails Nathan. Just as my old man Jay got in his car to go home the feds rolled up on him and locked him up soon as they put the cuffs on him his secretary Teresa called me. Soon as we arrived at the penthouse, I'm sitting at a large bar filled with chatter, smoke and hard beats flowing out the speakers.

I knew the number because Jay always call me from his car shop, I pick up the phone thinking it's him calling me back. I asked, "what you forgot to tell me something, baby."

She replied, "this is not Jay this is Teresa the feds just arrested Jay and five others of his workers here at the shop, They didn't lock me up because they I had nothing to do with the indictment they had on the others."

"What get the fuck out of here!"

CUTTING THE HEART OUT OF THE CHAIN GANG NIGGAS

"Well, thank you Teresa. Are you all right?"

"Yes, I'm okay just a little shook up that's all, Almasi."

"Did they shut the shop down?"

"No, they just took them out of here that's all what do you want me to do?"

"I want you to close up for right now and you're going to run the shop while he's in jail okay."

"Me, run the shop."

"Yes, you're going to run the shop while he's away. I'm going to send my son Little Boom and Carlo Cash to help you, so you got nothing to worry about. Jay will be home soon as I know what's going on alright, Teresa."

"I know you can do it. I'll call you tomorrow and let you know what's going on okay just go home and chill out."

"Okay Almasi, I'll talk to you tomorrow, goodbye."

Soon as I hung up with her. I turn to Dun-Dun, sitting right next to me at, the bar with a drink in his hand and a blunt in his other hand talking shit.

I announced, "Jay just got knocked by the fucking feds. His secretary Teresa just called me and told me."

"What?"

"Yeah, it just happened I have to call Mitch to find out what his bail is if they do give it to him." I make the call Mitch picks up after three rings.

"Yo, what's up Mitch?"

"Hey what's up Almasi? What's up with you?"

"Look the feds just locked up my man Jay. I need you to go see what his bail is so I can get him the fuck up out of there okay."

"Sure, I'm on it right now Almasi. I'll call you to let you know if they set bail for him or not goodbye."

Soon as I hung up with the lawyer Mitch Mookie came walking up with Jane Doe and her crew, I bump fist with all of them.

Mookie whispers in my ear, "your mom Dotty is dead, and the cops want you to come down to the 17th district and answer a few questions for them." *He just looks at me with his eyes getting wide.*

"Oh yeah, well there going have to fucking wait the feds just locked Jay up."

"Get the fuck out of here! Did you call Mitch?"

"Yeah, I just got off the phone with him let me holla at Jane Doe right quick I have some shit for her to do."

"Okay, but if you need me, I'll be here and let me know before I split, sis."

"I will **Ndugu** *(brother)." I wave Jane Doe over towards me.* Jane Doe told her people to stay back as she came and sat next to me, "what's up, girl?"

"I'm good what's up with you. I heard the good news about Black Giovanni being dead what the next move Ma."

I answered, "I want you to pull the heart right out of the fucking Chain gang right about now. Remember when you told me your really close to John Knotty sister name Bryah."

"Yeah, I can link up with her tonight." *She looks at me with wide eyes and a smirk on her grill puffing on her cigarette looking up at me.*

"Yeah, link up with her tonight and give her some new travel plans to fucking ghetto heaven for me, please."

"I sure can girlfriend that's a done deal."

"And I really do want to bring me her fucking heart too Jane I want you to cut it right out her fucking chest too."

"You got it, Almasi. I have to tell you something too."

"Yeah what's that Jane?"

"Your Lawyer Mitch is working with that Nigga Bookey that down with the chain gang so watch you back around him."

"How you know this shit?"

"He doesn't know me when I was out with my man Saggy, I seen him eating with Bookey's wife Dana at that fancy ass joint on top of the fucking comcast building. I told you I know all them Niggas because I use to fuck with Crazy Pauile before I was down with BSN. He got locked up and join them in jail him and Bookey was road Dawgs and crime partners."

"Okay thanks Jane. I can't lie when Damon told me you wanted to come back into the fold, I wanted to kill you I was wrong about you. I'm sorry."

"You don't have to apologize Jasper had me all fucked up for real like I told you I don't blame you. Look I want you to get ready for Canada I want you to run shit there after I plan my flag out that bitch."

"Yeah, I would love that shit, Almasi. When is that jumping off?"

"I'm setting it up first of the year so that's in another week or so after I give you the green light. I'm need for you to put your big girl panties on and boss the fuck up like I know you should."

We both started laughing. "I just send that fucking fat ass motherfucker Mitch to see about Jay's bail about a couple hours ago."

"Look to show you I'm not lying about this motherfucker watch he say it no bail for him and he's going want you to meet him or some shit like that watch what I'm telling you Ma."

"He's trying to set you up don't go for the bull shit. He's a fat ass snake take care of his ass right away Almasi."

"Don't roll out yet I'm going to call up my other lawyer Tony Garcia right quick and send him to bail out Jay."

"Yo Jane, you ever seen Tony before?"

"No, only Jimmy and Mitch when we have to bail Niggas out."

"Girl, this man is fucking fine good thing I'm hooked up with Jay and I'm a loyal bitch because this Nigga can get some for sure." We both start giggling like young ass schoolgirls. I show her a picture of him on my phone.

Jane , "oh your right he is one hunk of a fucking man girl. My man Saggy would break my neck just looking at that motherfucker." We both started giggling as I make my call to my lawyer Tony Garcia,

I told him to get with Carlo Cash to get the loot to bail my man out and to bring him here where I'm at in the penthouse. After I was done talking with Jane Doe, she she was rolling out to take care of that shit I wanted her to do. Dun- Dun came back over to me and asked, "did you hear anything yet on Jay?"

I replied, "no, not yet." I told him to call Tanya over to me I need to holla at her for me please.

Tanya came over to me real smooth I told her to sit down please she sat down with a cooler in her hand and a cigarette cocked in her thick lips. I asked, "do you think your young boys is ready to put in some real work?"

Tanya replied, "that's all they been waiting on is the call Almasi."

I , "okay after I bail out Jay and go to South Philly and talk to the cops, I need for them to take care of Mitch fat ass for me."

"Yeah that sounds good I'm get them on standby right now if you want."

"Yeah do that for me baby girl show them what he looks like and smoke his fat ass tonight."

"You got it, Ma. I'm on top of that shit."

"Now what's up with you have to go talk to the cops?"

"My ass hole of a so-called crackhead mother was killed, and they think I did It, I guess I really don't give a fuck I have an alibi for that shit."

Tanya started laughing making the call to Big De Shawn and his crew. I'm sitting back waiting on the news about Jay two hours later my phone rings its Mitch I quickly hit the button and asked, "what's up Mitch? You get him out."

"No, I'm really sorry they it's no bail for him at this time look I might can talk to one of the judges I know can we meet up tonight?"

I replied, "yeah, but after I go to South Philly to talk to the cops."

"About what, Almasi?"

"My mother Dotty was killed, and they want to talk to me about it."

"Do you need me to go with you or something?"

Almasi 2
Queen of The Streets
By Dartanya A. Williams Sr.

"I can meet you at your house right quick."

I replied, "No, I got Tony Garcia for that Mitch I'll call you when I come from South Philly alright. Sure, thing but I could have taken, care of that for you Almasi."

"No, I'm good I'll call you soon as I'm coming out of the police station all right."

I hang up the phone looks like I done fucked up his plans for setting me up for funky ass Dotty's murder. Soon as I go to meet him, he plans the gun in my house, and he call the cops on My black ass I don't think so.

Two hours later. Then I looked up and I see my boo Jay walking with Tony Garcia I jumped up from the bar right into Jays arms, "I'm so glad to see you baby. Are you all right?"

We started kissing I suddenly stopped, and I bumped fist with Tony "thank you so much!"

"You know I got you Almasi."

"Would you like a drink or something Tony?" *Waving his arms in the air with a smile on his handsome dark face.*

"No, I'm good let me know when you ready to go to the police station with you."

Jay looks at me and asked, "police station for what?"

"Look my crackhead mother Dotty got killed and they think I have something to do with it."

"Wow, I know you didn't like her, but I know dam well you didn't kill her ass."

"I'll tell you all about it on the way there these motherfuckers are trying to set me up with her murder."

"Who's that baby? Come on I'll tell you on the way." I stand up walking over and wave Poochie and Blood Eye over letting them know I'm ready to roll. I toss the keys to Poochie, "you're driving, Blood Eye your, going inside with me when we get there. your one of my eight alibis."

He just nodded his head and walked outside with us to my whip soon as we got outside, I told Tony to lead the way were right behind him. Popping up from one the car's in the parking lot is some shadowy figures all I see is the muzzle flash from a machine gun **Kactacka rata tat tat tat!**

Jay jump on top of me. Tony my lawyer ducked down in his car Poochie and Blood Eye quickly ducked down, but they were returning fire at the same time spitting hot shit. **Kapacka! Kapacka! Kapacka! Boom! Boom! Boom!** I'm trying to get up pulling my pistol from the back of my jeans.

Jay is yelling at me to stay down all I see is sparks and muzzle flash spitting Jay is pulling me under the car holding his gun. When I looked up, I see Dun- Dun, Mookie, Ty- Kim, Tanya Gats, Black Duke, Jimmy Goon, Crazy Jamel, Stomp, Bango, Yokey, Chrome, Damon Gee and Willie Whack- Whack with their guns and machine guns running out shooting at the men who came at us the men started running away fast. *I'm thinking to myself why they would try to get me knowing that I got all these people to protect me it like a fucking suicide mission.* I yelled out to everybody to run it's a fucking trap of some kind run! Everybody started running and **Kaboom!** One of the cars in the parking lot exploded near us. Then another car blew up behind us just missing us **Kadoom!** And another one in front of us **Boom!** Me and Jay ran clear of the explosions two more cars blew up **Kaboom! Kaboom!** My heart is racing looking around to see who else made it with the thick black smoke and flames shooting up in the air. I looked up I see Tanya then I see Dun- Dun, Jimmy Goon Willie Whack- Whack, Damon Gee, Ty- Kim and Crazy Jamel. I don't see Black Duke and my lawyer Tony Garcia, Yokey, Mookie or Stomp.

I asked, "Jay where the fuck is Duke?"

"I don't know baby I hope he made it."

Running out the from all the flames and black smoke behind him is Bango then I see Black Duke on fire Me, Blood Eye and Poochie and Jay run over to him taking off our coats putting out the flames.

All I Can Think About is Payback on a Nigga's Ass

I'm on my knees looking down at him he's all burned up and he took his last breath. He died right in front of all our faces. The fire men where there about 15 minutes later to put out the fires. The ass hole fucking cops came about twenty minutes later asking us questions up the ass. Most of my crew got the hell out of there and the rest of us who did stay Me, Jay, Poochie, Blood Eye Damon Gee and Chrome put away our guns and shit in the after math. Black Duke, Yokey, Stomp, Tony Garcia and Mookie were all dead.

Meanwhile at the same time Jagger and his crew along with some Niggas from S.O.S. Patty Racks, Fat Jacob, Ron Gucci, Donzilla and Chaz Money.

They all arrived at the Zulu's brown stone joint on Diamond street. Their dressed in all black with bullet proof vest and black mask toting machine guns. Its Jagger, Flip Diddy Patty Racks and Fat Jacob is on the right-hand side of the door. Steve Swiga and Gun Ho Moe, Chaz Money and Ron Gucci is on the left and the back door is Little Bay- Bay, Frank Iilly and Donzilla. They all have on earpieces radio set on with Jagger screaming, everyone is listening to him, **"Moshi kila kitu kinachotembea** *Smoke everything moving." Gun Ho Moe yelled,* **"Wacha Tuan glie** *Let's Rock!"* **Kadoom!** *Flip Diddy rushing in after they blew the door off the fucking hinges.*

Jagger is right by his side on the right Patty Racks, Steve Swiga, Fat Jacob, Ron Gucci and Gun Ho Moe on the left they came in their guns blazing mowing everything down that was moving. Along with Donzilla, Frank Iilly and Little Bay- Bay coming in the back door, then working their way up the steps it was a bloody mess. Until they all reach the top. They wipe out the whole house in less than twenty minutes the Zulu's never knew what hit them. Jagger could not find a hat box, after he cut his head off, so he put Mikey Zulu head in a Dog Food bag. He did put a trash bag over it for it leaking blood. When he brought it to me, I put it in my freezer and the only good thing was that Reggie Zulu Jay's cousin was out of town when it all went down. I'll have a lot shit to explain to him about when I had all of them killed.

Plus, he didn't know about Mikey Zulu setting us up when we got there or we both would have been dead. Mikey Zulu knew if he would have told him he would not been down with that shit. I found out later that Derick Zulu was also out of town when the shit went down, he ran right to the FBI.

*With all that shit going on Jane Doe was hanging out with that girl Bryah and her so called bodyguards Fat Nick and Boo-Boo trusted Jane Doe. After they hung out all night smoking and drinking and having a good time. They drop them off in front of Bryah's house there both drunk as Boo-Boo and Fat Nick is parking the car soon as Bryah when to open the door. **Boom! Boom! Boom!** Jane Doe pulled out her Glock nine and shot Bryah in the back of her head three time making sure she was dead. She wanted to cut her heart out like I told her to do but she didn't have time to do it. The two so called bodyguards jump out the car looking around for Jane Doe she was gone in the darkness.*

After a real bloody night, we had four of my men dead and my new lawyer on top of it. I never seen that shit coming those fucking Russian ass holes got us real good plus we spent six hours in the police station with Jake funky ass answering questions about what happen that night. The only good thing was when me and Jay got home Tanya did send them young boys who wanted to get put on took care of that Mitch backstabbing ass and the Zulu's are all dead too. Me and Jay went to bed and got a few hours of sleep. Six that evening Aunt-Tee came banging on our bedroom door.

I woke up and asked, "what is it Aunt-Tee were trying to get some rest we been up most the fucking night because of the ass hole cops asking us a million and one questions.

Aunt-Tee replied, "I'm sorry baby, but it's the police they need to talk to you." "Okay, I'll be out in a few minutes."

"Okay, I'll tell them."

Jay sat up in the bed looking at me and asked, "you want me to come with you?"

"No baby you wait here I can handle this shit you got enough to fucking worry about."

"I do, but I want to be with you when you talk to these ass holes."

"I'm good baby just sit back when you go back to court?"

"In three months from now I'm going to need a good lawyer."

"Don't worry you will have one of the best that money can buy, handsome."

He giggles I kiss him putting on my house coat and Jay smacks me on the ass as I walk towards the door quickly. I came out with a straight face I was really pissed off, but I held my real feelings back looking at these two sell out Niggas. I really hate these two- homicide detectives Darrell Johnson and his partner detective Karim Towns. Two Niggas with a badge it isn't nothing worst then a Nigga with a little power.

"Yes, how can I help you two today?"

Detective Johnson smirked, "well if it isn't our Favorite dope dealer Sharonda Miller. Oh, my bad Almasi Glock Mommy. Both men began laughing in my face.

I barked, "oh you better watch what you say to me Nigga. The last cops talking greasy to me did not get a chance to see the fucking new year."

Detective Johnson went to jump at me, but Poochie and Blood Eye step in front of him blocking his way. His partner detective Towns is pulling him back and snapped, "look here, bitch were not scared of you and your fucking low rent fucking thugs for hire, okay Where were you the other night between the hours of 10 and 11 O clock?"

"I was here at home."

Detective Johnson cut in, "can you prove that or anybody other than your paid goons can collaborate on that?"

"Yes, my husband to be."

Detective Towns , "that's not good enough he will lie for your no-good ass from the door!"

Detective Johnson chimed in, "why are we wasting our time here. Why don't we put the cuffs on this bitch and get it over with?"

I , "well, if you do you be wasting more time because my whole house has the best surveillance cameras equipment in the world. It will show that I was home when all that shit when down Nigga. Me and my lawyer will have a fucking field day with y'all ass in court! I don't think your raggedy ass department can afford to pay me with a two million-dollar lawsuit for harassment. So, you can go for it if you want to ass hole!"

Detective Johnson mimic my voice and asked, "can we look at that best in the world surveillance equipment than?"

"You really must be out your fucking mind not without a fucking warrant, Nigga! Now if you're not going to lock me up you can get the fuck out of my house right about now!" Detective Towns , "okay, were going to leave but I wanted to tell you they found one your flunky ass lawyer Mitch dead this morning. What you know about that? And where were you at?"

"You already know I was in the police station for six fucking hours. Why even ask me that shit?"

Detective Johnson pointed his finger and smirk, "well, it looks like your running out of fucking lawyers like your running out of men too! I want you to look at our faces really good because were the ones who is going to be taking your black ass down!"

I didn't say a word I just let them go out the door. I was pissed off all I could think about is some pay back on that ass. *I didn't know Jay was standing in the hallway watching the whole time with his gun behind his back, but he did not shoot them. I wish he did.*

Aunt-Tee La- Wadna came up grabbing me by my arms and told me, "come and let me make you something to eat. Fuck them Niggas."

I , "yeah, but I'm going to take care of them Niggas. You do know that shit, right?"

"I know but for right now I need for you to sit your ass in that chair over there and enjoy what I'm going to cook for you. And you Poochie and Blood Eye come sit y'all ass down while I make some coffee for y'all and something to eat!"

That's why I love Aunt-Tee lighting up the mood after dealing with some real ass hole cops coming at me like that. Before the new year came, I had to bury my friends it was sad each one of their wife's and girlfriends wanted different things for their love ones and I had to respect that. Black Duke one of my closest friends' wife Tya wanted a private thing and I paid for everything and she also wanted me to put her on so she can make her own money. So, I did but I told her the rules to everything. Yokey and Stomp had there funeral together. Mookie also had a private thing that's what La- Neesa wanted only thing with her was she wanted a lot of money even with her and I still being partners.

But I can see she's feeling some type of way about Mookie getting killed and I know she blames it all on me. Tony Garcia's woman Jenny hated me and told me not to come to his funeral and she would not take a dime of my money for his service. Two weeks when by faster than, you can blink your eyes. It's the first of the year and I had the sit down with the Haitians. Its January 2019. I took Dun- Dun Damon Gee and Jagger along with Blood Eye and Poochie with me to the sit down. We go to Toronto Canada Coyote takes us to this luxury building in downtown Toronto to meet up with Cougar Man the head of the Haitian gang called **Meute De loups** *meaning Wolf Pack in French.* We all go into this large room that was just off the hook. We all sit at this long table all of us sit on the left-hand side of the large beautiful room. Soon after Cougar man walks in with his large wild ass loud talking entourage, he's a tall dark skin dude not bad looking and his right-hand man name Vache that's French for Ox. This motherfucker is a giant but he's fucking ugly he only has a face a mother could love.

They all sit on the right-hand side of the long fancy ass wooden table. The, two of them came over towards me and the others shaking are hands and they quickly sat down. Cougar man gave me a look , "I heard you speak many languages."

"Just a few."

"Can you speak French?"

"I speak enough French that if you are talking shit about me, I know what you're talking about **Conduire** *Pimpin.*"

All of them started laughing that was the ice breaker. He , "I like that. Would y'all like something to drink? *He is pointing at two of the women in his large entourage.*

"Yes, I would like some beers for my boys and some Tangueray gin and bring us a lot of ice. I can drop on you 600 keys a month if you can handle it."

Cougar Man , "what 600 keys a month I would love that but I'm going to need more people to bag up all that shit."

"Not for nothing doe Cougar Man you have to step up your game and come up to the big leads. I got a lot of shit to sell brother and I think you're the man that can sling this shit." Vache chimed in, "when I was in New York I seen Niggas had drug factories with a bunch of women with nothing on bagging up drugs like a motherfucker."

"It was more than 50 or 60 of them not just 10 or 20 like we do."

I you're going to need about 70 or 80 people with that much heroin to bag. How soon can you drop off the dope? Next day air if you want? All of them started laughing.

"I can give you 600 keys at 20 a key will be 12,000,000."

"Are you sure you can do that Almasi?"

"Shit, I'm like Obama yes, we can!" They all started giggling and Cougar Man chimed in, "I like you so what's up with the cocaine 600?"

"No, 800."

Cougar Man , "oh shit! I'll give it to you at a good price 25,000 a key time 800 is 20,000,000. Most of the jet set crowd you have here want coke, so you get a lot more than the heroin.

"You know what I'm saying **Homme Cougar** *(French for Cougar Man)* **Allons chercher cet argent** *Let's get this money!*"

I spit a little French to his ass. They all burst out laughing. Cougar Man rubbed his hands together, "sounds good to me."

"Good, I can give you the whole thing upon delivery. All together that's 26,000,000."

His eyes widened and a big ass grin appeared on his face, "well I was hoping you would front me the heroin."

"Well if I do that it has to be the regular price at 27 or 28 a key that's still rock bottom prices shit in New York its 37 thousand a key."

"Now you're telling me if you front me the heroin its regular price, right?"

"Yes, that's the way I do business, brother."

"Now when I heard you was coming when Coyote told me about you, I'm thinking were going to have a real sweet deal here not pay regular price for anything."

Coyote stood up and raised his voice, "look I brought her here from Philly because you motherfuckers is paying more money for a bull shit product the product, she has. You will double your money back in less than a months' time because it the fucking best in the fucking world."

"So, you're wasting my fucking time here you guys have a piss poor product and you're just breaking even or you owe people for the shit your selling now if you don't make a deal here today you will stay fuckin broke." Vache is standing up like he was going to pull his pistol out of his jacket.

Coyote points at him , "if you're going to pull that shit out, I'll kill everything moving in this room. You better tell em Cougar Man. I will do it he doesn't fucking know me man."

"Yo Vache, go sit your ass down man!" Vache looks at him and then he looks at Coyote and he sits down. Cougar Man yeled at *Vache with the two women holding on to both his arms giggling and smiling.*

"What you trying to get all of us killed in here, Nigga. What's wrong with you! Okay "Coyote what do we do here to have common ground here, brother."

Me and Coyote huddled up for a few minutes and I finally speak, "okay here it is brother I'm going to front you the heroin, but you have to take more **Conduire** *(Pimpin)*. that way I get my money."

Cougar Man asked, "so how many keys do I have to take?"

"900 a month and no shorts each month or it will be tacked on after the end of the month."

"Now I can have my people come up here and help you bag all this shit up if you want me to."

Cougar Man replied, "yes, I would love that but not at the regular price mommy."

"Okay, I'll drop it down to 22 thousand for you."

"Okay, fuck it 20 thousand but you pay my peoples for bagging and have some where nice for them to live here."

"I can do that mommy, so we have a deal than right?"

"Yes, we have a deal."

Coyote jumped in, "I'll be on top of it. and if you don't meet up to your obligations with the people bagging shit or paying the money when it's dude you have to see me."

"So, what about the coke are you going to front that to me too?"

I answered, that's up to you but it's the same way you have to take more than 900 keys if I'm going to front it to you, If you don't pay us are money not only everything will stop Coyote will kill every last one of y'all. "

They already know not to fuck with Coyote when it comes to money. Vache came over to him and they were whispering to one another.

Then Cougar Man , "okay, this is what we're going to do we will take what you front us the heroin and the coke were going to pay for half and the rest when we get it. "

I , "okay, sounds like a deal to me."

Cougar man got up and walked over and shook hands with me. I asked, "where is my drink at Nigga?

He started laughing and so did the rest of his clique. We all had a good time eating laughing and drinking while we were there. The next stop is the sit down with the bikers, I know it's not going to be like this shit. *And I can't tell them about what kind of deal I'm going to cut with them* we all when back to the hotel after I cut the deal with the Meute De loups they don't know they will be working off that debt for a long time I get all them Niggas like that. When we got back to the hotel, I hit up Jay I missed him. I wish he could have come, but with him out on bail he could not leave the state. I told him everything went smooth and we brought out the whole floor so nobody could sneak the fuck up on us while were in Toronto. The next day Coyote call me asking, "that are meeting with the bikers is going to be out at this barn yard on the out skirts of Toronto. We had to start out a little early. I got myself together and I dressed warm because it was fucking cold there. I'm thinking it cold in Philly in the wintertime but up here it's like fucking ice station zebra up in this motherfucker.

I called everybody so they can be on point one thing I love about fucking with a lot of men they don't take all fucking day to get dressed like woman do. Poochie and Blood Eye came to my room first to get me then Coyote, Damon Gee, Jagger and Dun-Dun fell in and we all checked are guns and we rolled out at 11 A.M. on the dot. Coyote rides with me Poochie and Blood Eye with a truck we rented two trucks from the airport, but we had to take a private jet that way we can stay strapped the whole time. Damon Gee and Jagger road in the other truck. Poochie was driving with Coyote telling him how to get there and Damon Gee followed us all the way there. It took us about hour to get there and we were out in the fucking boom -docks like a motherfucker. We get there it's one road we ride up and eight bikers ride up on us stopping us right in the middle of the dirt road once we got off the highway. Two of the hairy ass dudes came walking up to the truck Poochie rolls the window down one of the straggly looking guys. Came up talking and introduce himself, "I'm Leather Neck. I'm the sergeant of arms I want you to follow me up to that barn over there. That's where Torch and all my other brothers will meet with you okay."

I replied, "okay just lead the way my man we will be right behind you." He looks all inside of the truck and they both go over to the other truck looking inside they jump back on their bikes waving for us to follow them up to the barn. I can see on one of their patches on his back and it read Metal Heads. The words were with a skull that's on fire in the middle of his leather jacket. On the bottom of it , Toronto we both ride inside of the barn and I see these men quickly closing the large barn doors. Then we see a bunch of bikes come riding up as we all get out the two trucks. We see them all standing on the left-hand side of the large space.

Coyote taps me on my arm, "come on just you the rest of y'all wait right here okay and don't move or act twitchy with these guys that will get us killed okay so be cool.

Me and Coyote walked up and its four guys are standing their they all hugged and shake hands with Coyote. I just stand there when he was done and he turned around and began to introduce me, "Torch this is Almasi. Almasi this is Torch the president of the Metal Head MC's."

He steps up shaking hands with me, "hi, you are doing."

"I'm good, Torch."

"Look, I told Coyote here we don't usually meet with black Mafia types, but he told me you are special, so I I'll meet with you."

I replied, "well that's good what is it you need because you would not meet with me unless you really needed something. I just might be that person to get it done."

"You want to know something I like that you get right to it no fucking four play."

"That what I do, my man."

"Okay, I need heroin and I need a shit load right now. What can you do about that?"

"Okay how many keys you need big man?"

"I need 300 keys to start with."

"You got the money we can talk big guy."

"Yeah, I got the money! What are you going to charge me for them Mommy?"

"Okay I'll charge you 20 a key so that's 6,000,000 dollars. You got that right now?

"I sure do, honey. Let me make a call."

I stepped to the side I pulled out my satellite phone and called Quan Kann.

I know his number by heart he picks up on the first ring, "hey, what's up girlfriend?"

"Hey home boy I need you?"

"Well, I'm good to go what you need girl. Only thing is I'm in Canada this time."

"So, I don't care if you are on the left coast it just takes a little longer but Canada, I can do it two hours but no more than 400 keys. I'm almost out to tomorrow, baby girl."

"Well hold the 400 and get it here to Toronto."

"Where?"

"Hold on."

I walked up to Torch and asked, "he's where?"

"Billy Bishop City airport."

Quan replied, "I hear him. I got a man there I can have it they're in one hour!"

I looked at him and announced, "he can have it they're in one hour."

"You mean to tell me he can have 300 keys of heroin in one hour?"

"No, that's 400 keys."

All of them raised their eyebrows and their mouths dropped opened.

Torch replied, "yeah, let's get it on!"

I replied, "good have your people there with the money. "

"What for 400 keys? I got enough for 300, Mommy."

I looked him in the face and answered, "you just owe me okay. Have the 6,000,000 their alright the past word is snowball."

"Yeah it will be their okay snowball!"

"Okay good, yo bring it Quan the password is snowball."

"Okay my people will have it there. I'll talk to you later."

"Thanks man. One!"

"You better be sending you people right now he's going to be there."

"Okay, yo Rock-O you go get the loot. Bob Wire and Bunky go with him the password is snowball." They jump on their bikes and ride off towards the left the other way with that loud sounds of them roaring out the door.

Torch walks back over to me, "I'm going to see if you that good black Mafia lady."

"I am and you will see Mister Biker man." he started laughing.

"I'll be in the truck with my peoples I'll wait until you get the call Torch."

"Okay, that's cool." Coyote winks his eye at me, and he goes on talking with him while he's bullshitting with them as other bikers come over as they gather together. I walked back to the truck with Jagger, Damon Gee, Blood Eye and Poochie.

Damon Gee asked, "what did he say?"

"He wanted 300 keys of heroin I got Quan to bring him 400 keys and they owe me on the rest of it he's bringing to Billy Bishop City airport."

"Okay were good he can get it their fast it not that far that motherfucker is one of the best." We all started laughing and we chit chat for a little while with one another an hour blaze passed, and Torch got the call.

He called out, "yo Almasi, come here for a minute please?" I winked my eye at all the guys saying it show time. All of them nodded their head and gave a small smile. As I walked over towards them real cocky like I asked, "did you get the call Mister Biker man?"

"Yes, I did everything is good and my man Bob Wire , "the quality is off the fucking charts."

"See not bad for a black Mafia type, right?"

"Yeah, I'm sorry for saying that it's that I don't know you, but I want to get to know you and do some business from here on out okay. "

"That sounds like what I want to here, Big Man. See, I'm not just a corner ass hood bitch my shit is international big guy. I can give you that every month if you want more let me know I got coke to if you are rolling with that type of shit just give me a call when your, ready."

I shake his hand Coyote came up patting him on the back announcing, "see what the fuck did I tell you brother?"

Coyote asked, "give me your phone Torch I'm going to give you her number and mine too okay."

"Sure, thing I'm going to need it, but I'll have to go to fucking war with the mob Greece balls if I buy coke off you. Her heroin is weak their cutting it too much it's making me lose customers, so I had to make a move."

I , "yeah, but you going to get new ones and more with my shit. I got it coming in from all over the world."

"Look give me a call when you want to make a move on the coke thing okay, I'm not going to send you into war. I know you need your peoples to move that shit."

Coyote , "shit don't y'all have five chapters of the Metal Heads."

"Yes, we do but I'll have to talk to the international president to make that kind of move. I don't have the authority to make that call."

I , "well go talk to your peoples after you been fucking with me a while then give me a call. I know its other people who do want to make that move."

"I'll call them, and I'll let you know like you after we been doing our thing together for a while."

"Sounds fair to me Torch I'll look forward to hearing from you soon, okay." *We shake hands.* "

"Oh yeah Almasi, I love the way you take care of business boss lady."

"That what everybody calls me boss lady.
We all started laughing.

"I'll holla at you later were going to get the fuck up out of here." I wave for Coyote to come he came walking by my side and announced, "he's going to be calling that international president sooner then he thinks."

"I know once they start with the shit were dropping on them." We both bump fists and jumped in the truck.

I look towards Poochie, "were all going the fuck home now are job here is done for now."

We drop the truck off at the airport and we flew back home it took us about three hours coming back. I rushed back home and when I opened the door I jumped into Jay's arms and we went right to the bedroom and started fucking. I dropped my bags right on the floor after were snorting coke and a few drinks. I put on my house coat and went and dragged my bags in the bedroom. Jay didn't get off his ass to give me a hand after he seen me huffing and puffing with them.

I yelled, "when was you going to get the hint, Nigga?"

"I did get up to help you honey God Damn."

"See your just like all the other Niggas out there in the street once we give y'all some pussy you don't want to do shit for us."

"Jay raised his eyebrow and chimed in, "oh yeah, that's what you say to me baby for real!"

He runs up on me grabbing and lifting me up in the air. We both playing around he tossed me up on the bed and were wrestling around laughing and having fun when we both hear it's a big knock at the fucking door. *I'm like dam soon as I'm really enjoying myself and it's some bullshit going on.* I looked at my watch seeing what time it is for someone to be knocking on my fucking door this time of night. I go in the bedroom to get my phone to call Blood Eye it his turn to stay overnight. Soon as I get the phone to call him, I hear him running to see who knocking on the door like the fucking cops. I know Poochie is off duty but he's in the back room with my sister Robin fucking. I could not ask him to get the door. I quickly walked over to the right where I have all the screens for my cameras on the wall to see who the fuck is it.

Little Boom is Wilding Out

When I looked up at the TV screen, I see it's my son I'm thinking to myself what the fuck do he wants. I hope it's nothing wrong with the baby or Laquitta. Blood Eye opens the door it was my son Little Boom I walk out to talk to him. I ask, "Blood Eye where the fuck was you?"

"I was taking a shit. I'm sorry Almasi."

"I look up at my son saying now what the fuck do you want knocking on my door like you the fucking police."

"Look mom we need to talk!"

"Talk about what and take that fucking tone out your fucking voice, Nigga when you're talking to me."

"Why you didn't take me to Canada with you?"

"Because it was my thing and I set it up. What the fuck is I'm taking you to Canada with me for?"

"I wanted to go to be by your side making big deals that's why."

"Look I didn't want you in this game in the first place Boom."

"What do you think I ain't be cut out to do what y'all do?"

"Yes, I think your cut out for this work, but you have a little boy now you need to pull back a little on the shit you're doing, that's all."

"Mom none these guys respect me that why I want to do more shit that's all."

"Well who fucking told you that shit?"

"Chrome, he told me that I'm a snot nose punk hanging on to your coat tails trying to be a gangster."

"What you got into it with Chrome over what?"

I wanted him to make some collections that's when we got into it."

"Boom baby that's not your job I told Jimmy Goon to do that shit now that Black Duke is dead for him to step up and do it."

"Well I was thinking now that Black Duke is gone, I would step up and do shit."

"Look I told you before to stay in your fucking lane Nigga you were, the one who was in the fucking wrong. You just told me you and Chrome got into it you must handle that shit yourself. You're really going to look like a real bitch if I step to him about this shit then nobody really won't respect your young dumb ass."

"Well, I'm going to fucking kill him then."

"What you are talking about is crazy now you come here to tell me you get into it with one my men and now you are going to kill him because he calls you a snot nose punk."

"Yeah, I'm going to blow his fucking brains out because he did it in front of everybody and he toss me out of Mookie's club you gave it to him!"

"You don't know what the fuck your talking about Nigga. I'm going to give the club to La-Nesa she's his fucking wife for Christ Sake. Boom! Your wilding out on me."

"Mom, did you know she is talking really greasy about you behind your back? So, fuck her."

"Look, I'm going to sit up here with you an tell you what's what. You must work up to the shit. All my men worked their way up to where there at and it going to be the same with you! Do you fucking hear me Nigga? That's why they don't respect your ass you have to put in work. when I give it to you until then don't be in a fucking rush okay! Are you going to give me some work to do? "Yes, I will now go home to your wife to be and your little boy and thank God you have what you have, Nigga!"

"So, what about Chrome?"

"Did you hear what I ? You have to work that shit out with him as a man. I can't get into that shit. And where was Boobby Hill at when all this shit went down?"

He answered, "I was wilding, and he told me to wait my turn like everybody else in the outfit."

"He told you right and I know he's not going to Rat you out to me he's old school. I did not give you a green light to kill one of my men go work it out with him".

213

"I'm going to kill him if he puts his hands on me again, I'm telling you."

"Chill the fuck out that man will kill you matter of fact. Stay the fuck away from him. You hear me?"

"What about the new dudes you moved up?"

"So, what about it? What are you fucking hardheaded or something, Nigga? Now you getting to be just like your father was!"

"What?"

"Yeah, he didn't listen to me and he ran off with that no-good Ho bitch and he killed all his fucking so called bum ass friends who was fucking her!"

"That's what really happen or you just telling me that shit for me to chill out."

"Well I never lied to you, Nigga and if you don't believe me go up there to see him, he will tell you himself."

"That's what I'm going to do, too."

"Yeah, go get it from the horse's mouth Nigga now get the fuck out of my house. I'm tired babysitting your dumb ass you don't want to fucking listen to me! And don't get your dumb ass killed fucking with any of my men too! There all fucking tougher than a box of fucking nails Nigga there not soft like you."

"Yo BloodEye, kick this Nigga out for me, please. I'm tired of looking at him for real." Blood Eye started walking over towards him. He frowned up his face, "for real mom you're going to do this to me?"

Blood Eye came up and grabbed his arm, "I don't want to hurt you kid but your mom you got to go right now so let's go." He pushed Blood Eye and he puts his hands up, but he looks over at me right quick.

"Oh, you need her permission pussy come on!" I just nodded my head slowly he smiled and announced, "kid, you done fucked up!"

He suckered punched him right in his mouth. **Pow!**

Little Boom fell on the floor hard, but he got back up with his mouth bleeding putting his hands up looking over at me ready to fight.

Almasi 2
Queen of The Streets
By Dartanya A. Williams Sr.

I looked at Blood Eye and asked, "what are you waiting for, Nigga? A fucking golden invitation kick his ass!"

Why I that he ran at him Little Boom never knew what hit him a fucking truck or a bus. Knocking the shit out of him with a flurry of punches beating the shit out of him. Boom he would not give up still swinging but Blood Eye is too much for his ass this Nigga never been in a real fight in his whole fucking life. Jay came running out of the hallway I didn't know he was standing there getting in between them yelling, "that's enough kid he looks over at me and give him something. Not this baby."

"No, he has to work his way up like everybody else did baby and when I tell him no that what the fuck I mean, too. If he keeps doing that shit, he's going to be a bitch like his fucking father."

With his mouth all bloody looking at me he barked, "I'm not a Bitch! And I'm nothing like my father was!"

I yelled, "your father was jealous of me working my way up in the gang (BSN). Go up to the prison an ask him what happen he'll tell you motherfucker!"

He staggered towards the front door holding his mouth and his side. Jay goes to help him, and I yelled, "let him go he has to learn shit on his own, Jay. He wants this life just like us this what you get nothing but fucking lumps and bumps. He needs to understand that nobody fucking going to helping you." I turned to my son and continued, "I didn't want this life for you, Nigga but you want to be a fucking gangster this is part of it, Nigga."

Jay knew deep down inside I was right, this life is all fucked up and all of us came up the hard way. He had it to fucking easy all his life.

I yelled out as he went out of the door, "don't forget your fucking rounds tomorrow, Nigga. Just because you got your ass kicked don't mean you don't do your fucking job!"

Jay walked behind him watched him walk and closed the door behind him. Jay came over and he hugged me and whisper in my ear, "that boy just might surprise you one day." "Well, until he does this is the way it's going to be!"

215

I go get my phone from off the table and I call Booby Hill. He picked up after it rings about ten times answering, "who is this?"

"This is Almasi, look how is the job watching my son?"

"He's fucking hardheaded but I'm on it. Why?"

"I was just asking that's all look after y'all hook that deal up with the Fentanyl I'm going to need for you to work with Puerto Rican Joe, okay."

"Sure, thing your son too."

"Oh, hell yes him too."

"So how close is the deal? That's another reason why I called you up for. He didn't tell me shit and I open another whole new fucking pipeline."

"Were picking it up tomorrow he got a real good deal at 20 a key. We're picking up 500 keys that's 10,000,000."

"Okay, what account y'all took the money out of?"

"Carlo told us to take it out of miscellaneous, so it doesn't be no mix ups."

"Good I taught you well, Nigga."

"Okay, I holla at you later my Nigga, **Moja!** *(One)*"

"Moja!"

I hang up and I to Jay, "let's go back to bed and you can show me that trick you do with your tongue again."

We both started laughing and we go back in are bedroom. After we had some buck wild off the chain sex. Jay sat on the side of the bed and he to me, "why don't I get Crazy Monk to give Little Boom some military training since Crazy Monk want to get out the game. Get him to do that for you before he steps off from the outfit."

"Babe, that is a great idea."

I quickly got my phone and called up Crazy Monk and told him to train my son before he gets out the game. He announced, "he can do it, but he will not take it easy on him."

I , "I know that's what I want you to give him the same navy seal training that he got." Crazy Monk , "sure, I can do that when do you want me to do it."

I , "tonight, I want you to come get him. I want you to give me a progress report on him as well."

"Yeah, I can do that for you, Almasi. I'll come get him in one hour."

I called Little Boom up he picks up after three rings, "that Crazy Monk is coming to pick you up in one hour. So, you can have some navy seal training, okay."

"Yeah, I'm down for that he going to show me everything."

"Yes, and he will not take it easy on you. I showed you how to shoot he's going to show you how to really take care of yourself with some real mental toughness."

"I'm with that and I can do it."

"Good just make me proud, Nigga, okay Moja (One)"

"Moja!"

Within that hour just like he he came and picked Little Boom up from his house and for the next three months Crazy Monk took my son through some rigorous training and he told me he was doing good too.

It's Too Much Heat on Us Right Now!

The next morning, I got up around 11 and Aunt-Tee La- Wanda is fixing all us something to eat. Me, Poochie, Blood Eye and Jay went to work and so did Robin. We all eat and it's time for me to get to work. Right before were ready to roll out the door her son Sonny was coming in the door while were going out. He bumps fist with all of us walking in to talk to his mother Aunt-Tee. We all know what he's coming to see her for only one thing and that's money. *Sonny is the type of dude who never has any money and he don't want to work for it neither.* Soon as I jump into my black Benz wagon, I get a text saying In Zulu Kwenzekile (*It's done*).

I know it was Dime Piece and Bop- Diglo who took care of Ted Schultz the head of the task force. They told me that they were going to text it to me in Zulu when I drop off the money with Tanya. These two Niggas look like a couple ghetto psychopaths, but they spoke five different languages. When I got to my home base, at Washington avenue warehouse. I felt funny when I walked in the door not seeing Black Duke, I felt sad again, but I played it off bumping fist with Jimmy Goon, I ask to step up now that Black Duke is gone. I took two of Big De Shawn guys who was working with Tanya two down ass killers name Mojo and Jaleam to work at the Warehouse with me.

I put Big DeShawn and Akbar with Tanya so she can train them with her. Gino Gats didn't like it, but I didn't give a fuck what he like I know what I was doing. Jimmy Goon is walking with me and announced, "some guy name Carl Crowbar came past here. He he wants to talk to you I told him to come back. I could not let anybody wait inside for you."

"Good now walk with me I have to talk to you Jimmy."

Jimmy open my office door for me. I close the door and sat down, he sat in the chair next to me.

He asked, "who is this guy, Almasi?"

"He was down with us and once apart of Rah- Killers crew. When he come make sure he's clean when he come back here with me. He been gone too long taking care of his sick kid for me to fully trust his ass. Where the fuck is Rah- Killer at any way?"

"She's working on something for me so she's on the low right now. Look, I need you to be on these new guys ass. They have to be at the top of their game at all times okay."

"You got it, Almasi."

Bango tapped on the door peeking his head in the door "those two-ass hole cops from homicide is here to talk to you and that light skin dude Carl Crowbar too."

"Okay, you take Carl into the conference room and tell Jamel to walk the two Dick heads back here to my office."

"I'm on it." He quickly walked away , "Jimmy, I need you to call Damon Gee right now and tell him **Nipatie Wakili** *(Get me a lawyer)."*

"Oh, I know that one that means get me a lawyer."

"So, you been studying than."

"Yes, I have Ma. My name is Jimmy Goon and don't mean I'm fucking dumb."

"you were Nigga, or I would not have asked you to step up for Black Duke."

We both started laughing as Jamel knocking on the door , "the detectives are here." They pushed him out of their way Jamel yelled, "man, don't put your fucking hands on me Nigga."

Detective Johnson stepped up and snapped, "what you say, Nigga. I don't put your fucking hands on me."

Soon as detective Johnson lunged at him to grab him Crazy Jamel side stepped him, and sucker punched him **Plow!** Knocking the shit out of him to the floor. At the same time detective Towns went to whip out his gun Crazy Jamel knocks his gun out his hand kicks him in the face **Kadoom!** He falls backwards on his ass and he kicks him in the head again knocking him out cold **Doom!**

I jumped up telling Jimmy get their guns and take Jamel crazy ass out the back door and get him the fuck out of here. I screamed, "hurry up!"

Jimmy quickly picked up both of their guns he looked up at me after he stuck both the guns in his jeans.

"What about that call to Damon Gee about that lawyer?"

"Yeah, do that after you get him out of here, I'm going to really need one after this shit!"

Jimmy quickly ran off with Crazy Jamel after ten minutes or so detective Johnson got up off the floor groaning holding his head and yelled, "you are under arrest!"

"What the fuck did I do?"

"You put that fucking animal on us bitch!"

"So, what are you going to fucking arrest me with your fucking fingers ass hole!"

I wave my hand for Blood Eye and Poochie to come watch my back just in case these two motherfuckers want to play ruff. Now both these ass hole cops are pissed off that Crazy Jamel knocked both them the fuck out. I should have stood over them and yelled it out like they did in the Friday movie. Detective Johnson is shaking his partner detective Towns he's still fucking groggy as he's helping him up off the floor shaking his head,

"what the hell happen?

"That black ass son of a bitch punched us the fuck out and took are guns!"

Detective Johnson is pointed at me screaming, "don't you fucking move."

He pulls his radio off his hip and he pressed it down hard as he continued looking up at the three of us.

He yelled, "this is Detective Johnson I need back up at 2301 Washington Avenue. We both have been assaulted."

The radio cracking loud and the voice yelled out, "10-4 were in route!" Five minutes later about four cop cars came and the patty wagon locking all of us up. Me, Jimmy Goon, the two new guys Mojo, Jaleam, Bango, Crowbar Carl, Blood Eye and Poochie. *I told everybody to be cool and don't give them a hard time we all be out before we know it. I called Damon Gee after 4 hours or so getting my phone call. He seen us all getting hauled off when he drove up. Damon Gee got us a lawyer name Joe Morgan a friend of his wife to be Dominique. He came and bail all of us out from the round house after about 9 hours. Damon Gee had Taz Money, Ty-Kim,*

Woo-Woo and Lurch with trucks to pick us all up in front of the round house on 8ᵗʰ street.

I told everybody to go home, but I went to my apartment building I own in New Jersey. I called up Jay and Aunt-Tee La-Wanda and I told both of them to meet me there. I also told Aunt-Tee to not have her son Sonny at my place. Crowbar Carl when straight to Las Vegas and linked up with Fly Ty. Blood Eye and Poochie came the next day I laid low there unknowing to me La-Nesa did some dirty ass shit behind my back. I found out about later she had a big stash of coke. That Mookie had before he got killed, she gave Jody Laquitta's stepfather who kept asking everybody around me to get put on. None of my people would not hook him up but La-Neesa gave him 15 keys of coke knowing he was going to fuck it up.

She went and talked to the D.E.A. A week blaze past but all I did was pace the floor chain smoking cigarettes, drinking Tanqueray gin and snorting coke every day. I worked the horn making sure everybody was doing their job. And my son even after when I let Blood Eye whip his ass was still on top of his job. Friday morning, I get a call from Rah-Killer I'm still half fucking sleep.

"Hey what's up, we have to meet sis."

"Okay, I'll text you the address. I'm in New Jersey laying low the cops are going buck wild."

"Yeah, I heard Crazy Jamel whip their ass really good. I also heard both Dick head cops got suspended because they both lost their Glock pistols that still have not turned up yet. that's why the going ape shit on us."

"I know I talk to Damon Gee yesterday he told me them asshole cops want their guns back but I'm not getting any of my money back we paid for fucking bail. Plus, we still have assault charges on us too."

"Look, I'll be there in a hour or so I have some really good news for you Moja(One)" "Moja." I sit up on the side of the bed and I quickly grab my smokes off the nightstand. Soon as I lit it up Jay sat up in the bed beside me and kissed my cheek, "good morning baby."

I kissed him and greeted him with, "well, good morning to you too, Mister Harry Handsome."

"Hey baby, light one for me, please."

I lit Jay a cigarette and handed it to him and asked, "are you going to work today?"

"Yeah, I'm going to go all the way up until my trial I told you that."

"Well, why don't you take off today it's Friday and spend the day with me."

"You want to know what I think I just might do that baby. Let me get washed and dressed and we can go out and get something to eat out on the town."

"Sounds good to me Miss thick and sexy." He hopped up off the bed and smacked me on my ass as I'm walking towards the bathroom. I jump in the shower and I got dressed. I checked my guns and put one behind my back of my jeans. And the one in my handbag never leaves home without them motherfuckers for real.

Now that I'm all set thinking I'm going to spend the day with my man. I walked in the kitchen while Jay was in the bathroom getting wash. Talking to Aunt-Tee she's sitting down drinking coffee.

"Hey, baby what do you want to eat?"

"I was just about to cook for everybody."

"Thanks Aunt-Tee but me and Jay are going to go out and eat something while were out." "Are you sure, baby?"

"Yes, were good plus you cook for us all the time just make something for yourself. I'll make sure the boys get something to eat while were out and we will be back later."

"Can I ask you while you don't want my son Sonny to come here to see me?" I didn't want to say I didn't trust him instead I , "I only want people I want to know I'm here let's just say that okay Aunt-Tee."

"Okay, hey do you boys want some coffee?" Poochie and Blood Eye looked up at me and I nodded my head yes. They both walked over to the kitchen area and sat down as Aunt-Tee set the cups in front of them she started pouring them some coffee with a smile on her face as always chit chatting with them back and forth. Then she puts the cream and sugar on the table, "here you are boys help yourself, on what you need over there."

222

I reached up on the sink getting my cup with the bold block letters that boss lady on it. Tanya gave it to me for Christmas I went and grabbed the pot and poured my own coffee and sat down waiting on Jay. Soon as Jay walked out and announced, "hey baby, I'm ready to go. **Tisssssssssssssss!"**

It's a loud sound of glass breaking on the left-hand side of the apartment I jumped up whipping out my gun along with Poochie and Blood Eye. They both jumped up guarding me and Jay Aunt-Tee quickly jumped up grabbing the remote off the counter knowing the drill from last time. We all are running towards the back room to the safe room. The four of us dash to the safe room Poochie and Blood Eye pushed us inside closing the door they both looked up.

On the right side the wall where the six large TV screen seeing where the intruder is at. *I also see him because I have TV screens up on the wall inside of the large safe room. Aunt-Tee is holding the remote waiting on my signal to hit the button.* They both see a tall white man with a black mask on his head with his long hair hanging down from his back holding a machine gun. He's creeping up the hallway slowly Blood Eye and Poochie both stand towards the right but they're both spread out staying low behind the walls near the living room. The tall man comes out quickly staying low soon as he came out Poochie and Blood Eye started spitting hot led at him. **Kapacka! Kapacka! Kapacka! Plow! Plow! Plow!** He ducked behind the wooden dresser still coming forward firing back soon as he got in the right spot, I yelled at Aunt-Tee, "Now!" She hit the button smiling **Shhhoooooopppppppp! Doom! Doom! Doom! Doom!** Simultaneously four thick steel fencing came up boxing the mask killer inside. He runs up kicking the steel fencing **Woom! Woom!** Trying to get out Blood Eye and Poochie ran up gunning him down **Kapacka! Kapacka! Plow! Plow!**

The impact from all the bullets made the tall mask man fall backwards on his ass. He's a bloody mess. Soon as I seen him fall on the floor, I yelled out, "that's all she wrote motherfucker!"

At the same time Aunt-Tee giving me a high five. Jay yelled, "we have to get the fuck out of here now!"

" I know we have to wait for Poochie and Blood Eye." Soon as I that they came running in the room as I hit the keypad code to let us out.I lead the way down the hallway to the room on the rig ht Blood Eye came in the room last, I tell him to close the door and reach up and hit that button at the top of the door for me on the left. He reaches up and hit the button long the wall in front of us the large bookshelf slide towards the right and it's a door.

Jay , "damn, baby you think of everything but what about the tall hairy dead ass hole in the living room area?"

"Fuck him this place isn't in my name let's just get the fuck out of here!"

I open the door and told Blood Eye, "just make sure you close the door behind you so the bookshelf will slide back into place."

"I got you, Almasi." The four of us quickly walked into the tunnel very quickly it leads across the street to a big tool shed. I go look under large plant pot getting the keys to another truck I have outside. I toss the keys to Poochie and told him to drive.

Jay , "what about the other truck?"

"I'll have Bango or one of them come pick it up. We have to leave in another car because of the cameras outside on the street." We all jump inside of the black GMC truck quickly. I sit up front with Poochie driving Blood Eye, Aunt-Tee and Jay sat in the back. I called Rah- Killer and told her to meet me at the penthouse she just that's cool. I hung up. Then I called up Ty- Kim to bring some men up to the penthouse to watch my back. I don't know who that motherfucker was a Russian or Armenian or whatever the fuck he is. Take us to the penthouse Poochie." It takes us about hour and a half to get to the penthouse. All I want is a drink to try to calm down,but I called Bango to come get the whip later on tonight he no problem he got me. Soon as we get there, I go right behind the bar pulling out the big green bottle of Tangueray gin from off the large row of bottles on the bar. I sat it on top the bar looking up at Jay blowing out air and I asked, "make me one too, baby."

Aunt-Tee chimed in, "yeah and me three shit!" Were all started laughing I make all of us a big drink knowing we all just narrowly escape death again. An hour later Me, Jay and Aunt-Tee was nice and fucking high. Rah-Killer came in the door all smiles, "What's up sis bumping fist with me looks like I'll join the party sitting next to me.

When I looked at her, she was all dolled up dressed like a one them hot in the ass chicks in the clubs or something.

"Well God damn look at you, girl. Wow your looking good I never seen you dressed like this before."

I just when and brought me a one way, ticket to Las Vegas and I'm one happy ass bitch." "Oh, really so it's done. He's dead."

"Yes, I'm sure of it he's dead you can check and see for yourself John Knotty is dead!"

I bump fist with her, "good work now you know I still have to check it out Rah."

"I know you are while you're doing that baby girl, I'll make me a drink right quick."

"Hold up sis *I put my hand up stopping her with a big Kool aid smile on her brown grill.* I got you girl just fall back for a few yo."

"Blood Eye could you please make Rah- Killer a drink for me please?" she just gave me some good news over here."

Blood Eye looked up at her smiling seeing how nice she's dressed. She looks good to him "Sure thing come on over here while I hook you up sexy to bad, you're playing on the other team with that fat ass of your girl. I'll give you something you'll never forget."

We all giggled. Rah -Killer , "oh yeah Nigga, ain't you married motherfucker?

"Yes, I am but I'm not fucking dead yet fuck that you look good girl." We all fell out laughing. I pulled out my phone calling Damon Gee to see if what Rah- Killer told me was true. The phone only rings one time when Jagger and some of his crew came walking in the door. Flip Diddy, Gun Ho Moe, and Frank Iilly. I put my finger up in the air for him to wait for a minute.

Damon Gee picks up and asked, "what's up boss lady?"

"Look, I'm here with Rah- Killer and she just told me that John Knotty is dead."

Almasi 2
Queen of The Streets
By Dartanya A. Williams Sr.

"Well good thing you called me because I was going to call you and tell you the same thing, but I had to double check to make sure."

"So, did you double check it yet Gee?"

"No let me call you back its only going to take a few minutes okay."

"Make sure you do that for me please Gee. I want to make sure before I give her my blessing to move on."

"I will let me make the call now Moja (*One*)!"

Soon as I hung up Jagger came up to me with a beer in his hand. "yo John Knotty got smoked last night!"

"Yeah you know who did it?"

"All I heard is this sexy big butt bitch came up on him and his whole crew and machine gunned his ass down took out five of them along with his funky ass."

Soon as he that I knew she did it the next person that's good with a machine gun is me. Damon Gee called me back saying yes it true he's dead and they some bitch did it and he hung up.

I stood up and I walk over to Rah- Killer, "so you really did it for me, sis? I hugged her and continued, " I knew you get the job done bitch! "

We both giggled and started play boxing with one another Rah-Killer I got something for you she reaches in her pocketbook pulling out a large zip lock bag of coke setting it on the bar and announced, "it time to get fucked up, girl!" Soon as we started laughing and shuffling the white powder on top of the smooth surface of the bar. Ty- Kim with his men Woo- Woo, Lurch and two new guys Sean Guns, Tony Gee and his two stepsons. *I gues he he was going to keep it all in the family just long as they can do the job.*

"Hey what up, Ty- Kim."

he hugged me and replied, "I'll put them on post right now and tell them what they have to do."

"Please do and when your done come over here and join us in the celebration."

"So, what are we celebrating Ma?"

"You didn't hear John Knotty is fucking dead!"

"Well, that some good news to hear but do you know who came at you today?"

"To tell you the truth I don't know if it was the Russians or Armenians."

"Ty- Kim, I think you need to find out because they already killed Black Duke, Nails Nathan Mookie, Stomp and Yokey."

"That's five good men, Almasi and I want some fucking Retribution. Do you trust me Ty- Kim?"

"Yes, I do, Almasi and for some years now too."

"Well, if you know me, I'm working on it as we speak, brother. Tell your men what they have to do, and you come back and sit with me and we will talk."

"Okay, I'll be right back to hear you out."

I wave Aunt-Tee to come closer while I'm making lines of the coke on top of the bar then I roll up a 100-dollar bill. I snort two lines real fast than I gulp down the rest of my drink and I hand Rah- Killer the 100-dollar bill while she is snorting up the coke. I called Coyote crazy ass up he picks up on the first ring and answered, "hey pretty lady what is it you need from me?"

I need for you to meet me at my penthouse place on city line avenue.

I Made You Believe What You Wanted to Believe

"Yeah, I know where it's at. I'm with your son right now taking care of a few more things I'll be there in about an hour."

"If you don't mine me asking what are you and my son doing?"

"Well were getting out all the orders we got from Puerto Rican Joe shit done doubled up once we got the Fentanyl flowing."

"Is X with y'all?"

"Yeah, he's here and so is Gino and Tanya send him here to give us a hand."

"**Nzuri (***Good).*"

"I have to tell you this were going to need more people to move this shit."

"Okay, were going to have to work on that I'll see you when you get here."

Aunt- Tee and jay is snorting the coke when Ty- Kim comes back I stand up and wave him to the side so I can talk to him. We walk to the tables by the window just me and him and I began with, "look, you been down with me for a long time so I'm going to tell you now that John Knotty is dead. I'm going to turn things over to Dun- Dun. So, I'm hoping you and your people will give him your full support after I make that move."

"Well you been in this shit for a long time now if that's going to make you happy, I'm all for it, Almasi."

"I just wanted to tell you first before it happens so your good with it."

"Yeah, I'm good with it. I'm just going to miss you and I know you going to look out for me before you roll right?"

"So, what is it you want your own things like Jagger and them did?"

"Yes, I think I earn it, Almasi."

"Your right you did earn it. I'll put that on the **Meza** *(Table)* before I roll out."

"So, what about you son? He's not going go off like Jasper did that time when you took over and Spider gave it to you."

"I already talk to him that if he's going to be in this shit, he has to work his way up like the rest of y'all did."

"Yeah, but he's real cocky and act like he's running shit now, Almasi. I don't want nobody to hurt him. Your right I'll get him under control Ty- Kim don't worry."

"Okay, if you say so I'll believe what you say but you know how Niggas is when they get power. I just need for you to look out for me when you split because I stood with you when this whole BSN shit fell apart."

"It's still a BSN it just that were not part of that shit right now because of what they did not us."

"Your right but now shit is changing again. I need to have my own shit flowing. I got you brother I never lied to you the whole time you been with me, right?"

"Yeah, that's true so you thought about what you want to do once you step down?"

"Yeah, I know just what I'm going to do and I'm going to enjoy every fucking minute of it too!" Jagger came over to the table where we were sitting at away from everybody at the bar.

"Excuse me, Almasi. I need to holla at you it's important."

Ty- Kim stood up "it's all good." He bumps fist with me and winked, "don't forget about me, Ma."

"I won't Ty I talk to you later okay."

Ty- Kim get up walking away and Jagger hung his head and spoke softly, "somebody just grabbed my sister, Tanya."

"Get the fuck out of here. I just came out of the jaws of death and now this shit!"

"What happen?"

Almasi 2
Queen of The Streets
By Dartanya A. Williams Sr.

"I just got a call from a Nigga and he sounds just like Gino Gats to me saying they have Tanya. I called her phone and it goes right to voice mail. Send some your people to make sure this shit is real."

"I did. I sent Little Bay- Bay and John Rocka they both they checked at all three of the warehouses. Fat Lou- Lou is at Sedgley avenue, Taz Money is at Nice town and Puerto Rican Joe is at the new one in the Northeast."

"I just talk to Coyote he that Tanya send Gino to give Puerto Rican Joe a hand."

I quickly call Coyote the phone rings two time and he picked up and announced, "I'm here, Almasi. I'm coming up right now."

"Good, I need to talk you about something." I hang up and a few minutes he's walking in the door I stood up waving him over towards us where were sitting at. Coyote quickly came over to the table and asked, "what's going on?"

"Jagger here thinks somebody grabbed his sister. You did talk to her?"

"Yeah, I told you she sent Gino over to give us a hand then he rolled out with her after we loaded all the trucks and planes. I have his number let me see if he's going to pick up!"

His phone just rings and rings. I looked at both and announced, "he's not picking up."

Coyote , "so what happen, Jagger?"

"Some Nigga calls me about a half an hour or so saying that he has Tanya."

I asked, "so how long ago did Gino leave y'all?"

"About two or three hours ago so you think it's him."

Jagger barked, "I know it's him!"

Coyote chimed in, "yeah, it could be him. Look, I'll take care of this for y'all give me your phone number."

Jagger read off his phone number 215 599-59 59."

"Okay."

Coyote pulls out his phone making a call, "yo, Koo- Koo Man put a trace on this number here 215 599-5959. You got it when somebody call you make sure to tell me where it is coming from okay you got me good one."

"Okay, I need both of y'all to sit tight when they call, I'll have them clocked in the meanwhile. Go get a drink and something to eat until they call or something. I got this shit. And you Almasi, you should have come to me with those two homicide ass hole cops came at you. I would have taken care of them for you from the door."

"I was not thinking shit was happing so fast."

"Well, just like Arturo told you I'm here to take care of shit up here we have a very big fucking investment in you, and we need for you to run it. I'll take care of all the bull shit coming your way."

We sit there for another hour or so I'm sitting on pens and needles these motherfuckers done snatch up my girl and I'm with Jagger thinking it's Gino Gats who has something to do with this shit. Jagger phone rings Coyote looks at him and whispered, "if that's them talk natural and real cool like."

Jagger nodding his head yes, he hits the button and answered, "hello."

"Yeah, listen to everything I tell you. Is Almasi there?"

"Yes, she's here. What does that have to do with my sister?"

"I'm going to tell you when you shut the fuck up. I want her to bring 30 million dollars to 54th and Parkside and to wait there for further instructions. You make sure she comes by herself with the money. You have two hours to get there or Tanya is dead!"

Jagger hands the phone up and he looks up at Coyote. He quickly calls Koo- Koo Man, "I know you got it right?"

"Yeah, I got it, and we can locate right where they're at when they come to pick up the money."

"Good." He hung up and gave me a quick glance, "okay, you need to get somebody to get this money together right about now. We don't have that much time, Almasi."

I asked, "what's the plan?'

"You go get the money together and I'll have my people there soon as they come to get it."

"That's the plan. Just do it trust me. I'm going to kill every one of them who did this shit, Almasi and make an example out of them. I'm going to show these Niggas we not anybody to be fucked with." He stormed out of the door. I pointed, "Jagger, I'm need two of your men to go pick this loot up, okay."

Jagger quickly walked over and grabbed Frank Iilly and Flip Diddy they are always on standby.

I , "Coo, I'm calling Jimmy Goon to take out the two duffle bags from the safe. I need y'all to get this money back here as quick as you can. Some Niggas snatched Tanya and were going to get her back. I'm going to make the call you two get in route right now." The two of them dashed out the door and I called Jimmy Goon he picks up after two rings.

"Hey what's up, Almasi? I heard the good news that John Knotty is dead."

"Yeah, were all very happy about that but check this out. I'm need you to go to the office and go down stair to the back safe and take out the two duffle bags and give them to Frank Iilly and Flip Diddy."

"Okay, I'm on it right now. I'm not too far from the office."

"Good, go do that because this is life and death here."

"What happen, Ma?"

"These ass holes kidnapped Tanya so we need that money right away Dawg."

"You can count on me, Almasi! Moja (One)!"

"Moja!"

An Hour and a half later.

Flip Diddy and Frank Iilly came in with the two big black duffle bags. I called Coyote telling him, "I got the money where you at?"

"Don't worry about that you're going to drive by yourself with your peoples not too far behind you."

"We're going to give them the appearance that you're by yourself with the money. I've done this shit a million times, so you must trust me on this, okay. I got this."

"I just don't want them to kill my girl. I'm more worry about you I want you to ask them for proof of life before you give them the money okay."

"I will what if they don't do it?"

"Then she's dead and they're going to try to grab you for more money, but that's not going to happen. I'll make sure of that."

"Get Jay to take your Aunt home and he hangs up."

I walked over to Rah- Killer telling her what's going on and I ask her if she's coming with us.

She yelled, "hell yes you know I got your back girl." We bumped fist with me smiling checking her guns.

So, I get myself together quickly I have not been this nervous about something like this in a long time. All the others strapped up super-fast as we all roll outside to the parking lot. I get in the black GMC truck I came there in Jagger put the bags in the back seat for me saying don't worry about shit I got your back looking me right in my eyes. I pull off and drive to Parkside avenue when I got there I didn't know if I was late or not. I just sit there looking around I didn't see anybody. It's fucking dark and freezing outside then I see somebody walking up to my window tapping on it. I roll the window down and this tall dark skin man with a long black coat and hat. I can't see his face too good and he hands me a phone and he quickly walk away. I roll the window back up and the phone rings with the heavy muffled voice, "I see you're here. Your fucking late steps out the truck and go sit on the bench about ten feet up the park road. Bring the money with you no tricks."

I step out the truck and button up my coat. I quickly open the back door and I grabbed the two duffle bags filled with money. I know damn well it's more than 30 million in this motherfucker, but Coyote told me he was going to make sure these motherfuckers are dead. So, I'm just thinking about getting Tanya back that's all. I'm playing this shit out to the fullest. I close the back door and I started walking up the path up the small hill to the bench towards the right. I sit down I'm looking all around not seeing any body and walking out from the shadows is a man dressed in all black holding a gun when he gets closer, I recognize who it is. "Ain't this a bitch, it's Spider."

I was in shock he sits next to me and asked, "what's up, Shorty?"

I can't lie I felt some type of way after seeing he's one the people who been trying to fuck me over all this time.

I looked at him and asked, "why the fuck is you doing this shit Spider?"

"This is the only way I could get you to meet with me now slide the money over here right quick."

"No, I want to see if Tanya is still alive."

"Give me the money and I'll have my people let her go. Come on now I don't have any time to talk shit and reminisce with your ass, Almasi."

"This is fucked up Spider you leave me with the top spot and then your people were all trying to fucking kill me after all this time I ran shit for y'all."

"Let me say you did a better job than I thought you was going to do. Matter of fact you did too much of a good fucking job to tell you the truth! That's why I'm here you had Bryah smoked, her brother John Knotty Killed, you had the shot caller in prison Black Giovanni killed and now I have to come here to kill you."

He points the gun in my face and barked, "give me the fucking money right now."

I screamed, "it was you who killed my mother and father wasn't it?"

"I don't have time for this soap opera horse shit, Almasi. I made you believe what you wanted to believe." *When I looked him in his eyes, I was hurt but he was right this Nigga had used me up to kill and made money for them. Now I'm trapped in this shit trying to get out the life.*

"Now slide the money over to me right now!"

"Why you're going to kill me anyway?"

"So just do it then motherfucker!"

He lifts his gun towards my head, "I'm going to tell you before I'll blow your fucking brains out. It was me who killed your mother and your father you, dumb bitch!"

Kapacka! *The sound of the shot rang out, but it was nobody out there in the deep fucking cold park.* Some of the blood slashed on the side of my face. It was cold and feeling eerie. The blood on the side of my face freaked me out, but I just watched his body slumped over and then falling to the ground face down **Doom!** I looked up and its Coyote with this camouflage net on him. He winked at me handing me a rag"here you go, wipe your face, pretty lady."

I did it real fast, but I still had his blood on my coat and still some of it on my face. I told you, I got your back he whistles loud. I can see the smoke from his mouth from the cold air outside. Out of the darkness I see this man holding on to Tanya walking up to us. I stood up as Tanya ran up hugging me, we both rocked back and forth near the park bench were both glad to still be alive. I , "where is Gino?"

"He's dead they killed him when he tried to put up a fight when they grabbed me."

"I was thinking he had something to do with the shit."

"No, he died trying to protect me, Almasi."

Coyote said, "ladies, we have to get the fuck up out of here right about now come on!" He continued, "oh yeah, this is my brother Koo- Koo Man."

He picks up the bags of money.

"Well, it nice to meet you, Koo- Koo and let do what the man and get the hell out of here!"

When I looked up and I see all my peoples with their guns and machine guns ready to go to war. They all looked up at me I can see in all their eyes their love for me. I wanted to hug every one of them. I wave and all over them waved back and I put my fist up in the air. They all did the same Koo- Koo Man put the bags of money in the back seat and he close the door back. He waves at all of us walking away into the cold and darkness he seen the hurt in my eyes. As Coyote he holds the door back door open for Tanya then he opens the door for me. I jumped in and he walked around and jumped behind the wheel. He took off into the dark cold air with the yellow Dall lights shining on the gritty cold streets. *While we were driving home to the condo, I was thinking all these years I put all this work for a Nigga who killed my family and he played me for a fool. I wanted to kill him my motherfuckin self is my only regret about all this shit. I know it's a few more snakes out there for me to get now. I seen Coyote crazy ass in action I have a few more ideas about getting that shit done.*

All I want to do now is get me something to eat and go to sleep. I called Jay to let him know that I'm all right he picks up on the first ring and asked, "you all right, baby."

"Yeah, I'm good. I know I'm fucking hungrier than three dogs I know that."

"Well, I got us some chicken wings from Wing Stop I picked it up on the way home."

For me, you and Aunt La-Wanda. I told her she cooks all the time and after the day we had I told her she can have the fucking night off."

"Okay, I can't wait to get home to tell you what happen tonight to me."

"Well, I'm here waiting on you, my love. Your sister been asking for you too. She just wants to see that Nigga Poochie not me."

We both laughed and I quickly hang up a few minutes later. I was coming in the door soon as Coyote drop me and Tanya off. Poochie and Blood Eye pulled up in the black Benz wagon. I told them get the bags from the back seat and put them in the house for me. Before I went in the house, they both came running up to me hugging me.

Poochie ran up on me and shouted, "Goddamn, I was thinking he was going to kill you. Coyote called all of us and told us to hang back so he can creep up and kill him."

Blood Eye chimed in, "we should have been used that son of a bitch to put in some work for us."

He hugs me and continued, "I'm so glad you alright, Almasi. My heart was racing 1000 times a fucking minute when that shit was going down."

"Let's go in the fucking house its cold out here. I love you, Niggas, too!" We all started laughing and we went in the house, but I just could not shake off what happen most of the night.

I looked up to this Nigga and he comes out the darkness to kill me and get paid too. I should have seen that shit coming in this fucked up game. Soon as I walked in the crib Jay came running up to me hugging me and asked, "are you all right?"

He can see the hurt in my eyes. But I just looked back at him, "I'm going to be all right baby. I'm going to be just fine don't you worry. I'll get over this shit." Then my sister Robin came running up to me, "I'm so glad to see you!"

"And I'm glad to see you too Miss big time lawyer!"

We hugged and she announced, "I got some good news for that sad face of yours here. I'm not sad what the fuck is you talking about."

"You forget I really know your ass look I wanted to tell you I'm pregnant."

"What?"

I looked up at Poochie , "oh wow now were really are family now Nigga."

I walked up and hugged him smiling.

He announced, "I'm glad you're happy about this, Almasi."

"You are fucking right. I'm happy about this shit it's one the best news I heard all day. I know you're a good man and you will take care of my sister. I know that for sure because I know who you are and where you come from."

She's in some really good hands we bumped fist then I hugged him.

"Thanks, Almasi. I always felt like real family with you."

We hugged as Aunt-Tee came up yelling, "welcome home and you know fucking well you're not leaving me out of this family thing we got going on here!"

We all started giggling loud. As we all walked to the kitchen with Aunt-Tee holding my hand,

"I'll heat up these wings, girl there not like mine but its fucking good, doe."

With her hand on her big hips and a cigarette hanging from her large lips smudged with her red lipstick. We sat and ate but my mind is still fucked up over Spider low life ass. After two weeks I got it all the way out of my mind, so I started thinking if he he was there to kill me if must be Nokey Blaze send him to do it.

Nokey Blaze is my next target and I'll get Coyote peoples to help me to do it. *But the only thing that's in the back of my mind is will Arturo and his peoples let me walk away from all this bull shit when I hand things over to Dun- Dun.*

Were all sitting at the kitchen table when we hear a big knock at the door. Blood Eye and Poochie jumped up with their gats in their hand quickly going to see who it is when they open the door. It was X he ran up and hugged me, "I heard what happen Tanya told me to stay at the warehouse and hold things down or I would have been right by your side, sis. I'm so glad your all right."

"Yeah, I'm good brother come have a seat and drink with us where is your wife at?"

"She's hanging out with her crazy ass girlfriends somewhere."

"So, what your drinking X?"

"I'll have a beer for right now, Shorty."

I started laughing.

"You know that's what that ass hole said to me when he came up on me holding a fucking gun in my face."

"Look Almasi, I could not tell you at the time that shit was not right with Spider at the time. You were to close to him I knew if I something to you, he would have killed me and my family. So, I got them the fuck out of Philly while the getting was good."

"I was wondering why you just got out your lucky he let you out to go to Miami."

"No, I was lucky because I found a bomb under my fucking whip the night I was going to roll. I knew it was him."

"Get the fuck out of here!"

"Yeah, good thing I checked that shit, or you would not be talking to me now. I'm sorry I could not tell you a lot sooner about that Nigga."

"It's cool, you and I will always be family, X."

We hugged one another, and we all sat at my kitchen table. We got fucked up with some weed, coke, champagne and a lot of fucking beer having a good time to the wee hours of the morning until the next day.

It's the beginning of February or so I called everybody into the **Meza** *table at the penthouse. I had Dun- Dun and his people sitting on the right and Jagger and his men sitting on the left room was filled with smoke and chatter.*

I yelled out for Booby Hill to turn down the music he did real quick standing next to Taz- Money. I had everybody there El Barero and his crew along with all the S.O.S crew with John Spartacus, Fat Lou- Lou and his peoples Jane Doe and her crew. Jagger and his crazy ass squad is in the place to be. Rah- Killer was chillin by herself Fat Wally and his crew is there now that there down with us the place is packed.

I banged on the table and began to speak, "I know all of you wanted to know why all of you are here we done been through so much together. I love every one of y'all who has been loyal and working hard for our family and your own family as well. So, I'm proud to tell y'all that are war with the chain gang is over for right now."

Everybody started clapping and banging on the tables. I continued, "And I'm all here to tell yawl I'm stepping down and Dun- Dun is going to be at the head of the Meza for here on out."

The whole room is stun now. "Before he comes up and give us a few words like I promise. Ty-Kim will have his own squad and my man Lou- Lou also will have his own thing. They've been working hard for me from day one and they deserve to have their own thing, but they will always be family. Dun- Dun the floor is yours, my brother." *Everybody is clapping loud as Dun- Dun steps up to the head of the table and I sit down on the right-hand side.* Dun- Dun , "thank you so much, Almasi. I like to say first that we really appreciate you and all you have done for all of us making us men in this game. We can hold are heads up in the streets with mad respect from everybody.

Everyone in the place started clapping and banging on the tables.

"I like to tell everybody in this room they have nothing to worry about now that I'm stepping up. And if anybody in this room don't know I was down when Almasi first put this shit together. There will be a lot of changes but most of what's going on will stay the same as that crazy ass flow of loot coming our way."

Everybody in the room started giggling loud and he continued, "Now I'm not much for making a speech but I can tell you that we will be stronger than ever and were going to stay on top of our game. I ask Damon Gee over here to stay on with for his counsel and he yes."

Damon Gee Stands up waving his hand smiling.

"And if anybody have any questions about some things. I want you to go to Jagger over here or Booby Hill now that's out the way. I want all of you to have a good time and remember **Walikuwa bado wakiua mchezo** *Were still killing this game!"*

Everyone yelled out, "**Na unamjua huyu mtu shit** *and you know this shit, man!" They all burst out in laughter.*

Dun- Dun , "for all of you who don't know I were still killing this game. And everybody back, and you know this shit man! Everybody go ahead and enjoy yourself it's on the house."

Everyone in the crowd is quickly heading towards the bar and the tables with the food and Dun- Dun walked over to me and whispered, "I need to holla at you about something right quick, sis."

We both walked to the back office away from everybody I sit at the desk looking up at him as he closed the door, "I don't trust your boy, El Barero."

"What?"

"Yeah him or fucking Ty- Kim or Chrome."

"Well you don't have to worry about Ty- Kim any more he got his own shit and as far as El Barero I think you got that shit all wrong Dun- Dun."

"And I don't know what's the thing you have with Chrome neither."

"Look I don't trust them Almasi when I get that feeling, I know I'm right."

"Well Damon Gee is going tell you you're wrong."

"I don't trust him all that much neither."

"For real Dun- Dun so why you ask him to be your consigliere than?"

"I have to keep shit solid until I make more changes that's why."

"Dun- Dun I hope you know what you're doing."

"Don't worry, sis. I got this shit all under control, okay. I'm bringing in all my own peoples in to run shit sis it's going to be real smooth trust me."

Now that I'm hearing all this shit, I might have really fucked up putting him at the head of the Meza (Table), wow.

"Please don't fuck this up, Dun- Dun!"

"I won't and don't tell Damon Gee on what we talked about please."

"No, you're not going to fuck him over later do that shit now that's the only thing I have to say before I step off. All the other shit you can do what you want to do."

"Okay, I'll do it now than."

He pulls out his phone hitting the speed dial Damon Gee picks up after four rings and I answer, "yo, what up?"

"Look I need to holla at you right quick in the back office with me and Almasi."

"Okay I'll be right there." After a few minutes Damon came in the office with a big smile on his face and asked, "you got something for me to do already, Dun- Dun?"

"Yes, have a seat look I been talking with Almasi and I told her that I'm bringing in my own peoples."

Damon Gee asked, "what that got to do with me, Dun- Dun?"

"Well I changed my mind I'm going to bring in Rico Salazar to be my consigliere I'm sorry man."

"Okay Dun- Dun I'm glad you're telling me now than a lot later shit."

I looked at Damon Gee, "I told him to tell you now than to fucking wait."

Dun- Dun walk up to Damon Gee to shake his hand, "no hard feelings, alright?"

"No, I'm good with it and good luck to you brother."

They shook hands but I can see Damon Gee was not good with this move, but he took it like a man doe. Damon Gee quickly head towards the front door of the office, 'hold up I'm walking out with you Gee. We both walked out of the office and I say to Damon Gee, "who the hell is Rico Salazar?"

'He's the head of TGB the Ghost boys that call themselves that because they be ghosting Niggas from off the streets really fucking fast. They move a lot of heroin that don't fuck with coke."

'So, what are you going to do now?"

"Well Fly Ty holler at me but I told him that I was going to be working with Dun- Dun so I'll still see if that jobs still open because you're getting out the game, but I still have to work."

'I know but you have to know I done put in my time Damon."

"I know I'm not mad at you do what you have to do, Boss lady.You deserve to do what you want to do you been at it for a long time."

Rah- Killer came up to me and patted me on the shoulder, " well you free now girl so what are you going to do?"

" I brought a real nice place in Arizona. I'm flying out there tonight."

Damon Gee , "look, I'm going to get the fuck out of here alright. Almasi make sure you call me okay." He hugs me and he quickly heads towards the door.

Rah- Killer , "what the fuck is wrong with him?"

"Dun- Dun brings in his own peoples so he's not going to be his consigliere for the outfit."

Damn, that's fucked up right after he named him to fucking do it."

"Well he was going to do it later, so I told Dun- Dun to do it now than fucking later."

"So, who is going to do it then?"

"Some dude name Rico Salazar."

"What get the fuck out of here?"

"Yeah that who he's bringing in to do it."

"Well that nice cut you get every month is going be fucking gone once he steps in watch!"

"For real Rah don't say that shit."

"I'm telling you he's going to stop your money watch what I tell you girl."

Soon as she that it made me start thinking than Rah- Killer elbows me, "that's him right there."

She nodded her head towards where he was standing at the bar with Dun- Dun and his new bodyguards. Little Luke and Fat Jimmy there laughing and carrying on having a good time. Rah- Killer , "you know that's the same Nigga your sister Robin got him off that murder case some time back."

"For real that's him."

"Yeah that's him girl. So, when do you go to Las Vegas?"

"One week from now I'm packing my shit I'm almost done."

Soon as she said that Dun- Dun came over to where we were standing at, "yo, Almasi. I want you to meet Rico Salazar."

Soon as I seen this dude, I got bad vibes from this Nigga down in my soul. He stuck his hand out at me and greeted me with, "it's so nice to finally meet you. Your sister is one hell of a fucking lawyer."

I shake his hand, "nice to meet you as well."

He asked, "why don't you have a drink with us?"

"No, I can't I have to get up out of here and get my grandson."

"Okay, maybe another time than. Well, it's nice to meet you, Glock Mommy. Live in the flesh you're a fucking legend in the game."

"Why, thank you and I be seeing you around and good luck to you."

I bump fist with him and Dun- Dun. I wave for Blood Eye and Poochie over. I need to get up out of there. I was playing it off, but I think I just killed everything we build up over the years. I think shit is going to get ugly, but I need a fucking break from this shit for real. Rah- Killer hugged me and whisper in my ear, "I'll call you, Sis. I love you."

"I love you too baby girl."

Poochie and Blood Eye walked by my side with my bags I quickly head toward the door. I , "Poochie make sure you check our whip before we pull off."

"You got it, Almasi and now that you're staying here with my sister you better watch your back."

"I think I just might have made the wrong move putting Dun-Dun at the head of the Meza (Table) over here with this Rico dude with him.

Blood Eye , "I think so too there going to fuck everything up from the door. I give it six months tops if you ask me."

None of us laughed we just all looked at one another soon as he it. We all walk up to my Benz wagon Poochie put some of my bags down pulling out the keys he was about to hit the remote I shouted, "don't do that, yet!" *We all quickly back up from the Benz wagon looking at one another.* I pulled out my phone and I called up Taz-Money he picks up after four rings and asked, "what's up,Almasi?"

'Look, do me a favor right quick?

'What's that, Almasi?"

'Come out here don't tell anybody where you're going and go get your truck for me." "Okay, I'm on my way." A few minutes went by and Taz- Money came outside getting his kitted-up Tahoe truck pulling up fast and yelled, "come on y'all. We all jumped in with my bags.

I , "when you get a little way from the truck, I want you to hit the remote. Soon as Taz-Money pulls off really fast we got about ten feet away from my black Benz truck." **Kaboom!**

It shook Taz- Money truck we all felt it I yelled, "you see that shit they just wanted me dead fuck stepping down."

Taz- Money yelled, "those no-good motherfuckers!"

As we all looked back seeing the flames growing higher with black smoke.

Almasi 2
Queen of The Streets
By Dartanya A. Williams Sr.

Poochie asked, "how you know that they were going to put a bomb on your whip?"

"Only one word I can say to you Poochie greed!"

Blood Eye chimed in and asked, "you don't think Dun- Dun was behind that shit do you Almasi?"

"Yes, I do! He will swear to God he had nothing to do with that shit."

Taz- Money , "where I'm I am taking you to, Almasi?"

"The airport, Taz and I want you to not tell anybody that you took me there for your own safety okay."

"Your right! I see how there working after I seen your truck blown up there some dirty ass motherfuckers."

"Just keep your head down and watch your ass Taz and you too Poochie. I want you to be around to take care of that baby your about to have my Nigga." We all giggled. We reach the airport I told Taz- Money which hanger to go to on the far left for me to get on a private jet. I rented me and Blood Eye got out along with Poochie with my bags and Blood Eye had his backpack on his big shoulders. I hugged him and repeated again, "watch your ass, Nigga!"

"I will him and Blood Eye bump chest." I tell Taz to step out the truck he did really fast I hugged him and patted him on the back, "take care of yourself. I holla at you later, okay." The pilot came over to me and asked, "are you Miss Miller?"

"Yes, that's me."

"Okay were already right this way." Blood Eye is right by my side carrying my bags as we both get on the luxury jet. I wish Jay could have come with me, but he cannot leave the state. I told him fuck them come with me he no he did not want to risk getting locked up again he he will sneak out there after a little while. Aunt- Tee , she wanted to stay here in Philly too so me and Blood Eye are going to Arizona.

to this ranch I brought a few months ago called Sun Dance. I only told Jay about it and no one else until I was ready to roll out. I can't wait to see it not on a computer to see and live in it for real. I lean back than I hear this banging on the door soon as the jet door when up I jumped up running to the cock pit with the pilot saying open the door back up! hurry up he lets the door back down it's Poochie yelling it two trucks driving up on us really hard and fast. I run off the jet along with Blood Eye we both pulling out are guns. I run over to Taz- Money "you have any machine guns in the back?"

"I sure do I'm always ready for war, Ma." Taz- Money quickly ran to the back of his kitted up Tahoe truck pulling out two AR-15 machine guns he hands me one and a full clip I slapped it in real quick soon as I did that I got the feeling I use to get in my BDC days. (The *Body Dropping Clique) I looked over at Blood Eye he got both his pistols out. Getting ready to fuck shit up for real. Along with Poochie and his two Glocks in his hands and fire in his eyes to kill shit.* I yelled to the pilot to go in his office and stay low. This tall blonde hair motherfucker is scared to death running his tall white stiff ass to his office. I stepped up getting in my gun stance along with Poochie, Taz- Money and Blood Eye as the trucks came riding up hard the two trucks stopped right in front of the Jet hanger and jumping out of the first truck is Puerto Rican Joe, X and Willie Whack- Whack. They all yelled, "don't shoot!"

"Hold up it's us!"

Jumping out the second truck is Ty- Kim and his two step- sons Tony Gee and Seany Guns. I yelled, "hold your fire boys!"

Taz- Money asked, "you sure it's not a trick!"

I , "it's cool and I grabbed the front of his machine gun and repeated, "it is cool, okay! Taz thanks for being there for me. I will never forget it, brother. Chill the fuck out."

I do not blame him after my Benz wagon got blown the fuck up. I hugged him as everybody walked up with their hands up.

Puerto Rican Joe chimed in and shouted, "you're not going to leave town without giving me a fucking hug or something."

"How the fuck you know I was here, Nigga?"

"You know I always find out shit in situations like this you should know that shit by now!"

He came over and hugged me than X and the others hugged me one by one.

I chuckled and announced, "y'all Niggas are lucky. I was going to smoke your ass!" All of them busted out laughing.

"Well, now that you guys see that I'm getting on my way safely. I might just get the fuck out of here and check out my new place in one piece. Now could one of y'all go in the office and get the pilot Mister blonde hair blue eyes fly guy that I'm ready to go."

"Ty- Kim and Yo Tony Gee go get the white boy out the office for her hurry up!" He quickly walked to the end of the Jet hanger to the office on the left-hand side grabbing him up in his collar pulling on him. When Ty Kim seen what he was doing when they came out of the office.

Ty-Kim yelled, "don't rough that man up he has to fly the fucking jet man let him go!" All of us is laughing the pilot came up to me, "let try this again Miss Miller."

"Yes, this time I think we're going to be more successful what is your name?"

"My name is Ray."

"Okay, Ray were getting the fuck out of here, my man and my friends will make sure that I'm fine."

Ray *looked at every one and nodded,* "well, I can see that for sure."

I waved for Blood Eye to come with me he just bumps fist with all the fellas and came up behind me getting on to the luxury Jet again leaning back. *I can see the look on Blood Eye's face checking out the light brown leather chairs on the jet the shit is sharp I have to say. I have been on jets like this one too many times, but I got a kick out seeing him rubbing the seats and leaning back enjoying himself.*

Before Ray when into the cock pit he its champagne over there and some fresh Caesar salad and chicken nuggets on the gold dining tray, "if you guys want something to eat."

Me and Blood Eye ate some the chicken nuggets and the Caesar salad, and we drank two bottles of champagne we were snorting some coke and smoke three blunts too it took us four hours to get there. After we landed, we went to this five-star hotel checked in and we got some sleep. We both were really tired and fucking high when we got off the jet.

We got up the next day and I was excited to see my new place. We ate breakfast and I called the woman name Dana Reed she was my contact to show me the place.

and if I like it, they will get the rest of the money the same day. *I did all of this on my own I did not trust La- Nesa ass anymore. She had been acting funny after Mookie got killed like it was my fault or something.* Blood Eye will move his family out here as well if I like the place and he can get a place of his own too. He was excited about that. Soon as I called her, she knew I was coming it only took her 20 minutes to come pick us up we drove to the place and it is fucking magnificent something right out of my dreams. Lots of land two Jacuzzis one inside and one outside near the pool shaped like a Spanish guitar. A beautiful long bar pool side and an outside fireplace with a large patio area. It also came with the grill and the inside of the house is fucking is breathtaking with eight bedrooms. We stopped back in the living room when Dana was showing me around and I yelled,

"I'll take it!"

Dana chimed in with, "that's good I'm so glad you like the place. We can go to my office right now and do some paperwork after that I'll give you the keys."

I ask her after we do the paperwork could she take me to a luxury car rental place she knows. She answered, "sure, I would love to Miss Miller."

We ride back to her office it was nice too. We took care of the paperwork and I transferred her the loot right after that she took me to Mister Big Deals luxury motors and I rented a Bentley GT coop white on white. I told Blood Eye to wait in the office while I look and see what I want on the show room floor. I was like a kid in a candy shop for real I see about five different ones I wanted. After I picked out what I wanted the owner Mister Big Deals Jonny Smooth, he is an older plum black dude that managed a few rappers that went big time. He offered to show me around town."

I told him that I was good but thanks for the offer, but my man is a real Jealous type of Nigga. He smirked looking me up and down, "Well what he doesn't know won't hurt him, baby!"

"Look I tried telling you nicely, but you don't look like you got enough Viagara to fuck with this pussy here big man. So, calm the fuck down alright."

"I like you, Ma you got fire. I bet you're the same way in bed a real wild cat."

"Now, if I told my man Jay Black the way you're talking to me he'll kick your ass so bad you be wearing your ass for a hat!"

"Hold up your man is thee Jay Black from North Philly?"

"Yes, thee Jay Black he has over six car dealerships just like you, Fat ass!"

"Hold up, Ma! I did not know that you were Jay Black's lady. I am really sorry about that."

"I'm thinking you're just another hot fly looking Shorty that's down with whatever you know. I am really sorry Ma."

I can see in his eyes he really did know Jay. I saw the fear in his eyes. Jay might be nice and sweet with me, but this Nigga done did his share of fucking dirt out here on the streets now. I pull out my phone and his eyes get wide.

"Hey, look here, baby girl. I am really sorry for the way I behaved just put the phone down Ma and I'll let you have the whip for a month free. Just do not tell your man what I to you, please."

I just smirked at him and announced, sounds good, but a couple of months would be better than just one, big man."

"Okay, I'm with that and welcome to Arizona, Ma."

He gives me that phony smile of his he does not know I'm going to Bogart his shit and not pay him a fucking dime and he better not say a fucking word about it, or he'll get smoked. I called Dana asking her where the liquor store was at. Me and Blood Eye stocked up on some liquor filling both bars inside and outside my new place it was already furnished. I already had two ounces of coke on me in my coach bag and only an ounce of weed but I'll have Tanya mail me some more. We went back to my new place and we both got fucked up pool side at this beautiful place I just copped. I am loving it nothing, but sun, weed coke and drinks. Every day in Arizona went by fast, I face time Laquitta every other day to see my grandson. Baheam he is getting so big he is a real hand full just like his father was when he was a baby. I facetime Jay all the time as well he did come some weekends. He did sneak out there to check it out so we can Christian the place right with a lot of hot sex and some deep down real hard-core gangster fucking. Me and Jay were like two minks in fucking heat. *I mean we were fucking all over my new place pool side, the Jacuzzis twice, the bedroom the living room by the fireplace in the hallway and crazy Romanic shit. This before I put in all the cameras and shit. You know I put in one hell of an alarm system in that motherfucker ten times better than at my other joints.*

Two weeks later Blood Eye moved his family to Arizona they all love it out here. I used the same agent Dana to hook his place up at another gated community. Blood Eye saved up his chips to get this joint. His wife Mary was over the moon when she saw the place. Blood Eye place was not too far from my ranch. I hired a few people to help me keep the place up like Miss Marie Sanchez. She cooks her ass off, and she cleans good as well. She asks me to hire her son Juan who just got out of prison when I saw him. He looks like a gang banger with all his tattoos and shit, but I gave him a chance. I told her if he fucks up he was out of here. *I told her like that, but she doesn't know I'll smoke his ass from the door.* But he is working out fine so far. Him and Blood Eye get along like good thug brothers.

Jay met him and their cool too they tell each other fucking war stories when they are getting high talking shit to one another. My drops of money are coming in regular every month with Carlo Cash. So far and I do not ask him how things are going in Philly. because at this point, I don't give a fuck neither. Only thing I heard was my son came back into the fold but he's not rolling with Booby Hill anymore. They fell out over some money or something now he is down with John Spartacus and the S.O.S Smash on site clique and now he is a fucking beast.

Three months goes by like a dream and by May of 2019. My dream quickly turned into a fucking nightmare. It is Friday night this was one of the weekends Jay sneaks up to the ranch after me and him had some buck wild off the chain sex. We went out by the pool to chill and we are getting high pool side at the bar. It is me Jay, Juan and his lady Melanie Blood Eye and his wife. Mary when I get the call. I am feeling good. I get the phone and I know the voice right off the bat it is Tanya.

"Hello, Almasi! How have you been doing? So, you know who this is?"

"Come on now, Tanya I know your voice. it is good to hear from you, girl!"

"Well it's good to hear from you, too, but I didn't call you with any good news doe."

"What happen?"

"Shit done went off the fucking rails here. Aunt La-Wanda is dead and Little Boom is going the fuck off."

"What the fuck did you say?"

"I Aunt-Tee is dead and so is her son Sonny and her old man Reggie they killed them in your condo. The homicide detectives want to talk to you so you can give them the code to your surveillance tapes so they can know who did it."

"Who the fuck did it!"

"Six of Rico Salazar men but two of them are dead. Poochie came over to check on her and he killed two of them and the rest of them got away now it is a fucking war."

"Where is my sister Robin at?"

"I just put her on a jet she should be there in a couple more hours or so along with Laquitta and your grandson Baheam. We want them to be safe, and I got the surveillance tapes do not worry. I am way ahead of you."

"Good work baby girl and hold on to them until I get there and give them to me and keep this shit under your hat Tanya, thank you."

"I'll call you back to find out who is on who side but I have to get Blood Eye to go pick them up. I'll call you right back."

I quickly go up to Blood Eye, "look dawg, I need you to go to the airport and pick up my sister and my daughter- in law Laquitta with the baby for me please."

"Sure thing, Almasi. I didn't know they were coming out here."

"Neither did I, hey Juan you go with him, okay."

He just nods his head, "yes, Jay came over to me saying what happen, Almasi, baby?"

Tears ran down my face and I took a deep sob. "Aunt La-Wanda is dead they just got killed by Rico Salazar men at the house."

"Oh my God. No!"

"Yeah, I just got off the phone with Tanya she told me things is off the fucking rails there."

Then my phone rings the call is out of the area I get it any way I answer, " hello."

"Hey, what's up, Almasi. this is Eddie."

"Fast Eddie?"

"Yes, it's me. Look, I know you turned shit over to Dun- Dun but I have to tell you this they just locked up some guy name Jody Wilson. I believe he's your daughter in law's stepfather."

"Yeah. What about him?"

"I got nothing to do with that low life project Nigga."

"I know that, but the feds don't they just busted his ass with eight keys of shit and there trying to link it to your organization."

"We never put that Nigga on at all Eddie. Who the fuck would give that Nigga anything he's an real ass hole for real?"

"I know your girl La-Nesa did that shit. Not only did she give him the coke she when straight to Dylan Thompson with D.E.A. and his team knowing he was going to fuck it up she made sure that he did as well."

"Well, I'm going to fucking make sure she gets what coming to her. She's not on the streets."

"So, where the fuck is, she at?"

"She just got locked up for this section eight scam the judge was so pissed off at her fucking over elderly people he denied her bail. She up in Philadelphia Federal detention center."

"Thanks Eddie, I'll make sure you get paid for this."

"No, I don't want a dime for this one, Almasi. You been good to me. I'm looking out like you looked out for me. If I hear any more, I'll let you know talk to you later." A blunt hanging from his sexy lips. Look come walk with me while I tell you this shit were walking towards the house I began to speak, "look, I just got some more bad news this low life Nigga La- Nesa gave some coke to Jody just got locked up and there trying to link that shit to my peoples."

"What? Who is the Nigga?"

"Laquitta's stepfather name Jody."

"You think he's going to talk?"

"Yeah, I do think he's going to talk."

"He's a lightweight, Nigga. He can't do any real time he's a fishcake Nigga all they have to do is put a little pressure on his ass and he'll fall apart."

"So, what are you going to do?"

"I'm going to call around and see if we have any peoples in PFDC. So, we can take care of La- Nesa ass for setting us up in the first place."

"What about the shit going down in Philly what are you going to do about that shit?"

"I'm going to have to fly back to Philly and find out what is what on the ground."

"I know you do, but I think it's all a set up to get you out in the open to kill you Almasi. If you ask me and my trial is coming up next month too. Do not worry about it, baby. I will keep you clear from the bull shit okay. I'll figure out something out trust me."

Two hours later my sister Robin and Laquitta with the baby sleep laying his head on her shoulder came walking in the door Laquitta coming up to me hugging me. Then Robin came up to me hugging me as well saying wow you place is really nice but it's fucking hot out this motherfucker. I looked both them in the face saying are you alright? Robin, Yes, I'm good but I'm worry about Poochie with all this new bull shit going on. Laquitta, I feel the same way Little Boom is going off that they killed Aunt La- Wanda I don't want him to get hurt. I he'll be just fine baby look Blood Eye show them to their rooms for me please. I point at Laquitta saying look baby when you get settle in, I need to holla at you about something okay. She just nods her head yes. I pull out my phone walking into my bedroom with me waving at Jay to follow me. I quickly call my son Little Boom to find out what the fuck is going on back in Philly.

His phone rings three times and he pick up and asked, "what's up mom? I am glad you called."

"You got to be real with me, Boom baby. What the fuck is going on there?"

"Mom, things are all fucked up. I hate to tell your boy Dun- Dun is just a figure head. Rico Salazar is running one half and Puerto Rican Joe is running the other half."

"Yeah, what side is Fat Wally and his crew are on?"

"There down with us Puerto Rican Joe. He really stepped up his game mom if it weren't for him Rico and his Ghost boys would run everything, but they can't fuck with us for real."

"So, what happen with Aunt-Tee getting killed?"

"They were trying to find out where you were at, but Aunt La-Wanda would not tell them where you were at that's what Poochie told me what happen."

"What happen with you and Booby Hill?"

"He's down with Dun- Dun and that fucking Rico Salazar motherfucker he tried to light bag me then he sends his boys to take me out. Me, Donzilla, Ron Gucci, Patty Racks, and Jacob Fats took care of their ass."

"Booby Hill is the only one that got away."

"Okay, I'm going to call you back."

"Are you coming back to Philly?"

"I'm going have to but don't tell anybody okay."

"Okay mom is Laquitta and the baby there?"

"Yes, there safe, bab.y I'll call you back all right one."

"Moja(One)." I quickly hit up Jagger to make sure my son story is on the up and up. He picked up on the first ring.

"Yo, what's up, sis?"

"I was doing good until I heard the fucking news about Aunt-Tee. My heart is fucking broken. I love that woman she always looked out for me from day one."

"I know she was good people I went to check up on her these fucking thugs was in the crib, so when they came out the door, I smoke two of them. The rest of them got away. What they do to her Jagger? They fucked her up bad it looked like they were torturing her trying to get her to talk about something."

"Like what, doe?"

"Maybe to find out where you were laying your head. You already know they tried to take you out when you stepped down."

"That's fucked up. So, what about this shit with Booby Hill and my son Little Boom?" "Look. your son has been a little too cocky in the past, but he is a whole new dude now after his training he got from Crazy Monk. This time he was in the right. Booby Hill is on some other shit now that he been fucking with Dun- Dun and Rico. He's a real greedy motherfucker now. Him, Ticky and Gee Dawg. Yeah them Niggas done flip the strip on y'all for real. Yeah, they even got into it with Jane Doe's crew too after they send them to do a hit and Booby Hill did not pay them for it. You know Jane Doe went the fuck off if they didn't have too many men Jane Doe would have killed him."

"Yeah, so what's up with Fat Wally and his crew?"

"There down with us they know where their bread is buttered at their cool, Almasi. I would not lie for his fat ass that Nigga done change too, Sis." He took a pause and then continued,

"I can say he has been a real good soldier so far. Him and his peoples you would never think we were mortal enemies not too long ago."

"Have you heard from my brother Mustafa?"

"Yeah, he's working out really good with us Almasi. He hooked up that deal with Charlie Champlain on the West coast him, Puerto Rican Joe, El Barero, X, Fritz Burger and John Spartacus is the best of friends now that monster flow is coming in along with your boy Quan Kauu that Vietnamese cat."

"That's good to hear. Listen, I'm coming back to Philly, but you have to keep it on the fucking low."

Almasi 2
Queen of The Streets
By Dartanya A. Williams Sr.

"I won't say a fucking word, sis just let me know where you going to land, and I'll be there to pick you up okay."

"I'll text it to you when I get in the air tonight, okay."

"I'll be there sis Moja(One)"

"Moja!"

I hang up with him and I looked over at Jay and announced, "I have to have somebody here to watch over my sister Robin and Laquitta while I go back to Philly."

"Call your boy Willie Whack- Whack or why you didn't ask Jagger to send a few of his men here while your there."

"You know that's a good fucking idea that way none of them Niggas could back door me thanks, baby. You always help me out with all this bull shit, and I ran up and kissed him." He replied, "I'm looking for a little more than that later on."

"Well, that's going have to be on hol bedcause I'm going back to Philly."

"Soon as I can get somebody here to watch over Laquitta the baby and Robin." I still have my phone in my hand I quickly dialed Jagger back.

"Yeah sis, what you forget to ask me?"

"I forgot to ask you I need two good men here at my ranch to watch my baby sister my daughter in law and my grandbaby."

"No problem, sis. I will send Little Bay- Bay and Gun Ho Moe."

"Good, I like Gun Ho Moe that Nigga is no joke with a gun. He is just as good as me with one."

"Don't let him hear you say that because he thinks he's better than everybody he is good." "Yeah, he's not better than me don't you ever forget that shit, Nigga."

"Okay, I can set up something like what y'all did with Miss Octavia and we can find the fuck out."

"Yeah, you do that shit after all this bull shit is over. We can do this shit and do not put your money on your boy because you are going to fucking lose, Nigga. You are ready know I am fucking good now motherfucker."

"Yeah, whatever now. I'll do that now how are you going to get my boys over to where you're at, sis."

"Tell your boys to go to Elite Flight at hanger 15 on the international side of the airport tell them to ask for Ray or Mick. I will have a private jet to fly them here it's a four-hour flight here to Arizona."

"I'm on it right now. I'll make sure they get there I'll drop them off and I'll text you when there in flight."

"Thank you, Jagger. I can always count on you, brother. You know I love you. I love you too sis let me go get these Niggas so I can get them there Moja(One)"

"Moja!" I quickly called Elite Flight and I talk to Mick letting him know that two of my people is coming. and to take out the money from off the card. I just used with them on file. He did it fast and it when through nice and smooth. I thanked him, and I hung up. Jay asked, "Am I flying back with you when you're ready to go?"

"Yes, baby. I need for you to be clear of this shit your trial is next month. So, you can't be in all this bull shit that about to go down."

"Yeah, but I want to help you take these motherfuckers out because this is going to be a whole lot more then with the chain Gang because there on the inside of your organization and there dug in deep."

"Look, we have too many soldiers were going fuck them Niggas up really good." *I started thinking about Aunt Tee and I started crying. The tears just started flowing down my face like somebody turned on the water Fossett at full blast. Jay stood up over me wiping the tears from my eyes hugging me.*

"You can't think like that baby you have to outthink these Niggas like you did them chain gang dudes along with some might and a whole lot of fucking Witt to kick some ass."

"Your right, baby it is just that they done killed my family and I want every last one them motherfuckers to pay with their life."

"You're getting all fucking emotional about this shit you still have to have your head in the game here."

"They don't call them motherfuckers the Ghost boys for nothing. You must think okay, call around with your peoples and find their weak spots then make your move. You are not in that BDC *Body Dropping Clique* any fucking more. You are a boss, so start thinking hard on what you can do to them. Like you been doing baby I'll make some calls as well and we can beat them at their own game."

"Your right I'm just hurt right now that's all I want to kill everything moving."

Jay held me in his arms I feel so safe and he is right I had to get my shit together. I kept thinking about Aunt-Tee La-Wanda getting killed because she was connected to me. It is a fucking shame. Now don't let your men see you like this! *He wipes some more tears from my eyes, and I started focusing on the task at hand. I kiss Jay on the lips, and I let him go.*

"Yo Jay, I'm going to the back room and talk to this girl right quick so I can know what to do about that shit as well."

"Yeah, it is good to do that, but don't forget to call around and see what you can dig up on these Ghost boys. I heard their thick as shit that is the only thing, I know about them."

"So, who told you that?"

"Poochie told me when he was coming past the house when you were here."

"Okay, Let me go holla at this girl I'll be back."

I quickly walk towards the back room to talk to Laquitta when I reach her room and I see her sitting on the bed crying holding the phone up to her head. I peek inside the room and I asked, "what's wrong, baby?"

She looks me right in the eyes with tears running down her pretty brown face and replied, "somebody just killed my mother La-Vonne."

"What? Get the fuck out of here for what, doe?"

"My cousin Kimmy because they say my stepfather Jody is snitching to the D.E.A." "Look, I need to talk to you Laquitta, please."

"Alright, hey Kimmy, I'll call you back thanks, cuz."

She hangs up looking up at me as tears are still streaming down her face.

"You talk to Boom."

"Yeah, but he didn't want to talk, too much he told me not to worry."

"He told you right my son knows how to handle himself, baby."

"I know that, but I'm still worry about him regardless I love him."

"What you know about your stepfather's peoples he hangs around?"

"Who Peanut, Fat Jake and Chico is a bunch of fucking low lives. If you ask me, Miss Almasi excuse my language."

I just giggled.

"That's alright, just call me, Almasi, okay."

"I know their scum bags for sure. Do you know where they hang out at or where they live at?"

"I know where two of them hang out at this dive bar at Girard Avenue and I can write down two of their address because when Jody use to get drunk my mother use to send me to go pick his no-good ass up."

"From what I hear from you that you don't like him all that much. I just put up with his ass because of my mother. I do not know why she loved that Nigga so much he was just a small-time ass hole crook."

"Write down those two addresses down for me please and his last name too. I'm so sorry to hear about your mother and don't you worry about nothing I'll take care of all her arrangements when I get back to Philly."

I point towards the desk on the right-hand side of the large bedroom where it some paper and a pen. She quickly goes get it and writes down the two addresses while she is still crying. Soon as she was done writing she looks up at me. When she is done writing she announced, "I'm coming with you."

"No, you're not your staying here where its safe and I'll let you know when you can come back to Philly."

"You will let me know when it's cool to come back, right?"

"Yes, I will baby."

She hands me the piece of paper with the addresses on them I quickly look at it and I stick it in my pocket. I walked over and hugged her, "if you know anything about me, they will all pay for killing your mother for sure."

"I know that you're no joke. I knew that before I even hooked up with your son and I know you're not going to take no mercy on them assholes."

"I want them to burn in hell."

"And they will burn in hell when I'm done with them baby, trust me."

I bump fist with her, and I walked over and kissed my grandson while he was still sleep. I walked back into my bedroom so I can make them calls. Without Damon Gee I feel a little handicap. I sit on the bed next to Jay and I call Ty- Kim. He picked up after four rings.

"Hey, what up boss lady? How have you been?"

"I was doing fucking great until I got the call about my Aunt-Tee. I know that was really fucked up."

"I heard about that. I was sick to death after hearing that shit you have my deepest condolences, Almasi."

"I know you and her, was really tight."

"Why, thank you. Ty- Kim."

"I called to ask you about what you know about the Ghost boys.

"Well they got their shit together selling heroin but only thing they are down with the white mob the Esposito family. They are backing them up they are their foot soldiers in the dope game."

Soon as he that I got a flash back me and my crew smoke Fat Neck Nicky Esposito and his family. Now I know why they wanted to kill me when I wanted to step down, they got the order from them.

"I can tell you that shit and their number two-man Crab hand Frank and his brother Big Rosco got over 200 soldiers on the street. Maybe another 100 wannabees. Niggas following them and over a 1000 Niggas down with them behind bars I know that much." "Do you know who their top dawg behind bars is?"

"Yeah, his name is Rusty Long. They say he killed 80 men on the streets and over 100 behind bars."

"I have one more question Ty. Did you hear about Jody getting locked up?"

"Yeah, but he's not down with what we have going on who gave that dumb motherfucker that much coke?"

"La-Nesa did it and she when to the D.E.A. To make sure he fucked it up to."

"But she must be long gone by now we have to take her monkey ass out fast."

"Check this shit out, she's in PFDC as we speak, my Nigga. Do, we have anybody on the inside to get to her ass?"

"I sure do, Almasi."

"Who then?"

"Remember when you send us on that Emillano Vargas hit."

"Yeah, what about it, Ty- Kim?"

"Well, the girl name Cambria the one I had to stop Chrome from killing in the spot.

She got locked up with 100 keys of coke and a million dollars in cash. They have her in there."

"Oh yeah, do you think she will do it for us?"

"Sure, she will do it she's already running shit up in there if I get in touch with her. She will do it for me. I am the one who had Chrome back up off her."

"But you had on a fucking mask she's not going to know it was you Ty- Kim? Are you sure this shit is going to work? I want La-Nesa ass dead before she starts talking too."

"She knows it was us somebody told her after we let her go look, I'll take care of it for you Almasi, trust me."

"Okay, Ty- Kim if it doesn't work please let me know what the fuck is going on right away."

"I got you, sis. I'll send in my peoples to holla at her she will do it."

"Well, thank you, Ty- Kim. I am glad I called you."

"Oh, for sure, Almasi you know I'm still family, sis."

 "Now, I have to see about some other shit too."

"Like what it sounds like you are coming back to clean shit up with the mess Dun- Dun fucking made."

"I'm going to have to or I'll get cleaned up with the people I was dealing with. Like who, Coyote and his thugs?"

"No, the motherfucker he works for his name is Arturo."

"Well I know you will get the shit done and I'm right there to help you out, Ma."

"Thank you, Ty- Kim. I holla at you later and let me know what that chick Cambria have to say."

"I will Almasi, Moja *(One)*."

"Moja! I get a text on my phone from Jagger that *my peoples are in the air.*

I text him back *the addressed at the airport where to pick me up at.* Jay is sitting right next to me listening to everything. He touches my face, "see, you're a boss bitch getting shit done. Now call up one them crooked ass cops you still have on the payroll and see what going on with Jody stupid ghetto ass."

I go in my dresser draw getting my satellite phone. I sit back down on the bed next to Jay who now rubbing my shoulders. I quickly call detective Don Wilson he picks up after four rings and yelled, well long time no hear from Almasi. What's up with you?"

"I need some information from you detective. Well I hope I can help you. What is it you want to know about my dear?"

"I want to know if this ass hole there to trying to link to my people's name Jody Sanders the D.E.A got his ass."

"Okay. give me a few hours and I will call you back at this number. I will tell you what I found out okay."

"Sure, thing Don. I'll talk to you then." I hang up bumping fist with Jay.

"Babe, lets pack are shit up so we can get ready to get the fuck out of here."

Me and Jay packed our clothes, have a few drinks and snorted some coke laughing and talking about shit other than the fucking dirty ass game. Soon as we were done Gun Ho Moe and Little Bay- Bay arrived. Blood Eye came banging on the door letting me know that they were there. I open the bedroom door and answered, "good and I need you to help us with our bags. Where they at?"

"They're at the bar near the pool outside with the others."

Me, Jay and Blood Eye carrying our bags along with Jay. I tell them to leave them by the front door while I go out and talk to them.

"Jay and Blood Eye let me talk to them by myself, please."

They both just nod their heads yes. I walk out to my large patio area near the bar I say to Juan, Melanie and Mary.

"I have to talk to them alone please could you guys step into the house for me please so we can talk."

They also nod their heads yes walking back into the house as I wave over Little Bay- Bay and Gun Ho Moe.

They both sit down on the bar stools looking up at me one with a beer in his hand and the other puffing on his Newport. I began, "look my people's life is in y'all hands please don't let me down.

Gun Ho Moe chimed in, "we got you Almasi."

Both bump fist with me.

"Give me y'all phones I'm going to give you both my numbers so you can call me if shit jumps off. Let me know right away. And I want you to keep an eye on that kid Juan he might sell us out for money. I don't know him all that good okay. Now his mother is cool but, I still want you to keep an eye on her as well."

Gun Ho Moe replied, "I know just what you're saying, Almasi don't trust nobody."

"You got that one fucking right brother and I bump fist with him."

I quickly walked to get out of there I go in the house soon as I get to the front door. Jay looked at me and announced, "somebody in the parking lot in front of the house."

"Who is it?"

"He his name is Jewy he he works for Arturo and he wants to talk to you."

"Okay, wait here. I'll be right back." Jay yelled, "no, I'm going with you!"

Blood Eye also chimed in, "me too!"

"Look y'all, it's cool, I'll be right back okay just stay here."

Jay yelled, "No! I'm walking with you fuck that!"

I looked at both and no matter what I had to say I knew they were going with me, so I just gave in "all right, come on y'all."

Now the three of us is walking towards my parking lot in front of my ranch Blood Eye is on my left and Jay is on my right we all stroll up walking up towards us is big ass Zack and Jewy. I see four other guys I never seen before popping up out the darkness with machine guns. Zack announced, "look, it's all good Almasi Arturo just want to talk so your men can wait right here nothing is going to happen. We wanted to kill y'all we could take out the whole ranch in 15 minutes, okay so tell you people to fall back."

I looked up at Jay not saying a word he kissed me on the cheek and Blood Eye looked at all of them and yelled, "yeah, you might take out the whole ranch, but I'll kill about half of y'all in the process!" Then he looks Zack right in his face with his gun out. Zack just smirked and lowered his tone, "it's cool, brother just be cool alright with his hands up in the air."

I just looked at Jay and Blood Eye, "it's alright y'all."

I started walking with Zack towards the long black limo not too far from where Jay and Blood Eye is standing at. I walked up to the limo with Zack he quickly opens the door and I jumped in Arturo smiles and greeted me, "hello pretty lady, I hated to come up here to talk to you, but I had to because things are really fucked up."

"Well, that's my fault because I was thinking I could pass it off to someone I came up with and thinking he could handle it. I'm going back to Philly to fix shit soon as I get back."

"Well that's good to know and if you're going to step down let me know first, please. I'm not trying to tell you how to run your thing but if you're going put someone into your spot make sure it's somebody like Puerto Rican Joe because he's the only one who saved your life."

He is running shit right and he knows what he is doing that kid Dun- Dun must go along with the people he brought in with him. You got to clean that shit up because you put him in your going have to take him out." He paused and then *he looked at me to see what I was going to say.*

Almasi 2
Queen of The Streets
By Dartanya A. Williams Sr.

I looked him back in his eyes and announced, "I'll take care of it personally, Arturo." "Good, I'm glad to hear it well I'm going to fly back to Caracas and I'll send you some more help some more of Coyote's men to help you out with this okay and then they will come back once you get the job done."

"Thank you, Arturo for being so understanding."

"It's not your fault that you are so loyal to the people you came up with, but people change over the years that what you have to know about firsthand. Look at what Spider tried to do to you after all them years you bust you ass for them. You already know your going have to take out. Nokey Blaze as well he's not going to sit back and let you run shit or retire. Your going have to get at him and take him out as well or he's going to get at you."

"You are right I have to get at him, and I will."

"Talk to Coyote and his brother Koo- Koo about that when you get back to Philly."

"I do want to step down Arturo I been at this shit for a very long time."

"Sure, I want you to fall back and enjoy yourself, but like I you have to put in somebody who is going to do the job right. Now you done fucked up one time please do not do it again. Most people I don't give them a second chance at this shit. I like you and I know you know what you're doing but you can't go by the time someone did with you go by who can get the job done that's what I do. Some of my people get upset with me all the time. I know who can do the job and the one who can't that's what you have to learn times change and people do too."

"Your right, Arturo I will do that."

"From my understanding that's why they put you at the head of the BSN that's why I came and started working with you. I knew you could do that job with all the shit you when through and yes I did my homework before I started fucking with you that what you have to do for now on okay."

"Your right I'm going to get up out of here and take care of that shit."

Almasi 2
Queen of The Streets
By Dartanya A. Williams Sr.

"I know you will good talk, Almasi call me after you take care of things. I know you going to get it done I see you soon, goodbye." I bump fist with him, and I step out of the long black limo and my wheels in my head was fucking turning like a motherfucker. I walked up to Jay and Blood Eye both hug me and we all started walking back towards the front door Jay so what happen?

I looked up at him and announced, "I have to take Dun-Dun out that's what happen." Blood Eye did not say a word he just smirked we quickly got our bags putting them inside of the white Bentley trunk. Blood Eye still smirking got behind the wheel Jay sat in the back with me and he took off. I to Blood Eye while he was driving up the road, "you didn't say goodbye to your wife."

He , "she knows what's up, I'll holla at her when I get back, she knows I have a job to do. She better do her fucking job taking care of my kids. Who is going to take your car back to the crib, Almasi?"

"I'll have Little Bay-Bay or Gun Ho Moe to take it back to the ranch."

It took us no time to get to the airport. I called Little Bay-Bay to come get my whip we quickly got on the private jet to get to Philly because I have a shit load of work to do. I have to get it done or I know I'm dead. While we were in the air, I started working the horn like I was on air force one or something. I called up Tanya and I told her to get my office ready and to call up Tee Cee from the Black Demon MC's and tell him give her six cases of hand grenades. She said was right on it. Then I called up Jimmy Goon and I told him to round up all the boys and make sure there at the office when I get there.

To make sure he keeps that shit tight within the gang. I hit up Jane Doe and I told her to meet me at the warehouse with her full crew. She told me she would be there and it's about time somebody is going to make a move on this Nigga! We both laughed and I hung up soon as I hang up with her. I called up Fast Eddie the crooked cop on my payroll and I told him to meet me later tonight so I can have a run down on all the Ghost Boys and some of their family.

I hit up Jagger and told him I was in the air and I'll be home in few hours and to bring all of his shooters with him. The four hours went by like a blur we touch down in Philly and I was all hyped up to get to work. When I stepped off the jet with Jay and Blood Eye, I seen Jagger came to the hanger with three trucks of down ass thug killers ready to go to work. In the first truck was Jagger, Steve Swiga and John Rocka. The second truck was Frank Iilly, Flip Diddy and his brother Fat Smoochy. The Third truck is my son Little Boom, Donzilla driving Ron Gucci and Levi Gats. I quickly pulled my son and his squad to the side. I quickly hug my, son and I bump fist with his crew "I need for y'all to go snatch Twanda Dun- Dun's wife she is staying at one of my condo's I own in Chestnut Hill. You know where it is at Boom. After you grab her ass take her to Sedley avenue warehouse call me when you get there."

My son nodded his head, yes. Little Boom replied, "don't worry. Mom we got this shit." I winked my eye at him as they quickly rolled out the door, I know I have to make my first move on this ass hole. I bump fist with Jagger stepping up and asked, you ready to take this shit back over boss lady"

I replied, "You better fucking know it!"

Jagger quickly helped Blood Eye with the bags, and he asked, "you with us, Sis in this truck?"

He waves his hand towards Frank Iilly, Fat Smoochy Jagger yelling, "I want y'all to follow us and keep your fucking eyes open where are we going first, Almasi?"

"My office on Washington avenue then I'm going to Luxury Golden Towers."

Jagger shouted, "you all hear that and nobody else better not know about it or I'll kill you myself."

Everybody nodding their heads yes. Then Jagger yelled out loud with his fist in the air, **"Wacha Tuondoke sasa** (*Let's move out now*)!"

Everyone started moving quickly as I walked with Jagger to the truck with Jay and Blood Eye by my side. We all quickly jump inside of the truck and head towards the freeway to my office. Meanwhile my son and his crew went and close in on the condo in Chestnut Hill. One smart thing my son did on the way there they called in for more men to help them out thinking to himself that she just might be heavily guarded. So, he called for Lorenzo Large driving Jacob Fats, Mark Mongol in one truck. Killer Cody, Crazy Kyle and Patty Racks driving joined them in another truck. Soon as I got to my office in South Philly the three trucks, full of killers arrived at the condo. My son Little Boom called and talk to everyone on speaker telling them she's on the second floor before they got there. The all gear up dressed in all black with black mask and gloves on checking their machine guns ready to jump out and get busy.

Donzilla pulls up in the first truck at the front of the condo Little Boom, Ron Gucci and Levi Gats jumps out at the same time just like crack commandos. Jacob Fats and Mark Mongol jumped out with their machine guns in hand. Killer Cody and Crazy Kyle is running towards the back of the condo at the same time. The guards at the front of the condo are in shock because they never been in real street combat before the on slot of bullets is too much for them to handle the group of mask killers ripped into their ass immediately. **Kacapacka Rata tat tat tat!** *Ron Gucci Little Boom and Levi Gats smoke the first four men on post. They hit them in their face, chests, and legs shredding them like they were rag dolls hitting a chainsaw. Their blood and chunks of flesh slashed and cover the front of the building.*

The rest of the other four bodyguards on the inside of the condo don't want to come out and engage the black mask killers smoking motherfuckers.

left and right after they seen what happen to their friends getting picked off faster than an, blink of an eye. Jacob Fats and Mark Mongol came up joining Little Boom, Ron Gucci and Levi Gats blasting and ripping them apart these punk ass bodyguards never ran into some real gangsters putting down their murder game killing all of them in ten second flat. In the back of the condo its four bodyguards but two of them run inside and two stand and fight spitting hot shit soon as they see Crazy Kyle and Killer Cody coming towards them with hell fire on that ass.

They both stay low never stopping retuning fire, but they are more accurate when they take aim hitting each one of the men in the chest, head and neck blood flying everywhere as they fall to the ground with loud death screams. The two bodyguards who hauled ass inside ran right into Jacob Fats and Mark Mongol they both strayed them all over like the wooden ducks at the carnival game. Their bodies falling backwards to the floor with smoke blood and were all disemboweled from burning hot led shower. Ron Gucci Little Boom and Levi Gats are running up the stairwell to the second floor on the right-hand side. Little Boom knew just where to go leading the way up to the apartment door. **Boom!** *Little Boom kicking in the door lighting up the first two men taking aim with the help of Levi Gats and Ron Gucci they overwhelmed them with all their firepower another blood bath slaughterhouse special. Tawanda tried running with her little girls. Little Boom yelled, "don't run because I don't want to hurt you Twanda!"*

She stopped and looked at him and screamed, "I know that fucking voice Boom is that you, Nigga?"

Little Boom just came up on her fast with his machine gun in her face nice and calm then he mashed into her head and yelled, "don't move!"

He quickly reached in the back of her jeans taking her gun soon as he did that Mark Mongol and Jacob Fats ran up closer in their gun stance with cold death gleaming in their eyes. They both have her locked down pointing their machine guns at her she knows if she makes one wrong move, she is fucking dead like the God Mommy in Columbia drive by. Little Boom he points nice and smooth yelled, "Ron, Levi get the kids I got her go.

Jacob and Mark watch are backs as we roll out it just might be some more of them ass hole amateurs running around in here!

He looks at Ron and Levi with the two little cute girls Kya and Mala yelling, "okay, let's go!"

Killer Cody and Crazy Kyle came walking up Little Boom and yelled, "kill the cameras in the control room downstairs while we are getting the fuck out of here."

Killer Cody ran downstairs shooting all the camera equipment he ran outside before running to his truck and announced to Little Boom, "I took care of all the cameras when they all ran outside."

Little Boom grabbed Twanda by her arm with his machine gun by her side "I don't want to kill you, but if you try to run off, I will kill your ass and you know that shit bitch!"

Twanda screamed at the top of her lungs at all of them, "you Niggas are dead men fucking with me and my family. You know who the fuck I Am!"

Almasi 2
Queen of The Streets
By Dartanya A. Williams Sr.

Little Boom just looks at her not saying a word all of them were in shock knowing he would say something. He did not he just pulled her inside of the truck hard when Donzilla came pulling up fast. Ron and Levi got into the truck with the girls quickly and gently with Twanda never taking her eyes off them. While they were on their way to Sedley avenue warehouse I was setting up shop back at my office. I quickly called up Taz- Money so he can take Jay to the condo. He arrived fast within a few minutes of his team Little Ziggy and Big Booker with him to make sure nothing happened to Jay. When I looked around in the warehouse Tanya really took care of this place while I was gone. Soon as I walked in the door to my place, I felt good seeing Jimmy Goon, Crazy Jamel, and Bango. I bump fist with all of them. Jimmy Goon points to the new guys and began the introduction, "Almasi, this is Juba and Chaco my two nephews I brought them in while you were away."

"Okay brothers, welcome how is your Swahili?"

"Juba said mine is Nzuri (*Good*)!"

He looks over at Jimmy winking his eye at me with a wide smile.

"So, what about you, young brother? **Mgodi ni ngumu sana malkia** (*Mine is really tight to queen*)."

Everybody started laughing loud.

I looked up at Jimmy, "you really train these Niggas well. I like that shit Jim- Bo."

In a laughing voice he replied, and "you know it boss lady let me show you to your office.

It's just the way you left it!"

He walked with me to my office as my satellite phone started ringing soon as he opens the door for me. I answer it pointing at the door for Jimmy Goon to close it for me as he sat next to me and I leaned back in my big office chair.

It is my son Little Boom and he announced, "It's done we got her."

"Good make sure she doesn't get out of your sight, okay. I talk to you later."

I hang up and tapping on the door is Tanya I wave for Jimmy to get the door he lets her in bumping fist with her. She came over and I stood up to hug her.

"I am so glad to see you girl!"

"I'm so glad your back to take care of all this shit for real."

"That just why I am here, baby girl. How have you been?"

"I've been better I got them hand grenades you ask for in the back. I had the boys set them back there."

"Good, what did he say when you when to pick them up?"

"Tee Cee if you need any help to let him know."

"I just might have to take him up on that shit too hay do you have that tape with you from my condo with you."

"I sure do right here she show me the DVD in her hand just let me know when you're ready."

Soon as she told me that Crazy Jamel came and knocking on the door and he opens it up "Almasi, it's Puerto Rican Joe here to see you."

"Okay, thanks Jamel show him back here and make sure you take care of his men for me."

"You got it, Almasi."

Jamel came back with Puerto Rican Joe he walks in the door closing it behind him. I stood up to hug him,

I'm really happy to see you, Joe."

Puerto Rican Joe replied, "I'm glad to see you as well, but I'm sad that you had to come back here for all this bull shit."

"Please have a seat, my brother."

He bumps fist with Jimmy Goon smiling. Then he quickly grabs a seat sitting in front of me Tanya get up ready to go out the door.

"Where are you going. baby girl, I want you and Jimmy to hear this."

Puerto Rican Joe began, "well, I came past here to tell you I been holding shit down while your boy been really fucking up. He sent them motherfuckers to kill your aunt that was some foul shit that sparked a war with us. Your son really dug in their ass and I backed him up 100% because he was in the right the whole time."

"I really appreciate everything you have been doing Joe. I have to tell you this I talk to Arturo and he told me if I was going to step down to put you at the head of the Meza (Table)."

271

"I never met the man before."

"Well, Coyote told him all about your good works with the outfit."

"I'm going to step down and you're going to be the man when I do but first, I have to take care of the mistake I made six months ago."

All of us started laughing. "Okay, Tanya. I really don't want to see this shit but get the projector and put the shit on so we can see who killed my aunt La- Wanda."

Tanya quickly set up the projector and she puts in the DVD inside.

She quickly turns the lights off then she sits down with the remote and she points it at the projector. We all sit back in are chairs looking up at the wall we can see clear as a bell the four monsters beating and whipping on my aunt unmercifully blood flying all over the place with her screaming at the top of her lungs. Puerto Rican Joe and Tanya points out and started naming who was who.

Tanya chimed in, "see that's Big Rosco the one holding her and the one beating her to death is Sukey his brother."

I asked, "who is the other two goons fucking helping them."

Puerto Rican Joe points at the large projected images up on the wall and replied, "that's Crab Hand Frank the, real ugly motherfucker and the little one is Twiggy Jones he's a really sick fucker." *I watch them beating on my aunt, but she is putting up a fight. Auntie knows she cannot win but she fights any way.* As we all can see him shooting my aunt in the head along with Sukey. I could not even look but I see, it and it made me sick to my stomach. Watching all these big ass thugs beat and shoot an older woman like that. Before her final breath, my aunt La-Wanda yelled, "all you low life motherfuckers is going to die when my niece finds out about this shit!" *Her words cut me in half.*

I yelled out to Tanya to turn that shit off. "I've seen enough!"

She quickly turns it off and she turns the lights on, and she sits back down. Me Puerto Rican Joe, Tanya and Jimmy Goon just all look at one another not saying a word for a few minutes.

I know all of us is feeling the same thing fucking discussed.
Puerto Rican Joe stands up and announced, "well, were getting the
hell up out of here, Almasi. Let me know when you are going to make
your move on these motherfuckers."

"Don't worry I will and it's going to be real soon brother."

I stood up hugging him then Jimmy Goon bump fist opening
the door for him. Soon as I sat down my satellite phone rings, I
answer it quickly it's Ty- Kim and he greets me with, "what's up, sis? I
am glad your back."

"Me too, brother. What's up with you?"

"Well, I got to the girl Cambria and she told me said will do it,
but she wants money on the books and some when she gets out."

"Okay, I'll send you the money what is she talking about?"

"It's only so much money we can put on her books. I'll take care
of that, but she wants a million dollars, but she wants us to put it in
an account with her lawyer on the outside." "Okay, give her the
money we can use her down the line so make sure she gets that loot
go get it from Carlo make sure you get that done right away."

"Oh, I'm on it right now. I'm going to call her soon as I get off
the phone with you Ma." "Okay bro, I holla at you and thanks
Moja*(One)!* "

"Moja!"

Crazy Jamel came tapping on the door again and announce,
"Jane Doe and her crew is here."

"Good show them in I've been waiting on them."

Jane Doe came strolling in the room with her brother Buckey
Guns, Neck Bone and Tia Slim. I bump fist with all of them and from
out of nowhere the two Dick Head detectives came rushing in the
room along with them. Tanya stood up ready to pull her gun out I
quickly grabbed her hand and whispered, "don't do that, baby girl."

Detective Johnson jumped bad yelling in her face, "Oh, you
were going to pull a gun out on me, bitch!"

As he pulls out his gun holding it on Tanya and at the same time
his partner detective Towns whips out his pistol. All cocky with a
smirk on his face. Tanya pulled her gun all the way-out lightning, fast

along with Buckey Guns, Tia Slim, Neck Bone Jane Doe and Jimmy Goon pointing their guns at the two detectives. *I to myself where these two ass holes come from.* I look at both in a middle of this highly tensed Mexican standoff. Detective Johnson yelled out, "I know why your, back here putting together your fucking murder squads against you little ass hole friend Dun- Dun!"

Out of nowhere walking in between us is Coyote with no gun in his hand he is looked both detectives in their eyes get the fuck out of here right now!

"What they both don't notice he's getting closer to them. Detective Towns looks at him and asked, "who is this fucking clown with all the tattoos on his face?"

Coyote started smiling, "oh your calling me a clown when you two the last time you were here Crazy Jamel knock both y'all out and took your guns and you both were suspended so who is the real fucking clown here."

Detective Towns barked, "out your under-arrest clown face, Nigga!"

Coyote just smiled then he quickly grabbed both of the barrels of the two detective's guns snatch them from their hands and at the same time lifting both of his elbows upward hitting them under their chin knocking them to the floor. **Kaplang**! *Wow I know that shit hurts bad just with the expression on their fucking faces.* All of us is laughing our ass off seeing both falling on their ass hard. Coyote looked down on the two detectives holding their guns, "I ask you two assholes nicely the first time to leave the fuck from out of here now. If you walk out here this time without your guns both of you Dick head motherfuckers will lose your jobs!"

Detective Johnson yelled in his deep hard voice, "give us are shit back or you're going to be in some really deep shit you can't get out of!" *Were all still chuckling loud looking at these two hard -core detectives on the floor in my office like little kids begging for their guns.*

Detective Towns began to bargain with Coyote, "look we will both leave here but you have to give us are guns back okay."

Coyote barked, "I think your fucking lying but this is what I'm going to do I'll go outside, and I'll give you your guns without the clips, okay."

Detective Johnson yelled at the top of his lungs, "I don't fucking believe this tattoo face motherfucker Karim man." Soon as we get outside, he's going to fucking smoke us.

Detective Towns nervously began to speak, "I think my partner has a very good point he just might be right about this shit." Coyote puts both their guns in the front of his jeans as the two men are looking up at this huge muscular black man with tattoos all over his face.

Coyote asked, "what choice do you have either you walk out of here without your fucking guns and you both will be the fucking laughingstock of the whole fucking department. Plus, you both lose your fucking jobs and you can't feed those spoilt two rug rats you have Karim and your three teenagers you got Darrell."

They both look at one another soon as one of them was going to say something Coyote cut them off and Coyote continued, "I know everything about both of you two ass holes! Now stand up and walk towards the door slowly or I'll have everybody in this room put more holes in your ass then fucking swish cheese!"

Coyote pulls out the same two guns he took off of the two detectives and he yelled, "Stand the fuck up, right now and head out the door or I'll just nod my head and everybody in this room will put some hot shit in both of you two silly dilly motherfuckers."

The two detectives stand up quickly as Coyote points towards my office door with all of us is not laughing everybody have their guns on them. I lifted my gun higher and chuckled with each word that fell out of my mouth, "tell Jesus, I hi motherfucker!"

As Coyote walks them to the front door right before they were going to walk out the door Crazy Jamel pop back from out the back room looking them in the face waving bye to both of them with a big smirk on his grill. Coyote pushed both out the large gray steel door the minute they stepped out the door speeding up is a big Black GMC truck. It pulls up on the pavement as two of Coyote Goons Paco and Yaya jumps out with black mask and machine guns up in their face making them get into the truck very quickly. *They looked like they were going to cry like two bitch made Niggas.* Coyote jumps up in the front seat with his brother Koo- Koo Man behind the wheel taking off down the dark street. While we were laughing about what just happen, I send Jane Doe and her crew of killers to go take care of Jody's low life peoples with the information my soon to be daughter in law Laquitta gave me.

All of us got the fuck out of dodge while me, Blood Eye and Jagger drove back to my condo. On the way there I called up Fast Eddie and told him. I'll meet up with him the next day or so. Tanya and Jimmy Goon was driving behind us to make sure I got home alright. I got home nice and smooth. Poochie was there sitting in his car waiting on us Jagger called him so he can be on post. I was so glad to see him. I hugged him as the three of us went in the house and Jay was on the couch sleep trying to wait up for me. Isn't that so cute?

While I came in the house Koo-Koo Man and Coyote drove the two bitch made detectives out to this deep wooded area making them get out the truck as Yaya and Paco pushed them up this long dirt road going deeper into the woods. As they were walking in the cold dark woods detective Towns just stopped and yelled, "fuck it, kill me here if you're going to kill me!"

Yaya came up on him sticking the machine gun in his face and barked, "if that what's you want motherfucker!"

They didn't know that Coyote was behind them he started shooting towards the ground **Plow! Plow! Plow!** *Just missing detective Towns feet, he jumped as Coyote yelled,*

"keep walking Nigga until we tell you to stop. He looked back and started walking faster along with his partner detective Johnson. They walked them both another twenty feet and stopped at this big hole in the ground they already had dug. On top of the dirt pile they can see the two-shovel shining from the moon light up above. They both looked down in the deep dark hole soon as detective Towns went to leap at Yaya Coyote and Paco started shooting the two men mercilessly with their bodies shaking like a twig in a hurricane before their bloody bodies fell face first into the large dark hole.

Almasi 2
Queen of The Streets
By Dartanya A. Williams Sr.

Yaya jumped in, "damn y'all didn't let me get some of that shit." He looked down in the dark hole only seeing the smoke floating up from their bodies. Paco and Coyote started laughing loud.

Coyote spat on two men in the deep grave, "I wanted you to save your energy to toss some dirt on these two pieces of shit!"

You're a Double-Crossing Ass Bitch

We both were exhausted having a long ass day, so I made Jay come off the couch and come to bed with me. So, me and him had to have one of them wee hours in the morning wake up fucking encounter with him rubbing his huge third leg on the back of my fat ass. I was horny too, so I to myself what the hell. I kept feeling his hard-on rubbing up on me feeling so good making my Twat sticky and moist. So, I just opened my legs still laying down. I reached back giving him a good helping hand for him to plug into my super wet hot socket. So, we both can feel this electricity between us flowing. As I'm giving my sexy hot hardbody baby that most wonderful reach around he started ramming his thick hard tube stake into my sizzling hot muffin he didn't get his large dark meat all the way up in me and already I started moaning feeling his large strong hands grabbing my hips one up and one under pulling me closer to me nice and slow. I can feel each one of his strokes filling me with his man hood.

What I really was loving is feeling the head of his large Dick hitting the rim of my dripping wet coochie is tingling making all kinds of popping noise. *In between both of us making loud sexual sounds is like an, blazing eight alarm erotic symphony that can fills the whole condo and the one next door too.* Jay is bunny bumping me from the back pulling on my hair I'm groaning and pushing my, ass back on Big Jim and the twins and I don't have to be looking at him I know this Nigga got a big hump in his sexy dark back making all kind of faces rocking my hot pussy so good.

I can feel his hard erection going in and out of my hot wet cunt. This Nigga is pumping faster and faster while hanging on to me tighter that can mean only one thing this Nigga is about to cum. He doesn't even know I'm already there I beat him to the punch, and I let mine go and scream, "oh shit! Oooooooooooh!" I see huge white stars and the 4th of July firework gushing like a hot geyser in yellow stone park. Soon as Jay started feeling my hot love juice squirting all over his large love muscle and **Boom**! Jay yelled, grunted and curse in pleasure. He kept pushing into me as I felt his hot Jizsm all up in me sizzling like hot lava. Wow it made me feel like I was going to cum all over again. Jay lifted himself up and began kissing me on the lips. "Damn, that was good, baby!"

I know Mister Big Dick any time. We both chuckled as he flops back down on the bed blowing out air. I sit on the side of the bed and I reach for my pack of Newports. I light up two of them and I quickly hand Jay one of the cigarettes,

"thanks, baby."

We both are still trying to regain our composure. We are sweating like we ran the 100-yard dash. I walked towards the bathroom puffing on my cigarette like it was a joint floating on air in a climatic bliss. I took a shower and got dressed snorted a couple lines of raw ass white girl and a big glass of gin with a lot of ice soon as I was done. I told Jay that I was going to the warehouse to take care of a few things.

I never told him that I had snatch Twanda I should have told him about it, but I'll tell him about it later. I kiss him, check both my guns, Poochie and Jagger are in the front room sleep soon as I walked in the room, they both jumped up with their guns in their hands. I yelled,

"It's me motherfuckers get ready to roll out were going to the warehouse suit up brothers. Poochie go get Blood Eye from the back room and we can all go."

"okay, I'll go."

He quickly walked to the back room and banged on the door hard. Blood Eye jumped up walking to the door and screamed, "what the fuck do you want?"

"Yo, this is Poochie. Almasi is ready to roll to the warehouse. Let's go!"

"Okay, give me a few minutes and I'll be out Poochie."

Poochie yelled, "alright don't take too long man we have to go."

After a few minutes Blood Eye came out bump fist, "let's roll, Nigga!"

Blood Eye walked to Poochie and I toss Poochie the keys. He caught them in mid-air as the three of us walked out quickly to my truck in the driveway. Right before I open the door to get in my phone rings and it is Tachell.

Her voice is trembling, "Almasi, I need you right now please hurry these motherfuckers is trying to kill me!"

Her condo is not too far from mine it is on the other side of the courtyard about a good 100 feet away. So, I ran towards her door all out of breath with my pistol in my hand ready to smoke anything moving. Jagger Blood Eye and Poochie is right behind me I ran in the door that was wide open. Soon as I get all the way up in the large living room, I see a gun in my face and they yelled, "don't move."

When I looked up its Booby Hill standing next to Tachell with a gun in her hand with a big smirk on her face. Blood Eye, Jagger and Poochie are right behind me hauling ass.

From out of nowhere stepping out of the large space from both sides is some big chisel face gunmen they had the drop on us. We were covered from the left and right -hand side with Ticky, Gee Dawg and four Niggas we did not know. Named Guru, Black Bart, Beamer, Katar, Fat Roman and Billy Wild. All of them had machine guns pointed at all of us ready to rip our shit up if we just blinked.

Gee Dawg barked, "put your guns down right now or your fucking dead!"

None of us drop our guns with our eyes locked on every one of these low life motherfuckers. *I'm not going to lie I'm thinking this is it they got us in a tight motherfuckin spot here but, if I have to go. I promise I am taking more than a few Niggas to hell with me for sure.*

I yelled at the top of my lungs, "Tachell, you fucking double crossing little no good bitch! Everything I've done for your raggedy ass and you do this shit to me."

She replied with a sneer in her voice, "look who's talking okay. I'm going to say this one-time hand over your fucking guns now or were going to start spitting hot shit out this bitch!"

I yelled out, "where the fuck is X at? If you killed him, or we will start spitting out this bitch right now if you want you already know me, I will bang it, out with you, pussy ass Niggas!"

"He's too fucking stupid and loyal to your black ass. I'm getting mine right now and getting the fuck out of here after I kill your ass boss lady!"

All their gun men are giggling. Booby Hill quickly pulled her back, "we have to find out where they have Twanda at okay then we can kill them so chill out bitch."

She smirked and ran her tongue across her teeth. She glared at me while I am still holding on to my gun pointed up at them. Walking in the doorway leaning real cool is X.

Tachell is in shock it was him; he walks all the way inside the large living room looking at everyone. holding machine guns and guns on one another real calm. X just looks at everyone he just nods his head real cool with a wicked smile on his face looking at all of them.

Fat Roman, Billy Wild, Beamer, Black Bart and Katar turns their machine guns on Ticky, Gee Dawg, Booby Hill and Tachell they all have that surprise look on their faces soon as they see that they turned their machine guns on them. X walks up closer looking at all of them,"now drop your guns or all of you motherfuckers will get smoked where you stand!"

Soon as he said that Fat Lou- Lou, Fat Jacks, Gavin, Woo-Woo and Lurch toting machine gun came running in from the back door surrounding them now they look up seeing that they were out gunned. X yelled, "I'm not going to say it again, motherfuckers! Now hand over your fucking guns and put your hands up in the fucking air or you will get shot!"

Soon as he made an announcement that they all started handing over their guns and machine guns with a sad look on their grills. After they handed over all their weapons X walks up to his wife, he looked her in the face and asked, "so you were fucking Booby Hill the whole time since we been back here?" *I looked at X and I can see the hurt in his eyes.*

She just smirked cold as ice looking over at Booby Hill standing next to her like she didn't care. She did not say a word looking up at him. X pulls out is gun **Kapacka!** Shooting her right in the head her lifeless body fell backwards to the floor with blood gushing out of her head running across the pretty hardwood floor.

X quickly points his gun in Booby Hill face and barked, "so, you think I was not going to find out you was fucking my wife, Nigga."

Booby Hill lip trembled, and he uttered, "she was coming on to me, man. I can't help if you can't keep your bitch in line man!"

"You want to know what you're right, Nigga, but I still have to do this shit to you!" **Kapacka!**

Booby Hill fell sideways on the floor next to Tachell in a large pool of blood. X waves me over to him when I stood next to him, he asked, "what do you want to do with the others?

I just had to get my revenge on these Niggas after my man Katar told me they were here to set you up to find out where you had Twanda. He also told me what was going on with my no-good ass wife fucking this Nigga. Those stupid ass motherfuckers did not know Katar and his crew was down with me from the joint (Jail). They've been working with me every day when I came back here to Philly making mad paper."

All of them started laughing I smiled bumping fist with him and Katar and his crew right quick showing them some love for helping me out.

I looked over at Blood Eye, Poochie and Jagger waved my hand for them to come over to me. Soon as they walked over to where I was at, I pointed at Gee Dawg and Ticky All three of them with their guns in hand took aim **Plow! Boom! Packa! Packa!** Each one of them shooting them Blood Eye shot Gee Dawg in the throat he fell to his knees with the blood gushing out and he fell face first. Poochie shot Ticky in his face he fell sideways on the floor on top of Gee Dawg. Jagger shot each one of them in the head for the Coup De Grace after they hit the floor. Their blood and skull fragment splashed and exploded all along the nice hard wood floors. I walked over and hugged Fat Lou- Lou, Woo- Woo Gavin and Lurch.

"It's good to see my boys. What's up as y'all can see I'm back in town to take care of a few things."

They all started giggling loud.

Almasi 2
Queen of The Streets
By Dartanya A. Williams Sr.

"Well, we all need to get the fuck out of here. Don't worry, I'll clean all this shit up you and your men can get out of here."

"Thanks, X man. I hug him as me, Poochie Blood Eye and Jagger quickly went out of the back door. So, nobody seen us walking back around to the courtyard the back way to my truck."

We did it nice and smooth as we quickly jump in my Benz truck. Jagger sat in the back with me Blood Eye sitting up front with Poochie driving to Sedgley Avenue warehouse. It takes us about hour to get there we park outside the huge bob wire gate in the darkness. When we pull up, I see my son have his peoples on post. Poochie is about to get out to walk up to the gate. I announced, "hold up let me call him before we go in."

I pull out my phone and my son Little Boom. The phone is ringing when these big thug Niggas are coming outside the gate and towards the truck checking us out. One of the men looked at me and announced, "it's Almasi, it's cool."

I see him quickly talking into his headset. I looked out it's that young boy Akbar with Mojo. Akbar is holding his ear listening to Donzilla on the other end. He quickly walked up to the truck and uttering, "were going to walk you in Almasi right this way."

I stepped out with Jagger right by my side Blood Eye joined us with Poochie bringing up the rear we walked inside the door on the right where it two more men Tone and Jaleam Akbar bump fist with both.

As we all walked toward the warehouse through this large dirt yard and piled up cars in stacks up rows. When I get up to the big green steel door, I bang on it hard a few minutes later the door opened, and I see Jacob Fats. He bumps fist with all of us.

"I got it from here boys go back on post."

Akbar and Mojo nods their head and walk back as Jacob Fats wave us into the large warehouse. He takes us to the back space where Little Boom is sitting at this steel table with Donzilla and Patty Racks eating breakfast. Little Boom looked up and greeted me, "hey mom, what's up y'all want something to eat?"

"No, I'm good baby is everything alright?"

"Everything is fine, Mom."

He stood up and walked over to me. He gave me a hug and then he bumps fist with Poochie, Blood Eye and Jagger who land they all bull shittin with one another.

I asked, "where is Twanda at?"

She right over there he points they have her hand cuffed to a pipe in the deep right-hand side of the large space with a bag over her head sitting in a chair. And where are the kids? There in the room next to her eating Patty just fed them. I walked over to Twanda checking her out she knew someone was there, but I did not say a word. Then I walked over and looked in on the kids in this little room with bars on the door. They were both sitting at this little table they made for them there eating. I walked back over to the table where my son is sitting and I began to whisper, "look I'm going to call Dun-Dun with my demands. You know how you're going to do this?"

"Yes, but I wish I could get with Crazy Monk so he can make me a couple devices when we make the switch. I can make the devices for you Crazy Monk showed me how to do that shit as well and I'm good now." *I looked him right in his eyes.*

"Are you sure you can do this baby?"

"Yes, I can do it only thing what about the kids?"

"Well, you make sure the thing goes off before the kids get in the car that's all."

"Yeah, I can do that."

"Good, then that's what we're going to do then. I'll start working on them devices right now I have everything I need right here."

"Perfect, I see you later on and I'll give you the rest of the game plan on how were going to kill this Nigga."

I hugged him, "Good job, I holla at you later."

We quickly head towards the door the three of us get to the whip and we drive back to my condo so I can get some rest and put together my plan on how I'm going to take this motherfucker out tonight. *While I'm sitting on the couch watching sport center with my boo Jay later on that afternoon Detective Don Wilson called me on my satellite phone and let me know he has some information for me on some of the Ghost Boys.*

"Go get a pen so you can write this down."

I whisper to Jay real quick hand me a pen and some paper, please baby."

Jay quickly goes over to his computer area on the left-hand side of the room grabbing a yellow legal pad and a pen handing it to me. I wink my eye at him blowing a kiss at him. s "okay, Don go ahead."

Tyrone Jones aka Twiggy, his mother Belinda and brother Mike lives at 12th & Cambridge but Twiggy stay at the President house on City Line Avenue. Samuel Irving aka Sukey He live with his wife Jada and his mother Pam in Bala Cynwyd 20001 Church House Lane."

"Okay I got it go head."

"Rosco James aka Big Rosco is also in Bala Cynwyd. He lives at 4499 Montgomery Road. I got nothing on Crab Hand Frank yet, but I did get their top money man who run things with Rico Salazar. His name is Larry Whitehead aka Loopy he's at One Brown street condo suite two one right next to your place."

"What?"

"You heard me right he right next door to one of the condos you rent. You have a picture of what he looks like?"

"I do. I'll send it to you on your I phone hold on."

A few minutes go by and Bing! I look at my I phone.

"I never seen this Nigga before. That's him Almasi. Do, he knows I have a condo next to his?"

"No, as far as I know look Almasi they're not that sophisticated there really good at killing people but there just building their organization. A bunch of old heads in the game tried to help them get it together but none of them listen. They think they know everything like most young boys out here their just dumb Niggas selling a lot of dope for the mafia."

"Thank you, Don for everything."

"Well, I have one more thing to tell you but it's some bad news."

"What is it?"

"Danielle Crazy Monk's wife is working with the FBI."

"What?"

"Yes, she broke up with him while you were in Arizona."

"Why nobody told me about this shit."

"This just happen Almasi. Can we get to her?"

"No, but I'll work on something."

"Please do I'll make it worth your while if you do Don."

"I'll try Almasi that's the best I can do and be careful out there the police is going ape shit over those two homicide detectives that are missing."

"Okay thanks, Don."

Soon as I hung up, I tell Jay what was going on.

Jay thinks I should get those two pros Dime Piece and Bop-Diglo to take care of their top money man. I kissed him on the cheek because my man always has brilliant ideas. My rang and its Dun-Dun.

"Well hello, Dun Dun."

His voice is full of rage and he barked into the phone, "hell is low just like you Almasi and that's just where you're going if you put your hands on my family, bitch."

My Kids don't have anything to do with the Bullshit We Do!

"You are a backstabbing ass Judas, but I wanted to hear your sorry ass out they will be your fucking last words Nigga."

"Look, I already know its player to player, gangster to gangster shit from here on out it's on, but my kids don't have nothing to do with this bull shit we do."

"Your right about that but when you and your people tried to blow me the fuck up and killed my aunt when she did not have nothing to do with it neither."

"True, now I know you and me, are not family anymore but all I'm asking to leave my kids out of this shit."

I just held the phone not saying anything. I've done some bad shit all this time I've been in this fucked up game, but I never killed any kids on purpose."

I'm not a fucking monster even doe I have to be some time not giving a fuck.

"Dunn, your kids will be spared but your one dead motherfucker. Believe that!"

I hang up the phone. I looked over at Jay and asked, "would you let the kids go?"

"Yeah, I would let them go him and his wife I'll smoke their ass but not the kids."

"So, what should I do then?"

"Call up fast Eddie or one of them and have the kids dropped off at the fire station or something that's all."

That gave me a great idea on what I'm going to do with the kids. I know what to do I pick up the phone I called my son up. He picked up after the phone rings three times and asked, "what's up Mom"

"Look get one your people to drop off Dun- Dun kids at Chuck E. Cheese on Roosevelt boulevard in the next hour or so. I want one of your people to follow their ass and find out where he is hiding out at. I love the way you think mom I got somebody who is really good at that shit Jerry Lit."

"Okay, sounds good to me make sure he doesn't fuck it up."

"He won't Mom. He is one of the best."

"Who are you going to use to take the kids?"

"I'll get Patty Racks, to do it the kids like her but what happen?"

"Dun- Dun called me saying that his kids have nothing to do with the bull shit we do." "True that, but nobody else in this game would give him his kids back doe mom but I love this plan. It is fucking smart."

"I know this is his weakness we find out where he's at and we fuck their ass. Now you know why I'm running this shit."

"Your, right mom but don't worry I'll make sure this shit gets done."

From out of the blue I get a call from Crazy Chaz a Capo from the outlaw faction of the Philly mob I asked, "how the fuck you get this number?"

He replied, "an old head gave it to me. Listen Billy the Kid Vanzetti wants to talk to you about a few things."

"Tell him if he's willing to come to me, I'll listen to what he has to say."

"Okay that's what I'll tell him sweetheart you have a good night.'

I hang up with this motherfucker I know what Billy the Kid Vanzetti wants right from the door revenge on the Esposito family for almost killing him. He is the only one who survive the hit on his wife and kids. From orders of Pauly Hair Trigger Esposito. Back in my BDC days me and my crew killed his father Nicky Fat Neck Esposito, so I know I'm at the top of their hit list and Rico Salazar is their handpicked Nigga working for them. while I was waiting on my son to get that done.

Jane Doe and her crew tracked down one of Jody's boys name, Peanut. He was coming from his girlfriend house Latoya at 12 & Huntington Soon. As he came out of the house to go to his whip parked about two cars from the house driving up fast is Jane Doe behind the wheel. The sliding door open up in a blink of an eye. Bucky, Neck Bone and Tia Slim light his ass up with their machine guns spitting hell fury in the daytime. **Baaarrraattttt!** *They hit Peanut with so many bullets his body shakes violently as his bloody body fall backwards to the cold ground. He is ripped to fucking shreds and his guts hanging out from his body in chunks. He is smoking like a broke stove as the big black van speeds off down the street disappearing in the cold crowded violent city.*

Two weeks later we had a private service in Chestnut Hill for my Aunt tee La-Wanda her son Sonny and her boyfriend Reggie. Just friends and family seeing her in that casket hit me harder knowing she die just loving cooking and cleaning for me. What really surprised me is that I see my aunt Lisa Dotty's sister came with my brother Mustafa I didn't think they knew one another. He also brought his brother Big Billy Bob, his daughter's Tye, Delilah and Nikkya all of them are very pretty with great personalities. I never met them before. But Billy Bob first seen me he it was like seeing a ghost or something telling me. I looked just like my mother Teja and he pulled out a picture of my mother showing it to me as he cried hugging me. He was right I look just like her I ask him to give me a copy of the picture and he sure. He also he get blown up to a larger size.

It was nice to meet real family and then Mustafa's sister De-Wanda showed up as well and I met her, and she was nice too.

She told me she was doing her thing in Las Vegas after she that I knew this was not just some chance encounter Mustafa wanted me to help her out I was cool with that I was not mad at them. It was nice to meet family and the funny thing about it was all of them are in the drug game. They all gave me their information so we all stay in contact with each other My people had shit locked down I didn't want no cops or FBI slipping in there, but we knew they were all outside taking pictures, but we made it really hard for them. I was in a daze the whole time with sadness Jay was by my side to console me the whole time.

That same day later inside of the Philadelphia Federal Detention Center the women inmates where lining up for lunch. La- Nesa is in the middle of the line with her tray of food when Cambria comes up behind her Bam! Bam! Bam! Bam! She stabbing La- Nesa in the neck four times she falls to the floor shaking with blood gushing from her neck as Cambria slips into the crowd and she quickly handing the shiv(Homemade knife) to one of her home girls Big Belinda. When the guards ran over to help La- Nesa bleeding on the floor she was taking her last

289

breath. By the time the guards came with a stretcher to give her medical attention she was dead. A Half an hour after that when down I got the call from Ty- Kim. While I was talking to people at the funeral announced, **Imefanywa** *(It's done)."*

Asante*(Thanks)."*

Two hours later when I got back home from the funeral my son called me after making Dun- Dun sweat for a whole week like I told him to wait.

Little Boom, "Patty Racks is about to drop off Kya and Mala inside of Chuck E. Cheese."

"Is your man on the job?"

"Yes, he's right on it, mom."

"Good I'll talk to you later on tonight."

"I hit Dun- Dun up he picks up on the first ring saying you can go pick your kids up at Chuck E. Cheese Nigga."

"How I know this is not a trick to get me out in the open. I'm not fucking dumb you know Almasi."

"Well send your peoples or something I don't give a fuck your kids will be there motherfucker!" I hang up.

"I should have sent a fucking hit team there, but I didn't want anything to happen to them kids I'm not a fucking monster no matter what people think about me. I'm still working the horn I call up Willie Whack- Whack to see where his head is at. I have not heard from him in a while. He picks up after the phone rang five times.

"Hey, what's up, sis? How the hell are you?"

"I'm good I have not heard from you in a while, Nigga."

"Well were going to hang it up, I just been chillin. Well I'm back in town to clean shit up."

"I knew you be back after Dun- Dun been fucking up and I did not want to work for his young dumb ass at all. Fly Ty ask me to go to Las Vegas with him, but I told him, no I was good."

"Well, I need you, big guy is you going to come in and put in some work for me, Nigga?" "Oh, hell yes, I'm in what you need for me to do."

"I need for you to meet some of my peoples at my phone store you know where it's at right."

"Yes, I do what time you want me to come?"

Almasi 2
Queen of The Streets
By Dartanya A. Williams Sr.

"Come at six when the store is closing come in the back, I'll have someone let you in. All the tools you need will be there okay don't make your move on these Niggas on the list until 11 P.M."

"Okay, I got you! Moja *(One)"*

"Moja."

I hung up and I quickly called El Barero he picks up after the phone rings four times I answered, "Big Man, what's up with you?"

He recognizes my voice and cheerfully said, "yo, what's up boss lady? What's up with you?"

"Well, I'm back in town and I need you brother."

"Sure, whatever you need. I'm there for you what you need me to do?"

"Look, I have to be real careful because we had a couple asshole cops smoked so I need for you to send a couple of your guys to meet Willie Whack- Whack at my phone store at six o' clock. He's going to have a few addresses. I want these Niggas dead before the night is over."

"Who are they Ghost Boys?"

"Yeah, I want them to become real fucking ghost you know what I'm saying."

We both started laughing.

"I got you Almasi. I'll send Mister Pete, Butter and Maro three of my best men on it." "Thanks, Big Man. I'll meet up with you next week to talk about things okay."

"Sounds good to me, Ma, I talk to you than goodbye."

I called Miss Cookie that work at the store and I tell her to hang around later tonight and open the back door for Willie.

"Sure, I'll take care of it, Miss Miller."

Cleaning House

"Good, I'll take care of you with this week paycheck thank you baby." I *quickly called up Tanya to pick up the list with the addresses to take it to Willie Whack- Whack and the others to hit these Niggas.* An hour later while I'm watching TV the Family Business on BET some hot gangster shit while I'm doing some real gangster shit in real life. Dun- Dun sent his bodyguards Little Luke and Fat Jimmy when Patty Racks seen them, she got the fuck out of there. The kids Mala and Kya was playing in the playground area with the other kids. Little Luke tried to be slick asking the kids to point out the person who brought them there, but she was in the wind for them to know what they looked like when they pulled up. What they didn't know is my son's man Jerry Lit follow them back to Wyncote and my son was right. This guy was fucking good he took pictures of the house and sent them to my son. Little Boom called me up letting me know where they are saying at and he was ready to go with everybody. I get up off the couch and I walked over to where Jagger, Blood Eye and Poochie is on post in the front of the house chilling smoking cigarettes and drinking coffee. The smart thing Jagger did he called in Taz- Money, the two new guys he put on in the gang.

Named Crazy Paco and Midnight in the back of the house on post locking shit down. I went and spoke to Jagger Blood Eye and Poochie.

"I got him where I want him. I'm sending my son and his peoples to wipe their ass out." All of them smirked I looked all of them in the face and continued, "after this is done Puerto Rican Joe is going to be at the head of the Meza(table). And I'm going to need for y'all to keep working with him, but I also want you to grow and do your thing and take care of your families." All of them are nodding their head yes, *but I can see the respect they have for me just by listening. They all understand about me stepping down again, but they do know all the time I put into this shit. It's time for me to get out but I have to clean house before I go, or*

Almasi 2
Queen of The Streets
By Dartanya A. Williams Sr.

I'll be dead for fucking up. I put up a so-called friend I came up with in the game. But in this wicked ass game you cannot make too many mistakes, or you will pay for them with your life.

"Just pass that on to everybody for me and I love each and every one of y'all and know that shit is for real. **Kushikilia Kuwa chini** *(Hold it down).*" *I pat each one of them on the arm and chest with my fist.*

"**Keep up kazi nuri***(Keep up the good work).*"

I went and sat next to Jay I took a little nap laying my head on his shoulder it's 11.P.M. I picked up my phone from off the coffee table and made the call to my phone, "**Kuwaua Wote** *(Kill them all)!*"

*I hung up and everyone made their move all at the same time. Willie Whack- Whack along with Big De Sean, Akbar, Butter Mister Pete and Maro. They close in on the president house on city line avenue there all around on the 5th floor three on the left and three on the right-hand side of the large brown door ready to bum rush their ass. Willie Whack- Whack points to the big man Akbar to kick the door in Akbar runs back a little and **Boom!*** Big De Sean rush in first with Willie Whack- Whack Butter right behind him spitting on the left at the same time is Akbar Mister Pete and Maro spitting hot shit on the right with their machine guns. **Kapacka rata tat tat tatt! Kapackata!**

They killed Mike Twiggy's little brother watching TV and his mother Belinda in the kitchen cooking dinner. Twiggy's three fearless goons came out fighting Tony Rome, Jay-Mack and Kay- Dog spitting back with their Glocks but the on slot of bullets is too much for the three thug gun men all shot the fuck up. As all three men are dead on the floor in a large pool of their own blood gush out their bodies thick soaked into the carpet on the floor. While Twiggy Jones jumped out the window making it to the next floor balcony and got in the fucking wind. Willie Whack- Whack said to everyone **Wacha tuzungushe** *(Let's Roll)! Big De Sean asked, "what he say?"*

Akbar walked up to him and repeated, "let's roll."

Willie Whack -Whack got up in his face and whispered, "he's new like you and he knows a little Swahili when we get back you better be studying, or I'll kick your ass every time I see you." As they all ran out of the apartment towards the exit door. Soon as they got to the ground floor two cop cars flashing their blue and red lights.

Meanwhile at the same time at the large house in Wyncote where Dun-Dun is hiding out at parked outside the house Patty Racks is behind the wheel of the black GMC truck as Little Boom Donzilla, Ron Gucci, Jacob Fats jump out like blood thirsty savages born to kill shit. They kicked in the front door with their machine guns spitting hot led all you see is muzzle flash going back in forth in the fire fight. Even after Little Boom and his S.O. S. Smash on Sight squad killed the first eight men in a matter of seconds they still were putting up one hell of a fight. With just a few men trying to stop the mask killers in all black coming at them killing everything that moves. Mark Mongol, Killer Cody, Levi Gats and Crazy Kyle running toward the back of the house at the same time. The four men had an easier time killing the four men at the back door making it inside of the house faster than a flash of light **Barrrrttttaaaaa!**

Killing the next three men posted inside of the house.

Little Boom and his squad finally broke through killing the last six men who put up a good fight. Even though they lack manpower they all went out hard like real fucking Gees going for it. Dun- Dun held his machine gun in his hand as he panics watching all the men bombard his home the surveillance cameras. Its only four men left himself, Little Luke, Fat Jimmy and Jimmy's brother Casper.

Casper yelled, "why are we still here? We can make it out to the tunnel come on Dun-Dun!"

"We can't because we will get trap down there because the tunnel is not finished that's why ass hole."

"Why you never finished it man what the fucks up with that shit with all the fucking money you were making God dam?"

"I didn't have time man I was running a huge organization Nigga that's not easy to do. I never had the time to get back and get this shit done Casper man what do you want me to say Nigga?"

Little Luke replied, "they don't know that we can hide down there until there gone man Casper is right."

Dun- Dun whispered, "only thing we can do is to shoot it out with them."

Fat Jimmy turned up his lips and hissed, "man your fucking crazy it's a hundred motherfuckers out there, Dun- Dun, man."

"So, what are you going to do Fat ass give yourself up? There here to kill all of us and that is just what they're going to do man!"

Fat Jimmy barked, "man, if you would have not let Rico Salazar run this shit into the ground we would not be in this fucking mess."

Dun- Dun looked him in the face,"it's too late to point fingers at one another we all have to fight. I am not going out like a bitch it is what it is motherfucker!"

Casper yelled, "well, fuck you. I'm out of here."

He quickly ran towards the back of the room pushing the button on the side of the wall as the large Fancy ass bookcase slides over towards the left and he ran inside as the bookcase slides back in place. Dun- Dun looked at Fat Jimmy and Little Luke and asked, "so what are y'all going to do?"

Fat Jimmy, "I'll take my shot at the tunnel soon as he when to run towards the large wooden bookcase. **Kaboom!**"

The large door blew off flying in the air rushing in the door is Little Boom, Donzilla Jacob Fats and Ron Gucci on the right along with Crazy Kyle, Levi Gats and Mark Mongol came in the door machine guns blazing spraying the whole room with bullets **Kapacktacka! Baaarrrttttaaa! Tackapacka**!

The first to get hit was Fat Jimmy the barrage of bullets cut him in half like a hot knife through butter. Little Luke tried to put up a fight, but he was hit so many times in the face removing his whole jaw from his face in big chunks. Parts of his face hit the walls and floor falling backwards in a bloody mess on the floor. Dun- Dun lifted his machine gun shooting but he also was hit so many times with the on slot of bullets ripping his arm from his body. He fell face first on the floor screaming in excruciating pain. Little Boom put up his fist for everyone to stop shooting. He stood over his bloody bullet riddled body with his machine gun in his hand pointing at his head barely alive gasping for air. He yelled, "this is for my mom, Nigga!"

Kapackataka! He shot him in the back of his head as his skull fragments flying everywhere and half of his brains hung outside of his head. The rest of it is scattered all over the floor looking like little pink peanuts. Little Boom pulls out his phone taking pictures of Dun-Dun's bloody corpse. Then Little Boom quickly took pictures of Little Luke and Fat Jimmy mangled bloody remains on the floor and they got out of there as quickly as they came. Casper laid low until everyone was gone, he was the only one who made it out that house alive to tell the tale.

Back at City Avenue the two cop cars think they have their suspects trapped in Willie Whack- Whack told everyone to stay back inside of the exit door. He quickly came up putting up his hands in the air like he was surrendering. While the four cops jump out of their cars all cocky with their guns out. The tall white cop yelling saying keep your hands up in the fucking air and come out slowly motherfucker! Willie Whack- Whack just was getting closer to them to smoke their ass. then he quickly fell, backwards flopping to the ground in the dark parking lot. All four of the cops started shooting at him. **Plow! Plow! Plow! Plow! Plow!**

The cops could not see him well in the dark and they were shooting at will.

Willie Whack-Whack super-fast whipped out his two machine guns under his long black coat at the same time pointing upward. **Kapackatapack!** He hit the two of the cops up front in the face and chest falling backwards to the ground dead instantly both of their eyes were wide and their mouth wide opened. **Doom! Doom!**

The other two cops quickly ran and took cover behind their police cars after seeing that on the left and right- hand side both them. They both were scarred. He quickly rolled over to his feet tossing two hand grenades on the left at the cop behind his car shooting and two hand grenades on the right. **Kaboom! Kaboom! Kaboom! Kaboom!**

He blew up the rest of the cops that were shooting at him. Their bloody body parts were scattered all over the parking lot like leaves on an autumn day in the park. Their body parks are all on top of cars windshields and splashed all over on the cold black asphalt the chunks were smoking like a steamy pile of dog shit. Willie Whack- Whack ran back to the exit door and yelled, "come on let's go!"

As the flames and smoking is flying up in the air out of control as Willie Whack- Whack and his crew of killers make their escape from off the scene in the mist of all the chaos going on with firetrucks and police cars arriving on the scene. After they were flying up the expressway.

Willie Whack- Whack with his hit team of killers made two more targets, I had him kill Sukey and his mother Pam in their Bala Cynwyd mansion. When the two trucks pulled up real quietly Sukey is sitting up in his front room getting his Dick sucked from his rich white girlfriend, Dana. You could tell she was fascinated with big black tools and snorting heroin all the time. The cute little millennial couple never knew what hit them it happened so fast. Springing up out the darkness is Willie Whack- Whack Butter, Maro, and Mister Pete shot out the large picture window **Tisssssszzzzzz!** Running in the crib shooting him up in his lavish front room **Barrrraaattttt!** Soon as they shot the two lovers up on the couch his mother Pam pulling up in her white Volvo coming from seeing one her boy toys in the city on the late-night tip. Big De Sean and Akbar on post outside seen the white Volvo pulls up in the parking spot on the side of the large house the two of them stepped up out the dark and lit her ass **Kapackataka!**

It was blood all over the windows and her wig was in the back seat filled with blood with half her dome with it. They all moved quickly in dark jumping in their trucks heading out to the next target not too far from where they were at.

They creeped up in the dark to Big Rosco large house they check out and seen how many people they have on post all around the house then sprang into action. They took care of the bodyguards first one by one killing them with knives real stealth like not to tip Big

Rosco off. Big Rosco is in the house he was in the kitchen making himself a smoke turkey and cheese sandwich with all the works when he heard the door kicked in hard. **Kaboom!** He quickly whipped out his pistol rushing towards where he heard the booming sound, but he did not know that Akbar and Big DeSean creeped in the back door. They were behind him they open fire on him **Barrraaattttt! tat tat tat!** He hit him in the back, down to his ass and legs ripping his shit up bad with meat hanging out from the back of legs. The blood jetting out everywhere as he fell forward to the floor bleeding and screaming in deep pain, they stepped up fast standing over him yelling for them not to kill him finishing him off **Baaarrraaatttt!**

At the same time Willie Whack- Whack Mister Pete and Maro are running up the stairway his wife Sweet Thelma a known big-time heroin dealer in the bathtub high out her mine after shooting two bags of some good shit. Willie Whack- Whack kicked the door in **Kaplang!** Mister Pete ran in with his Glock shooting her in both eye's and one inside of her chest. He lifeless body just slide down inside of the tub making her bath water deep red bloody bubbles bath.

Willie Whack- Whack and his team got ghost in the darkness with only the sounds of crickets chirping on the lawn along with their eight bodyguards dead scattered like dead flies all over the large mansion. An hour after all of that when down he texts me in big bold letters on my I phone IMEFANYWA *(It's done)! I did the same thing with Arturo phone I text him writing it's done. He text me back a big black thumbs up.*

Three hours later when Little Boom, Donzilla, Patty Racks, Ron Gucci, Jacob Fats, Killer Cody, Levi Gats and Crazy Kyle came back to the warehouse at Sedley avenue. They all walked to the back of the warehouse where they had her at and they all stand in front of Twanda Donzilla pulled the bag from off her head. Patty Racks pulled out her gun screamed, "I'll do it! "

Twanda yelled, "all of you motherfuckers is dead fucking with me! "

Donzilla looked at Patty Racks nodded his head, "you're right, baby girl, go ahead and kill this bitch right now!"

*Twanda yelled, "fuck y'all, Niggas!" **Packa!***

Patty Racks shot her in the head Twanda body falls backwards but the handcuffs on her right arm is holding her up leaning back not hitting the ground with the blood dripping from her head.

Donzilla looked over at Little Boom "your mom came up with a good plan so we would not have to do this shit to them kids."

The only smart thing Dun-Dun did was he sent his kids to his Aunt Janet's spot in New York with one his side chicks name Amy. The next day the cops found Sukey and his mother Pam dead. Big Rosco and his wife Sweet Thelma dead they really didn't care about two dead Nigga dope dealers but everybody know they both were working for the white mob and on the low all the crooked cops on their pay roll is on the organized crime unit. Fast Eddie gave me the whole run down and I know their coming after me next now that I clean house from out of my organization. That was those crackers whole plans from the door with Rico Salazar and their top dope dealing flunky ass Nigga. Working for Pauly Hair Trigger Esposito was to kill me and take over my business.

The white Mafia motherfuckers I put out of fucking heroin business tried to back door me and underestimate me again. Their peoples paid with their lives, but everybody in Philly now a days know that they do not have the power they once had like back in the days. I can get to all of them quicker than a rabbit gets fucked. Dun- Dun dumb ass never knew what was up just wanted money being so fucking greedy. He was ignorant to the history I had with these mafia ass holes. He didn't know he wasn't going to see a fucking dime after they got dug in and they would have eventually killed him too. Twiggy Jones got away he jumped on the first thing smoking getting out of town.

So did the money man Loopy once he got the news about Dun-Dun, Twiggy and Sukey. Rico Salazar was pissed, and all his peoples advised him to get out of town as well.

He said he was not going to run.

I was loving it because this give me more time to get at him as well, but his bitch ass did get out of town. A week later after talking all that tough Tony bull shit if he would have stayed a little longer, he would be dead as well.

I only went back to Arizona on the weekends. I had my sister Robin come back to Philly along with Laquitta and my grand baby Baheam. Little Bay- Bay and Gun Ho Moe, did a great job watching my peoples. I took care of them with

*a little something extra for their pockets. I paid for Laquitta mother La-Vonne
funeral. I got my son's man Jerry Lit to keep an eye for Fat Jake and Chico low
life ass. One of them did show up Chico he just came to be down for the party after
the funeral just like a Nigga.*

*That Nigga had a good time partying getting high and eating good and
motherfucker even got laid with one the chicken heads around the way ho name
Pookey who came to the funeral looking for a good time just like Chico sorry ass.
Its late-night Chico feeling good right after he done got himself some pussy, he is
coming out his house on 22nd street near Lehigh soon as he steps of the porch*
Kapacka!

*Little Boom stepped out of the shadow with a black mask and black gloves
and blows his brains out. Patty Racks came pulling up in a black GMC truck
Little Boom quickly jumps in the truck bumping fist with Patty Racks He pulled
off down the Dull yellow cold lit street. We already know that they were the ones
who killed Laquitta's mother La-Vonne knowing Jody is snitchin for the
D.E.A. We been looking for one more Nigga out there named Fat Jake, but he
was dead. He was killed by some junkies knowing he was holding a little
something showing off for women at the bar who set his ass up from the door. They
took the dope off him and they killed him in his car he had no ID on him and he
is in the morgue as John Doe. For months before they laid him out in Potter's field
with a number spray painted on top of a wooden box. After Judy head about his
crew and his wife getting killed. He refused to testify for the D.E.A. They gave
him ten years right off the bat and he still was labeled as a snitch when he when
inside, so he had to take P.C. Protective Custody.*

Making a deal with Billy the Kid

It's the end of May and before I step down again and let Puerto Rican Joe take over. I hooked up a sit down with Billy The Kid Vanzetti at my condo in Chestnut Hill. After I had him checked out good. I had Jimmy Goon set up security for me he had some the new guys Juba Chaco along with Crazy Jamel on the front door. He had X and his crew Katar, Fat Roman, Black Bart, Beamer and Billy Wild outside standing all around spread out and straped up. I had Blood Eye, Jimmy Goon Poochie on my left and on the right of me I had Jagger, Puerto Rican Joe my son Little Boom and Tanya. Behind us is Taz- Money and his clique Little Ziggy Dime Bag Benny. One of his new guys who just got out of jail, his sister Jill's son and Big Booker As I'm sitting in my favorite big chair my son's crew is outside as well with Donzilla, Patty Racks, Ron Gucci and Jacob Fats are all out of sight just in case shit jumps off.

Billy The Kid Vanzetti came in with his best friend and Capo Crazy Chaz Deluca, Crazy Chaz, his brother Sal The Bulldozer Deluca and he looked like one too. Johnny Smokestacks Daniello, Frankie Fast Track Di Fronzo and Ricky Hot Sticks Santino. They all came in strolling like they some bad ass motherfuckers from South Philly, but I already know these grease ball wise guys better not say anything slick or out the way or their fucking dead.

Soon as Billy The Kid Vanzetti walked in the door with his hands up in the air. "Hey,
I finally get a chance to meet the queen of the streets Almasi live in the flesh."
He came up shaking my hand when I stood up and Billy The Kid Vanzetti pointed at his people and introduce them, "this is my associates here this is my Capo Chaz, his brother Sal The Bulldozer and this is Frankie Fast Track, Ricky Hot Sticks and last but not least Johnny Smokestacks."

Almasi 2
Queen of The Streets
By Dartanya A. Williams Sr.

My son Little Boom and Jimmy Goon bring chairs they set up two chairs for Billy The Kid and Crazy Chaz right in front of me and they set up the other chairs on the left-hand side for his men.

"Gentlemen, please have a seat so we can talk business."

I lit up a cigarette and continued, "would you guys like a drink or something?"

Billy The Kid replied, "sure, I would like a cold beer that would be great. I pointed towards Tanya she quickly walked towards the bar getting the beers out of the see-through refrigerator behind the bar."

She handed each one of them a cold beer.

"Wow, this is a nice joint you have here, Almasi? What it set you back?"

"37.4 Million. I own the one across the street too that one was 40. The fucking fat greedy ass Jew who sold it to me when up on the price to see if I had the loot. He had a fucking heart attack when I put the cash on his fucked up wooden desk. He knocked off the pictures with his ugly ass wife and kids on the fucking floor hauling ass out the fucking door when I gave him the loot.

All of them started giggling.

"So, what you want to talk to me about Billy? I'm not trying to be smart but I'm really busy over here."

Sal The Bulldozer snarled, "what you say, you nigga?"

Billy The Kid cuts him off and yelled, "keep your fucking mouth shut, Sal!"

I snapped, "you better tell your boy over there to watch his mouth in here and I'm not going to say it twice you dig."

He looked over at him and pointed his finger, "don't worry he won't say shit! Look we have a common enemy over here the fucking Espositos."

"Yeah, we do, but I took care of them motherfuckers. They better not come stepping to me again or I'll wipe out the whole fucking Italian boot the next time they come at me and my peoples."

Sal The Bulldozer jumps up yelled, "fuck this shit with this black bitch talking shit about Italians!"

Almasi 2
Queen of The Streets
By Dartanya A. Williams Sr.

In the blink of an eye Jagger pops up with a 45 automatic and then Puerto Rican Joe jumps up with two Glocks. My son Little Boom with a AR15 machine Gun and Tanya with Springfield M1A machine gun sticking it in Sal The Bulldozer face. Puerto Rican Joe barked, "you better watch your mouth in here you Wop. When you're talking to our queen!"

"Look around you will never get out of here alive!"

All of them looked around and everyone had their machine guns pointed at them.

I looked up at all of them,"I told you to watch your fucking mouth in here when you're talking to me. Now our meeting is over, "get the fuck out of here!"

Billy The Kid Vanzetti jumps up with his hands up in the air and yelled, "wait a minute we can work this shit out!"

Frank Fast Track, Ricky Hot Sticks Crazy Chaz and Sal The Bulldozer are pulling out their guns. Johnny Smokestacks is the only one not pulling his gun out waving his hands at all his peoples.

He yelled, "you guys better sit down and chill the fuck out with that just look around you!" When they all looked up Taz- Money, Big Booker Dime Bag Benny, Little Ziggy is in back of them along with Juba Chaco, Jimmy Goon and Tanya is in front of them with their guns and machine guns on all of them."

I announced, "you better listen to your friend you will never get out of here alive if shit jumps off Billy."

He smirked,

"I've been in some really wild shoot outs like this and made it out of those fucking joints, Glock Mommy."

I laughed, "not like this motherfucker!"

He looked up again and out of nowhere, Bango, Crazy Jamel, Woo- Woo, Lurch, Fat Smoochy, Killer Cody, Crazy Kyle, Levi Gats, Mark Mongol, Willie Whack- Whack Midnight and Crazy Paco."

All of them have their machine guns pointed at them with that cold glare in their eyes burning ready to kill anything moving. If one of them just as much as fart their fucking dead.

"I have twenty more hard-core soldiers outside. You'll never make it out of here alive Billy The Kid."

He looked around and he started laughing lowering his gun. He ordered his men to lower the fucking metal boys!

All of them lower their guns but Sal The Bulldozer , "fuck that shit he is jumping, from side to side with his pistol."

"You better talk to your boy he's going to get all of you motherfuckers killed up in here for real."

Billy The Kid quickly walked over grabbing the front of his gun "come on brother we know you have heart but don't be a fucking fool okay. When you see someone with a better hand. Men, it's cool and stand down."

Billy took the gun out of his hand turning towards me and asked, "so, what are we going to do here? I came here to just talk Almasi. I did not mean for all this bullshit to happen, okay. Can we just sit and rap about this shit, please?"

"Sure, but your people have to understand were not going for none of that disrespectful shit you guys are always spitting."

"I understand that I didn't come here for us to disrespect you or any of your peoples." "I'm sorry about this. Okay tell your boy here to wait outside and I want all of you to put your guns down and we might give it a dry run or something."

"I did warn y'all when you first came in here to watch your mouth it's a new day. It's none of that bullshit from back in the days going on in here, okay. It's 2019 not 1919 you feel me. **Di solo alla tua gente essereforte** (*Just tell your people to be cool*)."

"Epossiamo fare molti soldi insieme (*And we can make a lot of money together*)"

He looks at me ,"I'm impressed. I didn't know you spoke Italian Almasi."

He does not know I'm just learning that shit.

I replied,

"It's a lot you don't know about me, Billy."

"You said a fucking mouth full right there, sister. Could you excuse me for a minute while I talk to my man here?"

He pulls Sal the Bulldozer by his arm pissed off towards the front door while Juba Chaco and Jimmy Goon walks behind them. Nobody else moved still in their gun stances, ready to smoke a motherfucker from the door. I love seeing this shit because this show me the discipline. All our people have the training is paying off. Billy The Kid Vanzetti is arguing with Sal The Bulldozer when he gets him outside and screamed at the top of his lungs, "what are you fucking crazy? Are you trying to get us fucking killed in here or what!"

Sal The Bulldozer yelled, "I can't believe your bowing down to those Niggas in there?"

"You want to know what you're on a fucking suicide mission or something Sal?"

"Your brother Chaz thinks he's black and the rest of your family. Are stuck in the 1950's or something you can't see pass color? The only fucking color I see is man is fucking green and I want to see a lot of it! They have a huge pipeline connection of Fentanyl and cocaine. I'm going to make a big fat deal with these guys if you like it or not while you're stuck in the fucking past piss poor broke crying talking shit about back in the days."

They walked towards their car parked outside and he pushed him in the back seat of the black Lincoln town car, "you're done when we get back. You go find another crew to be a part of because your fucking sick and he slams the car door **Boom!**"

While Billy The Kid is walking back towards the front door, he's looking around seeing all the men I had all around the condo. He walks back in and Johnny Smokestacks is smoking a blunt with me Puerto Rican Joe and Crazy Chaz.

He walked up and asked, "yo, did I miss my turn? over here or what with his hands up in the air smiling."

All of us started laughing he seen that all our men fell back and was cool. I passed the blunt to him and continued, "yo, your man has a fucking problem, Billy man."

Billy The Kid replied, "I know and I'm really sorry about that shit. If I knew that shit, I would had never brought his ass with me,

Almasi. Don't worry you will never see his ass when we talk business, he passes the blunt to Frankie Fast Track.

"I can use another cold beer right about now."

"Sure, Tanya could you get those cold beers for us please baby. Tanya quickly came with the beers passing them out to everyone Ricky Hot Sticks, "I heard you guys got the best raw dog coke flowing out here on the streets today."

"Check this shit out, Boss. He waves to Tanya, "give us that fat zip up of **Pigo**(Blow) for us sweetheart, please."

Crazy Chaz asked, "Pigo?"

Puerto Rican Joe answered, "yeah, Pigo that's Swahili for blow."

"Well, let it flow with the motherfuckin Pigo!"

We all started laughing and that really broke the ice with all of us as Tanya walked up shaking the large zip lock bag of cocaine filled up to the top. I pointed at Little Boom, him and Crazy Jamel set up a square glass table in front of all of us. As Tanya poured a large pile of the cocaine on top of it and laid out a bunch of cut off straws near the pile along with some playing cards to chop up the white powder.

"Okay, Ricky check it out and let me know what you think?"

He stood up getting one of the cards and the cut off straws off the table.

"I don't mind if I do."

He makes around four lines shuffling and chopping the white powder than he started snorting up the coke after making about four lines. He puts his head back holding his nose, "wow! That is some good shit, Ma!"

Crazy Chaz stood up next grabbing a card and a straw making about six lines on top of the glass surface. He quickly snorted it up and shook his head holding his nose, "yeah, this is good to go for sure!"

"Damn, that's some really good raw dog shit right there."

I turned to Billy The Kid, "it's your turn now, my man."

"Oh, I'm with it from the door."

Almasi 2
Queen of The Streets
By Dartanya A. Williams Sr.

He steps up making five lines and snorts up the four and the last one he blows in his mouth. I watch the look on his face when he stood back and started smiling. He quickly started drinking his beer and asked, "where did y'all get that shit from?"

I replied, "Mount Olympus, brother."

They all started laughing.

Billy The Kid asked, "how much are you going to sell it to us a key? I can give it to you for 27,000 dollars a key."

He looks over at Crazy Chaz and nodded his head, "that's a good price how many keys can you give us?"

I replied, "how many you want?"

"200 keys."

"Okay, than at 27 a key that's 5,400,000. "

Billy The Kid replied, "okay, that's cool. What about the fentanyl and what are you going to give it to me at?"

"Wow, that shit is kind of fucking expensive I can give it to you at 30 a key. We sell them at 35."

"Wow can you do better than that?"

"Well, I can if you are buying enough of it how much do you want?" He looks over at Crazy Chaz asked, "100 keys?"

"I tell you what I'll sell it to you at 25 a key, 300 keys are 7,500,000 and you give me half 3,750,000 now today. I will front you the coke now. You can't beat that fucking deal."

Billy The Kid rubbed his hands together, "that is a hell of a deal. So, when you want the other half of the loot?" "I'll give you the next four months to pay us off in small installments, so it doesn't bust your balls doing it and in the meanwhile your making a lot of money. I need you guys to pay me on time please and to take a little more coke I'm fronting you that's all."

"Okay, how much more coke?"

I need for you to take 500 keys instead of 200 that way we both can see our money you know what I'm saying *Mio Amico* (My Friend)."

"Yeah, I can do that sweetheart."

Almasi 2
Queen of The Streets
By Dartanya A. Williams Sr.

"Good, I'm glad we can come to a better understanding instead of all that racial shit the only color you and me, have to worry about is green."

"That's just what I was saying to my peoples. How does this work mommy?"

I answered, "it will be smooth as a baby's ass, Billy."

I pointed at Jimmy Goon, "that's Jimmy."

He steps up waving. He will have his men over their Jamel and Bango. *Jimmy points at both with all of them looking to* pick up the loot from you where you choose for it to be at. They are like clockwork so make sure your people are tight because I know my people are okay.

"Yeah, my people are on top of their game too."

"I know I did my homework on y'all, but I was kind of shocked with you bringing your boy out there in the car with you."

"Well you can pick your friends, but you can't pick your family you know but I think this is going to be a great working relationship here. Let me go out and get the money from out the car I be right back."

"I'll come with you." *I see the two of them talking and they came right back with a black suitcase. I pointed to Tanya to take it from them she walks over to the table on the right-hand side counting. She sticks it in the money counting machine with Jagger helping her.*

Soon as she was done Tanya looking over to me and announced, "it's 3,000,000 here." "Okay now that is done when do I get my goodies, Almasi?

"Have a seat honey and give me an address where you want it and I'll have it there while we have some more drink and snort some more blow. "

Billy The Kid mouth dropped, and he blurted out, "you mean to tell me you can have 500 keys of coke and 300 keys of Fentanyl in an hour."

I smirked and wink with a smile, "A half an hour or less."

All of them looking up at me smiling and giggling.

"This is some shit I want to see."

308

Frankie Fast Track giggling chimed, "yeah, me too."

I replied, "you guys want to put a friendly little bet on the shit or what?"

Johnny Smokestacks blurted out, "I'll take some that action sweetheart reaching in his pocket pulling out a hundred-dollar bill."

He chimed in, "yeah, let's have a little fun over here I want to see this shit."

Setting it down on top of the glass table with the coke on top of it.

"Billy, okay call your peoples where you wanted at."

He pulls out his phone and makes the call, "yo, Carmen **Presto arrivera qualcosa da te** (I'm going to have something coming to you really soon)"

Carmen repied, "**OK, Staro attento** (Okay I'll be on the lookout for it) **Richiamami quando lo ricevi** (Okay call me back when you get it)."

He hangs up and he looks over at me and continued, "okay, were on he pulls out his business card, "he's there waiting take it here handing the card to me smiling."

I looked at him, "okay, hold on I make my call and I stood up and announced, "it on its way right now."

I've bend over getting me a straw making lines with his business card and I snorted up the four lines of the coke. I sat back down and signal with a hand wave for Tanya, "give me another beer please, baby and see if they want another one too for me."

Tanya came back handing me my beer and to all the guys snorting coke along with me one by one. Before I even finished my beer twenty minutes later Billy The Kid phone started ringing, I looked at him, "there it is right there."

He smiled holding the phone to his head "Carmen, are we good?"

"So far so good were still checking it out let me call you back when were all done Skipper."

Billy The Kid looked at me and asked, "how the fuck did you do that?"

"Black magic, baby!" They fell out laughing we had a few more drinks and snorted some more coke. Carmen call him back "everything was good."

They also tested the drugs too everything was good to go.

I told him, "you guys lost the bet, but you can take that sample bag with you and your money you put down to bet."

All of them started laughing with Billy The Kid Vanzetti giggled, "you're alright, Almasi Thank you."

"I was just fucking with you guys on the delivery shit my peoples are fast and don't fuck around when it comes to making money you know what I'm saying."

Billy The Kid stood up "well, this has been nice, but we have to get out of here and start working to give you some of that money back."

He bumps fist with me and so do the rest of his men smiling and giggling.

I to my people," Will you make sure these guys get out of here safely. Have a good day and don't forget what I about being on time with the loot okay."

Billy The Kid replied, "oh, were just like you guys we don't fuck around when it comes to making money, sweetheart." I waved goodbye to them as Chaco, Juba, Jagger, Tanya and Crazy Jamel walked them to their car when they jumped in Sal The Bulldozer was not in the car, he rolled out pissed off at Billy The Kid Vanzetti. Billy the Kid is thinking where did this ass hole went to.

This Trial is Bullshit

It's the middle of June the weather is getting really nice outside. Puerto Rican Joe is at the head of the Meza(table), but I stayed in Philly because I know it's not over with these Ghost boys' motherfuckers. Plus, I had to stay with Jay to be by his side for his trial he always supports me when shit goes down, so I had to stand in his corner. It's a week before Jay's trial starts his lawyer Jason Jackson is one of the best lawyers in the country and his own team cost a fucking grip too. When we met up in his office in center city at 15 and Locust street right before the trial we get some really bad news the guy he have as one his managers the dude Day- Day at his car dealership was a fucking FBI agent. He had been working with him for the last two years. Jay was in shock once he found that shit out. Jason , "he has got enough evidence to put him away for the next thirty years."

Jay looks at him and asked, "what other options do I have other than going to trial?"

"Well, I hate to say his to you and I know you would never do it, but you could cooperate and give them some higher up people you get your supply from."

Jay yelled, "no fucking way I'll do that shit."

"Okay, I can go to the D.A. and ask him for you to plead guilty and you do twenty years." "What? Twenty years fuck that shit!"

"Well that's the only thing that will be on the table for you. I don't know what to tell you."

"No, I want to fight this shit."

"Look, you got two guys that are FBI agents working with you handling drugs and cash you can't win this shit."

"What two FBI agents you just told me it was one who is the other one?"

He picks up his file saying the guy name is Smooth Sammy.

"What? Smooth Sammy is an FBI agent isn't this a bitch?"

"So, what do you want to do here?"

He puts his hand up in the air looking at Jay. Jay leaned forward and announced,

"Look, I have a plan here if you're willing to listen to me here."

"Okay, let's hear your plan here, brother."

"I don't think you know this or not. I have some powerful people in my corner, and we can dig up all kinds of shit on the FBI agents that are testifying against me. Now if you hang in there with me, we can turn this shit around on their ass if you willing to stay as my lawyer and trust me."

"Well, let me think about that there my brother."

I , "we don't have time for that shit right now. Are you in or out on this shit or what?" The lawyer looks at me and answered, "I know who you are and what you can do if you think we can pull this shit off on them. I'm in."

"Good, that's what I want to here for my baby Jay here."

"Okay, I'll see you tomorrow in court." He shook hands with Jay and then me as we stand up. Jay and I went to work when we got home. I called up Layne West so he can dig up some shit on them two fucking FBI agents and see if that shit works. I know he's going to charge us up being something last minute, but we really didn't care at this point he he would be right over. While we were waiting on him me and Jay started getting high. Jay made the drinks at the bar. While I pulled the coke out from my pocketbook setting it on top of the coffee table. I pulled out the zip lock bag out and I dump some out on top of the table making fat lines for me and Jay. He sat next to me and handed me my drink gin on the rocks.

I take a quick sip of my drink while still shuffling the white powder on top of the coffee table. Jay rolls up a hundred-dollar bill snorting two of the fat lines then he hands me the hundred-dollar bill putting his head back leaning back on the couch. I snort up two lines and I can feel the effect of the raw coke right away were getting our groove on flying high when an hour later Layne West show up at the spot and we tell him what we wanted him to do. He he can do it, but he can't guarantee that it's going to get him off but will fuck up their career for sure. We both looked at one another and blurted out, "that's what we want." He he needs nine racks to get started. I went in the back to my safe in the middle room and I get it for him. I put it in a plastic bag from out of the kitchen when I handed to him, I asked him, "when will we hear from you?"

"Give me one week."

He bumps fist with me than Jay and then Layne West went out the door. *But this time I have to say I got a funny feeling about this whole plan it could backfire up our ass.*

Me and Jay finished getting high. We got nice and fucked up and took it to the bedroom. I took off all of my clothes and I jumped on top of Jay. I rode his ass like fucking Sally Star riding a wild black bucking bronco. Wow, this Nigga sent me into another fucking cum coma while sweating up a storm my whole body was tingling. After I came about four times, I pulled out some more coke getting high with Jay. I got a call in the wee hours in the morning it scared me because when you get that call at this time in the morning it's never any fucking good news at all. Jay looks up at me with that look to right after he was bend over snorting coke from off the nightstand.

So, I pick up my phone and it's Fly Ty and asked, "what's up, sis?"

I knew his voice right off the bat and I answered, "I'm good Fly Guy. What's up with you, Mister Las Vegas."

"Too tell you the truth it's fucking rough out here for real. Oh yeah so what's going on why is it so rough out there."

"I'm not going to lie to you Almasi. I need some help with these motherfuckers out here I heard you chase them Ghost boys the fuck out of town."

Fly Ty laughed.

"Yeah, you know me I always got something for a Nigga's ass who tried to fuck me."

"Look, I'm not going to beat around the bush here. I need your help bad with the Mexican Cartel there trying to push me out. I have nobody I can count on to have our back."

"I'm not going to lie to you, Ty. I'm trying to get out of all this shit the only reason I came back because I fucked up by putting Dun-Dun at the head of the Meza(table). I had to clean that shit up or I would have got smoked my God damn self from my plug."

"I know you want to step down, but could you please give me a hand and I can cut you in on some really big shit I got going on out here. This whole town is made of fucking money I'm telling you, Almasi."

"Look, you know I'll help you out. I'm not worry about money with you and me were family but I'm in the middle of my man Jay's trial here."

"We can help each other Almasi you help me get the cartel off our ass so we can operate. I'll help you put that snake ass Nigga Rico Salazar in the fucking ground. Is that a deal? "Sounds good to me let me go talk to some of my peoples and you call me back. We will see what we come up with okay."

"Thank you, Almasi. I'll holla back at you later **Moja***(One)*."

"Moja!"

Monday morning the trial starts, and they just pick the jury. Jason and his team he thinks this would be the jury that will be the best for us in Jay's defense. The angle was set up in all this bullshit and they were out to get him because he's Almasi aka Glock mommy boyfriend. *Even though the FBI and the D.E.A. want to be all on top of my ass with all their allegation I never been convicted of a crime in my life. I been in the game most of my life. That is why I know it's time to get out of this shit before my luck runs the fuck out.*

Day one went well Jason Jackson his other two partners in the firm Reba Waters and Anthony Hernandez were really good but I know the other side was going to drop the bomb on us and we never heard a word back from Layne West yet. Day three came and I felt nervous when we got up because I know this was the day, they were going to bring out the big guns and put them on their witness that day. We got up early like we did every morning before going to court soon as we were heading out the door Layne West popped up standing by the car with Poochie and Blood Eye ready to drive us to the court house located in down town center city. Layne handed me a large thick yellow envelope. He looked at me and Jay "give this to Jay's lawyer and for him to have the FBI witness read every detail. He bumps fist with both of us smiling and he quickly walked off. *He knew they were watching us the whole time we were leaving the condo. We were staying at*

314

my condo at One Brown street, so we didn't have to drive to far plus I did not want them to know my other spots where we were laying are head at.

After La-Nesa was killed in prison I had Tanya Bring me Stephanie one of La-Nesa top workers at the real estate office. I ask her if she wanted to move up now that I am taking over the whole thing now that she's dead.

She yelled at the top of her lungs, "hell yes."

So, I put everything in her name and I'm the silent partner. She knows what would happen to her if she crosses me. I did the same thing with all the hair shops with this girl name Joann one of Mookie side chicks. I had Stephanie hook me up some more spots around the Philly area, so nobody knows the one place where I stay at.

The Shit Did Not work

I called Jason up soon as we got in the whip, he to bring it to his office so they can break it down. he also is going to delay the trial so they can have time to go through all the documents. So, we took the envelope to him at his office as fast as we could, and he called up judge John Turner telling him he had some personal shit going on with him and could we start back up on Friday. The judge agreed knowing that Jason is a hard-working lawyer he respected. After he got off the phone with the judge Jason told us to go home and relax while he looks through the documents that we just gave him.

That weekend me and Jay really got into each other having sex twice each day, *but it was different this time because in the back of my mind is this could be the last time in a long time me and him could be making love. So, to me this was a little more special every time we climaxed together. I really love this man and I do not know what I'll do if he gets convicted. I hate to say it, but if he does, I know I will be next in their crosshairs. But the shit is like Michael Corleone every time I think I'm out somebody pulls my black ass right back in this bull shit.*

We are getting high with drugs and booze to try to take the trial off are mind. Monday came fast and when they put on their witness.

The first FBI agent they put up on the stand, we knew him as Day- Day his real name was David Allen this Nigga had on a dark blue suit looking clean cut when we know he's one dirty ass motherfucker from the door. He got up there on the stand and told the story of Jay selling drugs and how he washed his cash and he seen all this first-hand. He working with him for the last two years his manager in two of Jay's dealership the one in Philly and the one in Atlanta. When Jay's lawyer got to question him, he asks him about his self being on drugs and about his four baby mothers he had selling drugs for him as an undercover agent. Mister David Allen began stuttering. Then he asks him about the 10,000,000 dollars he hidden from the FBI selling drugs and the eight people he killed posing as a drug dealer he was done after that. Before he got off the stand, we knew he was fired from his job and he would be under more investigations. He had all the baby mamas he had still selling drugs to this day while he is still married to his wife Debbie. They have three kids and she is also pregnant sitting up in the courtroom hearing all this shit about her husband. *I see that look on her face and I know that feeling of betrayal boiling under her skin.*

Anthony Hernandez came up next questioning him about him selling information to other drug dealers as well. Anthony was killing it after hearing all that the jury was all into it mesmerized. Monday, they didn't want to put Sammy Smooth his real name Samuel Thompson on the stand until they really check out everything he did. So, they don't get burned again with a rogue FBI agent him and David Allen were working together. So, we were adjourned until the next day. I'm thinking this shit was going to work for us, so we were so happy when we went home. The next day on Tuesday they brought on Sammy Smooths handler a FBI agent name Norman Murphy and we had nothing on him, and he told the story of Jay letting Sammy as the manager of two of his car dealerships making sure that the workers put the drugs where all into the trap cars at three more of his dealerships. They had wiretaps and video tape of ten transactions they showed the jury. Jason Jackson did question him really hard and he also told the jury everything he was saying was hear say, but the jury was already all into what he was talking about with all the money and drugs and where they were going to. At the end of the day we did put up one hell of a fight and we got two FBI agents get fired because they found out about Sammy Smooth stealing money as well and he had five bodies, but all of that shit we had on them did not help us at all.

On Thursday we had closing arguments and we both still we thinking Jay was going to get out of this shit because Jason Jackson went up there and killed the shit. But on Friday afternoon Judge John Turner told us to rise as he asked the jury, "what is your verdict?"

Queen of The Streets
By Dartanya A. Williams Sr.

The tall young white dude the foremen of the jury , "we find Jaylan Black guilty."

I was numb I could not hear shit after I heard this white dude say guilty, but Jay just stood there with no type of emotion with that cold look in his eyes. When the two guards took him in custody.

He kissed me and whispered in my ear, "don't worry about me baby I'll be alright."

I wanted to cry but I would not give them fucking devils the satisfaction. I had to come back on Monday for Jay's sentencing. I was pissed off for real I was in a daze walking out of there. I felt so hollow seeing the smiles on the prosecutors faces but I played it off keeping my head up doe. It is one the most fucked up days of my life right now and they know it. *Walking out of there I felt like I was under water walking in slow motion. I'm looking, at the people on the jury with some deep hate and all the people sitting in the court room as well.*

I'm thought to myself what the fuck am I going to do now? I can't front I really want to cry but I'm holding it all in. Jason Jackson his lawyer began talking to me, but I can't really hear him because I just can't believe what just happen. When I did hear some of what he was saying was that he was trying to tell us that they really wanted to convict Jay and there is nothing we can do about it now. I'm still in denial and I felt like I got hit by a fucking Mack truck.

I'm thinking about going to Las Vegas

Riding back home I felt fucked up without Jay. I told Poochie and Blood Eye that they found him guilty. Poochie and Blood Eye could see it all over my face.

Poochie blurted out, "that's fucked up, Ma."

Poochie drove us home I was so fucking upset about this shit it seems like I'm losing all the people that are close to me. Frist Aunt-Tee now Jay I was in a deep funk all weekend. I talk to my sister Robin about it and I got it off my chest, but I'm still fucked up in the head about it. She made me feel better showing me some of the baby clothes her and Poochie was buying for their baby on the way. Poochie came and told me that him and my sister been looking for their own place. I was happy for them and Robin stomach was getting bigger it won't be long before she drops that load. Robin called up Laquitta to bring my grand baby to the house and I must say that did put me in a better mood.

I was thinking to myself what I'm I going to do after they give Jay his time will I go back to Arizona to my ranch or what? Robin knew what to do to get me out that funky ass mood I was in with my grandbaby Baheam. I love him so much.

The next day Saturday afternoon I got a call from my aunt Lisa Dotty's sister she she wanted to see me. I told her I would send a car to come pick her up to bring her to the house. I sent Blood Eye to go pick her up and I was so glad to see her. She stayed all day with me, my grandson and Laquitta then out of the blue she dropped it on me saying why don't you let me stay with you and take care of you like La- Wanda did for me.

"That sound good to me." I was really happy about it. Plus, I really trust her, we been tight for a lot of years, but I told her I just don't stay here. I also have a place in Arizona and if she's cool, with coming back and forth some time the job is hers. She it was cool with her.

She began by saying, "now that she's going to be cleaning and cooking for me, she was going to make a big Sunday dinner for me, Robin, Laquitta, Blood Eye, and Poochie." She was all excited about fixing this big dinner for us, so I had Blood Eye to take her out shopping for the food. While I was playing with the baby, I get a call from Fly Ty and he announced he was close to tracking down Rico Salazar. He when he picks him up, he's going to let me know.

I , "that's good."

I told him the bad news about Jay getting convicted on Friday and he was sorry to hear that news.

"Almasi, what are you going to do?"

I replied, "I have to get up some more loot and fight on his appeal. That's the only thing I can do for right now. "

"Sis, yo, keep your head up and I should have some really good news for you real soon I got something cooking."

"Good, how is Rah-Killer and Damon Gee?"

"They're loving Las Vegas why don't you come out here and check it out for yourself and come have a good time."

I replied, "I just might do that shit."

He , "yeah right, you're not coming out here."

I answered, "yes, I will just let me get Jay set up with everything he needs, and I'll be out there in a couple weeks."

He , "I'll be waiting on you." We both laughed and talked a little more and I hung up. I made the best of my weekend with Jay still on my mind. My aunt Lisa fried chicken, made collard greens and some wild rice it was off the hook. This woman can cook her ass off like she from down south or something for real. We all sat at the table laughing and talking that made me feel a hell of a lot better. It made me not think about what's going to happen on Monday. I didn't stay up to late because I know I have to be in court for Jay's sentencing.

The next day I get up early to get myself together so I can go to court, and I did something I didn't do in a long time and that's pray that they don't give him that much time. But no matter what I'll stay by him and fight to the bitter end. I'm washed and dressed Poochie and Blood Eye is ready to go and I'm nervous as shit.

Almasi 2
Queen of The Streets
By Dartanya A. Williams Sr.

What is really fucked up it's a beautiful day outside and I'm going to hear some real fucked up news about the man I love. He may be sent away for a long time. I hop in the whip and we drive downtown soon as I come up in the courtroom these motherfuckers are all happy knowing their fucking enjoying this shit. I meet up with Jason Jackson, Anthony Hernandez and Reba Waters their faces tell it all real fucking sad, so I know they were going to throw the fucking book at Jay's ass. They brought Jay out I blow a kiss at him he throws one back at me and he winks his eye letting me know that he's alright. They did not make us wait long judge John Turner asks him to rise while he pronounce sentence.

I stand up with all of them at the table looking on the judge Jaylen Black I sentenced you to 360 months in federal prison. I started adding that shit up in my head quickly. I blurt out, "oh shit that's 30 fucking years."

It was like I got hit with a fucking sledgehammer right in my chest I could not hear all the other bull shit the judge was saying to him. Then the two fat ass guards one black and one white who grabbed him. I ran towards him he yelled at the two men,

"hold up for a minute." The men stopped in front of me.

"I'll call you soon as I can baby, I love you." He went to reach over to kiss me the two big ass greasy ugly ass motherfuckers snatched him back and dragged him out of the courtroom.

I ran up to Jason Jackson and yelled, "you're going to have to work on his appeal right away."

He , "I don't want to take any more of your money, Almasi."

I have a few colleagues that can work on it for you come past my office next week and I'll give you their cards and you can pick one of them. I'll tell you if they can do a good job for you." I just looked at him with my eyes on fire. I wanted to sucker punch that bitch made motherfucker right there on the fucking spot. Instead I walked close to him and barked, "you're going to work on his appeal or you're going to be one sorry ass Nigga." I pointed my finger in his grill while he was backing up.

Reba Water stepped up fast with a serious look on her dark brown face and announced, "I'll work on it for you I'm just about to go on my own, so I'll be happy to do it for you Almasi."

I replied with a smirk, "Good, meet up with me next week and I'll drop some loot on you to start working on it okay."

Jason Jackson looks at both of us with that funny ass expression on his black smug privilege face of his. He just walked past me and her not saying a word. I shake hands with her. She smiled "I know we can get him off on the appeal, but it's going to take some time now."

She looks me right in my eyes. "I know Rebecca just get the shit done."

"Almasi, will we both walked out of the courtroom together."

I didn't even look at them devil motherfuckers on the other side walking out smiling and giggling because I would smoke their ass just thinking about it. I go outside getting some air after what just happen. Poochie walked up and asked, "you ready to go."

"Yes!"

"What happen, Almasi?"

"They gave him 360 months."

"So how many years is that?"

I answered, "that's 30 years. where is Blood Eye at?"

He went around the corner to get a hot dog from the stand. I looked in my bag getting my smokes, lighting up a cigarette and I see one of the cracker ass prosecutors with his cheap ass blue suit on walking pass me smiling in my fucking face.

"Poochie, I'm going to the car call Blood Eye and tell him to hurry the fuck up!"

I didn't want to be there any longer than I have to be because I'm going to get locked up for fucking up one of these cracker ass motherfuckers.

He called him and he came running around the corner and we quickly went to the parking lot and we got the fuck out of there. Now I know I'm going to Las Vegas I call up Elite flight. I told Ray the pilot and half owner of the company I'm flying out tonight to Las

Vegas. He he'll be ready for me. Then I called Fly-Ty up telling him I'll be out there tonight. He sounded happy about it, "Almasi, I will pick you up at the airport and text me before we land."

"Fly Ty that sounds good. see you soon Nigga."

We both laughed and I hung up. Soon as I got home, I told my Aunt Lisa to pack up her shit she's going to Las Vegas with me.

"I have to go home and get the rest of my clothes, girl. I'm down with this shit. Oh yeah, let's go."

"Look, I'll get Blood Eye to take you in the car to your crib okay and you come back here ready to go okay now hurry the fuck up and don't take all day!"

"Oh, hell yes, I never been to Las Vegas before." She was all giddy about going to Las Vegas. I went into my bedroom locking the door and I started packing up my shit, but I broke down and started crying when I was alone. I didn't want anybody to know and I didn't let people know how bad this hurt. I got myself together ready to go.

Every day in Las Vegas was just like Mardi Gras

My Aunt Lisa came back with her clothes and she started getting high with me until it was time to go. Poochie helps us with our bags. Blood Eye was ready to go with his clothes we all jump in the truck as Poochie drop us off at the airport. He's staying at the crib with my sister Robin. The three of us Me, Aunt Lisa and Blood Eye flew out at 7:45 P.M. All the way there we partied our ass off smoking blunts, drinking gin, champagne and snorting a shit load of coke too. We were eating wing dings and this banging ass Caesars salad Ray's wife made. I text Fly Ty where to pick us up at after I got the information from Ray our pilot. When we landed, we were nice and fucking high as a kite all fucking night.

Fly-Ty came in two trucks and we met his gun men working for him he introduced, us to Jazz, Cadillac Mack, Black Jo- Jo, and Silky Celine.

Then when I see Rah- Killer step out of the next truck smiling her ass off I jumped into her arms. Damon Gee and I introduce Aunt Lisa to the two of them. After they picked us up it was like a blur we partied, went out to dinner and all the shows in Las Vegas every night was like fucking Mardi Gras. Fly- Ty and his people show us the best time we could ever have in our life. The only business I talked about with Fly- Ty was so he could put on my brother Mustafa's sister De-Wanda my long-lost Aunt who is in the game with some major weight. Mustafa he will be responsible for her because he he knows she's really good at what she does. He has not let us down yet, so his word is good as gold.

I talked to John Spartacus the head of S.O.S. Smash on site crew about him sending some his hard-core soldiers to help Fly- Ty out so they can back off the Mexican cartel so they can operate and he does for a piece of the action. I had a ball From Monday to Monday I really need that time off just for a little while made me get that bull shit that happen to Jay off my mind just for a little while.

I flew back to Philly to talk to Reba Waters and I gave her some loot to work on Jay's appeal. I flew back out to go see him in Leavenworth Federal penitentiary in Kansas and I took my Aunt Lisa and Blood Eye with me. I made sure he had money on his books and everything he needs while he's doing his time. He was happy to see us. I went back to Arizona to check on my ranch Sun Dance and I chilled out for a while.

The Italians in Canada starts some shit

Three months go past quick it's September of 2019 everything is going smooth. I'm getting my drops Puerto Rican Joe told me that even things are going well with Billy The Kid Vanzetti peoples. The money is flowing in and they paid off their drug debt with the fentanyl I gave them and then some with the coke we fronted them. I got some good news from Detective Don Wilson he told me that Danielle Crazy Monk's wife who went to talk to the FBI they found out she was a drug attic and pathological liar they could not use any of her testimony against me. So that was a bullet I dodge but I never seen this other shit that happens doe.

The Lombardi family in Canada is piss off and at war with the biker gang. The Metal Head MCs once their national president gave the green light for them to step up production with the heroin and Fentanyl making money hand over fist. That took all the Lombardi family's business because the product is ten times better than what the Italians were selling. So, Gino Lombardi reach out to the five families in New York for help and they went to talk to the family in Philly asking them for their help to put an end to the suppliers to the bikers in Canada. They needed to find out who they are and to kill every one of them who are doing it. Now after their big sit down with New York and Canada mafia heads Pauly Hair Trigger Esposito had no fucking clue who were supplying the bikers. All he knew was that it was some niggers from Caracas was flooding the market with heroin, cocaine and Fentanyl.

The next night Pauly Hair Trigger Esposito's Capo name Jonathan Big John Galgano ran into Sal The Bulldozer in a bar called the dug out on 9th & Christian street. While there sitting in a booth in the corner drinking beer Sal The Bulldozer tells him about Billy The Kid Vanzetti hooked up with these Niggas selling coke heroin and Fentanyl and there making a shit load of money. He also told them that they throw him out of the crew for getting smart with the black bitch who were running things.

A light bulb goes off in his head and he called out to the bartender, "hey bartender bring my man here another beer for my friend over here." The bartender quickly gets the beer for him knowing he is in the mob, so they wait on him hand and foot. He puts the beer on the table and walks away quickly.

Big John looks Sal The Bulldozer in the eyes and asked, "who is this black bitch your talking about Sal?"

"Her name is Almasi. They call her Glock Mommy or whatever."

The gang she runs use to be called the BSN The Black Syndicate Nation now it's some MMC bull shit or whatever. I don't know where these niggers come up with these names. Big John replied, "I know that bitch she's the same bitch who killed Pauly Hair Trigger father Fat Neck Nicky."

"Wow, I didn't know that shit."

"So, what you were with them when Billy The Kid Vanzetti made the fucking deal with this nigger bitch?"

"Yeah, I was right there in that large ass beautiful condo where they did the fucking deal man now. I wish I kept my fucking big mouth shut because now those motherfuckers are fucking rolling in dough now."

"How many people do you think she got?"

"Wow, Big John those niggers got a fucking army I know that shit, but somebody told me she's retired or some shit like that."

"So, who is running their gang?"

"I don't know John all I know is Billy told me they have a large pipeline of cocaine and Fentanyl."

"Would you know some of them if you see them?"

"Yeah, I would know them. Why?"

"I'm going to need you to help me out with this shit on finding some of them and taking care of some of these niggers that's why. I want to get some of Billy The Kids people too." "I don't know about that shit. Big John Billy The Kid Vanzetti is my cousin man I can't do that shit."

"Oh yeah, the same kind of cousin who cuts you out of a fucking million-dollar deal right?" He looks Sal The Bulldozer in the face.

"How are you with money? I bet you a dollar to a donut your fucking broke. Right?"

"Yes, I am. I hate to say that shit. "

"Yeah and how are things at home? I know your wife is up your ass about bringing some fucking money into the house right, Sal."

"Yeah, were fucking arguing every God dam day about that shit. Matter fact that why I'm in here now. We just got into it about paying the fucking bills."

"Why do this shit to yourself Sal? It's time you got some of your fucking self-respect back in that big fucking bone head of yours!"

Big John reach in his pocket and hand him a big knot of bills, ",Sal all you have to do is point out some of these fucking mutts from Billy's crew for us and a few of the niggers in this bitch gang that's all."

Sal The Bulldozer is looking up at Big John still holding the money in his hand.

"Look what the fuck are you doing? Put the fucking money in your pocket, man. You already know Billy The Kid Vanzetti is an outlaw faction of this thing of ours New York backs us up not them."

"You can come in with us and be a fucking made man when this shit is over with Sal. For real will you go and talk to Pauly for me so we can get that shit done for me."

"Yeah, I tell you what meet me here tomorrow around one I'll come pick you up and we both can go talk to him together about it. What do you say Sal?" smiling.

"Yes, I'll do it." Big John stood up Sal stood up as well and he hugs him   "I'm so glad we can come to an understanding here."

The Haitians Fucked up

It's the end of September and all I'm doing is laying back and enjoying myself. I have Laquitta fly to my ranch on some weekends with my grand baby. That's the only real joy I get, and I miss Jay. I talk to him on the phone every other day and I go see him once a month to make sure he's cool. Tanya keeps me up on what is going on in the streets she told me that in Canada shit is heating up and in Las Vegas. She told me John Spartacus and S.O.S Smash on Site is kicking ass fucking up the Sinaloa cartel who all were in shock not knowing who they were.

The smart thing John Spartacus did was hooking up a sit down with Puerto Rican Joe and Charlie Champlane from the West coast who have all the connection with the gangs. Charlie Champlane is so powerful he had a direct line to the Colombians the Garcia family. He gets his Fentanyl from my peoples with my son's hook up with Tiger Mi from the Chinese mob. After not getting payments from the Haitians for none of the product they were receiving. Coyote warn their ass when I cut the deal with them and they took it to far. They owe us for the coke, Heroin, Fentanyl and the oxycodone pills. What happen is Cougar Man from the Meute De Loups? We had a sit down with Crazy Carlo Lombardi the son of the mob boss Big Papa Lombardi and his goon squad threatening him.

His gang cut off the deal with my peoples the MMC. Money Making Conglomerate and why they did it because almost all the mob in Canada had the police in their back pocket and they would get shut down and locked up. Plus, they told them they had to buy the weak product they had off them. Coyote went off he brought his crew up there and Puerto Rican Joe sent two crews to back him up. He also sent X crew with Katar, Billy Wild, Beamer, Black Bart, Fat Roman. He also sends my son Little Boom's crew Donzilla, Patty Racks, Ron Gucci, Mark Mongol, Levi Gats, Crazy Kyle and Killer Cody. Soon as my son and Coyote touchdown they went and talked to all the ethnic gang leaders from Canada getting them all together at the docks. Its Big Giorgio Bella the Greek who ran the docks James Mc Mulley aka Jack Skully of the Irish mob and Ice Gee from the blacks Canada Niggas they called them self the BSH Black Strong Hold.

All of them had one thing in common they hated the Italian mob like the bikers. But it was one Biker gang that worked hand and hand with the Italian Mob in Canada, and they were called the Star's and Bar's MC's. Little Boom is standing next to Coyote he knows all of them Coyote to all of the men standing there, "look, I came here to tell all of y'all that were here to take out the fucking Haitians. so whatever business you have with them it going to be all fucked up."

Big Giorgio with his face all twisted up started yelling at the top of his lungs, "those motherfuckers owe me a lot of money if you kill them all I can't get paid, Coyote man." Coyote , "don't worry Georgio, I'll take care of you and you know that shit so calm the fuck down all right! I'm just giving you motherfuckers a heads up and the deal of a fucking lifetime on top of that shit."

Ice Gee replied, "yeah, like what?"

"Were here to take care of the Haitians but were going to have to smoke some Wops while we're here too. They crossed us, and they must pay for that shit with their life you know what I mean."

Ice Gee , "so what's the deal stop beating around the fucking bush Coyote. I want to hear why we should be helping you out with this bullshit?"

All of them started laughing.

"I have a shit load of heroin from Caracas on that ship over there if you willing to help us out you will get 200 extra keys of pure heroin to do as you please with."

Jack Skully looked up at him and raised his eyebrow, "your just bull shitting us, right?" Coyote looked him right in his face and gave wide grin, "all of you know me and you know I don't bullshit when it comes to dope."

They all looked at him and knew what he is true.

Ice Gee chimed in, "I can use the loot for some of that dope but if y'all give me 200 keys of that dope to mix with 200 keys of that Fentanyl. I'll have all of my goons out to kill everything moving."

Coyote looks over at Little Boom "done!"

"Get your men I will have them give you half now and the other half when the job is done. Do we have a deal?"

Ice Gee walked up to Little Boom s and shook his hand and yelled, "hell yes let get this shit on!"

Coyote looked over at the others and asked, "so are you in or out?"

Jack Skully nodded his head and replied, "I'm in, but I want some cocaine with mine." Coyote shouted, "okay, get your men now. Giorgio what do you have to say about this?"

"Yes, I'm in but when this is all done, I want a bigger piece of the city to operate."

"Good, we will talk about that once we take over this motherfucker okay let's go to work." Coyote got his men Koo- Koo Man, Paco and Yaya to make sure they got half of the drugs they promise all of them four hours later. When it got dark all of them unleashed hell on the whole city of Toronto.

The Haitians didn't know what fucking hit them they blew up five of their hair shops, eight of their bars and four of their food markets. All of the Haitians scattered like roaches when the lights came on in all the chaos. The Canadian police didn't know what the fuck what was going on. All they knew was it was a big gang war and they had to deal with it. Cougar Man got out of town going to his people home in the United States relocating to South Carolina. A week later Ice Gee and his gang tracked down Vache in a cabin in the woods shooting him so many times his body could not be recognized. In that same week something historical happens all three of the ethnic gangs all worked together wiping out the rest of the Haitians gang members. They also killed over ten of Crazy Carlo's men and they took over all of their territory. Crazy Carlo Lombardi and his father

Big Papa both got out of town for fear of getting killed they fled to New York for protection.

By the first week in October of 2019 the ethnic gangs along with my peoples S.O.S & The MMC chased the Italian Mob out of Canada. When I heard that I could not stop laughing my ass off I knew they didn't have the balls or the power. They talk a tough game but when it comes down to it, they are some bitch made motherfuckers at the end of the day. After that they had the Stars and Bars biker gang on the run as well with the help of their arch enemies the Metal Head MC's loving every minute of it. But back home Billy The

Kid Vanzetti quickly had a sit down with Puerto Rican Joe asking for more help after five of his men getting killed in one month time and he's really hurt that his own cousin Sal The Bulldozer is helping them kill his peoples on the streets of Philly. Puerto Rican Joe looked him right in the face and announced, "your cousin got to go!"

Billy The Kid Vanzetti with tears in his eyes pleaded, "I know but he would feel better if you took care of it."

Puerto Rican Joe just looked up at Tanya "we can accommodate you on this request. Isn't that right Miss Tanya Gats?

She smirked and replied, "we sure can brother."

That same night Puerto Rican Joe sent Tanya Gats,Woo- Woo, Lurch, Midnight, Crazy Paco and Killer Cody to take care of Sal The Bulldozer after getting the information from Billy The Kid Vanzetti where he lay his head at 9th & Porter street. He also sent Fat Smoochy, Bango, Crazy Jamel, Levi Gats, Mark Mangol and Crazy Kyle. The two-wheel men on that job were Taz- Money and Jerry Iilly to smoke Big John Galgano after Puerto Rican Joe had a long talk with Crazy Chaz Billy The Kid Vanzitti's Capo. He wanted revenge because one of the men who were killed was his best friend, he grew up with Dan Slick Danny Dee Terracciano who was his best man in his wedding.

It's 9:34 P.M. Big John Galgano is in the car with his driver Anthony Skinny Tony Simonelli. He parked his car at 10th & Bigler in front his large beautiful red brick home popping up out of the darkness in back of them is Levi Gats, Bango and Mark Mangol with machine guns and running up in front of him is Crazy Kyle, Fat Smoochy and Crazy Jamel also had their choppers blasting the two men in the black Mercedes-Benz ripping it to shreds with hot led. All you see is muzzle flash from the tips of all their machine guns. Lighting their ass up good blood and glass flying everywhere and the sound of the men death screams turn into whimpers and a gurgling sound of the two men choking off their own blood.

Two trucks quickly drove up as the three men in the front jump in and the three men in the back got ghost from the set as fast as they came. All his neighbors came out after the men sped off down the street in the deep glare of the Dall yellow streetlights burning rubber. They all come out to see the gruesome sight of the two men bullet riddle bodies calling the police. They gathered gossiping to one another as the news trucks came up reporting on a new gangland style murder in the city of Philadelphia. Later that night Sal The Bulldozer came home drunk in his new car dark blue Cadillac Escalade he brought with the money he made fingering Billy The Kid Vanzetti's men.

Soon as he parked his truck he's about to get out and speeding up the street with Woo- Woo behind the wheel on the dark green van Tanya Gats in the passenger seat with a MP-5 machine gun pointing right at his head. Soon as she started spitting bullets into his face and chest at the same time Lurch, Midnight, Crazy Paco and Killer Cody is shooting from out the sliding door of the van. They hit him so many times his body is shaking up and down like a rag doll in a tornado.

They hit him in every part of his body, but his feet making a bloody mess with blood and glass scattered all over the ground in front of the luxury SUV. It is all fucked up and smoking like a campfire in the summertime. As the shooters speed up the street making their getaway into the concrete jungle. Hours later when Pauly

Hair Trigger Esposito got the news from one of his Capo named Dominick The Dark Horse Castellano Pauly he jumped up tossing his 50-inch TV on the floor screaming at the top of his lungs, " I want that black bitch dead! "

I have to say October was a very good month for all of my peoples right after getting the news about Sal The Bulldozer and Big John Galgano getting smoked most of the cartel muscle in Las Vegas got locked up and killed by S.O.S. So, they had to back up off of Fly - Ty peoples plus with S.O.S. Kicking a lot of ass out there. It looks like they done won the first round of their battle with their powerful rivals. *That shit just show me if I had all of MMC out there we could take over out there, but I'm fucking retired now for good. I hope so I can't keep that kind of thinking in my head but sometime I can't help it as I laughed to myself.*

After my son Little Boom was done with all that shit in Canada, he called me and he was coming to see me. Two weeks later it the end of October Little Boom flew in to see me at my ranch Sun Dance. I showed him around when he came, and we sat down and talked for lunch Miss Marie cook for us chicken tortillas. I love them. When Juan came in to work. I introduced my son to him after we were done eating and Miss Marie when in the other room. My son whisper to me, "young dude is shady mom do not trust his ass."

I to him, "I got my eye on his ass if he makes one wrong move, I'll put a bullet in his brown tattoo ass."

We laughed and he looked at me, "I have to tell you something mom."

"What is it?"

"Look, I went to go see my father in prison."

"Oh, you did what made you do that son?"

"You told me to go see him remember after you let Blood Eye kick my ass."

"Yeah but I was just fucking with you so what happen when you when to go see him?"

"You were right he told me he was jealous of you making good money and rank moving up in the world in the gang."

His father was holding him back from doing the same it was driving him crazy.

"Well, I was fucking with you when I told you that, but I did tell you the truth, Boom." "Well, me and him are cool now. I've been putting money on his books and I'm helping him with a lawyer for his appeal."

"Yeah, well that good it's too bad he had to go to prison to have a relationship with you but I'm glad you and him are hitting it off. Do you really think he got a chance to get out?"

"Well, he told me he does so I'll go with what he told me."

"Okay, that's why you came out here to tell me?"

"Yes, and that I'm down with S.O.S. full time now and I'm moving up in rank now John wants me to run shit. *I'm looking at him in his eyes.*"

Little Boom get some pay back on that ass

"Okay, that's good but don't do it blindly like I did it. When I was down with BSN you hear me keep your eyes open with all of them Niggas okay."

"I will, Mom I'm not going to let them use me up so I will keep my eyes open wide with these Niggas for sure."

"Good, I don't want you to let them Niggas play you for a fool like they did me."

"Yeah, but you ran shit doe, Mom. So, don't let them think they played you mom you were just too fucking smart for them."

"Good thing I was, or they would have fucked me really good too!"

We both started snickered.

"I heard about Jay that was real fucked up mom."

"Yeah, it is. I miss him so much."

"I'm hoping he can get out on the appeal it's a lot of fucking money, but I really don't care just as long as I can get him out. Now it's time I ask you the same thing you ask me Do you think he got a chance to get out on appeal, Mom?

He looked me right into my eyes good.

"Yeah, I do we already got two FBI ass holes fired so I know the next time we will get him out."

"Okay I hear you so are you going to say retired this time around?"

"I really hope so I really done with this game right about now with all of this dumb shit going on."

"I hear you so who is here with you?"

"Blood Eye and your Aunt Lisa."

"Get the fuck out of here I have not seen her in years. Where she at?"

"She over Blood Eye place with his wife Mary busing it up their real good friends now how long are you staying here?"

"For about two or three weeks I need some time off after putting in all that work, I been doing."

"I heard that's why S.O.S. wants you down with them they told me you're a fucking beast now."

"Well thanks to you and Crazy Monk I am now."

Later that day my Aunt Lisa came back to the house kicking it with Little Boom she was so glad to see him. Boom he kept eyeing Blood Eye up and down looking for that rematch. I knew I could not stop them, and my son wanted to get that shit off his chest. So, it's around midnight it's me, my Aunt Lisa and Little Boom is at the bar near the pool listing to some smoking hot hip hop and R&B music feeling good getting are groove on.

Were all having a good time snorting coke with a large pile of it on top of the bar and all of us drinking beer, doing shots of Tequila, smoking some weed getting fucking twisted. I saq that the two of them Blood Eye and my son Little Boom are eyeing each other all fucking night. I'm just hoping nothing jumps the fuck off, but we were all getting fucked up. When Little Boom put down his beer on the counter and he hands Aunt Lisa his blunt then he took his shirt off putting it on the back of the bar stool and he set his pistol on the seat. *Now I have not seen my son without his shirt off in a long time I can see he's been working out and he has all these new tattoos. The one on his chest with the large S.O.S and three stars told it all. He's a stone-cold killer now. I know that from what John Spartacus told me about his gang and what the stars stand for when they were in prison soldiers get one Capo get two and war lords get three.* He came up on Blood Eye "I have to do this shit Dawg!"

He suckers punch him right in his face. Blood Eye fell back almost hitting the ground He's pissed off he looks up at me real fast and I just put my hands up in the air letting him know he have to fight my son. Aunt Lisa went to jump in between the two of them I pulled her back by both her arms and told her, " "this is some shit between the both of them they are men let them hash this shit out okay! You just go sit your little narrow black ass down out the way and let them fight."

Blood Eye ran towards Little Boom swinging hard at his head Little Boom ducks it and came up with an upper cut hitting Blood Eye right up under his chin **Kook!** Rocking the shit out of him. Making Blood Eye fall back right on his ass hard. **Boom!** He jumps up putting his hands up looking over at me again. I yelled, "hey your going has to fuck him up like you did last time bro. Don't look at me get to it motherfucker as I'm pointing at him sipping on my beer."

He put his hands up I can see in his eyes that he didn't want to fight because Little Boom done had some training. Now he's a much better fighter now after he done been in more than a few fights rolling with the S.O.S. Gang where they make you fight within their clique just for fucking ghetto entertainment on the daily. Blood Eye came at him fast and hard swinging hay makers at him missing Little Boom with every punch. Little Boom started jabbing at Blood Eye tagging him in his face **Boom! Packa! Bloow!** Fucking up his eye bleeding. Little Boom started dancing soon as Blood Eye came up to hit him Little Boom sweep kick him with his left leg and he fell on his ass **Kaboom!**

Soon as Blood Eye when to lift his head to push himself up from off the ground Little Boom came an, stepped up swinging a thunderous right cross on his jaw **Plow!** Knocking him out cold.

He looked over at me and announced, "that's another reason I came over to see you, so I get me some pay back on this Nigga."

Then he looks down at Blood Eye he is stretched out on the ground.

I turned to Aunt Lisa and asked her to go get a bottle of that ammonia from under the sink and a rag for me.

Little Boom walked over towards the bar and asked, "you want another beer, Mom?" "Yeah, get three of them out one for Aunt Lisa and Blood Eye over here after I wake his ass up."

Aunt Lisa came back with the rag and the ammonia standing in front of me. I told her, "okay, put some of it on the fucking rag and put it under his nose for me. Do you think you can do that shit for me please Aunt Lisa?"

She looks up at me and nodded her head yes.

"Okay, I got it." She walks over to where he's laid out at, she put some of the ammonia on the rag, "not too much now Aunt-Tee now put it under his nose alright."

Aunt Lisa squats down in front of him she gently puts the rag with the ammonia under his nose and he jumps up so fast making Aunt Lisa fall back on her ass Boom! Me and my son start laughing our ass off. Blood Eye jumped up swinging his arms like he was still fighting. I'm sitting at the bar and I yelled, "the fight is over man!"

I stood up and walked over to Blood Eye and handed him the beer.

"Here you go brother drink this you will be alright.

Blood Eye looked up at me and asked, "what the fuck happen?" His eyes were all glassy.

I answer with a chuckle, "Little Boom knocked you out that's what happen. Just drink this and calm your ass down man its fucking hot out here, brother."

He knocks the beer out my hand the beer falls breaking scatted glass is on the ground he's yelled, "I didn't want to fucking fight him in the first place!"

"Blood eye, I know you're a little mad right now, but you better chill the fuck out with all that base in your voice, motherfucker!"

He jumps to his feet and yelled, "fuck you, Almasi!"

I yelled back, "go and cool the fuck off before you catch another bad break, Nigga!"

He quickly walks towards the house "okay that's the way you going to talk to me after all this time fuck this shit!"

I help Aunt Lisa up from off the ground and , "Nigga, you are going to be all right he just mad Little Boom got his pay back on him after I told him to kick little Boom's ass some time back that's all it's all good baby."

Aunt Lisa chimed in, "let me go get a broom to clean that shit up."

"Shit Auntie, I should make Blood Eye clean that shit up he's the one who knocked it out my fucking hand."

Almasi 2
Queen of The Streets
By Dartanya A. Williams Sr.

Twenty minutes five later after he got off the phone with his wife Mary. Blood Eye came up out the house with a gun in his hand strolling hard towards us while the three of us are sitting at the bar near the pool. I see the gun in his hand I quickly get my gun I cocked it back and I stood up pointing it at him and screamed, "you just lose your fucking mind coming out here pulling a fucking gun on us Nigga!"

"No, I'm out here with a fucking gun to set shit straight between me and your son so get the fuck out of my way, Almasi."

"Seriously, you're going to let that fight throw away all the friendship we have for one another Nigga. You're going let your pride toss all that shit to the side for your fucking ego man for real Blood Eye man."

Aunt Lisa came and ran up to him, "look here Blood Eye I got your wife here on the phone she's on her way up here right now I'll put her on speaker for you."

Aunt Lisa hits the button we all can hear her voice "Bobby don't do this shit just go calm down please Bobby!"

"I don't know what happen there but it's not worth putting your life on the line baby! Baby. I'm almost there am driving up to the ranch as we speak am in the car coming to you after you talk to me after it happen. I'm on my way okay please don't do anything!"

Blood Eye yelled, "hang that shit up I don't want to hear that bull shit!"

Aunt Lisa hung up the phone up and walked back towards the bar sitting down pulling out her gun sitting it in her lap holding it.

I stood right in front of him with my gun in his face and snarled, "I'm not going to let you kill my son for some bull shit Blood Eye. Man, your high or whatever go sit your ass down somewhere before something happens!"

Blood Eye yelled, "get the fuck out of my way, Almasi. You just don't understand it's a fucking street Nigga thing!"

My son Little Boom sat at the bar cool and calm a beer in one hand and his gun in the other looking up at him with a deep smirk on his dark grill. I'm yelling in his face, "no Blood Eye man you need to get you mind right motherfucker! Go take your ass back in the house before somebody gets hurt Blood Eye come on!"

He went to take aim I got my gun pointed at his head and from out of nowhere I hear this woman screaming voice, "no Bobby! No don't do this shit!" He backs up looking over towards his left and its' his wife Mary begging, "please baby don't do this shit."

He waves her back and screamed, "I got to do this get the fuck out my way, Almasi!" Mary runs and jumps right in front of his line of fire with tears in her eye begging him saying please Bobby don't fuck up everything we build. Blood Eye yelled, "fuck this shit he shoved Mary into me making both of us fall back from the very hard shove." **Kapacka! Kapacka! Kapacka! Kapacka!** Little Boom shot Blood Eye four times two in the head and two slugs to the chest before he could get one shot off. His bloody body fell backwards on the ground. Mary jumps up running over to his bloody corpse on the ground and the blood is gushing out fast. She dives right on top of him crying and waling than she looks up and screamed at my son, "you killed my baby! You killed my baby! Noooooo! Bobby oh my God no!"

I cut in "Come on Mary it nothing you can do for him. Now he's gone. I have to talk to you about this shit it was all one big misunderstanding now."

She jumps up she's covered in Blood Eye's blood all over her hands, chest and some on her face. "Noooooo! You just want to cover this shit up you and your son is going to pay for this shit! Your all just a bunch of fucking dope dealing murderers! I'm going to tell the cops everything what happen that you started this fight between them. It just as much your fault he's dead as that motherfucker right there who pulled the trigger!"

She's pointed at my son with his gun in his hand and I can see the blood dripping off of her fingers as she is pointed at him.

I began to calmly say, "wait a minute now, Mary why don't you come over here get yourself a drink or something and calm the fuck down, okay."

341

I'm pulling her by the hand so she can chill the fuck out so she can hear me out as well. She quickly pulls away from me and screamed at the top of her lungs, "no, I don't want to hear that bull shit you're not talking me out of this shit. I'm going to the cops fuck that shit! She started running towards the door. **Packa! Kapow!**

I shot her in the back of the head where you can see her brains hanging out from the back dripping out. My Aunt Lisa shot her in her upper back area making a large hole where you can see the chunks of meat hanging out. Her body fell sideways near the stone walkway to the house. My Aunt Lisa came walking up still holding her gun and shrugged her shoulders, "well, you tried to talk to her dumb ass it's just to fucking bad."

I replied, "only one thing I don't have a cleaner out here to get rid of the fucking bodies." My son answered, "I got a guy he's fucking good too he's from New Mexico right next door I got this shit don't worry." He winked his eye at me.

I asked, "are you sure Boom?"

"I'll call him, hold on mom." He has his head pressed to his phone walking way a little then he comes back.

"Mom, he wants 90,000 dollars."

"Okay, tell him to hurry up to this is fucked up y'all."

I quickly go into my video tape surveillance room I took out the two DVDs. I took them out and I snapped both in half and I turned it off until the cleaner comes and clean up this fucking mess. Now I'm not high anymore. I walked back out to the pool area where my Aunt Lisa is sitting at the bar drinking beer with a cigar cocked in the side of her lips, still holding her gun. I sit next to her, "you know no what's fucked up what about their kids."

"Well, they're both with Mary's mother in Philly for them to go to school. So, you don't have to worry about them there in good hands."

An hour later my son man came his name was Mister Rubin came in a big delivery truck outside of my gate. He walked to the door ringing the doorbell my son get the door shaking hands with him and asked, "are you ready?"

"Yeah, let me get my mother so you guys can get to work. "

"Yes, can I ask you something before you go get your mother?"

"Yeah what's that, Mister Rubin."

"Is your mother Almasi Glock Mommy from the BSN?"

"Well she's not down with the BSN anymore. She's doing her own thing but yeah that's her."

"Wow, I can't wait to meet her."

"Okay, I'll be right back." Little Boom came and got me while this guy was at the door. "Mom, you have to pay him before he gets started this is the way he works."

"Okay, let me go get the loot."

I quickly go to my safe in my bedroom and took the loot out. I walked with my son to the front door I want to see the guy I am giving my money to. At first glance he looks like a fucking bookkeeper or something, but he was dressed in all black with some really fly gear on doe.

He shakes my hand and greets me, "hello, it nice to meet you. I'm Mister Rubin I did some work for your son and his crew not too long ago, but I never met a living legend before. I'm always doing work for all of these new jack guys in the game. I heard so many stories about you. The one I love the most is the strawberry bridge hit y'all did on the Gorilla Boulevard gangsters that was some masterful work."

"Yeah, that was some really hairy shit doe but that's when the BDC was at the top of our game."

"Yes, you guys were the fucking best if you ask me."

"Well, thanks Mister Rubin here is your money. I'll like for you to get this shit done right away for me. Mister Rubin pushed the money back to me saying this one is on me okay this way. I can say I did some work for you."

"Are you sure about this Mister Rubin?"

"Yes, I'm sure this is on me I'm a big fan of you work. Your son never told me who you were. I'm really mad at his ass for not telling who you were well it's time to get to work. Here is my card you can call me if you need me again and the next time I'll charge you. This time it's free I'll pay my people out of my own pocket please show me where is the bodies at."

I walked him out to the pool area showing him where the bodies were at, he looked "okay, just open the gate up for us, please and we can get to work." I went and showed my son how to open the gate with the panel near the kitchen counter. He hits it, open the gate and they went to work. They moved fast because he had eight men working and they did not fuck around. They cleaned up the two bodies with all the blood in less than a half an hour time. He came up and asked could have some coke after seeing so much of it on the bar. I answered, "sure, I went to the back room and I brought out to him a big zip lock bag of cocaine.

He was happy "thank you so much, Glock Mommy. I'm so glad to meet you good night." He shook my hand and jumped in the truck and was gone. *What I found out later his wife is a writer of gangster books and her name is Sharon Rubin. She was writing a book about the BSN in its heyday. That's why this guy knew so much about all the shit we'd done in the game.*

I put my surveillance system back on. I walked out to check out their work and it was like it never happen. I was fucking tired now, so I went to bed now. I was thinking about who I was going to get to watch my back now. The whole thing was just fucked up, but when you pride is bigger than your commonsense you will surely lose your fucking life fast in this deadly game.

I don't trust this Nigga

This was so fucked up I really like Blood Eye I didn't know he was so fucking hardheaded. I never knew he would go out like that, but he did that fucking crazy shit. My Aunt Lisa and Boom stayed up listening to music getting high by the pool still partying. The next day I called Jagger up telling him about what happen with Blood Eye tripping and my son killed him. He told me he was going to send Gun Ho Moe and Fat Smoochy Flip Diddy's brother to watch my back, but he told me that Fat Smoochy is like Damon Gee. He knows a whole lot of Niggas in the streets and he's a walking talking gangster encyclopedia. He knows all the gangs back rounds and their history by heart. Jagger I'm going to love this guy because this Nigga is super smart. So, I send my son to go pick them up from the airport later that afternoon. I notice that when Juan came in to work that day, he was acting funny.

I ask his Mother Miss Maria what was up with him she his P.O. been riding his ass. About a drug test he failed, and they were giving him one more chance or they were going to send him back to prison. To me that sounded like a bunch of bullshit to me. I was played it off, but I kept my eye on this motherfucker. I like Miss Maria but if her son does something. I will blow his fucking head off for real. Now Gun Ho Moe and Fat Smoochy arrive at the house and I was so glad to see them I had my aunt Lisa show them to their rooms and I had Miss Maria and Juan to go pick up some liquor extra food and beer to fill up the bars outside. It's November I know it's super fucking cold back in Philly but out here it's like 80 and 90 every day. I fucking love it out here.

I'm in the kitchen eating a banging ass fruit salad and my Aunt Lisa made for the two of us. I'm watching TV, but the sound is down but when I look up, I see the news flash. I tell my Aunt Lisa to turn it up hearing the television announcer , "reputed mobster Billy The Kid Vanzetti from the outlaw faction of the mafia was shot up on the freeway in Philadelphia and he's in critical condition at Jefferson hospital."

I sit back and to myself, "wow, they got to Billy's ass I hope he pulls through."

Then my phone rings I pick it up fast and I answer, "it's Jagger."

He asked, "yo, boss lady did my boys make it there alright?"

"Yeah, I had my Aunt Lisa show them to their rooms."

"Okay, good check this out I got a call from one of your old heads from back in the days he wants a sit down so he can warn us about something."

"Yeah, so who the fuck is it Jagger?"

"It's Trevor Tee he he wants to talk."

"Did you run it by Puerto Rican Joe yet?"

"No not yet."

"Well, run it pass him because I don't trust that Nigga, he's up to something him and Nokey Blaze were really tight."

"That's why I called you I knew that shit sounded fishy."

"Yeah, be careful I don't trust that guy he got something up his fucking sleeve."

"Okay, Almasi. I'm going to call Puerto Rican Joe and tell him what's going on. Thanks Moja(One)."

"Moja. I hang up looking over to my Aunt Lisa and told her, "fucking Trevor Tee called up Jagger he wants to talk about something."

Aunt Lisa smirked, "that's a fucking trap from the door." Gun Ho Moe and Fat Smoochy walked up and I ask them to have a seat. They both sit down, "y'all want something to eat my Aunt Lisa can fix it for y'all?"

Gun Ho Moe replied, "I'm good thank you. I ate on the jet. Fat Smoochy also chimed "I would love some of that fruit salad y'all was having."

My Aunt Lisa , "coming right up brother."

"Gentlemen, I really can't talk now but when you done eating your salad. I need to holla at you one on one Smoochy okay. Moe

346

knows what to do around here being out here before. If y'all need anything just let me know." My Aunt Lisa sat the fruit salad in front of him on the table. I stood up and waved for Gun Ho Moe to follow me out to the deck area. We walked out to my long bar near the pool I sit down, and I point to the seat for him to sit down.

"Look, I want to keep an eye on that motherfucker Juan he's been acting funny all fucking day long."

"I got you, Almasi. I need to ask you what happen with Blood Eye?"

"Him and my son got into it some time back and Blood Eye whipped his ass now as you know Boom got some training and been putting in mad work with S.O.S.

So, he wanted to get his pay back on him with another fight but this time Little Boom kicked his ass. His ego could not take it they had a shootout and my son killed him. Mary came and saw Blood Eye dead. She went off and she was going to the cops so me and my Aunt Lisa smoked her ass."

Little Boom walks over towards us Gun Ho Moe stands up shaking his hand smiling. They bump chest as their shaking hands.

"Look, I just was telling Moe over here what happen last night."

Little Boom , "man, that Nigga was tripping so y'all my mother's new bodyguards now?"

Gun Ho Moe answered, "yeah, me and Fat Smoochy. You don't have to worry we will not be fucking tripping like Blood Eye."

We all started laughing as Fat Smoochy came walking out towards the bar area.

"Fat Smoochy I was telling Moe over here what happen to Blood Eye."

"Well Almasi, I really didn't know him all that good. I just knew he was working with Lou- Lou and Gavin."

"This is what happen he got too fucking high. My son over here gave him a beat down on some pay back shit they had a shootout and he lost now that motherfucker is smoking blunts with Lucifer. *We all started giggling.*

Almasi 2
Queen of The Streets
By Dartanya A. Williams Sr.

"Well, I'm going to show y'all my surveillance equipment and how to work. It is your job is to watch my back."

Fat Smoochy began, "can I say something, Almasi?"

"Go head Smoochy and speak freely, brother."

"Well, I'm thinking you were going to have some more men with all the shit going on in Philly."

"Like what Smoochy spit it all out."

"I heard what's left of the Chain gang and the Ghost Boys link up together. They Big Cyrus and Twiggy Jones put all the shit together with the help of Nokey Blaze's son MGR Blaze *Machine Gun Ronny*."

"Where you hear all this shit from?"

"My man Max Stacks he told me they tried to kill Trevor Tee he they shot him all up, but he lived and he's looking for some pay back on Nokey Blaze for betraying him." "Wow, Jagger you knew you shit, thanks."

I went behind the bar getting some cold beers for everyone setting them on top of the bar and I quickly called Puerto Rican Joe. The phone rings three times and he picked up, "yo Joe, this is Almasi. Did Jagger call you yet?"

"Yeah, I just got off the phone with him he was telling me that Trevor Tee wants to talk or some bull shit like that."

"Yeah, but I just found out that Nokey Blaze tried to kill him that's why he wants to talk."

"Oh yeah so, it's real than."

"Yeah and I also heard that the Chain gang and the Ghost boys are working together so you know who their coming after us."

"Yeah, you better know it because we done kicked their ass and chase them out of fucking town. So, I know there salty about that shit. I'm going to put everybody on high alert thanks, Almasi."

"Your welcome, brother you know I had to hit you up soon as I heard it my Nigga."

"You know a fucking lot to be retired, Almasi."

348

I looked over at Fat Smoochy "well, I got good people around me that's all just let me know when Trevor Tee reach out to you, okay."

I sure will and thanks again. Moja (One)"

"Moja!"

I take Gun Ho Moe and Fat Smoochy to my surveillance room showing them how to work the equipment. I show them around the ranch. I told them I wanted to get some horses soon, but for right now just to keep up maintaining the land. It is so beautiful and peaceful out here. I took them to the bank with me so I can pick up my drop. I keep some of it in the bank. I take some with me so I can put in my safe so I can have some cash on hand so I can take care of things. We all sat down and had dinner together my Aunt Lisa made beef short ribs and she also made this seafood salad that was so delicious we all ate like fucking Vikings. We laughed and had a good time eating all together after partying a little too hard other night I went to bed early.

The next day when I got up around 10A.M. I get a call from my housekeeper Marie crying telling me her son Juan was dead. She he was killed by his gang he told her that they wanted him to help set me up to get robbed and Juan did not want to do it because you treated me and him so good. So, they killed him for not doing it.

I gave her my condolences and I would take care of all his arrangements. She thanked me and she did not talk to the police about what her son was up to or about his gang. Marie expressed she wanted to talk to me about taking care of them for her. I told her sure I will make sure that those people who killed her son will pay. Marie in between deep sobs, "thank you so much, Miss Miller."

I told her to give me the information where her son body is at and I'll make sure that he's taking care of the right way. She thanked me again and I hang up with her. I knew it was something up with him when he came to work that day. I got washed and dressed and did my hair so as I step out to the kitchen Fat Smoochy and Gun Ho Moe is sitting down drinking coffee with my Aunt Lisa I greeted everyone with good morning.

Almasi 2
Queen of The Streets
By Dartanya A. Williams Sr.

I sit down, but I see Gun Ho Moe jump up pulling out both his pistols. He quickly hit the button to the gate close on the counter **Doom!**

He yelled out, "mask intruders at the front gate and back gate. Smoochy you take care of them motherfuckers at the back gate. Soon as I zap there ass when I hit the electricity I'm going to give you a running start go!"

Fat Smoochy quickly picked up his machine gun and started running I never thought his fat ass could move that fast. Me and my Aunt Lisa stood up pulling out our guns looking at the large TV monitors along my wall on the left from my surveillance system. Gun Ho Moe hits the switch zapping the shit out of the four men trying to clime the gate outside. and the three men at the back gate at the same time soon. As they got shocked me and Aunt Lisa fell out laughing watching them yelling falling from off the gate all at the same time. Fat Smoochy was outside of the back gate super-fast we see him spitting bullets at them he hits all three of their asses. A few minutes after that Gun Ho Moe came out with his two Glocks popping off hitting each one them trying to get up after getting burned the fuck up. From the electricity flowing from the front gate. Gun Ho Moe is picking them off one by one. I told Aunt Lisa, "why she didn't pop some fucking popcorn for this shit over here."

We both giggled our ass off, and Gun Ho Moe pulled out his pack of cigarettes sticking one of them in his thick dark lips lighting it up. Then he pulls out his phone and called me. I picked it and saw that that they got them all Moe.

Yes, I did their all dead they look like local ass hole gang bangers I think you better call a cleaner if you have one around here.

"Yeah, I got one a good one too."

My son walks in the kitchen and asked, "what's happening?"

I looked at him "everything Nigga you missed all the fucking action these gang banging ass holes just tried to run up in here."

Aunt Lisa agreed, "yeah, but Smoochy and Gun Ho Moe smoked their ass in about two minutes fucking flat!"

Little Boom yelled, "I bet you a million fucking dollars your little tattoo helper had something to do with it. I knew that guy looked fucking shady!"

Were all chuckled while drinking coffee and smoking cigarettes telling more jokes like it was a real shocking experience for their ass.

I told Boom that Juan was dead, and his gang killed him for not setting me up to get robbed but he did not want to do it, so they smoked him. I just got off the phone with his mother those assholes out there. I know his home boys. Now I must call your boy Mister Rubin. Little Boom laughed, "oh no, that's your boy now that motherfucker was going to cum on himself after he met you."

All of us started laughing as I quickly called my newest fan Mister Rubin the cleaner. "Well it took Mister Rubin about an hour to get to the ranch were all sitting in the kitchen eating breakfast. Aunt Lisa made it for all of us while we were waiting on Mister Rubin and his crew to come clean up the dog shit outside of my front and back gate. It was seven bodies all together."

Mister Rubin came up in the kitchen "wow, something smells really good in here."

I , "would you like something to eat, Mister Rubin?"

"Why I sure would, and I have the time because those guys aren't going anywhere. Good thing you live so far apart from your neighbors as he sits down smiling at everybody. Aunt Lisa fixed his food and set a plate right in front of him.

"Here you go I got you some eggs, turkey bacon grits and butter biscuits."

"Why, thank you my dear this here meal is fit for a king over here. He started eating as those dark wicked eyes of his is filled with joy. James Brown song is on the radio playing in the background *Get on up*. I went in the back to get Mister Rubin his money when I get the call I looked at the caller ID. Soon as I see that code name. I know it's from Puerto Rican Joe and I picked up fast and asked, "yo, what's up, Joe?"

"You were right on the money, sis with all that information. I'm having the sit down with Trevor Tee tomorrow in Nice town."

"Okay, that sound good after you talk to him let me know what he's talking about and I can tell you if he's trying to set you up or not."

"Okay, I will look. I have some bad news to report to you, Ma. The Italian's killed your home boy Quan Kauu. Man, he was a good dude, I'm going to miss his ass."

"He delivered his drugs faster than the fucking wind blows. I'm telling you, sis."

"Wow, that's fucked up! Do you know who going to take his place in his organization?" "No, not yet. I can still get heroin from Coyote's people, but there not as fast as Quan was."

"Yeah, you better know it he was the best maybe when you hook up with Quan's successor he can be like Quan. He was alright with me. I holla at you later Joe."

"I have to go get some shit done Moja*(One).*"

"**Baadae Ma***(Later Ma).*" I walked out my bedroom back into the kitchen with the money in a plastic bag from the shoe store. I hand it to him he sets it on the table in front of him finishing his food smacking his lips. After he was done, he stood up

"well, it's time to make the donuts."

He picked up the plastic bag with the loot walking out to his truck and his men jumped out and started cleaning up the bodies at the front gate. They went around back cleaning up at the rest of the gang banging ass holes from off my property. Blood, guts, shells and all they were all done in about an hour and a half. After he was done Mister Rubin came back in the house asking could I do him a favor one day by meeting his wife the writer. I told him I don't know about that because I didn't want to incriminate myself. His never said that she just wants to meet you no questions or interview. I told him I would think about it.

He said, "okay, I'll tell her what you , and he walked back out to the truck taking his time." He jumped on and they took off.

I pulled out my phone and called Jagger up sitting in the kitchen while my Aunt Lisa was washing dishes from that big breakfast, she made for all of us. Fat Smoochy and Gun Ho Moe were helping her clean up to some old soul music blasting on the radio. He picks up after it rang three times, he greeted me, "what's up, boss lady?"

"Look, I got some great information from your boy, Fat Smoochy that the Chain gang and the Ghost boys linked up together so I'm going to need more people to watch my back out here."

"Well, if you feel that way, I'll send out two more guys if you want."

"Yes, I do. I think I should have more men because more shit is about to jump off."

"Okay, I'll send you Maximo and Dallin both of these guys are stone cold killers there really good, but they know how to follow orders to the tee trust me."

"Are you sure now Jagger?"

"You know I'm not sending you no fuck ups your way to watch your ass. You should know that, sis. I would not do that shit to you Ma."

"I know you won't because you know I'll kick your ass Nigga!"
 We both laughed.

"Thanks, Jagger man I can always count on you, brother."

"No sweat, sis. You know I got your back they should be there in the next five hours or so. I know where to send them to fly out. Same shit, right?"

"Yeah, but send me some weed with them for me."

"Sure thing I got you I talk to you later if you need anything else just hit me up, boss lady Moja *(One)."*

"**Kwaheri***(Goodbye)"*

I looked up at Gun Ho Moe and asked, "what you know about these two dude Jagger is send me Maximo and Dallin?"

 Gun Ho Moe looked me right in the face and answered, they are good men, a little young and crazy but there loyal you don't have to worry about them. **Nzuri** *(Good)* but you're going to train them when they get here. **Kuhakikisha** *(Sure)* Almasi. The two men Jagger send out came later that evening Gun Ho Moe showed them around the ranch.

Snatching Nokey Blaze wife brought us so much hell

Gun Ho Moe showed them where all the guns and ammo were at, the surveillance room, how to work shit and he made sure they had it down pack. They both seem to be all right so far; I'll break their ass in really good over the coming weeks. A week blaze passes my son Little Boom went back to Philly while he was there with me, in Arizona he did not want to go, but he he had to get back to work. He even showed the new guys Maximo and Dallin a few things about fighting with knves and how to use all kinds of machine guns.

They both looked up to my son hearing about his reputation back in Philly with S.O.S As a real killer and a gangster's gangster. *I knew once I hooked him up with Crazy Monk, he would be one bad motherfucker, but it looks like I might have created a real fucking monster doe.* When I got the call from Puerto Rican Joe on Tuesday afternoon while I was looking for a new housekeeper on my computer because Miss Maria Sanchez quit after burying her son.

"I took care of everything like I told her, and she is a nice lady. He told me he made a deal with Trevor Tee so I'm one step closer to taking out Nokey Blaze. Now that he put two of our mortal enemies together to come at us to kill us now. I have to think about this shit. I was supposed to be fucking retired three weeks ago, and it went by fast like a blur.

It's the first week of December I had a few people apply for the housekeeping job. I didn't like them too much until this older Black woman name Miss Zola came to the house. I interview her and I liked her from the door. She was tough, resourceful and most of all incredibly wise. She told me she was from Mississippi and she also told me that she had six grown children and nine grand kids. I hired her on the spot after talking with her. I introduced her to my Aunt Lisa soon as I did that my phone started ringing, I told her excuse me for a minute. I answer the phone and its Poochie yelling with excitement, telling me that Robin is about to have the baby. He was driving her to the hospital as we were speaking.

I stood up and yelled in the phone, "oh my God please keep your eyes on the road and get her there in one piece. Call me back when she has the baby, I'm so happy for you, Nigga. Now go take care of my sister now, bye."

I looked at Miss Zola and explained, "my sister is having her first baby. I'm so excited for her. So, do you want to say here, or you be coming in every day. "Well, I was hoping I could stay here I just lost my house." She lowered her eyes. "I'm so sorry to hear that, Miss Zola but welcome to your new home okay. I'll have my Aunt Lisa show you to your room." I stood up shook her hand she looked like she was going to cry shaking my hand back with both her hands.

"So, I wanted to ask you when do I get paid?"

"You get paid every two weeks on Friday and you get 1,500 every two weeks. She looked at me and blinked twice, "What? Are you sure?"

"What's that's not enough?"

She started giggling, "Oh, that will be just fine, Miss Miller."

Now if you need some money at the end of the day, I can hook you up to make sure you're alright to take care of a few things. *I can tell by looking in her face without telling me she was having a very hard time right now in her life, but I know she's very proud and strong.* Yes, Miss Miller I do need a little something. Well I'll have my Aunt Lisa will go with you to pick up your things where you're staying and she will make sure you get a little something okay. Thank you so much again. I looked up at her saying Robin is about to have the baby. I know I heard Poochie through the dam phone he was talking so fucking loud. We all started laughing my Aunt Lisa took Miss Zola to go get her things where she was staying at. Soon as they when out the door my phone rings when I looked at the caller ID saying Jack Porter Joe's fake cell phone name, I knew it was Puerto Rican Joe. I pick it up fast saying what's up Joe? He I have some very good news for you we have Nokey Blaze wife Zelda. What your bull shitting me right? No, I'm not kidding you we have her. I'm flying out there tonight Joe. Okay I'll be looking out for you when you get here.

Good I'll have Jagger and his peoples to come get me I see you when I get there Moja*(One)* **Ndiyo***(Yeah)!* I quickly when to my bedroom so I can pack a bag to go to Philly I quickly call Jagger he picks up on the first ring saying I knew you be calling me soon as I heard the news. about them snatching up Nokey Blaze wife. Well you know where to come get me I'll text you when I'm about to touch down. Okay you know I'll be there with my troops Ma I see you soon Moja*(One* **) Baadae***(Later)!* I packed my, bags and my Aunt Lisa came back with Miss Zola I pulled Aunt Lisa to the side while Miss Zola was moving into her new room. I take her out on the patio saying look I have to go to Philly to take care of some shit I need for you to hold shit down here while I'm gone. Okay but how long will you be gone doe. Just a couple days I be right back you're in charge here I'm going to take Gun Ho Moe and Fat Smoochy with me keep your eyes open on these new guys for me okay. I got you Almasi don't worry about nothing alright. Good I know I can always depend on you Aunt-Tee. I hug her as we both started giggling. We both rocked back and forth hugging one another then we both do a high five and we point at each other at the same time that's our thing we been doing that for years now. I walked out where Gun Ho Moe and Fat Smoochy on post near the front of my ranch I bump fist with both of them saying look I need y'all to pack up y'all shit and go with me to Philly for a few days so get yourself together so we can fly out tonight. They both nodded their heads yes as I when to get ready to go so I change my clothes and I do my hair and load up my guns. Gun Ho Moe and Fat Smoochy packed up their shit a couple hours later we were all ready to roll out my Aunt Lisa drive us to the airport in the white Bentley. *And all the time I had this whip I didn't give that fat motherfucker Jonny Smooth from Mister Big Deal's luxury motors a fucking dime.*

We jump on the jet my man Ray had his wife's famous Caesar salad I don't know how she does it but it's off the hook along with

the chicken nuggets. I just drunk beer I didn't snort or smoke nothing
I really wanted to be on my game for this shit. Soon as we took off in
the air my sister Robin call me telling me she had a little boy and his
name is Leo after our father who was killed. I talk to both of them
Poochie and Robin for a while telling them how proud I was of both
of them and they both they were going to get married I that was
beautiful and I got off the phone with them to get myself together
and go to the bathroom. It took us four hours to get to Philly but
soon as I stepped off the jet inside of the huge hanger I knew it, was
something funky in the fucking air not just the refinery up the road
pumping out all the foul shit on a daily basis killing people without
them fucking knowing it. Jagger and his shooters are all jump out
their trucks I seen some new guys with him I didn't see before. Jagger,
Flip Diddy, John Rocka and Little Bay- Bay came over to me I
hugged each one them because their family to me. Jagger sis I want
you to meet some of these new Niggas he's pointing at them saying
this is Kenny Cobra, Hamza, Big Bryee and Smoky Sam I bump fist
with all of them really fast at the same time Gun Ho Moe and Fat
Smoochy is bumping chest with all of them with the two of them
knowing everybody in the click. Jagger broke up the big thug brother
reunion by puts his fist up in the air saying loud **Wacha tuangalie**
(Let's Roll out)! But all of them at the same time yelled back really
loud Ee(Yep)! Just at that moment I felt the new thing with all of
them, but I can tell they were a really tight crew. Jagger waves us over
towards him and I jump in the first truck with Jagger and my guys
sitting in the back of the truck we quickly drive to the nice town
warehouse it took us an hour to get there we pull up and I see about
eight guys on the outside of the warehouse. We all jump out in the
dock area Jagger Flip Diddy and John Rocka step up banging on the
large steel doors. Soon as the door open, I see Tanya along with Taz-
Money I hug both of them really fast as I see Big De Shawn, Akbar,
Mojo, Midnight, Juba came up bumping fist with me.

Jimmy Goon came up hugging me saying right this way my
queen. He walks me to the back of the room, and I see her looking up
at me with her eyes on fucking fire burning a fucking hole right

through me like glass is Zelda. The queen of fucking mean right in front of me looking as evil as ever. She's screaming at me I knew you had something to do with this shit! I see they have one of her hands handcuffed to this iron chair in front of this smooth steel table. I told her relax bitch I had nothing to do with this shit I want your husband dead not you okay but if you keep talking shit I will put a bullet in that fat ass thick head of yours. Everybody started giggling loud. Then walking in the room is Puerto Rican Joe he came up hugging me saying I heard you just touch down you already know Fat Jacks and Chaco his new bodyguards I shook both their hands smiling. Puerto Rican Joe Trevor Tee is right behind me he came up saying hey what's up he bump fist with me. saying dam, I never knew you would blow the fuck up like you did and become the biggest gangster in Philly Wow I feel so proud to know you for real. I thanks Tee. Zelda yelling out you both are going to be dead before the month is over trust me! Trevor Tee walked over to her **Wam!** He slapped the shit out of her yelling shut the fuck up you better hope we cut a deal because you're the one who is going to die bitch! Zelda screaming out well kill me now motherfucker because my husband will never bow down to you low rate want, to be gangster ass Niggas! **Kook!** Trevor Tee slugged her right in the fucking mouth really hard and blood is running out her mouth. Trevor Tee phone rings he quickly answers the phone and I can see in his eyes that Dred he quickly walked away from the table where we were at then I see the tears in his eyes as he walked away really fast. I ran behind him along with Puerto Rican Joe I what the fuck happen Tee. He looked up at both of us with the tears in his eyes flowing even more somebody just shot up my mother's house and she's in the hospital I have to go I'll be back later! He quickly rushed out the door I look at Puerto Rican Joe saying you know if his mother dies, he's coming back here to kill that bitch you do know that right?

Yeah but we can't let him do that shit until we get Nokey Blaze out in the open and kill his ass. Soon as he said that his phone started ringing, he gets it right in front of me saying, "yo, what's up" What?

Get the fuck out of here I'm on my way! *His face was in shock* I looked at him saying what the fuck is going on now. I don't know but somebody just blew up my mother in laws house up with my wife and kids inside. What? Yeah, I have to go it seem like there hitting us everywhere. You know what we have to do hit there ass back. I know but I have to go see about my peoples I'll start calling everybody to make moves while I'm on my way, but we have to find where the fuck their peoples are at too. Don't worry I got a guy that knows a whole lot of shit I quickly ran over to Fat Smoochy saying come with us! Me Fat Smoochy with Puerto Rican Joe jump in his truck with him driving like crazy. Gun Ho Moe Fat Jacks and Chaco all jumped in the second truck following behind us with Fat Jacks behind the wheel. Now we quickly driving to front street to Puerto Rican Joe's mother in law house name Big Mary. So Fat Smoochy is running down where a lot of where these Niggas live and where they hang out at. I'm writing all this shit down on my phone and I have to say this Nigga mind was like a fucking super computer spitting out information after he was done I called up Jane Doe crew to make some moves on these Niggas while they been making moves on us most the night. I also got Jagger and his men to hit a few of the joins Fat Smoochy told me about before we reached Puerto Rican Joe's mother in law house it was burned down to the fucking ground. The cops and firemen were all still out there when we walked up this big fat white cop told him when he ran up asking what happen that was his mother in law's house he that everyone that was in the house were dead. It was like I got numb after hearing that shit looking over at Puerto Rican Joe's face in deep anger and shock of this news.

His mother in law Big Mary, his wife Stephanie, his son 12 years old Luca and his baby girl Brie 5 years old. His whole family died in the fire of the explosion this was so sad. Puerto Rican Joe lost it he when the fuck off the cop told him to go to the morgue to ID the bodies and that he was sorry for his lost. Puerto Rican Joe with tears in his eyes when to go do what the cop told him not knowing who he was.

Death is Everywhere Tonight

Plus, he wanted to get the fuck out of there before the detectives were coming on the scene asking us all kind of fucking questions up the ass. I looked around and it was so many people out there crying and weeping in the crowd. So, me, him and Fat Smoochy quickly walked back to his truck where he parked it to go to the Philadelphia examiner's office in university city near 34th street with Fat Jacks, Chaco and Gun Ho Moe following us in the second truck. I told Puerto Rican Joe why he doesn't let Fat Smoochy drive. He handed him the keys with that blank look on his brown grill this was one hell of a fucking hurt piece. His family was his whole world and they took it away from him in one night. We got in the truck and I told Fat Smoochy where to go to get there Puerto Rican Joe to me sitting next to me in the truck that he was going to call up Dime Piece and Bopdiglo to kill every last one of Nokey Blaze family and that Nigga had kids all over the fucking place. I told him that's going to be a shit load of money.

He , I don't give a fuck. I have money. I have to get some fucking get back."

"I feel you on this shit and that I'm with you 100%."

While we were driving to University city Jane Doe crew road up on one of Nokey Blaze kids house named Tony Blaze. He's 25 years old young, cocky and very arrogant in Penn Rose Park a wannabe tough guy because of who his father is, but he had a different mother name Janice he had about a good ten baby mamas drama on the streets of Philly. He promised him a bigger spot in BSN, but for right now he had him and his boys selling coke for him in that South West Philly area. Tony Blaze and his crew were all sitting in the garage area Tia Slim was behind the wheel. She drove up and stop not too far from where all of Tony Blaze. His crew were all out there drinking and getting high they never knew what hit them. They jumped out of the truck with masks on dressed in all black from head to toe is Jane

Doe with Heckler &Kock machine MR556A1 gun. Her brother
Bucky Guns has a Daniel Defense M4 Carbines and Neckbone has an
AK-47. Soon as they ran up on them quickly quietly and
professionally one of Tony Blaze boys name Dodee. Seeing them to
react to pull his gun out yelled, "it's a hit!"

A few of Tony Blaze people got some shots off it was like Niggas
with a pop guns versus true professional killers with their tools of
death and destruction doing what they do best.

Tony Blaze crew was in shock trying to shoot back but that was
just about it. After that it was a slew of hot led pumped in their ass
Barrrraattttt! Kackaptaka! Tat tat tat ! Raaaaattttttkacka! Bullets
were flying everywhere all you see is muzzle flash spitting hell fire
from its tips killing all six men and three women. They hit them so
many times it ripped the flesh from all their bodies they all looked like
piles of hamburger meat laying out on the driveway smoking. Jane
Doe and her crew quickly jump back in the truck with Tia Slim
pulling up behind the wheel and taking off up the street in the
darkness hitting the expressway. They are burning up the black top to
their next target as all the bodies lying in pools of blood and shells all
over the fucking place.

We reached the Philadelphia examiner's office known to
everyone in the city as the last stop. I told Fat Smoochy to stay with
the truck and to keep his eyes open and to call us if anything jumped
off. Puerto Rican Joe called up Fat Jacks, Chaco and Gun Ho Moe to
keep an eye out as well.

Me and Puerto Rican Joe got out of the truck and walked inside
of the place.

To tell you the truth I did not want to go up in there, but I went
in there with my friend. He went up to the desk and talk to this
heavyset pretty face black lady. I waited for him as he walked with her
to the back, I did not go with him back there that was just too much
for me to bear. While waiting I got a text from Jane Doe that **Moja
chini mbili kwenda**(One down two to go) with a skull and cross

362

bones emoji. *I text her back* **Nzuri Dada** *(Good sister). I waited for Puerto Rican Joe to come out a half an hour later* was wiping the tears from his eyes, "come on, let's go."

I called Fat Smoochy to bring the truck around soon as we jumped in the truck and took off, we can see the police detective's cars pulling in the parking lot. I told Fat Smoochy to floor it towards the expressway and he did with Fat Jacks in the other truck right behind us. We make it across the bridge before you get to the expressway ramp Fat Smoochy Jumps on with Fat Jacks in the other truck right behind us we just ducked that bull shit with the cops. I tell Fat Smoochy to drive to my condo on City line avenue it takes about a half hour with traffic was not that bad. we made it there and I tell him where to park. Before I get out of the truck, I touch Puerto Rican Joe shoulder, "Bruh, you need to stay with us at the condo and get some rest. Plus, nobody knows your there because more shit is about to jump off.

"What about Zelda at the warehouse?"

"Just tell your peoples not to let Trevor Tee ass in there until you come that's all, Nigga you're the one in fucking charge."

His eyes were glossy, "I really don't want to do this shit anymore!"

"You just need some rest you had one hell of a night, Joe. It's just too much death around us tonight and I'm sorry about your family."

"Well, coming from you I appreciate that, but I'm at a real lost and your right I do need to get some rest."

"I'll call Tanya or one of them Niggas to keep Trevor Tee ass out of there until I get back there."

We waited for Gun Ho Moe, Chaco and Fat Jacks in the parking lot as they all helped with my bags. Gun Ho Moe and Fat Smoochy get their own bags as I'm pulling out my keys from out my bag. we all walked inside, and this tall white dude walked up to us and asked, "yes, may I help you!" *He said it with a snappy arrogance.*

I replied, "were fine, sir. I'm Miss Miller I'm the owner what's your name?"

"My name is Heath. I don't mean any disrespect, but I have to check with the manager."

"No problem, Heath! Do what you have to do, baby. Who are you going to call? Layton is he on working?"

"Yes, he is. I'll call him he picks up the phone sitting on the front desk. He held the phone up to his head staring at all of us rolling his eyes like a little bitch. After about ten minutes Layton came out from the back and greeted us, "oh it's so nice to see you again Miss Miller. How are you doing?"

"I'm great. I'm in town for a short time and me and my friends want to go up to 2a, and 2b my private suite."

"Why sure can I help you with your bags?"

"Why yes." He waves over towards Heath to help him with our bags. I can see the look on this white dude face carrying our bags. This motherfucker after we got off the elevator, he just tossed bags in front of the first door hard with his face all twisted up like he was mad.

Soon as he did that, I ,

"you want to know what go get your shit and get the fuck out of here, okay!"

He glared at me and mumbled something slick under his breath. Gun Ho Moe quickly grabbed his ass by his arm I walked up and sucker punched his ass **Plow!**

I yelled, "you racist ass pussy!"

I tagged his ass good right on his fucking jaw. He hit the floor **Boom!** Looked up at Layton "I want you to march this motherfucker out of my building, okay."

"Yes, right away!"

Soon as Layton went to help Heath up off the floor, he pushed Layton hand away and jump up. He came and lunged towards me and Gun Ho Moe we spun around **Kapacka! Packa!** We shot Heath right in the middle of his head and Fat Smoochy shot him in the chest making a large hole the size of a tangerine with the meat hanging out. The blood and his brain fragments are dripping on the back of the wall. Layton stood there in shock with his mouth open about to shit on himself.

Gun Ho Moe pointed his gun to him, "do we have a problem here?"

Layton with his hands up in the air shouted, "I don't have a problem, please don't kill me."

Gun Ho Moe looks over at me Layton is trembling. I thought to myself why take a chance I just nodded my head yes **Kapacka!** Gun Ho Moe shot Layton in his eye his lifeless body fell sideways into the wall with the drag marks of blood from his body along the wall. I looked up at Gun Ho Moe and Fat Smoochy.

"Call up Jimmy Goon and his people to clean this fucking mess up for me, please."

Gun Ho Moe pulled out his phone "Goddamn, this cock sucker here done shit on himself. He fucking stinks!"

Gun Ho Moe called up Jimmy Goon and his crew to come clean the shit up. They arrive here kind of fast with Crazy Jamel, Midnight and the new guy Nicky Wolf. They clean up all the blood wrapped up the bodies in thick wide cellophane wrap and even dug the bullets out of the wall. I watch them work here and there after it was all done Jimmy Goon just waved at me and they were gone. I went inside of 2a with Puerto Rican Joe, Gun Ho Moe and Fat Smoochy. Fat Jacks and Chaco entered next door into 2b. I asked Fat Smoochy to go get us something to eat some bake chicken, green beans and some mash potatoes and some Heineken beer at the deli. We all ate together in my room, but I can see that Puerto Rican Joe was emotionally drained. I could expect that he just lost his whole family. He ate a little and went to his room. Chaco and Fat Jacks also went to their room then I received the news that Jagger and his crew hit Big Cyrus Mom from the chain gang that they killed her and her old man Mister James in North Philly in a very brutal fashion. They also hit Twiggy Jones's close cousin Lewis Jones they were more like brothers than cousins and his mother Miss Pat. They killed both in their home in West Oak Lane the whole house looked like the house of horrors with blood everywhere.

To tell you the truth I didn't even feel good about this pay back shit I just went to bed after hearing it. The next day I get a call from Tanya Gats at 10:30 A.M. I sit up in the bed trying to knock the cob weds off my brain. I quickly reach up on my nightstand grabbed my pack of smokes lighting up a Newport.

"Yeah, what's up baby girl?"

"I just wanted to tell you that the police are looking for Puerto Rican Joe they they have some questions to ask him that's all."

"You know that's a bunch of bull shit right."

"I know that but, that what they told us when we got stopped last night when we were coming home but they didn't lock none of us up they let us go."

"Look meet me at the warehouse at Washington avenue get Jimmy Goon and his crew to be there, okay."

"Alright, I see you later **Moja***(One)*"

"**Kwaheri***(Goodbye)." I go get washed and dressed I check my guns and I get my bags setting them near the door thinking of what's going to happen after Nokey Blaze find out about his son and his crew getting smoked.* I go wake up Gun Ho Moe and Fat Smoochy so we can go to South Philly they when and got their shit together. But when I when to get Puerto Rican Joe up I go knocking on the door he asked, "who is it?"

I answered, "it's me. I'm coming in are you dressed?"

"Hold on let me put my pants on, okay."

A few minutes past and he , "alright, come on in Almasi."

I open the door and I walked in. He's sitting on the bed with his head hung low, "what are you doing? We have to go to South Philly to finish with this bull shit with Nokey Blaze and Zelda."

"Look, I'm going to tell you like this Almasi. I'm staying right here today to get my mind right."

I wanted to yell at him, but I just replied, "I'll call you later on tonight."

He just waved and laid back down on the bed I walked out the door slowly I walked over to Gun Ho Moe and I'll told him to go next door, so Fat Jacks and Chaco keep an eye on Puerto Rican Joe

366

ass. *I knew once he didn't want to get up out of the bed that's he didn't want to be at the head of the Meza(Table) any more. I don't fucking blame him for real.*

I knew I would have to find someone to take his place before I fly back to Arizona than I'm going to have to run it across Arturo. Soon as the two of them come over to watch Puerto Rican Joe I was going to get the fuck up out of there.

Ten minutes later Chaco and Fat Jacks came over I told them to keep a good eye on him. Don't let him kill himself either and give me the keys to one of the trucks Fat Jacks hands over Gun Ho Moe the keys and snapped, "take my truck, don't fuck it up."

Gun Ho Moe replied, "don't worry about it I'll have somebody drop it back off to you, brother. You know were family, baby."

We bumped fist with him and Chaco smiling. Both of them they would keep an eye on him I had Gun Ho Moe help me with my bags him along with Fat Smoochy we took the second truck and we drove to South Philly it took us about hour and a half traffic was all fucked up jammed bumper to fucking bumper. When we made it to the warehouse Crazy Jamel open the door and he greeted me, "what's up, boss lady?"

I hugged him and replied, "it's good to be back home just for a little while. I walked inside and Tanya Gats was there with Jimmy Goon and his men."

I spoke and waved towards Tanya Gats.

"Tanya, I need to talk to you, baby girl."

"Sure, Almasi." She walked with me puffing on her cigarette cocked to the side of her thick lips. I asked Gun Ho Moe and Fat Smoochy to wait right outside for me for a few while I holler at Tanya Gats about some shit. I told Tanya to close the door behind herself.

"I have something important to ask you so please have a seat." She sat down with a peculiar look on her face.

"What is it you want to ask me, Almasi?"

"How do you feel about being at the head of the Meza(Table)?"

"No, my brother would be next up not me."

"It's not about who is next I did that before and things got all fucked up. I learned that I have to have someone who can do the job

367

not about who is next up. I found the shit out the fucking hard way. I'll call your brother and tell him about it trust me it will be cool with him watch the phone rings three times.

Jagger asked, "what's up, boss lady?"

I put it on speaker look I want to tap your sister here to be at the head of the Meza (Table)."

"I think that would be beautiful I think she perfect to do the job, Almasi."

"That what I was telling her I fucked up putting Dun- Dun at the head of the Meza(Table) this time I have someone I know can do the fucking job."

Jagger yelled with excitement, "you have my blessing sis go head and take the job. Almasi is right you the one for the job, Sis."

Tanya Gats , "well, alright then, I'll do it."

"Good as you know Puerto Rican Joe is out of it after last night, I don't fucking blame him. I hate to say it, but life goes on in this fucked up game."

Tanya Gats asked, "so when will this start?"

"After I talk to Puerto Rican Joe and Arturo so just be ready when it all goes down all right. Thanks Jagger man, I'll holler at you later about this and good job last night."

"Why thanks sis that what we do best Almasi smoke Niggas who cross us."

"You better know it, look I'm glad I called you so I could get that shit straight with your sister letting her know she the right person for the job. I holler at you later **Moja**(One) **Baadae**(Later)."

Soon as I hung up with Jagger. Crazy Jamel came knocking on the door and then rushes in, "your boy Coyote is here."

Coyote walked in the door with his two goons Paco and Yaya I stood up and I hugged him.

"Where the fuck you been at Nigga?"

I point at Yaya "close that door for me please." He does it quickly. Coyote sit on top of my desk and asked, "I just got back from Caracas and I barely got out there with my fucking life."

"Why what happen?"

"The Colombians made a move on us and Arturo is dead."

"What?"

"The big man is dead so what the fuck are we supposed to do about a fucking plug now?" "I don't know because Tito Quito and Eloy Rodas took over in Caracas now and their both running with the Colombians."

"So, what about Tony Bolivar that's who Arturo was working for right?"

"Yeah, but he went out of the country. I don't know so what every happen with Rico Salazar?"

"We never track him down my peoples was working on it I have not heard anything yet. I heard about the Ghost Boys and the Chain gang motherfuckers linked up together and they killed Puerto Rican Joe's whole family how is he holding up."

/

Almasi 2
Queen of The Streets
By Dartanya A. Williams Sr.

He might be the one who fucking framing me for murder

"I hate to say it, but he's all fucked up in the head."

"I would be too if my whole family got blown the fuck up." My phone rings I looked at the caller ID and its detective Don Wilson I'm thinking to myself why is he calling me on my fucking cell phone. I pick it up and answer, " yo, what the fuck is you doing calling me on this phone motherfucker!"

"Look, Almasi calm the hell down I called you to tell you that the FBI and the police are right outside your door to take you and the others into custody."

"For what?"

"For murder your boyfriend's cousin Reggie Zulu sold you the fuck out and you killed them three men at Miss Octavia makeshift hospital joint."

"What get the fuck out of here!"

"Yeah and Miss Octavia is along with Reggie saying you killed her son Dashawn too."

"That's a fucking lie I didn't kill none of them people!" *I knew this motherfucker was recording this shit I quickly hang up.* **Boom!** I hear all these motherfuckers yelling FBI! I quickly jumped up opening the door. I yelled at Gun Ho Moe and Fat Smoochy, "hurry the fuck up and run in here it the fucking FBI!"

As they were grabbing Jimmy Goon Crazy Jamel, Midnight and Nicky Wolf. The two of them quickly ran into my office door I quickly closed the door and hit the button on the right-hand side the steel gate quickly slide down **Doom!** Follow me! I walked to the back of the room on the right-hand side I hit the top of the movie poster of Menace two Society and my large file cabinet slides to the left. It's a door to my tunnel to the other warehouse I quickly pushed everybody inside of the tunnel one bye one where the FBI is banging on the office door and they can't get inside. Tanya Gats, Gun Ho Moe, Fat Smoochy, Coyote, Yaya and Paco I went in last but soon as I when inside the large cabinet slide back in place and I can hear it **Woop.** We all are running down the long dark tunnel soon as we got to the end of it were all two blocks from where the FBI have the whole place surrounded. *What the FBI and everybody else didn't know I had a tunnel made when I brought the other warehouse next door to me for some shit like this going down.*

When we all came out of the tunnel it's right at 25th street bridge side when I came out last, I hit the button at the top of the entrance making it close back and sealing it close. I tell everybody quickly to turn off your phones they all did it as we all walked on the left I told everybody to follow me to the old garage that was my old hold up spot when I first was down with BSN. *When I open the door It still had that smell of oil and gasoline two trucks and a Ford sedan parked on the left-hand side and a black Dodge Ram van parked on the right-hand side all of them cover in dust but to me this place is full of old memories when we stepped inside.*

I locked the door back after letting everyone in. As we all are walking towards the back of the garage Coyote , "you want to know what I love your style. We both giggled and bumped fist smiling our ass off."

I joked, "El Chopo don't got shit on me, brother." Everybody started laughing. I pointed to Gun Ho Moe and Fat Smoochy to get some more chairs for all of us to sit down. Tanya Gats , "so, what are we going to do now, Almasi."

I answered, "we are going to lay low here until it gets dark and go to one of my condos too. I find out what the fuck is going on that's what we're going to do, baby girl."

Fat Smoochy and Gun Ho Moe put out the chairs at this little card table that's still back there it gave me a flash back when I first came back here with the gang back in the days. Everybody sat around after I took one them rags sitting on the side and cleaned the dust off it. *I quickly took my cell phone and broke it up knowing that they can track us down with this motherfucker. I decided I'm going to kill that asshole detective Don Wilson sending the FBI to come get me and as far as I know he might be the one who fucking framing me for murder.*

I looked up at everybody and announced, "this was one of our first hide out when BSN was tight as a frog's ass in water." *Everybody started chuckling. I told them a few stories about when we were doing all kinds of shit in the streets and how I started coming up in the game. What I really love about this time with everybody they were sitting up listening to me as if it was a banging ass gangster movie or something. This was real life shit that really went down in blood and a shit load of pain. After Five hours or so with me giving all of them the gangster bible the do's and don'ts, the pit fall's and the triumphs of the game. And as much as I want to get out of all this bull shit, I can say I did have fun doing this shit living my life while I was doing it. I might have got used up, but I took back all my power. I flip the script on all the motherfuckers who just thought I was just some dumb ass ghetto bitch with no future. I sure came along way. But I still have some ways to go in the fucking foul ass matrix. I don't know how I'm going to win I just know that I will win at the end of the day that's all I really know for sure.*

It was dark outside, and we made our move to get the fuck out of there. I show Gun Ho Moe where the keys were of the two trucks hitting the panel on the back wall on the right. I hit the button and the steel panel slide back and his eyes got wide. I , "you like that shit, right? He smiled as I handed him the keys, I told him to try one of them he jumps behind the wheel of the first truck and it started right up. I waved Fat Smoochy over telling him to help me with the doors on the outside. I instructed Tanya Gats Coyote, Yaya and Paco to get in the truck while me and Fat Smoochy open the doors of the garage with Gun Ho Moe driving it out quick. Fat Smoochy help me close the doors back fast and I told him to get in the truck. I locked up the place making sure everything was secure. I kept an eye out while I was doing this under the yellow dull lights under the bridge.

I jumped in the truck as Gun Ho Moe took off making a hard left turning up Tasker street heading towards the expressway ramp about seven blocks up on 31^{sr} street. I turned the radio on DMX's Ruff Ryders Anthem is on I turned it up as all of us is singing along with the song *stop,drop, shut em down open up shop! Ohh Noo, that's how ruff ryders roll!*

We all sang along having a good time while on the freeway and it's all jammed up with cars. An hour and half later it seem more like

372

two hours we make to my house in Chestnut Hill. Soon as we pull up in the parking area.

Tanya Gats mouth dropped open, "I didn't know you had a mansion, Almasi?"

I replied, "after you buy your first one this isn't going to be shit to you."

"well, I can't fucking wait this is off the fucking hook, Ma."

I laughed I was just like you the first time I seen Spiders big ass house it doesn't mean nothing now I'm on the fucking run. We all get out walking up to the long pathway to the front door. I pull out my ring of keys rattling while I'm trying to find the key to the door. I find it and I open the door, and everybody follows behind me.

"make you self at home y'all." We all walked into the large living room area I keep all my places furnish when I buy them. All of us sit down on the white couch set I had. I still remember when I brought this shit with La Nesa. I sit back lighting up a Newport blowing out smoke as there all looking around like they never seen a house like this before.

I before everybody gets to relaxed, I pointed at Smoochy, "you're going to have to go get us some food. I know it's not shit in here I have not been in here in a few months." Fat Smoochy , "I can do that I stood up and went to hand him some money."

"I got this, Ma don't worry about that!"

"It's a mall about a mile and half from here just buy enough food for about two weeks or so. I'll figure out the rest by the end of the week. Tanya Gats chimed in, "I'll go with him." "Good, keep your eyes open don't get relax because were up here I need for y'all to stay on your toes at all times as I sat back down."

"I want to look around this joint God Damn!"

I , "go right ahead Dawg don't get lost."

"Almasi, shit as big as this motherfucker is I just might."

All of us started laughing

He asked, "how many rooms is in here?"

"Only ten."

"Shit only ten ain't that a bitch!"

While we all were laughing, Fat Smoochy and Tanya headed out of the door to go get some food. I pulled out my satellite phone out of my coach bag. I'm looked over at Coyote and for the first time I see he has that lost look on his tattoo face.

I patted him on the shoulder, "it's going to be all right. Dawg trust me."

He smirked and sat back along with Paco and Yaya on the other end of the large L Shape couch set I have. The first person I called was my Aunt Lisa she picked up after the phone rings four times.

She , "yo, what's up, Almasi!"

"Every fucking thing."

"What happen?"

"They have a warrant out for me for murder so I'm going to have to lay low before I come back to Arizona."

"What murder get the fuck out of here for real?"

"Yeah, there fucking framing me for some shit I didn't fucking do."

"Yeah, you know how these motherfuckers play dirty!"

"Look, I'm telling you what's up I might can slip out of here after I make some calls. For right now I'm laying low until I can make a move. Just hold shit down for me and I'll call you back okay."

"Okay Almasi, you be careful you hear me girl."

"I will Aunt Lisa I talk to you later. One."

I called my son Little Boom he picks up on the first ring and shouted, "are you all right mom?"

"Yeah, I'm good that dirty motherfucker detective Don Wilson set me up for murder." "Who they got that's talking?"

"Jaylen cousin Reggie Zulu , I killed these motherfuckers at Miss Octavia makeshift hospital place. She was the one who killed them motherfuckers when they popped up out in the fucking dark when me and Jay when to go see the fucking Zulu's."

"Why is he doing that shit, Mom?"

"Because we found out the Zulu's were cutting side deal's and stealing money playing us and I had most of them killed. He was out of town when it happened, and he's pissed off we had his people killed."

"So what fuck is up with the old bitch, Miss Octavia? What's her beef?"

"Well, after the shooting contest with me and her son Dashawn came at us at Mookie's club and Gun Ho Moe smoked his ass trying to do a drive by. So, the FBI got the two of them putting all four murders on me."

"What you need for me to do?"

"I need for you to get word to Jay in prison and tell him what his cousin Reggie is up to trying to pin those fucking murders on me."

"I will I get somebody that can go up there and talk to him. Good and I want that cop detective Don Wilson dead too."

"You got it mom so what are you going to do in the mean while?"

"I'm going to fucking lay low and call this lawyer I have working on Jay's case and get shit straighten out. That is what I'm going to do. I knew it was some foul shit when you called me on the satellite phone who is with you?"

Tanya, Gun Ho Moe, Fat Smoochy, Coyote, Yaya and Paco.

"Where the fuck is Puerto Rican Joe is at, I been looking for his ass all fucking day!" "Trevor Tee is going the fuck off that he can't get in to kill that bitch Zelda because his mom died."

"Oh, shit I didn't know that shit did you did here about Puerto Rican Joe's family yet?" "Yeah, I did that's why I'm looking for him to make sure that Nigga is all right."

"He's all right he's laying low at one of my condo's let him chill so he can get his mind right."

"Look things are all fucked up now. I'm need for you and Jagger to hold shit down because some more shit jumped off too. The big man is dead to Arturo are plug."

"So where are we going to get are coke from now?"

"Don't worry about that right now just do what I told you, please. We will figure something out we always do Boom."

"Okay, I'll get on that shit right away and you call me if anything else jumps off, Mom. "What are we going to do about Trevor Tee?"

" Just make sure he don't kill Zelda that's all and tell him I'll call him I'll get his number from Joe just go take care of business for me please honey I talk to you later Moja*(One)* **Nakupenda***(I love you)*. I hang up with my son and I called up Carlo Cash so he can go bail out Jimmy goon and his men right away. I told him to call me when he gets them out.*

Fat Smoochy and Tanya came back from the store with all these bags of groceries. Fat Smoochy came up to me huffing and puffing with bags in his arms he announced he was going to cook.

I smiled, "what are you going to fix?"

He answered, "ghetto goulash."

Coyote blurted out, "what the fuck is ghetto Goulash?" All of us fell out laughing.

I jumped in and laughed, "its macaroni with ground beef and spaghetti sauce that's ghetto Goulash."

"Go right head brother and do your thing the kitchen is on the right-hand side you can't miss it."

"Yaya, why don't you give them a hand with the bags baby."

He stood up, "sure, I'll help out."

Paco got up and chimed in, "I'll give y'all a hand." He clapped his hands and stood. They all took the groceries in the large kitchen. I make another call and my lawyer Reba Waters that's works on Jay's appeal case for me. She picked up after it rings about five times.

"Reba Waters at law how can I help you?"

"Yes, this is Sharonda Miller. May I speak to Miss Waters, please? Could you please hold on Miss Miller?"

A few minutes later I hear her say, "well, hello Almasi, how are you doing?"

"I'm not doing to good somebody is trying to frame me for murder."

"Oh Yeah, who?"

"The FBI have a warrant for my arrest for the murder of four people I did not kill. They have two fucking jokers squeezing them who really killed these people and there trying to pin it on me."

"Were you there when it happened?"

"Yes, I was there but with the first three. This lady name Miss Octavia shot and killed those people right in front of us when these people popped up out the dark on us at her place."

"Do you have anybody else who was there when it happened?"

"Yes, my old man Jay but you know where he's at."

"Well as you know we can't use his testimony only. I can tell you is get that same guy y'all had to looked up all that stuff on the FBI agents on your case and turn yourself in and fight this when you get out on bail."

"I don't know about that Reba those crackers want to set me up from the door."

" Think about it Almasi it going to get worst the longer you stay out there on the run you have to get in front of it longer you out there on the run the guiltier you look."

"Okay I'll turn myself in. Are you going to be there with me right?"

"I'll be right by your side I rather you come in then having them hunt you down and kill you trying to stay on the run."

"Your right but I'm not scared to die but I'll come in."

"Okay what time are you coming in?"

"Tell them I'll turn myself in at One O'clock. I'll come to your office and we will take it from there."

"Good let me call them and find out a little more before I tell them that you are coming in first let me call you back Almasi."

I hang up thinking to myself should I really do this shit? I'm sitting back after a while I can smell the food cooking and it smells good to the aroma put some black soul into this house. I stood up to go into the kitchen Coyote walked up to me, "I didn't mean to be all up in your conversation but you're really going to turn yourself into the FBI."

"Yeah why?"

"Because I don't trust none of them motherfuckers that's why Almasi. You can go anywhere you want they would never find you because you have lots of paper to spend."

Almasi 2
Queen of The Streets
By Dartanya A. Williams Sr.

"I don't know how to tell you this Coyote but there not smarter than me I been in this game for almost twenty fucking years and never got locked up you want to know why.

"Yes, I would like to know, Ma. Because I don't underestimate nobody not even the FBI once you know that with a few other things I know. You will be alright now come on and let's get something to eat and stop fucking worrying about every little fucking thing.

It's going to be alright like I . He gave me a small smile and we both walked into my kitchen area.

Tanya is sitting at the large round white table on the right.

"I didn't know big man could throw down like this that goes to show you that you really don't know somebody like you think you do."

Fat Smoochy , "you got that one right, Almasi."

I asked, "who showed you how to cook Smoochy?"

He looked up at me with his eyes really wide "my mother Grace she could cook her ass off shit. It was six of us and we were really poor, but we would never know it the way my mom cooked. She showed me when I was around 10 years old.

I always hung around the kitchen for the entertainment of my mother she was off the hook. She was incredibly wise and fucking hilarious. I used to listen to her tell stories cuss people out on the phone and smoke two pack of cigarettes all at the same time. Is you mom still around? Oh yeah, she's still alive and kicking. She, went down south a few years ago. I go see her every year drop off some loot on her and talk and play card with her, but she cheats all the time."

We all started laughing while he's stirring the sauce with so much love now to me that's a good sign of a great cook for real. I asked, "where is Yaya and Paco at?"

Tanya answered, "they are out back in the yard smoking weed."

Fat Smoochy chimed, "you can call them in because the food is ready."

Tanya went to the large patio doors calling Paco and Yaya to come eat. Me and Tanya got the bowls from out the cabinets Fat

Smoochy started scooping out the ghetto Goulash that just smell so amazing. The whole kitchen is filled with this wonderful aroma that would make your mouth water before you even taste the food. Me and Tanya started serving everybody at the table were all sitting around eating laughing and having a good time with one another. Eating this down home soulful delicious food words just could not describe how good it really is. I looked over at Fat Smooch and complimented him, "wow you really put your foot in this pot for real."

Tanya , "you sure did. Man, this is really good!"

The whole kitchen is filled with chatter and laughter. Then from out of nowhere **Oooooffff! Oooofffff! Oooofffff!** All of us hit the deck fast and hard pulling out are guns. I looked up and Yaya was shot in the head falling backwards from the table the second shot hit Paco in the neck. The blood is gushing out from his fingers laying on the floor, the third one hit was Coyote in the upper arm. He's lying on the floor and yelled, "Motherfucker!"

He looked at me laying on the floor bleeding putting his finger to his lips for us to be quiet. He did not have to tell me fucking twice. He put up his hand and whispered, "Stay here don't move." He crawled towards the patio doors and he was doing something weird. he was like he was sniffing as he crawled slowly out the door with a trail of blood from his arm. I just turned my head to see where he was at, I could not see him anymore. Gun Ho Moe started to get up I I would not do that shit if I was you. He just looked at me not moving any more with his guns in his hand. Then all the sudden I see Coyote stand up super-fast getting in his gun stance **Kapacka! Kapacka! Kapacka!** Then I can hear like branches breaking and a loud thumping sound **Kadoom.** I quickly jumped up running towards the door and spoke softly.

He looked at me "I got that motherfucker, Almasi. Don't worry about it."

He quickly walked over to where the man fell out of the tree, I walked behind him still looking around because it might be more of them. Gun Ho Moe is running behind me along with Fat Smoochy and Tanya Gats were all standing over the dead body of the sniper bleeding out in the grass. I asked, "who is he Coyote? Don't fucking lie to me because nobody knows where here."

He looked me right in my eyes, "he's a **Hombres De la selva (Jungle Men)** their like CIA of Venezuela **Policia secreta** *(secret police)* .They came to track us down because we killed Tito Quito and Eloy Rodas whole family before we left. Caracas when everything when fucking sideways this asshole here name is Josbo. He was one of the men who trained us when we were kids, he was one of the best beside me.

I asked, "are you sure any more of them ass holes aren't going to pop up out the fucking woodwork on us?"

"I'm not going to lie to you as long as I'm with you they will until I'm dead. They will know when he doesn't report back in the next 24 hours or so. If he wanted to kill you and the others, he could have done it. He just wanted me and my crew dead for what we did."

"Look, you have to get patched up that looks pretty bad Coyote. I got your back because you saved my life when all that shit when down with Spider."

"Thanks, Almasi come on in the house while I call somebody to get that secret police ass hole from Caracas off my fucking grass." We all went into the house we all looked at Paco and Yaya on the floor dead. In a deep pool of blood near the table what was fucked up we had to go around them Yaya still had his fucking eyes open to me that's some spooky shit when people die like that. I told Fat Smoochy to get some plastic bags and cut them open to cover the window up. I went got my satellite Phone and I called up X because Jimmy goon and them are still the fuck in jail. I don't know if Carlo Cash got them out, yet he didn't call me yet. I told Tanya to go in the bathroom and get all them towels so we can help stop the bleeding from Coyote's arm. She quickly ran and brought back about eight of them. I quickly ripped his shirt and pressed it on his upper arm sitting him down at the same time.

I'm calling X. The phone rang three time and I ,

"yo, X man I need a really big favor from you."

He . "what's that Almasi?"

"Look, I'm up at the mansion in Chestnut Hill and I need for you to bring a crew up here to clean up three bodies two of Coyote men and the ass hole sniper that Coyote killed. "Sure, thing that's no problem, baby girl. I didn't know you were still in town. I thought you went back to Arizona after I heard about Puerto Rican Joe's family got blown up that's a fucking shame."

"Yeah, I know that's really fucked up. Well you better be careful too I know you heard that the Ghost boys and Chain gang Niggas is all working together, and I heard the big man is dead too Arturo."

"Who told you that?"

"Your son, look I'll be up there as soon as I can okay **Moja**(One)."

"**Sawa** (Okay)!"

Soon as I hung up with him, I called up Doctor Chow. He picks up on the first ring this motherfucker is always on the fucking hustle that's why I love this dude.

"Yo doctor Chow, I really need you to help out a friend of mine."

"Just tell me where you at and I'll be there sounding like a black dude motherfucker from around the way."

"I'm at my place in Chestnut Hill."

"I've been there before I'm not too far from you I be right their sweetheart.

"Thanks Doctor Chow, I made Coyote a drink and I let him snort some of the blow I had in my coach bag to kill some of the pain. I also snorted some for my fucking nerves with a cigarette cock in my lips. A half hour went past really fast and Doctor Chow is ringing the doorbell.

I told Gun Ho Moe to go let him in the crib he quickly walked to where Coyote is sitting not saying a word. He's going right to work pulling out his tools from his heavy ass black bag of his. Soon as he was done, he hands Coyote a hand full of pills saying take about four of them before you go to sleep. I hand him four stacks from out of my coach bag he bumps fist with me "it a pleasure doing business with you Almasi."

I told Fat Smoochy to take Coyote to the back room upstairs as he was doing that, I walked doctor Chow to the door soon as he was going out. X and his crew were pulling up in the workmen van. I'm standing in the doorway and its X, Katar, Billy Wild, Beamer, Black Bart and Fat Roman they all hug me as there coming in the door. X came up to me asking, "what up Shorty!" Were both laughing as I walked them to the where the bodies were at in the kitchen. I'm bull shitting with X while his crew is getting busy, I told Gun Ho Moe and Tanya to show them where the body was at in the yard area. It took them about a hour and half to clean it all up I ask them if they wanted something to eat they all no as I walked them to the door its dark outside now X , "looks like you going to have to go back into the saddle again and run shit they're not going let you retired, Ma."

"You want to fucking bet Arturo is dead.So, I can do what the fuck I want to do now."

"You're right I holler at you later Shorty you take care Moja(One)"

" **Nakupenda Ndugu**(I Love you brother)."

I walked back in the house closing the door and I went in the kitchen and wash up the dishes by myself listening to some old love songs on the radio thinking about my baby Jay. I was ready to go to bed I had one hell of a fucking day everybody when to bed too I show them to there, rooms where they can sleep at.

Dog and Pony Show

The next day I was awakened by the sun blazing through the window. I went to check on Coyote in the back room he was still knocked out sleep all the others had their door close, so I didn't bother them. I let them sleep while I worked the horn talking to my lawyer Reba Waters, she told me to relax today. Everything is set up for my surrender she did tell me that the press was going to be there so be ready for that she has nothing to do with that shit it's the FBI. I told her I'm not worry about that shit because I was working on my case as we speak. She she just wanted me to know what was going on, so I don't get blindsided. I told her it was cool, and I hung up with her. All that day all I did was get high drink and eat with everybody. I still made sure that Taz- Money was holding shit down and keeping an eye on Zelda's ass.

He , "he got it, don't worry."

I called up Puerto Rican Joe to check on him and he told me out of his mouth that he would no longer will be at the Meza(Table).

I to him that it was alright just for him to take care of himself. I sent Gun Ho Moe to go get my black Benz wagon at my Cheltenham condo. After I got off the phone with him, I was hoping he didn't try to kill himself. I went back to getting high after I took care of business the whole day went by in a fucking blur. I had a big feast with my crew Fat Smoochy cooked again he made fried Chicken wing dings with his homemade hot sauce. He joked he would give me his mother's recipe for five stacks. We all fell out laughing then he just quickly wrote it down on a small piece of paper and handed to me with a smile. I thanked him, but I was really touched. I didn't stay up late because it was my big day for another fucking perk walk with the FBI this time.

The next day I got up around 10 I got washed and dressed but I got fucking sharp for the camera. This time if they wanted to see a gangster, I'll show them South Philly best gangster living and breathing today. Soon as I got dressed in all black with my Jay Godfrey power suit, flat black Gianvito Rossi shoes. I put my hair in a pony tail with a diamond brooch for my hair, my large gold hoop earrings, my gold chain and name plate piece in all diamonds that read boss bitch.

Almasi 2
Queen of The Streets
By Dartanya A. Williams Sr.

I made me a drink gin on the rocks pour out a little coke on top of my dresser I snort up the four lines of coke I'm feeling it.

Then my phone rings I get it real fast and asked, "yo, what's up. "

"Yo, Mom. I got word to Jay and he , "don't worry about nothing he he will take care of Reggie. I also talked to Ty- Kim and he the FBI got her under protective custody, but he got things worked out to get to her. He has a few nurses who owe him big time."

"That sounds good, baby look I'm turning myself in today and as you know its going to be a perk walk to show all these cracker's think they got me."

Little Boom started chuckling, "nobody got my mom Almasi aka Glock mommy queen of the fucking streets."

"And you better know it. Look, I got to go. I love you."

"I love you too, Mom."

I quickly go downstairs Gun Ho Moe is dressed in all black and so is Fat Smoochy and Tanya Gats is waiting for me near the door. Tanya complimented me, "you look nice, Almasi."

"Thank you, baby. I'm going to look my best to get locked the fuck up."

We all started laughing. I continued, "Look, you stay here Tanya and look out for Coyote. Make sure he doesn't take too many of them fucking pills alright."

"I got you, Almasi.

She hugged me.

"I'll be back in few hours I got Carlo Cash with a big suitcase filled with money to meet me there to bail my black ass out." We all started laughing again. Gun Ho Moe open the door for me Fat Smoochy is right behind me as Tanya is in the doorway watching us get in the car. She waving as we pull off to go to downtown center city to Reba Waters office first then the federal building for the dog and pony show. It took us an hour half to Reba Waters office I see she was a little dressed up too she looked at me and asked, "you ready for this?"

"I was born ready for this shit, counselor."

She instructed to Fat Smoochy and Gun Ho Moe, "you two can be with us until we get to the building, then I'm need for you two to stay behind us and after we get inside your going have to fall back."

She looked at me, "okay, that's the plan, but if shit get fucked up y'all know what to do right." They both nodded their heads smiling.

"Ya'll waiting for me when I come out, I'm going to text y'all, okay."

We all leave and jump in my black Benz wagon it only took us ten minutes to get there. We park in the parking lot across the street from the federal building soon as we all started walking up all the cameras started flashing in my face we pushing them back as we keep moving forward towards the door Gun Ho Moe and Fat Smoochy quickly get in front of us pushing all the reporters back yelling at all of us all at the same time. Then they started running up with the TV cameras with the reporters came up pushing their microphones in our faces yelling questions, "like are you the black underworld queen!"

"Are you head of the black mafia here in Philadelphia? Is it true did you kill all three of them men inside of a makeshift hospital in North Philly over a bad crack deal? Is it true that you had something to do with two Philadelphia police officers being missing?"

Reba Waters stop right in front of the doors and stated, "we have no comment at this time after we come out, I will make a very brief comment thank you very much."

We quickly when inside soon as we walked in the building all the people had their eyes on me filled with deep hate. We get on the elevator and ride up to the third floor we get off its about ten FBI agents five on the right five to the left as we walk in this ugly ass old white man steps up to me "Sharonda Miller your under arrest for murder." That is the only part I heard. They had an FBI woman pat me down then she snatches my black coach bag off my arm. I wanted to sucker punch that bitch, but I pushed her. All of them wanted to jump on me, but Reba Waters jump in front of me shouted, "we came in here peacefully it no need for the rough stuff!" Special agent in charge Harold Green step in "she's right, calm down everybody we can all do this in a civil manor." They took me in the back took my fingerprints and my picture. The took me to their holding cell they made me take off my belt. Two hours later Carlo Cash came with the money 10 % of the million dollars bail they put on me he came up with the 100,000 cash they gladly took the money.

I'm walk back out with my lawyer Reba Waters with that tough North Philly smirk on her pretty brown grill where she's from soon as we step out. She steps out in front of all the cameras it was lights camera action.

"my client is 100% innocent of all these horrendous charges my client Sharonda Miller never been arrested in her life for nothing. She's a legitimate businesswoman and she a pillar of the community who is well respected and loved. All of this is one big smear campaign by the FBI on an African American woman in this city and they need to be a shame of themselves. And you will see when we have our day in court my client will be exonerated of all the charges thank you very much for your time have a good day!" *While Reba was doing her thing, I hit up Gun Ho Moe up texting him letting him know we were outside and to bring the car up in front of the building.* I saw the car pulling up on the side I tap her on her arms   "our ride is here let's go. Hey, your fucking good counselor!"

"I'm the best."

 We laughing running to the car parked on the side they don't let you stay long. We jump in Reba sat in the back with Fat Smoochy I got in the front with Gun Ho Moe behind the wheel and he took off like a fucking rocket. He made a giant fucking U turn on Market street like a wild man heading towards 5th street to hit the expressway. I'm laughing my ass off Gun Ho Moe , "what are they going to do lock us up for making a fucking U turn on Market street?"

Were all laughing as he hit the expressway ramp. We drive for about ten minutes and he yelled out, "some motherfucker is on our tail!"

Soon as he that a dark color sedan came speeding up with two mask men shooting at us **Boom! Plow!** Hitting the driver side window but what those dopes don't know that the whole fucking car is bullet proof.

Gun Ho Moe wickedly chuckled sticking his gun in the special slot on his side shooting back **Packa! Packa! Packa!** Hitting one of the mask men in the head he falls to the black top while were speeding up the expressway. As Gun Ho Moe and the mask men in the other car is exchanging bullets shooting back and forth at one another. Fat Smoochy wanted to get in on the action he yelled at Reba Waters to jump on the other side of him. She did as ask, and he sticks his gun in the slot shooting at the same car trying to pursue us. Each of them kept shooting until they hit the driver in his face and neck ripping half of his nose off and both his eyes blown out his fucking skull. As we see the car drift off toward the left fast and **Kaboom!**

It crashed into another car making it flip over and it's about eight car pileup cars are still flying all over the place with cars all hitting one another making loud thumping noises. It sounding like thunder falling from the fucking sky then from out of nowhere a car came hitting us from the driver side door **Kaplang!** Knocking us through the guard rail off the bridge. All I see is fucking water as where flying in the air then heading down super-fast into the water. My heart is in my ass by this time knowing that I'm going to die screaming at the top of my lungs then **Buuuusssssssshhhhhhhhhhhh!**

Mwisho Kwa Sasa (The End for Now)

Dedications

Just like all of my novels I like to thank God for letting me do what I really love to do and giving me the wisdom of knowing what my real purpose in life is and that's writing because there are so many people who never know their true purpose in life what God put them here for. And so many of us people of color is trapped into meaningless life's and jobs and never seek to make their dreams come true so I'm very blessed to be able to not only writing books but to also be putting them out independently with my own company I call Ni Jambo La publishing that means our thing in Swahili and to me that's nothing but the power of God that move me to that kind of motivation.

I dedicate this book to my father James Leroy Williams. I've been thinking about you a lately and every time I see my son Dartanya A. Williams Jr. Every time I talk to him about you, I feel bad you never met your grandson. Soon as we talk to make it happen it was too late God had other plans. Even though you have transitioned many years ago. I still have the memories of you being an intellectual black man in this wicked ass white man's world that did not see you as one and you were one hell of a man and a lot of your great qualities I have now. I know it comes from your DNA and you lived an extraordinary life and I think of you all the time and may your soul rest in peace Jimmy.

To Tamyara Brown, for all of your hard work and dedication on helping me with put my visions of greatness to life on the page as well as my brand with all of my works I know I could have not got it done without you and its beyond words of just saying thank you. You have made me a better writer in every way. I'm so glad you came into my life now. We are family now thank you sis and you're a great writer in your own right as well can't wait to read your next masterpiece.

To my wife Margaret, when we first started dating before we got married, I told you about my writing and you read my story and loved it. We stayed up talking about my book Dark Secrets and how much you love the character Detective Cassandra Wilson. Now were still doing that with my Almasi series with long deep conversations about the meaning and what I was trying to say about the struggles of every day black life tragedy joy and pain. Mere words cannot describe how much I love you for everything you have done for me in my life. I'm truly blessed to have you as my partner in crime my confidant, wife, and love of my life thank you baby for believing in me.

To Veda Mc Lean aka Rasheeda. I always thank you in every book I wrote for reading my stories when I was writing them in five subject spiral schoolbooks. When I could not afford a computer but you knew it was fire and compassion to tell my stories my way the voice for the voiceless from the streets you seen what the world needed unapologetic blackness the joy's the triumphs and pain of life in the day to day struggles of life raw Dawg without the bag. You gave me the courage to become a writer and I'm so glad you found your purpose becoming a writing professor at an university helping to spark other writers of the world to their full potential just like you did for me thank you so very much for everything.

I like to thank all of the people who read the last book Alexis, Vivian, Jermaine, Rob, Kat Daddy Love, Larry, Shakia, Craig, Chilly Ock, his wife Chrissy The Bomb Shell and so many others. I could not name you all and the other fans for all your love and support putting me on the map. You just don't know what this all means to me for helping me make my dreams come true. Thank you so very much. I like to say to everyone in these trouble dangerous times where are all living in now of days in the middle of a pandemic. I'm praying for all of my family, extended family members and friends to come out of all of this safe and sound and I know God will have the last word on guiding us all to live our best life's. And remember work hard on your dreams just don't dream.

Author Dartanya A. Williams Sr aka Deeluciano The Don.

Almasi 2
Queen of The Streets
By Dartanya A. Williams Sr.

Be sure to visit www.dartanyaawilliamssr.com **to read my Latest blogs, purchase merchandise and be sure to sign up for my email list.**

www.ingramcontent.com/pod-product-compliance
Lightning Source LLC
Chambersburg PA
CBHW070358260626
47161CB00001B/180